PHOEBE'S GIFT

BOOKS BY
JERRY S. EICHER

PHOEBE'S GIFT

JERRY S. EICHER

HARVEST HOUSE PUBLISHERS
EUGENE, OREGON

Scripture quotations are taken from the King James Version of the Bible.

Cover by Garborg Design Works

Cover Image © Dean Fikar, volgarivar, Cozy Nook / Bigstock

The author is represented by MacGregor Literary, Inc.

This is a work of fiction. Names, characters, places, and incidents are products of the author's imagination or are used fictitiously. Any resemblance to actual persons, living or dead, is entirely coincidental.

PHOEBE'S GIFT
Copyright © 2017 by Jerry S. Eicher
Published by Harvest House Publishers
Eugene, Oregon 97402
www.harvesthousepublishers.com

ISBN 978-0-7369-6932-1 (pbk.)
ISBN 978-0-7369-6933-8 (eBook)

Library of Congress Cataloging-in-Publication Data

Names: Eicher, Jerry S., author.
Title: Phoebe's gift / Jerry S. Eicher.
Description: Eugene, Oregon : Harvest House Publishers, [2017] | Series:
   Peace in the valley ; 2
Identifiers: LCCN 2017004441 (print) | LCCN 2017010977 (ebook) | ISBN
   9780736969321 (softcover) | ISBN 9780736969338 (ebook)
Subjects: LCSH: Amish—Fiction. | BISAC: FICTION / Christian / Romance. |
   GSAFD: Christian fiction. | Love stories.
Classification: LCC PS3605.I34 P48 2017 (print) | LCC PS3605.I34 (ebook) |
   DDC 813/.6—dc23
LC record available at https://lccn.loc.gov/2017004441

Printed in the United States of America

17 18 19 20 21 22 23 24 25 / LB-GL / 10 9 8 7 6 5 4 3 2 1

ONE

Phoebe Lapp entered the low-beamed barn and closed the rickety door behind her. Cobwebs laced the ceiling and hung on the highest rafters, where the haymow opened into the loft. Cleaning the barn was her responsibility, but there hadn't been enough hours in the day with the constant care Grandma had needed this past year. Now it didn't matter. Grandma Lapp was gone. Since the funeral, none of the family had complained about the barn's condition. They had mourned and comforted each other with the godly testimony Grandma had left behind. *Mamm* and *Daett* had departed an hour ago with two van-loads of relatives for the long journey back to Lancaster. Now silence followed the sorrow.

Phoebe jumped when a man appeared from the stalls in front of her. "David Fisher!" she exclaimed. "What are you doing here?"

He ducked his head. "Just checking on the ponies. Sorry if I'm disturbing you."

"No. I mean, that's okay," she stammered. "I'm collecting my thoughts after..." She waved her hand in the direction of the house, where the funeral had been held. "Of course you're here. Someone has to do the chores."

His smile was crooked. "I'll be going now. Do you know what happens from here? I mean, with the ponies?"

Phoebe shook her head. "That's a problem. No one has made any plans."

"Well, if I can be of any help, let me know. In the meantime, I'll continue to cover the chores until a decision is made on...I mean..." He searched for words. "We all knew Grandma Lapp would pass, but it was still kind of unexpected."

"Yes."

"I...Sometimes I...ah, I really should be going."

"It's very kind of you to help with the chores," she called after him. "Thanks so much."

"I'm more than glad to help out Grandma Lapp." He paused and ducked his head again. A moment later he vanished through the barn door.

Phoebe stared after him. David and his sister Ruth had a close relationship with Grandma Lapp and lived a mile south of her farm. Beyond that, Phoebe hadn't asked questions about the Fisher family. Grandma Lapp had run things her own way. Not that any of the family had complained. David was shy and carried the burden of the Fisher family's ne'er-do-well reputation in the valley—which wasn't fair, from what she could see. David had always performed his duties for Grandma. A man shouldn't be held accountable for his *daett*'s inability to run his farm efficiently.

A chorus of neighs from the horse stalls along the far end of the barn interrupted Phoebe's thoughts. The sound brought a smile to her face. Grandma's horses were known in the district. Her Assateague ponies were little wild horses from Maryland who had no business being in an Amish community nestled under the foothills of the Adirondack Mountains, but they were here nonetheless. Cousin Herman Yoder—Aunt Millie's husband's relative—had seen to that, although the idea must have come from Grandma. Cousin Herman wouldn't have been able to talk Grandma into something she didn't fully support.

Phoebe leaned over the wooden boards of the first stall and stroked the pony's nose. "Howdy, little one."

She had never been told their names. Grandma had not been well enough to explain such things or to say why she kept Assateague ponies as pets.

Phoebe moved on to the next stall. In the past year she had taken every precious second she could find away from her duties in the house to spend time with the ponies. They soothed her spirits as she cared for Grandma during her waning days. The ponies were small compared to a regular horse, sort of stuck in the middle like Phoebe. Here she was in her midtwenties with no prospects of marriage, and now her duties in the valley had drawn to a close. Several unmarried men in Lancaster had taken her home for Sunday evening dates before she came to the valley, but the relationships had all fizzled for one reason or another.

"Something will come up if I go back," Phoebe muttered. She opened the back barn door to release the three ponies from their stalls. She watched as they raced into the pasture, their heels lifted joyously at their newfound freedom. They were proud little creatures, half wild, and yet loving and tender once their hearts were won.

Why had Grandma asked Cousin Herman to buy the small horses? Grandma never did anything without a reason. Phoebe had been a child when Grandpa Tobias passed in a terrible farm accident, and afterward people said that Grandma had become eccentric—but that didn't explain the ponies. Maybe there were no answers, and the ponies would be disposed of along with the rest of the farm now that Grandma had gone to her rest. Phoebe would find out soon enough. Someone would be by this morning to begin the sale process, and she would have to make her own plans.

There was always the option of returning to Lancaster, and life would go on in *Mamm* and *Daett*'s old house outside of Gap. Her parents were ready to build a *dawdy haus* and turn the farm over to her youngest brother, Ernest, and his *frau*, Thelma, along with their three children. Perhaps some handsome unmarried man would notice her return from the valley. Phoebe smiled dreamily. She had never been in a rush, but the years were passing.

Her parents had hoped she would find a husband in the valley, but she'd been too busy with Grandma the last year to think about marriage. And whom would she have dated? The valley community was small, and the eligible young men who didn't have girlfriends were few and far between. David was available, but she and he didn't exactly fit. He was too shy for her timid ways, and his family had a poor reputation—whether he deserved it or not.

The little one-room schoolhouse on Peckville Road didn't have a schoolteacher for this term. She had overheard Fannie Fisher, the deacon's *frau*, say so this past Sunday. Phoebe could apply for the job, and if accepted, try her hand at teaching. Maybe that was what she should do. She was a baptized member of the community. She had always loved children, and she'd enjoyed her own school years. What other qualifications did she need?

For Phoebe, though, the shadows were more comfortable than the bright sunlight. Teaching school would place one in the full exposure of either the community's approval or dislike. On the plus side, she would have a drawing card when any unmarried men ventured into the valley in search of prospective wives.

Phoebe sighed. She gazed at the three ponies as they trotted across the pasture with their manes and tails flowing out behind them. How freely they lived, without a worry or concern in the world. She wanted to live like that. She wanted to move through life with both abandonment and certainty. Why could she not be like Grandma—bold, confident, and tenderhearted all at the same time? But she was no Grandma Lapp. She was plain Phoebe Lapp. There was no other way to look at things.

Phoebe jerked her head up when she heard buggy wheels in the driveway behind her. The ponies also noticed the new arrival and stood with their heads turned toward the barn, their ears perked up. Someone from the family had arrived. Uncle Homer, most likely.

Phoebe took slow steps toward the barn door before Uncle Homer burst through.

"There you are!" he exclaimed.

"*Yah*," Phoebe muttered, but Uncle Homer hurried on.

"Cousin Herman here has agreed to take the horses." Uncle Homer motioned over his shoulder with his beard. "And help us sell them."

Phoebe forced a smile. This was not unexpected, and it was the logical conclusion to Grandma's venture into owning the ponies.

Cousin Herman walked inside, tipped his hat, and smiled. "*Goot* morning, Phoebe. I'm sorry about the ponies and for the loss of the woman we all loved. I haven't had a chance to tell you personally."

"Thank you," she whispered.

"You have done *goot* taking care of Grandma Lapp this past year," Cousin Herman added. "She endeared herself to all of us, but to you especially, I suppose."

"We grew close, *yah*." Phoebe pressed back the tears. "She was a sweet grandma."

Both men nodded, and Cousin Herman continued. "She was a special woman."

"Like her Assateague ponies!" Uncle Homer snorted. "She was a little strange, but she was a *goot mamm*. I don't disagree with that."

"Yet look how you turned out," Cousin Herman teased.

Uncle Homer ignored the jab. He walked to the back barn door and hollered over his shoulder. "Maybe you can help call them in, Phoebe. We'll tie them to the back of my buggy. I think Herman and I can handle three little horses between the two of us."

Ponies, not horses. Phoebe wanted to correct her uncle, but why protest? Cousin Herman had stepped forward to help Uncle Homer, and she was clearly supposed to follow. Yet she knew she had to say something. Otherwise the moment would be lost forever.

"I'd like to keep the ponies," she croaked. *Where did this nerve come from?*

Uncle Homer's head whirled about. "Keep them? How would you do such a thing?"

Phoebe moved her hand around in a circle. "They can stay here in the barn until I find a place to live, and—"

"I don't think that's wise!" Uncle Homer proclaimed. He stroked his beard. "I never did agree with *Mamm*'s plan for these horses."

"Her plan!" Phoebe drew a sharp breath. "What plan?"

"She never told you?" Uncle Homer eyed her sharply. "I expected *Mamm* spent the last year filling your ears with her harebrained idea."

Phoebe stilled her rapid breathing. "What is this plan? I've wondered plenty myself."

"It's not going to happen," Uncle Homer said. "I told *Mamm* it was foolishness, but nothing could turn her from her fancies once she set her mind to them. And since *Daett*'s passing, who of us children could tell her no?"

Cousin Herman shrugged from the back barn door, his eyes locked on the ponies as if to say he bore no responsibility for Grandma's scheme.

"You'll have to tell me now," Phoebe told him. She couldn't believe her boldness this morning.

Uncle Homer continued. "We have a spare room at our house, and there is an opening for a schoolteacher this fall. You can take that job. We will speak no more about the horses."

"But...but...I will find out somehow, and then what?" Phoebe said. "Why are you doing this, Uncle Homer, when you know that Grandma's ideas were always right? She was the kindest, gentlest person any of us knew."

Uncle Homer flinched. Clearly her arrow had found the mark.

"I'm surprised she didn't tell you," he finally mused. "How can this be, Cousin Herman? You are the one who bought the horses for her."

"Hey, don't blame me!" Cousin Herman yelped. "I couldn't tell the woman no, and she didn't fully explain to me why she wanted them."

"Of course she didn't." Uncle Homer fixed a fierce gaze on the hapless Cousin Herman. "She paid you well, and you made fancy trips down to *Englisha* places. You even got your picture in the paper over it."

"Well, it...I...it wasn't my fault," Cousin Herman sputtered. "And what harm could come from humoring an old woman?"

"That much harm!" Uncle Homer gestured toward the ponies as they ran in the pasture. He turned back to Phoebe. "I thought for sure *Mamm* brought you up from Lancaster to carry on her dream."

"Really, Uncle. I have no idea what you are talking about."

"I guess that would be like her now that I think about it," Uncle Homer muttered. "Trusting in the Lord and getting her way as usual. Confound that woman."

"She was your *mamm*," Cousin Herman pointed out. He hid his smile with a quick turn of his head.

Uncle Homer still noticed. "I guess that's true," he grumbled.

"So are you going to tell me?" Phoebe clasped and unclasped her hands. What was this great secret? Grandma must have asked for her to move in from Lancaster for reasons beyond the obvious. Never had Phoebe imagined such a thing.

"You want to step right into your grandma's shoes," Uncle Homer said. "What makes you think you'd be up to it?"

Phoebe's heart pounded. "If Grandma thought I could do this—whatever it is—then I surely can."

Uncle Homer grunted. Somehow she said all the right things this morning.

"We are reading the will later," he continued. "But I am already aware of its contents. We were expecting *Mamm* to leave something to force our hand, but there is nothing. All the children will receive equal shares of the farm, which means..." He paused. "I really shouldn't be telling you this, Phoebe. How about we forget this conversation? Cousin Herman will take the ponies and sell them in no time, and you—"

Phoebe shook her head.

He sighed. "That's what I thought."

Cousin Herman spoke up. "I think your conscience is bothering you, Homer. You shouldn't have opposed your *mamm*'s plan to begin with. She might have lived a little longer with something worthwhile in her life."

"You always were on her side." Uncle Homer glared at Cousin Herman.

"Well, it was for a *goot* cause," Cousin Herman protested. "We live sheltered lives. We—"

"*Yah*, we've been over that," Uncle Homer interrupted. "You've never married, and you gallop all over the country at your leisure, so why speak to you of danger?"

Herman glanced at Phoebe. "Do you think she can handle it any better than Grandma Lapp? Or is Phoebe simply a way for you to ease your conscience?"

"It always was a harebrained idea," Uncle Homer muttered, obviously avoiding the question.

Phoebe's head spun, and no words came. She had no idea what the men were talking about.

"So why don't you make up your mind?" Cousin Herman stared out the back barn door. "Am I taking the ponies or not?"

"I have to think about this," Uncle Homer finally decided. "I'll drive you back, and we'll return this evening with the others to speak with Phoebe."

"I'm not coming. You're on your own with this," Cousin Herman declared. Both men said goodbye to Phoebe, and then Herman followed Uncle Homer out of the barn. Moments later, Phoebe listened to the buggy wheels rattling out of the driveway.

She stood without moving for a long time. Grandma thought she—timid Phoebe Lapp—could do something *wunderbah*, something worthy. There was no other way to look at this.

But what did Grandma want her to do?

TWO

Several hours later, Phoebe sat at the kitchen table in Grandma Lapp's empty house, a lunchtime bologna sandwich in hand and her eyes fixed on the kitchen wall. She wanted to force the hands on the clock to make the evening arrive, but there was nothing she could do but wait. She should have run after Uncle Homer this morning and demanded he tell her at once what Grandma's plan had been. There was a time when she would have dared, but that was...well, a long time ago. Even after her bold words to Uncle Homer about wanting to keep the ponies, she had reverted to her cautious self.

There was nothing she could do as the minutes ticked past in the silent house. She should be used to silence after her care of Grandma this past year, but this was the total absence of sound. What a relief it would be to hear Grandma's shallow breathing in the bedroom again. Or the sound of her faint cry for a glass of water, or the occasional request for food she struggled to consume.

Phoebe pulled her gaze from the wall and finished the sandwich. The evening would come in its own *goot* time, and the Lapp families would gather. Three of *Daett*'s siblings lived in the valley: Uncle Homer, Uncle Noah, and Aunt Millie, who had married Reuben Yoder. Between the three families, their children would fill the house, but that was the least of Phoebe's worries. She thought only of Grandma's dream, a dream that had stirred opposition in all of her relatives. So what was Phoebe Lapp's part in that plan? Apparently she had been summoned from Lancaster for reasons other than Grandma's care. Grandma's plan must have demanded a lot of courage. Had Grandma remembered how Phoebe once had been? Surely Grandma could not have known what happened in the schoolyard, or about the harsh words that had been spoken years ago.

Phoebe groaned and cleared the sandwich crumbs from the table. She knew she had to speak up this evening—to say to Uncle Homer and her family, "I am not up to this—whatever this is." She was a different girl now. She would say her piece, and they need not say anything else of the past or the present. The family could enjoy the evening together, and their time would not be wasted.

Phoebe squared her shoulders and dumped the crumbs into the wastebasket. She paused when she heard a knock on the front door. She hadn't heard the sound of a buggy pulling into the driveway, but she had been wrapped up in her own thoughts. Phoebe shook her apron clean and headed out of the kitchen. The door opened before she arrived, and David's face appeared.

He managed a smile. "Can I come in?"

"Sure." She waited. Maybe he had come back to pick up something he had left in the house.

David stood by the front door with his head down. "Your grandma was very dear to me, Phoebe," he finally said.

"I know. We all loved her."

"Ruth wanted to send her regrets, but she had to work at her job this morning cleaning homes." David gave Phoebe a quick glance.

She smiled gently. "Thank you both for your concern."

He hurried on. "I will certainly miss coming up here and seeing Grandma Lapp. I know that Ruth feels the same. Your grandma was kind to us." He paused, apparently caught up in his memories. "She could look past our family's strange ways when few could. I'm sorry for the way *Daett* is sometimes."

"That is not your fault, David."

"Thanks," he replied. He hesitated again. "But that is not what I came to talk about."

Phoebe motioned toward the couch. "Do you want to sit?"

He shook his head. "Your grandma told me something I was supposed to tell you after she passed. I tried to speak about it this morning in the barn, but I lost my courage. I hope what I have to say isn't too shocking or too sudden." He looked at her, doubt in his eyes. "If you would rather, I can come back in a few days, and we can talk then."

Phoebe stared at him. "Grandma gave you a message for me? Why wouldn't she tell me herself? I took care of her every day."

David glanced at floor. "I don't think she meant to offend you. Maybe...I don't know. One could often ask why your grandma did the things she did. For example, why did she befriend Ruth and me? She's the reason I joined the community when I did, and why Ruth hasn't jumped the fence yet with Ethan, that *Englisha* boyfriend of hers. But I suppose you know all that."

Phoebe nodded. David had never been this open before.

He continued. "Grandma told me my part of the plan, and I am supposed to see if you want to move any further with it. She gave me a year's wages in case you accept and everything else falls into place. But if it doesn't, Grandma told me to keep the money with the Lord's blessings."

Phoebe sat down on the couch and steadied herself. "So you know what Grandma's dream was?"

"I suppose so. She never called it her dream to me."

Phoebe motioned impatiently with her hand. "So tell me!"

David waited for a second. "This was all Grandma Lapp's idea, let me assure you—although Ruth mentioned something first after she became acquainted with Ethan's work at Child Protective Services."

"Just tell me, David," Phoebe whispered. "Please!"

"The ponies out there." David motioned toward the barn with his chin. "Grandma Lapp wanted to bring troubled children to the farm for a week at a time. She hoped to give them a taste of country life, and perhaps a touch of the Lord too." His face clouded. "But that's not something you can tell Child Protective Services. Ethan explained to Ruth the difficulties of obtaining secular support if the Amish were running the farm. There would be training for the person in charge. Things are touchy when the state pays for things. Even so, Grandma Lapp liked the idea of the Assateague ponies because they would entertain the children. It wasn't all settled yet, but the ponies were the start of her plan." David gestured toward the barn. "So now you know, and I'm just the messenger—although I do think it is a great idea."

Phoebe tried to breathe. "So Grandma wanted a working farm for troubled *Englisha* children?"

"Something like that."

"And you would help me run the place?"

"That is what Grandma Lapp wanted." He grimaced. "I hope you don't object. I would pull more than my share of the work if you gave me a chance."

"I'm sure you would," Phoebe assured him. "But it's not all my decision. The family's gathering tonight, and things will be decided then."

"That's fair," he agreed. "I hope they make the right choice."

She gave him a quick smile. "You can pray, I suppose. That wouldn't hurt. If the project does go through, this would be no small undertaking."

He nodded, his face sober. "So you knew nothing about this?"

She shook her head.

"I wonder why."

"It is confusing. Uncle Homer spoke with me this morning about some dream of Grandma's, but he wouldn't give me details. How did she keep so many secrets, David?"

He grinned. "Grandma Lapp was a *wunderbah* woman, Phoebe, but you already know that. I hope the Lord gives her a great reward for all the kindness she showed my sister and me. But she must have proceeded with caution on this farm idea, for which I don't blame her. Obviously your relatives have their doubts about it."

"Yes, they do. And I'm still dizzy with information, but I will let you know what the family decides."

"I'll see you later, then." David turned and slipped out as quietly as he had come.

Looking out the living room window, Phoebe watched him leave. So this was Grandma's secret. Grandma wanted her to work with David Fisher? Perhaps for David's sake as much as for her own? Grandma was into such things—horses and hurting souls. Did Phoebe have the courage? Even if Uncle Homer and the others gave their permission, such a project would disturb the community.

She was a faithful member of the church, and so was David. That should help. Unlike Ruth, David had ended his *rumspringa* long before Phoebe had arrived in the valley. Uncle Homer would know this, and he also knew about Grandma's wish. Likely Uncle Homer considered the idea this morning largely because of his high regard for his *mamm*.

Phoebe would have to wait for the evening to see how things would turn out. In the meantime, there were the cobwebs in the barn. It was a wonder Cousin Herman hadn't teased her this morning about its condition.

Phoebe left the house and pushed open the barn door to find a broom in the back storage room. She returned to the front of the barn, and with an old bandana wrapped across her face, she began to attack the cobwebs with vicious strokes of the broom.

THREE

Dusk had fallen outside the old farmhouse by the time Phoebe finished the last of her soup in the silent kitchen. She should have made enough for everyone, but that hadn't been part of Uncle Homer's instructions. The family would gather after supper to discuss Grandma's dream. They would decide then, Uncle Homer had said, but he intended to proceed with the plan. Why else would Uncle Homer gather the whole family? This was only so everyone would feel involved. But was she ready to pick up where Grandma had left off? That was the question that nagged her.

Running a farm to minister to needy *Englisha kinner* was so right on the one hand, and so unusual on the other. No one did such things. Once word trickled back to the community in Lancaster that she had received training from the *Englisha* to take on such a project, the whispers would start in spite of Grandma's sterling reputation. Phoebe could hear them already.

Phoebe couldn't settle down with a husband, and now look what she's doing.

Yah, is it any wonder she couldn't find a decent man? Pride is a hard thing to hide.

Our women have always been quiet and submissive. I thought Phoebe had changed her ways, but apparently not.

The words would sting, as those from the past had stung. They already did, and they hadn't even been spoken yet. Would she have the courage to face them, to say nothing of running the farm? Phoebe Lapp had vowed she'd never again do anything risky in her life. Somehow she had to find peace and the right answers...but how? Should she simply say no? Uncle Homer would likely be relieved. But could she let the opportunity slip away? A job of this impor-tance might never be offered to her again. Grandma really must have wanted this to happen for her to pay David a year's wages with-out any promise that Uncle Homer would agree to the plan. And clearly, Grandma had believed this was right for her granddaughter.

Phoebe stood and paced the kitchen floor as her thoughts whirled. She couldn't turn down this chance. If she walked away from this opportunity, she would look back in the years to come and wonder what could have been. In this job she could be herself again, and how many *Englisha kinner* might be helped if she had the courage to say yes?

Phoebe peered out the kitchen window toward the darkened barnyard, where the ponies had settled down for the night. They didn't know that the Lapp family would soon arrive, and heavy decisions would be laid on the table. David had seemed so level headed this afternoon, even with his shyness. Could she depend on David? Grandma had confidence in him. Why else had she already paid him to help? Phoebe would never have thought to ask the man, and Uncle Homer might object to that arrangement tonight. If he did, she would insist that David be involved. There was no other way. Grandma's plan must be implemented to its fullest or not at all.

And Grandma's dream would *not* fail.

Moments later the sound of horses' hooves beating on the pave-ment reached Phoebe. She popped the lid over the soup bowl. A few crumbs scattered on the floor, and Phoebe grabbed the broom from the closet to sweep them up. With the dustpan she gathered the debris and tossed it into the stove top. The flames came to life in a quick flash, and Phoebe slammed the lid back down with a bang.

As she was hanging the broom and dustpan back in the closet, the front door rattled and opened. No one knocked before Phoebe heard footsteps coming into the house. They were family members, and this was Grandma Lapp's home. Phoebe gave her apron another shake and pasted on a brave smile before entering the living room.

Aunt Mary and Aunt Hettie took off their wraps and greeted Phoebe with smiles of their own. Phoebe held out her hand, and they gave her their shawls.

"How are things going?" Aunt Mary asked as Phoebe retreated toward the bedroom.

"Okay." Phoebe tossed the word over her shoulder. "I just finished supper, but I can make more if anyone is hungry."

"Oh, no. Please don't bother," Aunt Mary assured her. "I was afraid you would prepare something. I told Homer he should have made the details of his plan for this evening plainer to you. We are not here to add an extra burden."

"I couldn't agree more," Aunt Hettie echoed.

Phoebe nodded and entered the bedroom with the shawls. No comment was needed. Her family planned to make this evening easy. For that she was grateful.

When she returned to the living room, Uncle Homer and Uncle Noah had entered. They tossed their hats and coats on the floor.

"*Goot* evening," Uncle Homer said. "We are back again."

"Hi, Phoebe," Uncle Noah added.

They all turned as the door opened, and Uncle Rueben entered with Aunt Millie behind him.

A chorus of "*goot* evening" went around the circle as everyone took their seats.

Phoebe found a chair, and once she was seated she clasped and unclasped her hands. This meeting was about her. Never had so much fuss been made about Phoebe Lapp's affairs. She took a deep breath and willed the pounding of her heart to cease.

"Well, we might as well begin since everyone's here," Uncle Homer said. He took a quick glance around the room. "Thanks for coming out on such short notice. I didn't know myself until this morning, and I had hoped this could be handled in some other way, but apparently..." Uncle Homer paused and then cleared his throat. "I'm not quite sure how this all began. I first heard about *Mamm*'s harebrained scheme when she sent Cousin Herman down to Maryland to buy some horses. I told Noah then about my feelings, and we both voiced our strong objections to *Mamm*, which—"

"And no one thought to tell me," Aunt Millie interrupted.

"Millie, I know you are my sister." Uncle Homer used his most patient tone. "But this was still a man's matter at the time, and *Mamm*—"

"You should have told me of your objections!" Aunt Millie insisted.

"Maybe that is true," Uncle Homer allowed. "But looking back is always easier than looking forward."

"We presumed the matter would blow over," Uncle Noah added.

Aunt Millie slid forward on the couch. "So let's start with what *Mamm* planned to do and stop beating around the bush. For Phoebe's sake."

"Millie, that's saying enough," Uncle Reuben warned.

Uncle Homer shrugged. "I suppose you are right, Millie. Phoebe doesn't know, so that is where we should begin. *Mamm* wanted to open a farm of some sort for troubled *Englisha* children, a place where they could come for a week or so and find peace away from their world of woe and turmoil."

"That's a *goot* idea!" Aunt Millie proclaimed.

Uncle Noah made a face. "That is exactly why you weren't asked. The men needed to think this through on their own."

Aunt Millie took a deep breath but remained silent.

Uncle Homer waited a few moments before he continued. "So this morning when Phoebe brought up the subject of keeping the horses, I thought she was asking about something *Mamm* had told her. Turns out *Mamm* hadn't mentioned her plan to Phoebe, but that's beside the point."

"It was a sign from the Lord," Aunt Millie got in edgewise.

Uncle Homer ignored her. "So I thought we should at least look into this idea. Of course, that's not saying we should follow the plan. Doing so would involve not just us three, but the rest of the children. We'd all have to invest our interest in the farm—not that most of us couldn't. From what I know, no one is hurting financially."

"I think it's a great idea," Aunt Millie said again.

Uncle Homer still ignored her. "So that's where we are, and it's where we left the conversation with Phoebe. So let's begin with you, Phoebe. Would you consider running the farm?"

All eyes turned toward Phoebe, and she clutched both sides of the chair. Somehow the words came out. "I...I mean...I really didn't know anything about this until today. I know that I'm the least likely person anyone would choose to do something like this, and that it's risky and all...but I do think we should follow Grandma's plan. If we don't...I mean, if *I* don't, I believe I'll always regret it."

Uncle Homer grunted. "You are right that the plan is risky. That's why Noah and I never thought much of it, and it's why we hoped it would all blow over." Uncle Homer glanced at his brother. "But it didn't, and here we are."

"I'd like to hear more from Phoebe," Aunt Millie said. "How did you arrive at your thinking, dear?"

Phoebe hesitated, and Uncle Noah spoke up. "Phoebe seems to know about the plan. How did that happen? Earlier today you said you did not."

Phoebe hung her head for a moment. "I was getting to that

point. David Fisher came by around lunchtime and told me that Grandma had already hired him on for this project. She paid him a year's wages, which he could keep regardless of whether or not the plan worked out. He said he was supposed to tell me on Grandma's behalf. Only Uncle Homer had beat David to it, or almost, as Uncle Homer didn't give me any details."

Uncle Noah and Uncle Homer exchanged glances. "So *Mamm* did make some plans," Uncle Noah said. He didn't appear too pleased.

"But she left most of the details up to us," Uncle Homer added. "Did you notice that?"

Uncle Noah grunted but said nothing more.

"I'm thinking your consciences are bothering both of you—and quite a bit," Aunt Millie said. "Am I guessing right?"

Silence greeted the question.

"Then we should proceed with the plan," Aunt Millie continued. "I'm sure Rueben isn't against leaving our share of the farm for *Mamm*'s worthy dream."

Rueben didn't think too long before he spoke. "It does sound like a worthy cause, although quite unusual. What if things go wrong? Who will be responsible?"

"That's just the problem," Uncle Homer told him. "And now there's this new part about David Fisher. I don't know about that."

Phoebe forced herself to speak. "Grandma wanted David to be part of the project, and I'm fine with that—even considering his family's reputation. I haven't seen that much of David this past year, but Grandma paid him to take care of the chores and the farmwork. He always did them well from what I could see." Phoebe paused, noticing every eye was fixed on her. Had she said too much?

"You'd be running the place, not David," Uncle Homer said.

"I...*yah*, sure," Phoebe stammered. "That's how it would need to be. I mean, you all have families, and I don't have anything else to do, and David would help out the way he did when Grandma was alive."

"You could take the community's schoolteaching job instead," Uncle Noah said. "That would be much more fitting than this wild venture."

"I know," Phoebe agreed, "but…" She didn't know how to explain.

Aunt Millie spoke up. "*Mamm* was a praying woman. We all grew up under her prayers and were greatly benefited. Perhaps her wishes were for others to be blessed with her faith also."

"That is one way to look at this," Uncle Noah allowed. "But that doesn't solve our problems."

"*Mamm* is with the Lord," Uncle Homer agreed. "So I'm expecting she has His ear now as much as she used to down here."

Silence fell. Everyone was looking at the floor, and a tear trickled down Aunt Millie's face. Her voice was hushed when she spoke. "My vote is for doing this—for letting Phoebe run the farm."

"If the farm could be self-supporting, I would agree," Uncle Homer added. "That would be important, and we could reevaluate after a year or so."

"If the Lord blesses it, surely the farm will be self-supporting," Aunt Millie told him. "And *Mamm* has paid David Fisher for a year already, so you don't have that expense to consider."

"David Fisher," Uncle Noah muttered, seemingly lost in own thoughts.

"*Mamm* was trying to help out their family," Aunt Millie told him. "That's what I am thinking. She did practically raise those two children."

"*Mamm* always had more faith in Leroy Fisher's children than I did," Uncle Noah replied.

"Then it's decided." Aunt Millie clapped her hands. "We will say no more about the Fisher family."

Both Uncle Homer and Uncle Noah grunted but otherwise remained silent.

"I guess it's in your hands now, dear." Aunt Millie turned to Phoebe. "Do you know anything about running a business?"

"Ah...I...no, but I feel sure I can learn."

"That's the spirit!" Aunt Millie chirped.

Both Uncle Homer and Uncle Noah appeared quite skeptical.

"You two can keep a close eye on things," Aunt Millie said, looking at her two brothers. Then she turned back to her niece. "That will be okay with you, won't it, Phoebe?"

"Of course! I mean, *yah*. I can use all the help I can get."

"You are so brave," Aunt Millie told her. "That must come from *Mamm*'s prayers too."

Phoebe opened her mouth to protest, but Uncle Homer spoke first. "We'll think about this and talk with the others. If they're in agreement, we'll send Millie over to tell you, Phoebe. You can proceed from there. Okay?"

Phoebe nodded as they turned their attention to other things. She should offer them something to drink from the kitchen, if her legs would hold her. Phoebe struggled to stand and lunged forward. As she walked toward the kitchen, Aunt Mary and Aunt Hettie were close behind her with concerned looks on their faces.

"That was some surprise!" Aunt Mary exclaimed. "No wonder you're at the edge of exhaustion. All of this on top of yesterday's funeral."

Aunt Hettie put out her hand and helped Phoebe sit at the table. "What were you planning to get in here?"

"I should serve something," Phoebe gasped. "Lemonade, maybe? I have some lemons in the refrigerator."

"You stay right there and don't move," Aunt Hettie ordered. "Mary and I will see to this."

Her aunts busied themselves at the counter as the conversation from the living room buzzed in the background. Aunt Mary and Aunt Hettie exchanged glances several times.

"I suppose you think us a strange family," Phoebe finally ventured.

"We married into it." Aunt Hettie attempted a laugh. "Your grandma did always seem extraordinary, but this..." She paused.

"Is going a little far," Phoebe finished.

Aunt Hettie smiled. "*Yah*, I suppose that's what I mean. And yet you have the courage to take on a farm. You must be a lot like your grandma."

"I'm not," Phoebe protested. "Not in the least. I..."

The two exchanged glances again.

"It's all Grandma's doing," Phoebe insisted. "She was a praying woman, but so are some of our other faithful people. It's not so strange to..."

Silence finished the statement. Praying or not, one didn't regularly go about starting up farms with Assateague ponies for troubled *Englisha* children.

"We will hope for the best," Aunt Mary finally said, "but don't miss the chance to take on that teaching job if you're in doubt. The school board has to find someone soon."

Phoebe nodded. The two older ladies worked in silence until the pitcher of lemonade was finished. Phoebe looked over at the sugar bowl and the freshly squeezed lemons scattered on the counter.

She took charge. This was her kitchen, after all. "I'll clean up later. Let's serve the lemonade."

Phoebe grabbed several glasses from the cabinet, and Aunt Hettie did likewise. Aunt Mary followed them into the living room with the pitcher of lemonade in her firm grasp.

FOUR

The following morning Phoebe awoke early before the dawn had blossomed in the eastern sky. She dressed, placed her kerosene lamp on the hardwood floor, and set out to clean the upstairs before breakfast. Her mind was in a whirl as she hurried down the hallway with her broom and dustpan. The day of Grandma's burial seemed two years instead of two days ago. So much had happened in the last forty-eight hours, as if a dam had broken and the water had rushed downstream to overflow the river's banks.

Phoebe took a firm grip on the broom handle. A few cobwebs she must have missed at the last cleaning hung at the far end of the hall. How could that have happened? She swatted at them before picking up crumbs some young cousin had doubtless left at lunch-time on the day of the funeral.

Phoebe paused to catch her breath. Only two days ago, every bedroom in the house had been packed to the hilt, with cots laid out in the hallways for the smaller children. Now silence reigned, with a stillness that crept into her bones. This old house was made for the patter of small feet and the rise and fall of excited voices. Generations had been raised here, and those who followed should also be so blessed.

Phoebe's heart still pounded at the thought of what Grandma's venture would bring. She didn't have to take the plunge. The place could be sold to an Amish family, and the home would be back to full use. On the other hand, she could follow the path that Grandma had laid out. *Englisha* young people would sleep here and run in these halls...perhaps tearing the place apart or burning it down as she slept restlessly downstairs.

Phoebe gasped as the awful image of flames flickered in her mind, and the dustpan clattered to the hardwood floor. Why hadn't she thought of this last night, instead of putting on a brave face in front of Uncle Homer and Uncle Noah? They would have been glad to relieve her of the responsibility and lay Grandma's dream to rest. But she hadn't expressed these fears, and now she couldn't back down. She must be brave. This was her chance—if she could keep up her courage for more than a few moments. What a timid soul she had become. What had possessed Grandma Lapp to think she was capable of such a huge, tremendously complicated, and perhaps impossible task?

Phoebe grabbed the dustpan from the floor and swept vigorously with the broom. The kerosene lamp flickered from the bursts of wind she created.

"This is enough!" Phoebe declared to the empty house. "Time for breakfast."

She gathered up the lamp and made her way down the stairs, where her foot stopped midstep. What would running a farm for *Englisha* young people do to her chances of finding a husband? The voices from the past rang in her ear. She'd be forever known as a risky case for any unmarried man seeking a decent *frau*.

Phoebe moaned. She couldn't give up the farm because of some unknown future that wasn't about to happen anyway. No Amish man was standing in line to ask her for a date. And the past was the past.

Phoebe forced her foot onward and held the lamp high. What awful choices life pushed on her. She plunked the lamp on the kitchen table.

"I'm making myself oatmeal. Something simple."

A few minutes later the water boiled, and Phoebe added dry oatmeal, along with cinnamon and raisins. She stirred while the mixture bubbled. When the prescribed five minutes had passed, she dipped the gooey goodness into a bowl and added brown sugar and milk. After a quick prayer of thanks, she began to eat.

Her mind still raced, so Phoebe quoted Scripture between bites. "Now unto him that is able to keep you from falling, and to present you faultless..." The holy text brought some peace.

She'd be perfectly happy if exact instructions were written down somewhere on what Phoebe Lapp and three ponies were supposed to accomplish. But, of course, there was nothing like that. There were only words that applied to all of mankind, and one had to work out the personal details. That's what Bishop Rufus had preached several times in his sermons since she arrived in the valley a year ago. She couldn't remember any particular instructions at home in Lancaster, but maybe things were different in a new community where the need to address fresh circumstances was more frequent—such as how to run a farm for *Englisha* young people.

Phoebe finished her bowl of oatmeal and slipped out into the brisk morning air. The summer day would soon see a rise in temperature, but things were still pleasant. The ponies had been out all night in the pasture. She had left the barn door open for them—if she remembered correctly. Everything had been such confusion last night. She had hardly gotten to bed herself. There had been no time for a final check on the ponies, but they would be okay. They were wild ponies at heart and used to fending for themselves. This was a fact that hadn't come up last night—thankfully. She was fairly certain that any mention of wildness would have been too much for either uncle to handle.

A chill ran up and down Phoebe's back. Maybe this was why she felt such an affinity with the ponies. She must have her own wild heart. Wasn't that exactly what Willie Mast had called her—a wicked, wild woman? The pain of the words had gone all the way through her open heart. That day, she had vowed to change. She thought she had buried herself, but she must have failed. Her heart had been there—well hidden, she thought—but apparently visible to the observant eyes of the Amish men she had dated. All of them must have seen her wildness, whether or not they could put the dreadful thought into words. An Amish *frau* with a wild heart was the last thing any of them wanted. How else could one explain why she was considered for this project? No doubt Grandma had also known and made her plans accordingly—which made a wild heart a *goot* thing if Grandma thought the Lord could use such a person.

Phoebe beat her forehead with the palm of her hand. What confusion—and things were only getting worse. Maybe the ponies would clear her head.

Phoebe entered the barn and found only stillness in the stalls. The occasional thread of cobweb still hung from the ceiling, accented by the low morning light in the window. She slipped through the barn and out the back door. The ponies greeted her with hearty whinnies from the pasture and raced up to nuzzle her with their outstretched necks.

"And a *goot* morning to you. I am glad to see you again, but you only want grain, I'm thinking. Is that it?"

They whinnied together, and Phoebe managed to laugh. "Coming right up, then."

She retreated into the barn, and they followed to wait with swishing tails as she filled three buckets with grain. They stuck their noses into their breakfast the moment she lowered the offerings to the ground.

"Better than swamp grass?" Phoebe teased.

She stroked their necks while they chewed hungrily. "I should name you. Maybe that would help me make up my mind...sort of transfer the ownership from Grandma to me. Do you think that would work?"

They chewed and plunged their noses back in their buckets.

"Let's see." Phoebe touched the mane of the brown pony with the white face and white tail. "I name thee Aladdin. Is that *goot*? Do you like that?"

The pony continued to chew. "Then Aladdin it will be," she told him.

"Now you, the all-white one. Shall it be Snow Cloud? *Yah*, I like that."

Snow Cloud neighed, and Phoebe laughed. "You agree, *yah*? A *goot* name." She stroked the horse's nose before Snow Cloud returned to the grain bucket.

"And now you." Phoebe stepped closer to the brown-and-white horse painted in splotches across the back. "How about Lady? Would you like that?" Phoebe studied the pony who chewed busily. "Lady it will be," she decided. "And now we're done."

She waited and petted them a few more minutes until the grain was gone. They left willingly, without prompting from her, as if they understood she had to move on.

Phoebe watched them trot back out to the pasture with the first of the sun's rays low on their backs. They seemed to sparkle and glow, but that wasn't possible. She wouldn't take this as some kind of sign as to what should be done. No, the answer must come from somewhere else. But from where? She had not gotten herself into this fix, and she couldn't get herself out.

Maybe she should take a brisk walk down to the graveyard and pay Grandma's burial site a visit. The dirt would still be piled high, with the grass trampled in a circle where hundreds of mourners had stood only two days ago.

She could hitch up Grandma's old driving horse. Misty stayed in the back pasture during the summer months, and one had to make the trip down and bring up the mare by hand. Misty didn't like to stir more than she had to. Nor did she like to trot on the roads. Phoebe only drove Misty when absolutely necessary, so a brisk walk down to the gravesite would be the best option. Even so, Grandma was in heaven by the Lord's side, and visiting her grave for reasons other than respect might not be wise.

She would wait and rack her brain because she couldn't help it, but she already knew no answer would come from that direction.

Phoebe stepped outside the barn and turned her face toward the rising sun. Who was she to think that she could minister to hearts torn and injured? She was a troubled soul in her own right.

"Oh, Grandma," she cried to the heavens. "What did you think you were doing? Are you tempting me?"

But this was no temptation. Grandma wasn't like that. Grandma was the epitome of kindness and goodness. Eccentric, *yah*! Grandma must have thought she could do this, but why? That was the question. Would Phoebe have to find the light on her own?

FIVE

David strode slowly up Burrell Road from his parents' place early on Saturday morning. He shouldn't bother Phoebe at this hour, but he couldn't help himself. Phoebe would be up by now. Surely a decision had been made about the pony farm. Phoebe had said she would tell him when it was, but he couldn't wait. He also wanted to see her again. He hardly dared to think such thoughts, or imagine that his love would ever be returned. Thankfully, Phoebe didn't know what lay in his heart—his deep admiration of her, his shortness of breath in her presence, his hope that stirred when he gazed into her eyes. He would never show his face in her presence again if she knew, and if the pony farm fell through, she would be gone from his life forever.

David walked with his eyes on the ground. Grandma Lapp must have known about his attraction to her granddaughter. Had Grandma approved? He had never been able to tell. He had wondered if this was what lay behind Grandma's request when she had asked if he would be involved in the farm project, but that hope had been dashed after his talk with Phoebe. Grandma would not have made such vague plans if she had considered him a serious suitor for Phoebe.

David lowered the brim of his hat when the first rays of the sun burst over the Adirondack foothills. How could he dream of winning Phoebe's affections? True, they were both Amish, and Phoebe had lived in the district for more than a year, but their similarities ended there. Phoebe came from a well-respected family, whose roots went deep into Lancaster. Phoebe's two uncles and aunt added much to the stability of the young community nestled in the shadow of the Adirondacks.

David's father, on the other hand, had always struggled financially and kept relationships on edge. Nothing that *Daett* touched seemed to bring about the desired result. If *Daett* planted corn, the timing was always off by a week or two. If *Daett* mowed hay, the rains always came two days later, right when the grass was dry and ready for the baler. *Daett* tried, but he failed. There was nothing David could do about the matter. Because of *Daett*'s attitude, his family's reputation as ne'er-do-wells was firmly established in the community.

Ruth didn't help matters. David's sister hadn't left her *rumspringa* when the normal time had arrived for young people to return. Ruth still dated that *Englisha* man, Ethan Thompson, off and on. David had done what he could. He had spoken with Ruth, but his words fell on deaf ears. He had joined the baptismal class three years ago, but that hadn't persuaded Ruth to follow his example either. Ruth had become fully bitter over their family's poor reputation, but leaving the community was no way to escape.

One was what one was. Like *Daett*, David never got the timing right. Even if this farm venture of Grandma Lapp's came to pass, he would be consigned to the status of Phoebe's hired help. What romance could bloom under those circumstances, even if the thought crossed Phoebe's mind?

Here he was, twenty-six years old, desperately in love with a young woman who hardly knew he existed. After the funeral he had gathered the courage to approach Phoebe with Grandma Lapp's message. He had hoped Phoebe would respond with a great burst of joy and happiness, but he should have known better. The whole project was risky. Of course he liked Grandma's dream. He was a Fisher and used to unconventional things. What else explained his openness to the idea while stable members of the community held back?

He would only expose himself further when he arrived this morning at Grandma's farm uninvited. What would he say, exactly?

"Have you made up your mind, Phoebe?"

Or worse: *"I really think you should do this, Phoebe."*

That's what he really wanted to say, but he felt he had no moral authority from which to speak. He really was crazy to reach for Phoebe Lapp's affections. To think he might someday ask for her hand in marriage. To imagine he could run a proper farm and provide a stable financial base for his family. How he dreamed. He was David Fisher, the ne'er-do-well's son. He had inherited his *daett's* faults, and if not for Grandma Lapp's kindness, he would have given up a long time ago.

Which didn't speak well for him. He should be a man and stand on his own two feet. Somewhere there was a woman who fit his status. He ought not reach for the impossible Phoebe Lapp.

David kicked a stone with his shoe, and its arc went high over the ditch before disappearing in the roadside grass with a rustle. *Mamm* had named him David when he was born in the hopes that, like the David of old, he would grow up to slay giants and make a difference in the world. *Mamm* had known there were many giants to slay in their family. So far he had failed to drop even one. Maybe that was the hope that stirred. Maybe there was still time. Maybe he could persuade Phoebe that this idea of Grandma Lapp's was the perfect venture. But considering his status, his assurance might emphasize all that was wrong about the project.

No one consulted a Fisher on when to mow hay or plant corn. Why should a Fisher be consulted on such a weighty question? A pony farm would take the support of the whole community. His opinion on the matter had best be left in the dark.

David kicked another stone and turned his steps into Grandma's driveway. If the pony farm didn't happen, this place would be sold and another Amish family would move in. But he would always remember this as Grandma Lapp's place. This was where he had first seen Phoebe's face, appearing like a dream that drifted up from Lancaster. On that day he had managed to hide the emotions that flooded through him.

Phoebe hadn't noticed because of her intense dedication to her grandmother's care. He was so obviously beneath her. Why Phoebe wasn't married, or had her wedding planned, he couldn't imagine. Phoebe hadn't even dated since her arrival in the community because all the eligible men were spoken for in the small valley.

He was the only bachelor left!

David glanced at the house but turned his steps toward the barn instead. He once had free access to the place, but that had changed. In the meantime, he could do the chores until something was decided. Phoebe might catch a glimpse of him from the kitchen window and expect his arrival at the front door later. He didn't dare head straight to the house.

David pushed open the barn door and entered. The cobwebs had been swept clean since he had been here last. Phoebe must have taken on the task now that she was freed from Grandma's care. Phoebe certainly wouldn't sit around with idle hands. David found the broom propped up in the corner with its straws askew.

A smile filled his face. Phoebe must have attacked the cobwebs with a fury to leave the broom in such a condition. Maybe she had been mortified that the task hadn't been completed before the funeral. Hundreds of mourners had been through the place, and a messy barn was always a disgrace. Maybe his family wasn't the only one who did things off schedule. Of course, Phoebe had a perfect excuse, but the Fishers usually didn't. David had been down here many times over the last year, and he could have taken the work on himself, but not once had the thought occurred to him.

He hurried on and whistled to the ponies at the back barn door. They perked their ears up and came toward him at a fast trot. He held out his hand. They nuzzled him and whinnied.

David chuckled. "I can't be spoiling you anymore, I'm afraid." A moment later he gave in. "Maybe just this once."

He retreated into the barn to fill a bucket with oats. Back outside, he held up the offering to each one in turn. They took greedy mouthfuls and munched with contented swishes of their tails.

"Enough now," David warned as he pulled the bucket back. All three of them followed him to the barn door, but he held them back before he slipped inside and closed the gate. Loud whinnies of protest filled the building, and he reached out to pat them on their heads.

David jumped when Phoebe spoke from behind him. "Spoiling the ponies, I see."

"I..." He searched for words.

Her smile was kind. "I'm just teasing. I've grown quite close to them myself." Phoebe reached over the gate to brush their long manes. "No more treats," she told them. "Enough for one day."

They seemed to understand and trotted back toward the pasture. David watched them go, keeping Phoebe in his side vision. Her beauty was even more pronounced this morning. She hadn't put her hair up yet, but had it wrapped in a handkerchief with stray strands all over her face. He had never seen her like this, nor had she spent time with the ponies when he was around.

"I named them." She sent another smile in his direction.

"So you...you are...you are moving forward with the pony farm?" The question burst out.

Her smile left. "I don't know yet, but I did name them."

"And what would those names be?"

"I named the white one Snow Cloud." She glanced at David. "Do you like that?"

He forced a smile. "That's perfect. She is like a snow cloud."

"*Yah*, that's what I thought. I named the brown one with the white face and tail Aladdin after the ancient tale of the rubbed lamp."

David suppressed his astonishment. "You have read that book?"

"Why do you ask? Do you think it's inappropriate for an Amish girl? A wild—"

"Of course not," he quickly assured her. "It's just that I've never seen this side of you. That's adventurous."

"I guess I am adventurous. Well, I used to be." Phoebe made a face. "I've not been adventurous for many years."

"But you came up from Lancaster to care for Grandma Lapp, and now you're considering this pony farm."

"I guess so," she said, but she didn't meet his gaze. "Do you still like the idea?"

He drew his breath in slowly before he answered. "I think you ought to honor your grandma's wishes."

"Do you think Grandma thought me capable of this?"

"I think you are capable of *anything* you set your mind to."

"Oh."

He looked away. "I trust your grandma."

A smile crept across her face. "That's sweet of you to say."

So you're doing this? The words almost slipped out. "And what is the last pony's name?" he asked instead.

A dreamy look had settled on Phoebe's face. "I settled on Lady for the other brown-and-white one. Do you like that?"

"I do. A lot."

She leaned on the gate as she looked at the distant ponies. "It would seem such a shame not to do what Grandma wanted."

He waited and said nothing.

"But I've never done anything like this before, and Uncle Homer and Uncle Noah aren't sure I'm up to it. They aren't even sure if the venture would serve the purposes of the community. What do you think?"

"Why are you asking me?" He didn't dare lift his gaze from the barnyard dirt.

"Because you would be a part of this whole thing. Didn't Grandma hire you?"

"She did. I like the idea very much, but maybe I should send Ruth up with her *Englisha* boyfriend. They could explain everything to you. Maybe that would help with the decision making?"

She hesitated for a moment. "I suppose that would be the place to begin, but I have to be honest, David. I need some clear direction beyond what the *Englisha* have to say. If you have any suggestions, please share them with me."

He kept his head down. "I will do so if I have some." What did a Fisher have to say that would be clear direction? "I only know that I am very interested in the project."

"That's means a lot. At least I know you would be fully on my side."

He tried to breathe evenly. She was on board. He had known she would be. "I will speak with Ruth and schedule a meeting."

She smiled. "And now I'd best get busy with my day."

"And I should get home. There's lots of Saturday chores."

"As there always are," she agreed as she followed him out of the barn.

He left her at the end of the walk with a quick glance in her direction, but Phoebe was on her way to toward the house with her head bowed and her loose hair strewn back over her shoulder. David pulled his gaze away and plunged his hands in his pockets to march resolutely down the road. Somehow this must work. But how? In the meantime, he loved the woman way too much, and that had no solution either.

SIX

Ruth Fisher paused on the front porch. She'd had an ulterior motive when she agreed to David's request, but he didn't need to know that.

"David!" she hollered. "We are going to speak with Phoebe now!"

David appeared from around the corner of the house with a worried look. "I know we went over all this yesterday evening, but please make sure Phoebe has all the facts. This has to work. Be sure you cast everything in the best light. I know you will, but this is important to me."

Ruth forced a smile. "You are way overwrought. Grandma Lapp was a kind woman, but she's gone. To expect Phoebe to simply step into her shoes is a little much."

David's concerned look grew. "That's what I mean. Don't say anything negative, Ruth. Don't even think it. Phoebe is..." He waved his hand about. "You know Grandma wanted this. She probably would have proceeded with your idea already if she hadn't become ill."

Ruth regarded him for a moment. "I know that, but it's not your problem. You have more up your sleeve than a simple concern for her pony farm."

He looked away.

"Phoebe's not really worth it," Ruth continued. "Take my word for it. You should try what I'm doing."

"See, there you go again. Please, Ruth. For my sake. I don't want you messing this up just because you don't think..."

She shrugged. "I'll do this for you anyway. And this was my idea originally, so why can't I defend it? Look what I've done already." Ruth motioned toward the lane, where an automobile turned into the Fishers' driveway. "I didn't ask Ethan to come, but rather his boss, Mrs. Broman. That way Phoebe will not..." Ruth left the sentence unfinished. "But I won't allow the community's rejection of Ethan to color this matter."

"Thank you," David replied, but he didn't appear convinced.

"I have to go."

The truth was, she had her own motives for her continued involvement in the pony farm. Ethan's opinion of her was at the heart of her effort this morning. He hadn't proposed after two years of off and on dating. Something held Ethan back. If she brought this deal to fruition, Ethan might see that not all Amish were Neanderthals from another time and place. He might fully open his heart to her and consider her worthy of a place at his side as his wife.

She had so much to overcome when it came to Ethan. The community had slighted her family since her childhood, and though she had only completed the eighth grade, Ethan had a college degree. But she loved the man. She could cook and sew and do a hundred other things any Amish housewife did. The problem was, an Amish homemaker wasn't what Ethan wanted. He came from another world with other priorities, none of which she had been trained to do. On this point Ethan was correct. She was a hopeless Neanderthal who couldn't find her way home in anything but a horse and buggy. David was happy in his world as a ne'er-do-well Fisher, but she was not. She wanted more than what the community offered.

Ruth pasted on a bright smile as she approached the automobile.

She greeted Mrs. Broman with a cheery, "*Goot* morning. It's so nice of you to do this for us."

"The pleasure is all mine," Mrs. Broman assured her. "I've known that Ethan was working on this project for some time, and I was honored when he asked if I would make the pitch to young Ms. Lapp. Her grandmother just died, right?"

"*Yah.*" Ruth opened the car door and hopped in. "She passed away last week. A very godly woman Grandma Lapp was, with a heart for people in need." She almost added, *for people like the Fishers.* But Ruth clamped her mouth shut.

"That is so encouraging to hear. The care the Amish show their own people is legendary. Who hasn't heard about their barn raisings and other community projects?"

Daett appeared momentarily at the barn door as Mrs. Broman turned the car around in the driveway. Mrs. Broman waved, and *Daett* retreated after a feeble swing of his hand. "Your father," Mrs. Broman stated more than asked.

"Yep!" Ruth forced a cheerful chirp. Thankfully *Daett* wasn't involved in this deal, or its doom would be sealed. He never got anything right and disagreed with everything.

"What does your father think about this proposed project?" Mrs. Broman asked as she accelerated north on Burrell Road.

"Oh, *Daett* isn't involved," Ruth said.

"But isn't everyone included in everything? Isn't that how the community works?"

"If it's a community project, *yah*, but this..." Ruth waved her hand. "This is more of a family affair—the Lapp family, that is. My brother and I are involved because we knew Grandma Lapp. But *Daett*..." Ruth stopped. Her chattering didn't convince anyone, but she still smiled brightly.

Mrs. Broman appeared skeptical. "You know we'd have to inspect the farm. There would also be forms and reports to fill out and schooling for the person in charge. I hope the community wouldn't object to government involvement."

"Oh, my brother is a solid church member, and he can do things like that," Ruth hurried to say. "He'll be working on the proposed farm full-time, and he enjoys that type of thing." Which could be true. She wasn't sure. David would enjoy anything if it kept him in the vicinity of Phoebe Lapp. "If the Lapp family approves the project, the community will approve," she finished.

"I'm just bringing up the point to emphasize the difficulties—"

"There's the driveway," Ruth interrupted. "You can tell Phoebe all of your concerns. I'm sure she'll have answers, but I don't want to speak out of turn."

"Of course," Mrs. Broman said as she parked beside the Lapp barn. "Is this an okay spot, do you think?" She glanced around as if she expected an assault from a team of horses or bearded men. *Daett* hadn't made a *goot* impression on the woman when they'd met, but what was surprising about that?

"There's Phoebe on the front porch now." Ruth jumped out of the vehicle, and Mrs. Broman followed slowly. Phoebe came down to the bottom of the porch steps to meet them.

"*Goot* morning." Phoebe greeted them with a nervous smile. "I'm Phoebe."

"And a good morning to you," Mrs. Broman returned. "I'm Wauneta. Are you expecting us?"

"*Yah*, come on inside." Phoebe turned to lead the way. "It is very kind of you to come and explain things to this ignorant Amish girl."

Don't say that, Ruth mouthed in Phoebe's direction, but Phoebe didn't seem to notice.

Mrs. Broman smiled. "I'm glad to hear of your interest in this project. You will do your grandmother proud, no doubt. This was her dream, correct?"

"*Yah*, Grandma Lapp. I cared for her this past year. She was dear to all of us." Phoebe ushered them through the front door and then motioned toward the couch. "If you will be seated, I'll get coffee. Or I could prepare hot chocolate if you prefer."

"Coffee's fine," Mrs. Broman replied as she made herself comfortable.

Ruth followed Phoebe into the kitchen, where they placed cups, sugar, and creamer on a tray. Phoebe led the way back to the living room with the coffeepot in her hand, and they set everything on a small table in front of the couch.

Once the coffee cups were filled, Mrs. Broman took a careful sip and pronounced, "It's excellent, Phoebe. I've never had Amish coffee before."

Phoebe brushed the praise away with a toss of her hand. "Coffee is coffee, I suppose."

Mrs. Broman smiled. "So where shall we begin?"

Ruth held her breath until Phoebe finally asked, "If you could fill me in on what the expectations are for the pony farm, maybe that would be helpful."

"Certainly," Mrs. Broman began. "We're looking for a farm where young children can come for a week at a time. These are troubled children—even physically abused, perhaps—but all of them would benefit from what a quiet place in the country could offer. There would be inspections of the farm, conducted primarily by myself or Ethan Thompson, and training for the person in charge. We're looking at property worthiness, cooking issues, and bedroom space. After that, we would begin sending a few children a week. Perhaps we could increase the number as time goes on and we all learn what works and what doesn't."

Phoebe appeared a little pale. "I've never done anything like this before. I've only cared for my grandma and my younger siblings, but I suppose the training would help." She finished with an apologetic laugh.

"But you can cook, wash, and keep house." Mrs. Broman chuckled. "The Amish know that naturally, don't they?"

Ruth jumped into the conversation. "Yes. We all do."

"That's what I thought," Mrs. Broman said. "Another issue of concern would be your business structure. But that shouldn't be a problem, considering how community minded the Amish are. Everyone oversees everyone else, don't they?"

"*Yah*, I suppose so," Phoebe allowed. "Exactly what are you referring to?"

"Something like a board," Ruth offered.

"What's a board?" Phoebe asked.

Ruth looked away, but Mrs. Broman explained patiently. "Surely you have older relatives who could form a business group to oversee the farm, offer you advice, and provide consultation if we have concerns with how things are going." Mrs. Broman smiled sweetly. "In a worst-case scenario, of course. You always have to be prepared for such things."

Phoebe nodded. "I do have two uncles and an aunt in the community. We already had a meeting last week about this, and my Aunt Millie told me this morning I could go ahead if I wanted to. They plan to allow the use of the farm since Grandma Lapp left a share to all of her children."

"A family business. There's nothing wrong with that, but families are notorious for not getting along. I guess you know that."

"Oh, we get along," Phoebe assured Mrs. Broman. "That's the least of my worries. Whether or not I should do this is the question. It is a little unusual for Amish people."

"I see." Mrs. Broman paused. "Of course, I don't get involved in those issues. You either have the farm here for our inspection and usage, or you don't. But let me say, unofficially, that I would welcome the existence of such a place, and I would see that you received all the help you need with the required paperwork. You would have a full house at all times. I would want the venture to succeed, and so does Ethan, who..." Mrs. Broman cast her gaze at Ruth. "You're not his fiancée, are you?"

"Not yet," Ruth chirped.

Mrs. Broman smiled. "My heart is with you on that one, Ruth. Ethan's not an easy man to nail down."

Ruth pressed her lips together as the conversation continued.

"They would bring their own clothing for the week, then?" Phoebe asked.

"Certainly," Mrs. Broman assured her.

"And will they all like Amish cooking?"

Mrs. Broman laughed. "Who doesn't? But if there are any special needs, we would let you know."

"I hope I'm up to that," Phoebe muttered.

Ruth jumped in again. "Any Amish woman can handle cooking if she has the recipe."

Mrs. Broman smiled, and Phoebe seemed satisfied.

"Can you give me a quick tour of the place?" Mrs. Broman asked. Her smile was kind.

Ruth waited while Phoebe took Mrs. Broman through the whole house, and then she followed the two other women out to the barn.

Phoebe called to the ponies, and they trotted up to the back barn door.

"Real Assateague ponies!" Mrs. Broman gushed. "And tame at that. But I've always heard they make great pets."

"One of Ruth's brothers, David, has taken care of them since I came," Phoebe offered. "And they have never misbehaved."

"You may have to get more of them if this idea takes off, you know," Mrs. Broman said.

Phoebe shook her head. "We'll take one step at a time for now. But I am so thankful that you came out and answered my questions."

"I wouldn't have wanted this any other way."

After a last nuzzle from the ponies, the party moved back to the car. Mrs. Broman handed Phoebe a stack of forms and papers to read.

"Just look these over and call me with any questions." Mrs. Broman's finger traced one of the pages. "No concern is too little."

"Thank you so much," Phoebe told her.

Mrs. Broman opened the car door and turned to Ruth. "Are we ready?"

"Ah...I believe I'll walk back home," Ruth told her. "I want to talk with Phoebe a little bit."

"See you later, then." Mrs. Broman climbed in her car and waved goodbye.

Phoebe groaned once the car was back out on 170. "My head is spinning! I think I'm going to faint."

"Here!" Ruth took the stack of paper from Phoebe's arm. "Does that help?"

"No, that's not the problem. Courage is my problem. I've been a coward for too long."

"You are not!" Ruth retorted. "You're a woman of strength, and Grandma Lapp was a praying woman."

"I wish Grandma were still here with her prayers," Phoebe said. "How much easier that would make things."

Ruth's thoughts raced. Should she confess what she knew? Snooping wasn't that bad a sin, and she was desperate to encourage Phoebe. "Grandma Lapp has some prayers written down," she admitted. "I looked through them once when the house was empty. I mean, I know how that sounds, but David and I were given the run of the place. We never misbehaved—"

"I believe you," Phoebe interrupted with a smile. "What did you find?"

"Grandma Lapp had a prayer book. They were *goot* prayers."

"Do you mean a prayer book like the ones at church?" Comprehension dawned on Phoebe's face.

"No, silly. Her own prayers."

"Her own prayers?" Phoebe appeared dumbfounded. "But where?"

Ruth shrugged. "I found a tablet sitting beside her bed on the dresser. I don't know where it is now."

"A prayer book." Phoebe seemed lost in thought. "Maybe Grandma left an answer."

"Maybe."

"Then I must find it." Phoebe grabbed the stack of papers from Ruth's arms and hurried up the walk. "Thank you for everything!" she hollered over her shoulder.

"You're welcome!" Ruth called back. She had done everything she could do. Ethan's opinion of her would not be advanced if this plan didn't work. Not after they had gone to all this trouble.

SEVEN

A week later, on Saturday morning, Phoebe again bustled about Grandma Lapp's old farmhouse with a dustpan and broom in her hand. Aunt Millie was due any minute for a visit, and the kitchen and living room floors must be spotless. The upstairs hadn't been swept since that early morning effort after the funeral, but a lot of dirt shouldn't have accumulated from her solitary activities. Still, a quick check wouldn't hurt. With all the idle time she'd had on her hands these past two weeks while she thought about the proposed pony farm, a clean house was the least Aunt Millie could expect.

Phoebe took the stairs two at a time. A quick glance around revealed a clean hallway. Maybe the bedrooms should be looked into? If nothing else, she might find the cranny where Grandma's mysterious prayer book was located. She'd spent every spare moment this week in a thorough search of the house, right up to the attic.

Grandma had a lifetime's worth of things stuck in every corner of the house. Somewhere Phoebe had missed the book—if Ruth's memory was correct. Ruth had seemed so certain.

Phoebe opened the first bedroom door to peer inside. The place was clean, but the book had to be either hidden or sitting in plain sight somewhere in the house. Phoebe pushed the broom under the bed and came up with a slight puff of dust that had gathered since her last cleaning. She gathered up the offending particles and proceeded to the next room. Twenty minutes later, the entire upstairs was spotless, but there still was no sign of a prayer journal.

Phoebe paused to listen. She heard the sound of buggy wheels in the driveway, meaning Aunt Millie was here. Maybe she knew where the book might be. If not, she might help with the pile of papers Mrs. Broman had left. Phoebe had set them out on the kitchen table downstairs and had been through each one until the words ran together. Even so, they had never made sense. The *Englisha* words about this and that were mumbo jumbo. Certainly not Amish sounding. Grandma's dream was doomed. Phoebe's courage had failed her again. Why couldn't she grab on to Grandma's vision and make this work?

Phoebe slowly made her way down the steps and hung the broom and dustpan in the hall closet. Aunt Millie had tied her horse and was halfway to the house when Phoebe stepped out on the front porch.

Aunt Millie waved. "*Goot* morning!"

"*Goot* morning!" Phoebe hollered back. She hurried toward her aunt.

The two embraced, and Aunt Millie held Phoebe at arm's length. "You are looking great."

Phoebe forced a laugh. "Why wouldn't I be?"

"Oh, you know why. You're living by yourself in this big old house, worrying about things, and trying to figure out what must be done. Am I not right?"

"Well, almost," Phoebe admitted. "I've been busy worrying. But I did tell you Sunday about the visit Ruth Fisher arranged with Mrs. Broman to give me the information I needed."

Aunt Millie took Phoebe's arm to lead the way toward the house.

"This plan shouldn't have been indulged in the first place. That's what we're thinking now—Homer, Noah, and I. I know I was very supportive that first evening, but are you really up to this, Phoebe? If it weren't for *Mamm's* memory…"

Phoebe drew a long breath.

Aunt Millie continued before Phoebe could answer. "You've lived in the valley this past year, dear, and you are a timid and cautious person. Isn't this—"

"I wasn't always this way."

"But you are now." Aunt Millie gave Phoebe a kind smile.

Phoebe pressed back the tears. "Grandma seems to think I can be someone else. Someone I used to be. I want to try, Aunt Millie. Deep down I do. I want to be like Grandma."

"We all want to be like her." Aunt Millie paused to take Phoebe in her arms and give her a quick hug. "Think of how the other evening I spoke up to my brothers when I should have been quiet. A meek and mild spirit is also what *Mamm* was, Phoebe."

Phoebe wiped her eyes. "Ruth told me about something that I think could play a big part in my decision."

"Your decision?" Aunt Millie looked at Phoebe. "I know we wanted you to make up your own mind, but we are also involved. The truth is, all of us are getting cold feet. This seems so…"

"*Yah*, impossible," Phoebe finished. "And yet Grandma wanted this. I know she did. I can see that most clearly when I'm speaking with David and Ruth."

"The Fishers!" Aunt Millie tugged on Phoebe's arm. "You know what the community thinks about that family. That's another thing. This is a Lapp decision."

"*Yah*, but Ruth told me something that we should look into. At least, that's what my heart tells me."

"Your heart!" Aunt Millie paused again in their walk toward the house. "This comes down to a question of the head—not the heart,

Phoebe. Take that from a woman who lets her heart get away from her at times. *Mamm*'s gone, and so is her dream. We all have to face the truth."

"Maybe," Phoebe allowed. "But first I'd like to find Grandma's prayer journal. The one where she wrote down her words to the Lord."

Aunt Millie paled but didn't answer.

"So you know about this?"

Aunt Millie looked away.

Phoebe gripped her arm. "Do you know where this tablet is? This...this prayer book?"

Aunt Millie faced her. "*Mamm* was a little strange in some ways, Phoebe. This is one of those times—writing down prayers in a book. You know how that would appear if such a tale got out to the community."

"I want to read them."

Aunt Millie hung her head for a moment. "I told *Mamm* I'd take the tablet home with me for safekeeping, but we both knew the real reason. I was afraid you would find the prayer book while you were taking care of her."

"Then I must read them. I am part of the family."

"You are the next generation. This is not something we wish to have passed on."

"But prayers? What can be wrong with prayers?"

As they arrived at the front porch, Aunt Millie sat down on the steps before she answered. "Writing them down, Phoebe! The answer is plain enough. What if the ministers heard of another prayer book in the community—one that was written by a woman?"

Phoebe met Aunt Millie's gaze squarely from the bottom of the porch steps. "If Grandma wrote them, I have a right to read them."

"You *are* like her," Aunt Millie muttered. "Can we just forget about this? I wish Ruth had never told you anything. Then you could go on with your life."

"Go on the way I am now?"

"There's nothing wrong with that."

"Do you know what was said to me when I was in school?"

Aunt Millie attempted a smile. "Children say things all the time. We are taught better as we grow older."

Phoebe tried another angle. "What about the pony farm?"

"We had best be forgetting that, I'm thinking."

"Not until I have read what Grandma wrote." Phoebe turned toward Aunt Millie's buggy. "Take me to your place right now so I can read these prayers."

Aunt Millie tugged again on her arm. "I understand how you feel, Phoebe, but it would have been best if Ruth had never seen them."

"But she did, and Grandma must not have been ashamed of what she wrote if she left it lying around for Ruth to read."

"I suppose *Mamm* wasn't," Aunt Millie allowed with a little smile. "And she seems to have chosen her friends well to carry on this dream of hers."

"Then there is something in there about the pony farm?"

Aunt Millie hesitated. "I'll bring the tablet to you, Phoebe. It's best that you read it over here. I don't want anyone else to know about it."

"Do Uncle Homer and Uncle Noah know?"

Aunt Millie nodded and turned to scurry back toward her buggy. Phoebe watched from the porch as Aunt Millie drove out onto Highway 170 and headed north at a fast trot. She retreated inside and stood in the kitchen doorway. What should she do with the time until Aunt Millie returned? Maybe make lunch? But twelve o'clock was still a few hours away. On Wednesday she had begun a dress pattern, which now sat on the dining room table. But could she focus enough to avoid mistakes? She would have to. She couldn't sit idly around.

Phoebe pulled up a chair and took a firm grip on her scissors.

She had already cut most of the pieces, but there were still two smaller ones left. She made the first cut and then paused to steady her hands. The sewing machine was buzzing by the time Aunt Millie drove back into the driveway. Phoebe kept her head bent over the whirling needle until Aunt Millie walked through the front door, a small parcel tucked under her arm.

Aunt Millie extended her hand as if she expected the tablet to leap out and bite her. "Here!"

"Did you have to explain your trip home?"

Aunt Millie forced a laugh. "My daughters presumed I was just scatterbrained and forgot something." Aunt Millie stopped with her gaze fixed on the unopened book.

"Where shall I start?" Phoebe asked.

"It's not fit reading, any of it. But there's plenty in there about the farm."

"You mean her dream?"

Aunt Millie nodded. "Read for yourself, dear. I know where one is. I'll show you."

Phoebe's hand trembled as she sat down in front of the sewing machine again. Aunt Millie found the page and then waited as Phoebe looked at it, her vision blurry. The pages were written in Grandma's handwriting. She knew from the letters Grandma used to write to *Mamm*.

"Read out loud," Aunt Millie ordered. "I would like to hear the words again while we're at it."

"'Dear God in heaven,'" Phoebe began. "'You are the great Redeemer of mankind and the One I so greatly love. You have become even more precious to me as life around me fades away and grows so very dim. I love my family and my dear Tobias, who is waiting by Your side, I am sure, but it is Your face that I long to see. Someday soon, I hope. Oh, the joy that flows over me when I think of that dawning morn, when the sun will come up upon that golden shore, and we shall never grow weary or weep again.'"

"Do you see what I mean?" Aunt Millie whispered. "Such prayers! Who has ever heard of such a thing?"

"But the dream of the farm," Phoebe replied. "Where is that?"

"It's coming up."

Phoebe read on as Aunt Millie waited in front of her. "'I thank You, dear Lord, for the vision of that land You gave me the other night. My eyes could only see so much of the glory before I was blinded, but soon I'm thinking I'll have better eyes with which to see. Oh, for that day to come soon...but all in Your will and in Your time. We have been given our days on this earth for reasons that only life over there will fully show. I know I have gained great treasures from the pain of this world, and for that I give You thanks. And for the dream You have given me in these last years of my life. I have raised my family, and I pray my dear Tobias will have kind words for me when we meet again, as he did in this life. I know I failed You many times, dear Lord, but You loved me and I loved You in return. For this I give thanks, and for the final burden that has been given to me. The marks of Your love are all over this dream of a farm that ministers to hurting children. I know what must be done. I saw that too. I have only my little farm down here on this earth, so feeble and frail, and yet something can be done to touch the sufferings of this world through my weak hands.'"

Aunt Millie's sharp intake of breath stopped Phoebe. She hurried on after Aunt Millie gave a little wave of her hand. "Don't pay me any mind. Just read."

"'I saw ponies right here on my farm, and the faces of children I didn't know riding on their backs. I saw laughter and smiles and hearts that were healing. I saw hope rising like clouds up to the heavens, and I saw evil slain with kindness, and wrongs made right with prayers offered at nighttime by our simple beds. I don't know, dear Lord, how possible that is. How could an Amish woman ever do such a thing, or how could my farm become a part of heaven's plan? But I thank You for letting me see what Your will is, and for allowing me to believe it can be done. Is this not what we are to pray for? And for this I do pray. Let it happen, Lord. Let my farm become a healing place for those who do not know Your love. Let me be the hands through which Your mercy touches a weary and a broken world. Amen.'"

Phoebe laid the tablet down and forced herself to breathe.

"Now you understand," Aunt Millie said. "No one must ever see this."

"But the dream *must* happen," Phoebe told her. "Grandma's dream. She believed I could do this."

"That's what I feared you would say," Aunt Millie said. She pulled out a chair beside the sewing machine and sighed deeply. "I know in my heart this is right, which is why I spoke up the other night so quickly." Aunt Millie wiped away tears. "I'm sorry that I doubted, Phoebe. You can do this. I know you can."

Phoebe reached for Aunt Millie's hand, and for a few moments they clung to each other.

EIGHT

The following morning Phoebe paced the living room floor in her best Sunday dress. She had changed more than an hour ago, right after going to the back pasture to bring Misty up and throw the harness on the horse. Eight o'clock was thirty minutes away, when she would leave for the Sunday services at Bishop Rufus's place.

Grandma's brown tablet lay on the kitchen table, right where she had placed it yesterday after Aunt Millie left. They had eaten lunch together and read again that explosive piece about Grandma's vision of the pony farm linked to her dream of heaven. Neither of them had dared read further after that. Aunt Millie had only stayed long enough to pack up a few things from the attic. What she would do with them, Aunt Millie hadn't said, but likely a fair distribution to all the siblings had already begun.

Phoebe was committed now. She really was. Aunt Millie knew it, and likely her uncles would learn of her decision today. It was hard to breathe, thinking about her new responsibilities and what Grandma claimed she had seen in the heavens. No wonder Aunt Millie had wanted the prayer book kept a secret. Uncle Homer and Uncle Noah might not know the full details, but they must have known the basics of what Grandma wrote. After all, they had allowed the pony farm idea to get this far. Her family had hoped she would be the one to give up on the plan, but she had found out what the others knew. She had read Grandma's prayers and heard her words of faith. She could be brave Phoebe Lapp again. If Grandma thought so, she could.

Phoebe trembled and sat down on a kitchen chair. She could approach bold thoughts, but the years had taken their toll. She was not bold the way Grandma had been. How Grandma's words had burned into her soul yesterday. Such confidence! To think that she could...

Phoebe reached for the tablet and flipped it open. She waited a moment before her eyes lit on the first page.

My thoughts and prayers before the Lord, dedicated this day on my eighteenth birthday, July 3, 1938. I am young yet, and I know I have much to learn, but I also know there is a God who watches the affairs of men. I hope with all my heart that I can prove pleasing in His sight. So my first prayer is, Lord, help me know what Your will is, and help me do that will. Beyond that, what can one do but give thanks? I am born into an Amish community who seeks to benefit each other in all ways, and to protect us from the world and keep awful things from happening in our lives. For this I give thanks, and for the love I feel in my heart for Mamm and Daett. There are ten of us right now, with another little one on the way. I am the second born, with my brother Milton being the oldest. May You help us all, and give us wisdom and strength for the journey through our lives.

Phoebe closed the tablet with a snap and leaped to her feet. How Grandma prayed. Honest and brutal cries of the heart were laced with a boldness that took one's breath away. Did *Mamm* know about this? She had to, but *Mamm* had never breathed a word about it to Phoebe or any of her siblings. The family had worked hard to cover up Grandma's eccentric ways. That seemed the logical explanation, but now Phoebe was held up by Grandma's strength.

Phoebe hurried out of the house without her shawl. The July air was warm, and there wouldn't be a chill in the air until late August—if she remembered correctly from her only year in the valley. Misty whinnied when Phoebe entered the barn. There was no sign of the ponies, but she had petted and fed them this morning when she brought Misty in from the back pasture. Phoebe stroked the mare's neck before leading her out of the stall to hitch her to the buggy. Minutes later she was headed north on Highway 170 toward Bishop Rufus's place on Highway 29. Deacon Matthew lived further north on the same road, which was where the church services would be held in two Sundays.

Phoebe jiggled the reins, and Misty increased her trot to a steady pace. Buggies gathered behind her, so Phoebe knew she wasn't late. Several girls leaned out of the open doors to wave to her, and Phoebe returned the greetings. By the time she arrived at Bishop Rufus's driveway, two buggies were in front of her and more than a half dozen were behind. She had to wait while the buggies unloaded the womenfolk at the end of the walk, but Misty didn't mind taking a break. The horse calmly reached down for a few blades of grass along the lane, and Phoebe let the reins go limp. She didn't worry about the appearance of her horse. None of her brothers would have tolerated a horse snatching breakfast in front of the house where a Sunday service was held. They would have kept the reins taut and would have protested if their horses tried such a stunt.

Phoebe smiled as she waited. She missed her family back in Lancaster, but the truth was that the peace of the valley had grown on her while she was busy with Grandma's care. She felt at home here. Phoebe jiggled the reins when the second buggy in front of her pulled off and headed toward the barn. When Misty reached for another mouthful of grass, she called out, "Come on, girl. Let's go."

Misty jerked her head up to lumber forward. Uncle Homer stepped out of the line of men beside the barn and hurried toward Phoebe's buggy.

He greeted her with a smile. "*Goot* morning! How are things going?"

"Okay. Has Aunt Millie spoken with you?"

He jerked his head. "Not here, Phoebe. We'll talk later."

"But—"

His look was sharp. "I'll be by next week, and we can go over things then."

She let out a long breath, knowing there was still hope. "Thank you," she muttered.

He hurried off with Misty without a backward glance. They would have to face the community eventually, and until then, Uncle Homer planned to keep as much under his hat as possible. But that was his way. Uncle Noah would support his brother fully, so she'd best watch her step with the women this morning. She wanted to blurt out the whole story to the first listening ear. Now she had been warned.

Aunt Millie met her at the mudroom door with a quick hug. "*Goot* morning," she whispered. "Don't say anything to anyone about the pony farm. Homer wants to break the news in his own way."

"At least he's not going back on his promise," Phoebe whispered back.

Aunt Millie gave her a quick look. "Has *Mamm*'s spirit already begun to influence you?"

That's not a bad thing, she wanted to say, but she couldn't breathe at the moment. Was she really like Grandma Lapp? Could she find her way back to the person she used to be?

Phoebe followed Aunt Millie into the kitchen with her head down. Bishop Rufus's *frau*, Mae, stood by the kitchen sink and whispered in Phoebe's ear, "You're still here. I was half expecting you'd be back in Lancaster by now."

Phoebe smiled. "Something has come up."

That seemed safe enough to say because Mae had obviously not been told about the pony farm plans. At least the bishop should have been told by now. Uncle Homer took secrecy too far. Everyone in the community must be told eventually, and the sooner the better.

Phoebe greeted the circle of women who stood around the kitchen. She finished a moment before Mae led the way into the living room for the start of the service. As the oldest single girl, her place was right behind the last of the married women. Sometimes the routine didn't work out exactly this way, but today everyone fell into place on schedule.

Phoebe kept her head down again for the walk to the end of the empty bench. She settled in and raised her head for a quick look around. David's face was right across from her on the unmarried men's bench. He gave her a smile, and Phoebe returned it. She would have to speak with him sometime this week. Perhaps before Uncle Homer made his visit. David had been patiently waiting for her to decide. She should have gone down to the Fishers' place yesterday afternoon with the news, but Leroy would have wanted to say his piece. That scene might not be pleasant, and she was still no Grandma Lapp.

Phoebe ducked her head as someone gave out the first song number and the singing began. The flow and ebb of the service surrounded her, and Phoebe drifted into a daze. Her courage was building. She could comfort herself with that thought. She would even dare read more of Grandma's prayer journal when she arrived back home. The pages seemed sacred and blessed all at once. Maybe that's how things were when the Lord placed His finger of blessing on a life. And here Phoebe was, being touched by Grandma's life and receiving direction after Grandma had gone to her reward.

Grandma must have planned this, and yet she had left huge gaps where things could have gone wrong if the Lord had so directed. What faith the woman had carried in her heart. If Phoebe could achieve that single virtue, she would consider her life blessed.

Phoebe snuck a quick look at David's face. His concentration was fixed on his songbook. She would have to work closely with him in the days ahead. Thankfully, he seemed dedicated to the faith, even if he suffered from the Fisher family's notorious reputation. She had confidence in Grandma's opinion. If Grandma trusted David enough to hire him, Phoebe would not complain.

She had been given a great gift by Grandma. Everything was slowly falling into place. She could feel it. Now if Bishop Rufus would add some further thought with his sermon today, the windows of heaven would truly be open. Phoebe held her breath for a few seconds as the ministers filed down from the upstairs and the singing stopped.

She listened intently to the first sermon. "This is grace," Minister Hostetler said, "this godly heritage we all have of Christian parents. We can pause often to look at the Lord's blessing not only in the heavens, but also on this earth. We all had praying parents who bent their knees before the Lord. This has an effect on those who come after them more than we can ever imagine."

Phoebe kept her gaze on Minister Hostetler's bearded face. Did the man know about Grandma Lapp's prayer book? Not likely. He wouldn't approve of such boldness or such plain speaking by a woman. And yet Grandma's life was affecting hers. Minister Hostetler couldn't disagree with that if he knew. The godly effects were there for everyone to see.

Phoebe ducked her head as the sermon ended and Bishop Rufus stood. "Let us bless the Lord and worship His great name. His works are from everlasting to everlasting, and His blessing without end. Each morning brings a new sun and a new outpouring of the goodness of the Lord. We should be thankful and praise His name from the rising of the sun to its setting. Blessed be His name."

As Phoebe listened, a smile crept across her face. Bishop Rufus didn't know about her new life either, but his words spoke to her. Indeed, this was one more sign from heaven that the Lord's blessing was upon Grandma's dream.

Phoebe caught David's glance and gave him a warm smile. They would labor together very well. That much was clear. David wasn't like his *daett*. Maybe the grace Grandma had left behind for the Lapp family would also bless the Fisher children. Perhaps Ruth could even be saved from making the terrible mistake of jumping the fence into the world.

Phoebe gave David another smile and settled in to listen as Bishop Rufus continued his sermon.

NINE

Phoebe hitched Misty to the buggy the following Tuesday morning and drove south on Highway 170. She could have chosen to walk the distance the way David did between the Fishers' house on Burrell Road and Grandma's farm, but her entrance into the Fishers' driveway would be more dignified considering the business at hand. David was of age, and he wouldn't need his *daett's* permission to work on the pony farm. Still, she wouldn't put it beyond Leroy to throw a fit if she gave him the slightest excuse. Things were going too well at the moment to allow problems to occur through carelessness.

Phoebe jiggled the reins as the horse settled into a slow trot. She would have to put forward a brave face this morning if Leroy confronted her. Leroy's bad management skills did not restrain the man's opinions. This much she knew from hearing the man hold forth on the lawn after the Sunday meetings. She would receive an earful of Leroy's thoughts on this wild adventure of hers, but she knew his anger would be better directed at her than at his son. While Uncle Homer broke the news to the community, this would be her chance to tell David. She could sit around the farm and wait for another visit from him, but that might take another week or two. David would have heard from someone else by then. She had wanted to speak with him after the Sunday evening hymn singing, but he was not an easy man to catch alone. Her courage was not large enough yet to march up to the man and broach the subject in front of others. Leroy was enough to handle at the moment.

"Whoa there," Phoebe called to Misty as she neared the Fishers' driveway. Misty almost came to a complete halt before she made the turn and lumbered up to the barn.

Leroy's frowning face appeared in the barn door. "I'm thinking someone didn't teach you to drive very well." He stroked his long beard. "You almost turned the buggy over trying to turn at the end of my driveway."

"I did not!" Phoebe retorted. "Misty's a slow horse, and there's nothing wrong with that."

"Sort of like her mistress, eh? Getting on up in years and going nowhere."

Phoebe gripped the reins until her fingers ached. Leroy's tongue was sharper than a spring plow blade. Maybe the community had been kind in their evaluation of him.

"Cat got your tongue too?" he continued. "I thought you'd be back in Lancaster by now. Or are you taking on the schoolteaching job this fall? Not that I think you should, but..."

"I didn't come to ask your opinion. I want to speak with David and with you."

"Oh, you do?" He stroked his beard again and contemplated her. "I didn't place you as having that kind of nerve. Now my son, I can see where he would get ideas, but I wasn't expecting you to come calling before he makes the first move. But I guess old maids from Lancaster are getting desperate these days." Leroy finished with a wicked grin. "I'll go tell him you are here."

"You would be completely wrong to think that," Phoebe snapped.

Leroy paused midstride to turn around. "So why would you be

calling—and late in the day, I might mention—when normal peo-ple are already busy?"

Phoebe fixed her gaze on Misty's long mane and lowered her voice. "I'm planning on telling you the reason, even if it is none of your business—but let me say this first. It's not about what you just said."

"Oh."

Phoebe resisted the urge to give him a fierce glare.

"I'm waiting."

"I want David here before I speak," she said.

He didn't move. "I want to know what this is about first."

"I will go and find David myself." Phoebe bit the words short. "I'm sure you have him working hard somewhere on one of your—" She stopped abruptly. She was clearly out of her place. "I'm sorry. I shouldn't be speaking like this."

"*Yah*, that is true. But you are a fiery one underneath that meek face of yours. I don't say that I object. David is much too laid-back for his own *goot*, so I see he knows what he's doing." Leroy grinned. "I'll be getting him then." With that, he vanished into the barn.

Phoebe tried to still the rapid beat of her heart. What in the world was wrong with her? She'd never had a temper before. Where had that angry response come from? Somehow she must bring her-self under control.

Leroy reappeared in the barn door with a sheepish David in tow. "Okay, spill it! What are you two up to?"

"*Daett*," David objected.

Leroy gave him a sharp look. "Not that I object to your interest in Phoebe, but she has something to say first."

"I…" David stalled.

"This is about a pony farm for *Englisha* children in need," Phoebe began. "If you'd listen for once instead of running around with your opinions already fixed, you'd hear what I have to say."

Leroy opened his mouth to speak, but Phoebe rushed on. "Grandma Lapp dreamed of opening her farm to troubled children, and she purchased three Assateague ponies with that intent. Though she didn't live to see her plan come to life, my uncles and Aunt Millie are fully behind the project. They think Grandma's dream is a worthy one, and something the Lord can bless. So that's what I want David for. He's already paid up with a year's wages, so if he could spare a moment this morning, we need to begin with the forms the state wants us to fill out."

"I'll be right up after I change," David said. He hurried off toward the house.

From the look on Leroy's face, he was not happy. "What did you just say? A pony farm? What ridiculous thing is that?"

"I have explained myself enough," she told him. "Uncle Homer will explain the rest."

He glared at her. "Do you think you can just run over me like that, Phoebe? Of all people. I mean, who are you? An old maid in the community who pretends she's so timid and meek. How else would you have the courage to take on this kind of *Englisha* project—whatever it is—and not make a complete disaster out of things? It sounds as though there will be *Englisha* children in your home, and they will have an influence on you and David and the community. The Lord only knows where this will end." Suddenly a sly grin filled Leroy's face. "But who would have thought the day would come when a Lapp woman would want my son?"

Phoebe took a deep breath. "David is a baptized and faithful member of our community! He has proven himself in the year I have known him. You have nothing to worry about. And it's *not* what you think!"

The grin didn't leave Leroy's face. "You do have the sharpest tongue, Phoebe. I can't say I'm surprised, but seeing is always believing, for sure."

"I am saying no more about this," she retorted.

He contemplated her with his hand on his beard. "Don't say I didn't warn you, Phoebe. I'm giving you a big look-out-for-danger signal. That's all I can say. This wild venture of yours will not work. You might even be dabbling in wickedness."

Phoebe trembled and clutched Misty's reins. "I'm sorry you feel the way you do, and I will take your words into account and be careful."

"This will take more than carefulness." As Leroy spoke, David ran out of the house and leaped into the buggy. Ruth had come out on the front porch to wave toward them, and Phoebe returned the greeting.

"Let's go," David whispered in Phoebe's ear.

Phoebe leaned out of the buggy to tell Leroy, "I'm sorry for my temper."

"So am I!" he called after her.

Phoebe focused straight ahead as she jiggled the reins. Ruth was still waving from the front porch, but Phoebe's hands were occupied. Thankfully, Misty set off at a decent trot and didn't stumble on the turn at the end of driveway.

"I'm sorry about *Daett*, but now I guess you know how he is."

"I guess there are always roses among the thorns."

David winced. "At least you have an optimistic view of life."

"This is not your fault, David. I don't know what's wrong with me this morning. I flew into a temper with your *daett*, and now... maybe he is right? Me and my tongue. Who would have thought it?"

"You said what needed saying, Phoebe. Don't regret one word."

"But you weren't there to hear all of it."

"I know what you said because I know you, and each word was lovely."

"I didn't know you had a flowery tongue." She gave him a pretend glare.

He laughed. "Maybe this is a morning of discoveries."

Phoebe sighed. "I suppose so, but thanks for the kind words. I need them to comfort my heart, which is bruised and scared right now. Your *daett* got to me."

"I'm sorry. I want to help with this project where I can."

"I'm sorry your *daett* is trying to throw me on you." She gave him a quick sideways glance.

"That's *Daett*. Don't mind him. He sees with narrow vision."

Phoebe managed a smile. "He certainly has no pony farm in sight, but I already suspected that."

"You can say that again."

Phoebe sobered. "Do you think he will seek to undermine the effort? Perhaps at the Sunday services with his opinions?"

"Do you think anyone will listen?"

"You do have a point. But I'm still sorry for my harsh words. He is your *daett*."

"*Yah*, he is." David shifted on his seat. "So what are we doing at your house this morning?"

"Forms, and I have my first class this week!" Phoebe turned to smile at him. "Are you *goot* with forms?"

"I can try. This pony farm really needs to work. Grandma Lapp wanted it."

"*Yah*, she did," Phoebe agreed as she pulled into Grandma's driveway. Aunt Millie's buggy was parked beside the barn, and Phoebe came to a stop beside it.

Aunt Millie leaned out to greet them brightly. "*Goot* morning!"

"Are you here to help?" Phoebe teased. "I just picked up David, and we're ready to tackle the forms and go from there."

"Your *mamm* and *daett* are coming this weekend," Aunt Millie said from inside her buggy. "That's what I came over to say."

David leaped down to unhitch Misty and stopped short. "Surely they are not against the plan."

"No, it's not that, but they are concerned," Aunt Millie told him.

"*Mamm* and *Daett* will support us if Uncle Homer is on board," Phoebe answered.

"I suppose so," Aunt Millie allowed. "I'm sure they just want to see if you're okay."

"And maybe help around the place," David said with a grin before taking off with Misty.

"He's mighty cheerful," Aunt Millie said once David and the horse had vanished into the barn.

Phoebe moved closer. "Maybe he's just happy I survived his *daett* this morning. Oh, Aunt Millie, I have never been so angry with a man in my life!"

Aunt Millie smiled. "You must be talking about Leroy Fisher."

"*Yah*. Do you know how unreasonable he can be? And the things he said! He really got to me."

"I wouldn't worry about the man," Aunt Millie assured Phoebe. "Some people are the way they are, but now you see why *Mamm* was so kind to the Fisher children."

Phoebe let out a long breath. "And David has to live with that all the time."

"That's one reason I'm glad this is working out—that, and for *Mamm*'s sake. She had her reasons and her prayers."

"*Yah*, I know. Do you want to come inside? We'll be working at the table all day on those awful forms."

Aunt Millie shook her head. "I have to get back, but I'll be in touch when your parents arrive. Can you put them up here?"

"Of course! I wouldn't want it any other way."

"You take care then." Aunt Millie jiggled the reins, and her horse trotted out of the lane.

David reappeared at the barn door, and Phoebe waited to walk with him up to the house. They entered and took their places at the kitchen table. David bent his head over the forms and began to fill them out. He muttered to himself, "Number of acres on the farm? Condition of the home? Year built? Number of bedrooms? Year barn was built? Number of stalls?" He seemed to know the answers without asking her, but he had been around Grandma's farm since his youth.

"What do you think our next step should be after we finish this?" she asked.

"The fences," he said without hesitation. "Some of the wires have come loose in the lower pasture, and we could use another divider in the front field. That would make it easier to manage the summer grass, as this is now primarily a pony farm."

"Do you think we will make it?"

He thought for a moment. "Grandma Lapp believed this would work. I'm willing to take my chances with her and with you."

"That is a *goot* answer. Will your *daett* make problems for you now that he knows?"

"*Daett* will be okay," he said, but his face darkened.

"I'm sorry. I didn't know things were like that between you."

He nodded and busied himself with the forms.

TEN

Early on Saturday afternoon, Phoebe drove south toward Little Falls at a steady trot. The class had gone well on Friday afternoon, so she could breathe a little easier. *Mamm* and *Daett* were due on the Greyhound bus at two o'clock, but she wanted plenty of time in case traffic held up Misty's already slow pace. At least the mare was a safe horse and didn't shy over every little thing the way some horses did. There was always something for which one could give thanks.

Aunt Millie had assured her yesterday after she came back from town that *Mamm* and *Daett* had made the trip up from Lancaster to encourage and support the pony farm effort. Phoebe didn't doubt Aunt Millie's evaluation of the matter, but still, she kept holding her breath, thinking something would go wrong at the last moment. They had planned a big supper tonight, and Uncle Homer and Uncle Noah and their families would come. Aunt Millie would be by the house before four o'clock to help with the meal preparations.

David had been busy at work behind the barn in the morning, and Phoebe had invited him to supper. He might as well join in since things were going so well. He had taken the forms down to Mrs. Broman at her offices in Utica with a hired driver on Wednesday. Phoebe had offered to travel with him, but he had refused. "I'll speak to Mrs. Broman after I've filed the federal forms at the library."

David knew much more than she had expected he would about the legal side of things. There were moments when he seemed to have thought all this through in detail—perhaps for months—which was possible. Grandma had given David plenty of warning of what might lie ahead, and his heart was in the project.

"Careful there," Phoebe called out to Misty as they made their way downhill into Little Falls.

She pulled up to a stop sign and turned left. Moments later, Misty trotted up to the bus stop, and Phoebe climbed down to secure the tie strap on a light pole. She waited beside the buggy with the swirl of city traffic all around her. The minutes ticked past until the long shape of the bus appeared from the north. Phoebe began to wave even before the vehicle ground to a halt and the doors opened.

Daett was the first to step out, with *Mamm* right behind him. Phoebe ran forward to embrace them while the bus driver went to unload their luggage.

"It is so *goot* to see you both!" Phoebe gushed. "How are you? And so soon after the funeral. Who would have thought?"

"*Yah*, who would have thought?" *Daett* agreed with a twinkle in his eye. "*Mamm* had more than a few secrets up her sleeve, it appears."

"You don't disapprove, do you?" Phoebe clung to his shirtsleeve. "Please tell me you approve."

"You know he does," *Mamm* told her. "Your *daett* has many of his *mamm*'s eccentric ways. In him they are just better hidden, that's all." *Mamm* tapped him lightly on the arm, and *Daett* grinned.

Phoebe let out a long breath. "I guess I should have known, but still..."

"We understand," *Mamm* assured her. "Now let's get back to your place. We want to hear all about this idea."

"To my place!" Phoebe exclaimed.

"It's just a term," *Mamm* told her. "Grandma's gone now, and things move on."

"But I don't..." Phoebe began to protest.

Daett silenced her with a look. "It's time for courage, daughter, and change. You have this in you."

"I've become such a timid soul," Phoebe whimpered. "I don't know how I'm surviving."

"You're doing fine," *Daett* told her as he led the way over to the buggy. He loaded the luggage and then untied Misty while the two women climbed up. *Daett* tossed them the reins and pulled himself up onto the buggy seat.

"Is this horse safe to drive?" he teased.

"*Daett*," Phoebe chided. "You're just trying to make me feel better. You know Grandma only had one horse and that Misty is slower than molasses in January."

"*Yah*, I know." *Daett* grinned. "But you've been through a lot these weeks since the funeral. I must say you're doing quite well."

"That's the real reason we came," *Mamm* whispered. "To see how you're doing."

"Oh, *Mamm*." Phoebe reached over the buggy seat to give her mother a quick hug. "This visit is so sweet. I'm sorry I was a little worried that you'd come to chew me out—"

"I am glad to see this happen," *Daett* interrupted. "If your grandma thought this was the right thing, then I trust her judgment. She was a praying woman, Phoebe. This is the truth. All of us children have been blessed and ministered to by her prayers."

Misty plodded slowly out of town on the long uphill grade. No one objected as silence settled over the buggy.

"Did you have a *goot* trip?" Phoebe finally asked.

"*Yah*," *Mamm* replied with a smile, but the silence returned quickly.

Phoebe broke the stillness again. "So are you worried about me? Be honest!"

"You're okay," *Mamm* assured her. She reached over the back of the buggy seat to pat Phoebe's arm. "Just relax. We're just getting used to our daughter and her new adventure, that's all."

"Is there a man involved here somewhere that we should know of?" *Daett* teased.

Phoebe laughed. "You know there is no man!"

"That's to their own shame," *Mamm* chided. "They don't know the treasure they are missing."

"I quite agree," *Daett* seconded. "And I was teasing, of course, but with all the other surprises you've been springing on us, I wondered if there was one more."

"There is no man." Phoebe didn't laugh this time. "In fact, I haven't even thought about dating and marriage since...well, this thing came up."

"So you're thinking a pony farm might be your life's work?" *Daett* turned around on the buggy seat.

"Maybe." Phoebe let out a long sigh. "Would that be so terrible? It was either running the farm or teaching school."

"So they did offer you the job?" *Daett* asked.

"No, but Uncle Homer mentioned something about the school-teaching job when selling the ponies first came up."

"They would have offered the position to you!" *Daett* proclaimed. "There's no question there."

Silence settled again as Misty lurched forward at a slow trot.

"Should I have taken the schoolteaching job, perhaps?"

"I'm sure *Daett* didn't mean for you to think he disapproves of you or Grandma's project," *Mamm* said at once.

Daett nodded. "I'm sorry, daughter. I'm just thinking things through out loud, but you have to admit this is quite an odd opportunity."

"*Yah*, I know," Phoebe admitted. "I'm not blaming you, and I do understand. I'm so out of my comfort zone, and yet I've been finding the strength and courage to go on."

Daett and *Mamm* exchanged glances.

"What?"

Mamm turned around in her seat again. "Your grandma had

a *goot* influence on many people while she lived. We just hadn't thought that things would go on after she passed. But why couldn't they?" *Mamm* smiled warmly. "So we're here to help you and to support you, and, *yah*, to see for ourselves the change in our daughter. What's wrong with that?"

Phoebe didn't say anything for a moment. "You should have seen me tangle with Leroy Fisher the other morning."

"Why? How did that go?" *Mamm* was all interest. Even *Daett* tilted his head sideways to hear better.

"I didn't know I had such a temper." Phoebe shivered. "My behavior was not *goot*, but the man goaded me something terrible by implying that I had come down to force myself into a relationship with David. He called me an old maid who was so hard up she had to resort to such measures." Phoebe's face flamed at the memory. "The nerve of the man."

Daett chuckled. "I wouldn't pay much attention to Leroy Fisher. He's known for his many opinions, which are backed up by little real-life experience. They don't last long, though. He'll be fine."

"He doesn't think much of this project, that's for sure."

"There you go," *Daett* said. "Leroy is usually off on both his timing and his purpose."

"Well, I will comfort myself then." Phoebe forced a smile. "But I discovered what a temper I have, which wasn't a pleasant experience."

"I'm sure it was merely a passing emotion." *Mamm* didn't appear worried. "You have always been so levelheaded and calm."

"I guess so." Phoebe took a deep breath. "I just hope it doesn't happen again."

"So tell me about David," *Daett* said as he turned into the driveway. "I heard that Grandma paid him for another year before she passed—yet she didn't tell you a thing?"

"That's right. But I'm not offended. Grandma's judgment has been correct so far. David has proven himself over and over again.

In fact, there he is now, working on the fence this morning even though I told him there was no rush. He also took all the papers to the lady at Child Protection Services—a Mrs. Broman—and everything looked splendid. They are doing an official inspection of the place late next week if everything continues to work out, and I passed my first training class with flying colors on Friday, the teacher claimed."

Daett didn't say anything as he pulled Misty to a stop and hopped out. David came around the corner of the barn with a big smile on his face. He shook hands with *Daett* and came over to *Mamm*. "Howdy," David greeted her. "Glad to see you back in the valley."

"We are glad to be back, and for a happier occasion this time," *Mamm* told him.

"*Yah*, Grandma Lapp was a sweet woman," David agreed. "Your daughter has astonished everyone by taking on this project."

Mamm gave Phoebe a warm smile. "*Yah*, that's what we've been hearing."

"She's an amazing woman, just like her Grandma," David said.

"Hey," Phoebe protested. "The daughter is standing right here."

David and *Mamm* laughed heartily.

"Can I get in on the joke?" *Daett* called from where he held Misty's bridle.

"Sorry! You're not hearing a word of that," Phoebe told him.

They all laughed this time, and David went to help *Daett* unhitch.

"There's a surprise in the house," Phoebe warned *Mamm* as they headed up the walk, the heavy suitcase grasped between them.

"And what would that be?"

"I can bring in the suitcase!" *Daett* called out before Phoebe could answer.

Mamm shook her head. "We're making it!" She lowered her voice to Phoebe. "So what's the surprise?"

"Everyone's coming over for supper. That's why the kitchen's such a mess. Aunt Millie is coming over at four, and probably other aunts as well—but they didn't tell me who."

Mamm lowered the suitcase, and her face glowed. "That *is* a surprise! That must mean they approve of the venture."

"I think you'd better let me carry that." David spoke from behind them. Phoebe jumped.

"Sorry. I didn't mean to scare you."

"That's a splendid idea," *Mamm* told him. "I overestimated my energy, and what little I have I'd best reserve for working in the kitchen."

"Ah, you're still young and spry," David teased, smiling broadly. He lifted the suitcase as if it weighed nothing at all. "Phoebe invited me for supper, which was very nice of her." He shot up the walk and deposited the suitcase inside while Phoebe caught her breath.

"That's quite a nice young man," *Mamm* commented.

"That's what I told you."

"I mean, in more ways than one."

"Don't go there, *Mamm*. David hasn't looked at me like that, and I wouldn't want him to. We have to work together, and that's that."

"Whatever you say," *Mamm* said with a smile. She marched up the walk after David. Phoebe followed her inside to where David had deposited the suitcase at the foot of the stairs. He had vanished, so he must have left through the mudroom door, which meant he had seen her disheveled kitchen. Well, that was that too. Kitchens became messy when one prepared to cook for four families at once.

"I want to see one thing before we dive into supper preparations," *Mamm* told her after a quick glance into the kitchen. "Grandma's prayer journal."

"You've never seen it?" Phoebe's mouth fell open.

"Maybe a little," *Mamm* admitted. "But I want a *goot* look now."

Phoebe led the way into her bedroom and handed over the tablet. *Mamm* paged through it quickly and seemed to settle on a date. Tears brimmed in her eyes as she read.

"What?" Phoebe asked when her mother had finished.

"It is as Millie said it would be." *Mamm* held out the tablet. "I mean, not this prayer, but the prayers *Mamm* wrote about us. This one was written on our wedding day."

Phoebe read silently.

Dear Lord, You are the One who always hears the cry of Your children. I come to You today not out of fear, but out of the great love I have in my heart for Ammon and Miriam. They have found something so precious in each other. I have watched them grow closer each day, as I am sure You also have. May Your grace be on them on this day of their sacred union. They will say vows to each other, and breathe holy words that carry the weight of the world and of eternity. I know they will hold each other tight as the years roll on—for as many as You give them. I also know that danger will come to threaten their union. Be there to help them in that hour. Touch them even now. Protect and seal today what will be written in glory as it is written on this earth. They will be man and wife, Ammon and Miriam. They will be made one, as their hearts are already one. Let life be kind to them, dear Lord.

Phoebe laid the tablet on the bed and wrapped her arms around her mother. They held each other until the front door slammed behind them.

ELEVEN

That Saturday evening after dusk had fallen, David leaned on Grandma Lapp's dining room table with a full plate of food in front of him. He had seated himself here many times before while Grandma served lunch or an early supper to Ruth and him. But the house had been silent then, broken only by the ticking of the grandfather clock against the living room wall. Now the sounds of conversation and laughter emanated from the four Lapp families and filled the whole house.

David smiled and listened in. No one paid him much attention, but he didn't mind. That he had been invited was an honor enough for one of Leroy Fisher's children. Ruth should be here to enjoy this with him, but of course that wasn't possible. She was out somewhere with her *Englisha* boyfriend. She wouldn't have come even if Phoebe had thought to include her.

David sobered and took a bite of mashed potatoes and gravy. Phoebe had spared no effort in the supper preparations—not with the arrival of her parents and the gathering of the Lapp siblings who lived in the valley. This was normal. He had to remind himself that his *daett*'s behavior made their family different. Members of the extended Fisher family lived in the valley to the west of Little Falls.

Daett's brothers were located in another district, and *Daett* made little effort to visit, except for a few Christmas breakfasts. They had gone twice in David's memory, and both times they had left early.

Phoebe's *daett* leaned across the dining room table to give David a warm smile. "I hear you're quite involved in this project."

David paused with his fork halfway to his mouth. "*Yah*. I'm excited about the venture."

"Do you think it's going to work?" Ammon's beard was so long it almost touched the dining room table.

David gathered his courage. Rarely did anyone ask his opinion. "I suppose you mean the money part—how much the state will pay, and whether we can make a go of it."

"That's a *goot* place to begin."

Two of Phoebe's uncles turned in their direction, apparently quite interested in what he would say.

David forced a smile. "Judging from the numbers Mrs. Broman has given me, there should be plenty of income even if Phoebe begins with only two or three children a week." He named off a number, and all three heads nodded.

"That's not bad," Ammon said. "What do you think, Homer? And you, Noah?"

Both grunted their agreement.

"Could it bring problems to the community?" Noah asked.

David thought for a moment. "I suppose that's not for me to answer. I only know how to run a farm and do the paperwork. Church questions are beyond me."

"Well said." Ammon took a bite from his plate and chewed slowly. "Where did you learn bookkeeping? Phoebe said you've been taking care of the forms so far."

David shrugged. "I loved math in school, and I keep the books at home."

Both Homer and Noah chuckled but stilled their laughter after

Ammon glanced at them. "I'm sure David doesn't make the final decisions with his *daett's* finances."

"Thank you," David managed. "I appreciate your understanding and for giving me a chance."

"You're welcome." Ammon smiled. "But *Mamm* made that choice, and you'll have to pull your full weight."

"I will work my hardest," David assured them. "And Phoebe made the final choice."

"I don't know about the future of this arrangement," Homer said.

Ammon laughed. "Phoebe will be consulting the two of you since I'm not around. Does that satisfy everyone?"

"That was already agreed upon," Noah said, and they all laughed this time.

"Welcome to the family," Ammon told David. "Don't mind our fussing. At the end of the day, we love one another."

"Like I said, I appreciate it." David kept his head down as the conversation moved on. He seemed to have passed some sort of test. What kind of test, he wasn't sure, but he was grateful to make it this far.

He glanced toward the heavens and muttered a silent *Thank You.* Tears threatened, but he suppressed them. This was a moment for rejoicing, not crying. If he could continue down this road, albeit slowly, perhaps his dream of winning Phoebe's affections would come to pass. The thought took his breath away, and he struggled to swallow.

Homer reached over to slap him on the back, and everyone roared with laughter. "Are you okay? I thought we were going to lose you."

David's face flamed at the thought of what these three brothers would say if they knew what crossed his mind—that Leroy Fisher's son dared to hope for Ammon Lapp's daughter. No doubt they would banish him from the house forever.

"You okay?" Homer asked again, his hand poised as if to thunder down once more.

"*Yah*, I'm..." Their laughter drowned out his words.

"If he survives your tender care, he'll be okay," Ammon quipped from across the table.

Phoebe appeared from the kitchen with pies in her hands. She flourished them about before sliding one onto the table. David was grateful the attention would be transferred from him to her.

"Now that is what I have been waiting for," Homer said. "Do I get the first piece?"

"Only if you've been nice all day," Phoebe teased.

"I have been a saint!" Homer declared, and the laughter rippled again.

"As a matter of fact, David gets the first piece." Phoebe turned toward him. "Because without his help, we wouldn't be where we are with the pony farm. He filed all the forms with Mrs. Broman, and we have an inspection coming next week. All thanks to David." Phoebe slid the pie plate into an empty spot in front of him. "So here. With many thanks from me and the whole Lapp family."

David kept his head down, and Homer slapped him on the back again. The man had a fierce pound, but it was all meant in fun.

David lifted his head before Phoebe walked away. "Thank you. I didn't do that much."

"Don't be modest." She gave him a sweet smile. "You've earned your keep."

"Oh my, praises are being sung in the young man's honor," Ammon declared with a big grin.

"I don't care about praises!" Homer roared in David's ear. "Are you going to help yourself to a piece of pie? Or are you going to take all evening? I'm starving."

"Don't take this to heart now." Noah leaned toward his brother to tease him next. "You can have praises sung to you someday."

David forced his hand to move as laughter rose and fell around him. The piece of pie nearly slid off his fork, but he managed to avoid disaster. "Here." He handed the pie plate to Homer.

Homer thumped him on the back again with one hand and maneuvered the pie with the other.

David joined in the laughter around the table. They finished their dessert, and the final prayer of thanks was offered. The men spilled onto the couches and chairs set up in the living room while the women did the dishes in the kitchen.

David lingered in the background. He should leave now and make a graceful exit. There had been enough *goot* things happening tonight to last him for a while. He shouldn't press his luck and mess up everything.

He began to move toward the front door when Homer hollered to him. "Take a seat, David. There's still one left, and the night is young."

"I should be getting home," he muttered, but they waved away his protest. Instead of leaving, he took the proffered chair.

He thought he could hear Phoebe's voice among the voices in the kitchen, but that wasn't possible. He had begun to imagine things in his happiness. This whole evening felt like something conjured up out of thin air, and yet it wasn't. This was real, and it was happening to him.

Moments later the women came in from the kitchen and took seats beside their husbands. Children moved in and out of the house at irregular intervals, with the front door slamming each time. *Daett* would have called for silence a long time ago or left for home. This was a new world for David, and its light just about blinded him.

He also couldn't breathe very well as Phoebe came in and pulled up a chair to sit beside him. He forced himself to glance at her and say, "Thanks again for your kind praise earlier. You know I don't do much."

"Let's not play that game," she said. Her tone was that of a sister.

"I couldn't do this without you, and that's no secret. You don't have to be so modest."

He looked away and didn't say anything. No one stared at them or acted as if Phoebe shouldn't be at his side. What did they think? That he had orchestrated their friendship? But he hadn't. Phoebe had chosen to sit beside him.

"So what do you think of my family?" she asked him with another warm smile.

"They are *wunderbah*!" he exclaimed, nearly choking on the words.

"Maybe you need Uncle Homer to thump you on the back again," she teased. "Did he nearly break your ribs?"

He joined in her laughter. "No, I was okay. The first time I wasn't expecting it, but by the second time…"

"You'll get used to my family," she said. "They seem to like you."

"I'm glad," he managed. "Are they okay with the pony farm?"

"They are. I had my worries, but everything seems to have worked itself out—at least for now. How, I'm not exactly sure, but my family is like that. They make decisions carefully, but once they are made, everyone is on board."

"That is different. But I'm glad."

She smiled again. "So am I, and I'm glad you are on board as well. Grandma knew what she was doing."

He looked away and willed his face to remain passive. Phoebe meant only to make him feel better. She knew how *Daett* was, and…

"My *daett* will be here all of next week, and I will finish my two classes," she told him. "Could you show him what needs to be fixed up? And explain about the money, of course." She gave him another smile. "*Daett* has *goot* advice when it comes to money, and I don't think we have plentiful funds to work with until the income begins to come in. Grandma left some money in her checking account that Uncle Homer has been letting me use, but that won't last very long."

"So everything needs to fall into place rather quickly?"

"*Yah*, but you have been doing a *goot* job so far. That's why I'm so grateful for your work. We really couldn't do this without you, David."

"Thank you," he said.

He didn't dare look at her. Phoebe might see the longing in his eyes. He wanted her praise, but more than that he wanted her affections. He could only dream her heart would turn toward him. He must not presume.

Phoebe stood. "Time to make popcorn. Do you want to help?"

"In the kitchen?" He nearly choked again.

"*Yah*. Are you *afraid* of the kitchen?" she teased.

No, of you, he almost said, but he smiled instead. "Of course I am. You'll have to teach me what to do."

"If you learn as quickly as you have so far, that shouldn't be a problem." She led the way and stopped in front of the stove to stoke the fire. "Up there." Phoebe motioned with her chin. "You get the popcorn popper, and I'll get the popcorn. The butter is in the fridge."

He retrieved the popper and set it down to get the butter. He guessed at the proper amount.

"Excellent!" she exclaimed as she came back with the popcorn kernels. "See, you already know." With a flourish, she emptied her cup of corn into the popper and stepped back. "There you go. Twirl away, and I'll get a bowl ready."

He fixed his gaze on the popcorn popper while the fire crackled in the stove beneath him. Phoebe meant nothing special by including him tonight in her popcorn making, just as she didn't with his work around the farm. He was included, and at present that was all he could expect.

"Thank You for that much, Lord," he whispered. Thankfully, the sound of his voice was drowned out by the exploding kernels of popcorn. Phoebe had the bowl ready for him when he took off the lid and tipped the popper sideways.

"Perfect!" Phoebe proclaimed, as the last kernel slid into the bowl. "Not one missed the mark."

"Shall I make some more?" he asked, his face turned away from hers.

"Sure! Maybe two more poppers full. I'll pass this out, and *Mamm* can help me with the orange juice."

David refilled the popper. He listened as she rattled the dishes and walked into the living room with the big bowl and smaller bowls for individual servings clutched in her hands. He watched her until she disappeared through the kitchen doorway. Thankfully, she didn't glance over her shoulder.

TWELVE

On Thursday morning, Ruth glanced at Ethan's handsome face and gave him a bright smile as they pulled into Grandma Lapp's driveway. "It's looking quite fixed-up and homelike, isn't it?" she chirped.

Ethan grinned. "We're looking at more than appearances, dear."

Ruth caught her breath. Ethan used endearments all the time, and they were nothing special, but still. To win all of Ethan's affection was a dream, but this was a step in the right direction.

She had walked up to the farm yesterday to make sure Phoebe had everything ready for the all-important state inspection today. As she and Ethan parked in front of the barn, Ammon appeared in the barn doorway with a question on his face.

"Is that the first sight that will greet the arriving children?" Ethan asked.

Ruth forced a smile. "You're teasing, right? This is quaint, and see? He's smiling."

Ethan laughed. "Relax, Ruth. You didn't have to come along to oversee my tour of the farm. I don't bite."

"But you might need..."

"Interpretation?" he finished for her. "Look. Just let go and let me ask the questions. They have to be asked, Ruth. And they aren't that difficult." Ethan held up his clipboard. "See? Standard state board forms, which I will fill in."

"I was very fond of Grandma Lapp," Ruth whispered. "I want this to work, Ethan."

"It will, dear." He hopped out of the truck to extent his hand to Ammon. "Good morning, sir. Ethan Thompson from Child Protective Services. I'm here for the scheduled inspection of the Lapp Family Farm." Ethan glanced at his clipboard.

Ammon chuckled. "A *goot* morning to you, and to you, Ruth." Ammon gave her a friendly smile. "I'm Ammon Lapp, but I won't be in charge of the farm. I'm just here for the week to get things up and running for my daughter, Phoebe. She and Ruth's brother David will run the place."

"I see," Ethan said. "Shall we begin with the barn and the horses?"

"We'd best wait for Phoebe," Ammon told him. "But here she comes now."

Ruth turned to see Phoebe hurrying down from the house with her white apron aflutter.

"What have we here? Amish Heidi?" Ethan muttered.

Ruth gave Ethan a quick glare, but Ammon didn't appear to have heard.

"Just teasing," Ethan said out of the corner of his mouth.

Ammon made the introductions. "This is Phoebe, my daughter. And this is Ethan Thompson, who is in charge of the inspection."

"Howdy." Ethan offered Phoebe a broad smile. "So you're the boss of this outfit—the Lapp Family Farm?"

Phoebe nodded her head. "*Yah*, I suppose so. That's what we all decided was the best name for it."

"Works for me." Ethan smiled again. "Shall we begin?" He motioned toward the barn. "Your father was about to lead the way before you made your appearance."

Phoebe took a deep breath. "We don't have everything ready yet, but I can show you what we do have. There are the ponies, and the barn, and..." She led the way through the barn door listing off all of the physical details around her. Ruth followed the group. Thankfully, Ethan seemed impressed so far—at least from what she could tell. This was what she had grown up with, so it was nothing new to her. Ethan, on the other hand, had been raised in New York City, and even after several years of living in a rural area, he still thought the country a little strange. Doubtless this was why Mrs. Broman had trusted him with the inspection. If he was impressed with the farm, he would present a glowing report, and Grandma Lapp's place would be approved.

Ruth hoped Ethan's opinion of her might also grow right along with his respect for her people. Here she planned to jump the fence, all while she used her past to make the leap. If Ethan thought her flawed because she was a country bumpkin, he would never give her a chance beyond the sporadic dates they had been on, when he had taken her out to eat at local restaurants.

Ethan was from another world, but in matters of the heart they were the same. She had to believe that. She could be a credit to him. She could love him as well as—and perhaps better than—any woman from his world. No doubt Ethan had plenty of girlfriends when he attended college. A handsome man like him would have girls gathered thick around him, though there was no girlfriend at present. At least, not that she knew of. Ethan simply took his time, which gave her the opportunity to demonstrate that she could be that special person in his life. Special enough to say wedding vows with him someday.

Ruth hugged herself as all three ponies trotted up to the back barn door. "Meet Snow Cloud, Lady, and Aladdin," Phoebe told Ethan. "They are as friendly as can be, and fully tame and gentle." Phoebe demonstrated by stroking each pony's neck in turn. They tossed their heads about and nuzzled her arm.

Ethan chuckled nervously. "They do seem friendly enough."

"Here, see for yourself."

Ruth held her breath as Ethan stroked the nearest pony's mane. All she needed was some fiasco right at this crucial moment to scare Ethan, and this adventure would be over. For example, an Amish person would understand a nip on the arm from a horse as an expression of playfulness or even affection, but Ethan probably wouldn't arrive at such a conclusion.

Why did she pursue an impossible future with him? Was it because she had no options in the community? The question stung painfully. She never tried to win the attentions of unmarried Amish men before they settled down with a girlfriend. The effort was hopeless. That's what she told herself. She was Leroy Fisher's daughter, and no one wanted such a woman as his *frau*.

Ethan was a fresh start, and in his world she could be transformed. He pulled at her heartstrings in a way that no man in the community ever had. That was the truth, and furthermore, no one would be overly surprised if she jumped the fence. They would nod their heads and say, "Well, she's Leroy Fisher's daughter."

Maybe she should show them how wrong they were and capture the affections of a community man. But who? They all had girlfriends at present. She should have explored that option earlier, but going back in time was impossible. In comparison, Ethan appeared an easy conquest. He was reasonable, kind, handsome, well educated, and charming. He took her breath away, all while her heart pounded furiously. She hid most of her feelings for him. Ethan had best be played with a gentle hand. That she had extracted a few dates out of him was already quite the accomplishment. She could tell by the looks on the faces of Mrs. Broman and Ethan's coworkers when she had stopped by the office a few times.

Several of the younger women had appeared downright jealous. That she, an Amish girl, could evoke such an emotion from an

Englisha woman was an amazement of the highest order, especially considering her family's reputation.

Ruth focused on the inspection as the party moved away from the ponies and toured the rest of the barn. She kept close enough to hear Ethan's responses to Phoebe's explanations. There was still no disapproval in his voice, and Phoebe did quite well with her descriptions.

"He seems like a nice man," Ammon said, startling Ruth out of her thoughts. "How long have you known this Ethan?"

"Oh, for some time." Ruth smiled brightly. "David and I met him at a…" Ruth paused. She was not about to mention the rock concert they had been to. "We were on our *rumspringa*. I still am."

"I see. But aren't you old enough to think about coming back?"

"Maybe old enough, but the heart has its reasons." She glanced meaningfully at Ethan.

"Him?" Ammon didn't appear surprised. "He is handsome enough, and smart and a *goot* catch, no doubt—for an *Englisha frau*!" Ammon regarded her for a moment. "You really should come back, Ruth. This is a chance you may not get twice in a row."

"What chance?"

Ammon didn't answer for a moment, as they watched Phoebe lead Ethan up to the hayloft. Ammon finally continued. "I know how difficult things have been for you and David in your growing-up years. I also know what my *mamm* did for the two of you. I have spoken to my brothers about this. How things were handled wasn't right in the past. We feel bad, and Phoebe is taking this risk now." Ammon smiled again. "My brothers and I thought it might be the time to offer you something a little risky, but we think it might work out for the best. Would you consider teaching school for the community this fall?"

"What?" Ruth jerked her head around. "But I'm not baptized."

"*Yah*, we know. And that's the risk, but *Mamm* invested a lot of time in David and you, and we trust her prayers a lot. Which I am sure you do too. *Mamm* was a praying woman who had the Lord's ear. There is no question there."

"But...but..." Ruth's head spun. They were outside the barn now, but it wasn't the fresh air that made her dizzy. "That would mean..." Well, it would mean a lot of things.

"You would be expected to join the baptismal class this fall," Ammon continued. "I'm sure that wouldn't be a problem for you, as it is high time you made the choice to come back. People would understand if you made your intentions known beforehand."

"You would hire me on as the community's schoolteacher?" Ruth rubbed her face with both hands.

Ammon chuckled. "I am glad to see that you are pleased, but I wouldn't exactly be the one hiring you. My brother Homer is on the school board."

"And he wants me as the community's schoolteacher?"

"Ruth, I know it hasn't always been easy growing up in your family, but the community doesn't hold you or David responsible for your *daett*'s reputation. Your brother is making a fresh start with this venture." Ammon paused at the pasture gate while Phoebe led Ethan farther down the dirt lane toward the back of the farm. "Why can't you do the same?"

"Because I..." The protest died on Ruth's lips.

"Do you really think this *Englisha* man will ask you to be his *frau* someday?" Ammon gave her a quick glance.

"Sooner than one of the community men." The words slipped out with all their bitterness.

Ammon sighed. "The Lord's ways are the Lord's ways, and a single life among the community's people is not a thing of dishonor. That's better than jumping the fence, Ruth. We had expected Phoebe to take the schoolteaching offer before the farm venture came up. Yet you are not being offered second best. You are being given a great honor. And beyond that, many of our schoolteachers eventually find decent husbands. Perhaps some widower, if no one else, will set his affections on you once he sees how well you run the schoolhouse. We believe you can do it."

"Teach school!" The words burst out. "Why, it's just that..."

"You will think about this, *yah*?" Ammon patted Ruth on the hand. "There is no rush, and things of value can't be rushed anyway. Homer is willing to speak with you whenever you are ready."

Ruth kept her gaze fixed on the distance horizon. Why didn't she turn this offer down on the spot? If she accepted it, she and Ethan would never be together. But could she just walk away? Could she give up her hopes of capturing Ethan's heart and settle down to a life as the community's schoolteacher, even with the honor such a position would bring?

Ammon gave her a kind smile as Phoebe and Ethan came back up the pasture lane. "This would be the Lord's best choice, Ruth. Think about that."

Ruth looked away and didn't answer. She would be respected as she had never been before. The job would change her life completely. Maybe she could give up Ethan for something real. But still...she loved him. How could one give up love?

"Sometimes the things of the world are only a mirage," Ammon added, as if reading her thoughts. "The things among the people of God are sure." Ammon fell silent as Phoebe and Ethan walked up to the gate.

"So what do you think?" Ruth forced herself to ask Ethan.

He grinned from ear to ear. "I'm impressed, to say the least. Phoebe answered all my questions, and her plan is well thought-out. Now for a quick walk through the house, and I think we'll be done."

"I'm glad you like it," Ruth told him, but he had already moved on with Phoebe in the lead.

"I think you'll do very well as the community's schoolteacher," Ammon told her, as if his words sealed the deal.

Ruth pressed her lips together and followed Phoebe and Ethan while Ammon returned to the barn. This was a once-in-a-lifetime offer, and Ammon must understand her shock. That she even considered a return from her *rumspringa* took her breath away, but Ammon spoke the truth.

Ethan was no sure thing.

THIRTEEN

On Friday evening the sunset stretched along the horizon in a long blaze of orange and yellows, with higher streaks of blue and green rising skyward. Phoebe stood with *Daett* in the barnyard as they gazed at the sight in silence, the ponies circling around them. The all-white horse, Snow Cloud, walked up beside her and lifted her head to whinny loudly toward the beauty splashed across the heavens.

Phoebe wrapped her hand around his neck and leaned against him. She wanted to cry and laugh all at the same time. This evening was a little too much, with such glory written in the heavens and things going so well with the farm. But now *Daett* and *Mamm* were leaving tomorrow for Lancaster. Did happiness and sadness always walk so close together?

Phoebe buried her face in the pony's mane, and *Daett* reached over to brush the long white hair. "Even the horses seem to praise the Lord tonight," he said.

"It is so beautiful." Phoebe let out a long breath. "This week has been so *wunderbah*. Having you and *Mamm* here, and passing the inspection yesterday. My classes are completed, and our license has been issued..."

"I agree. This has been a blessed week, and a clear sign of the Lord's *goot* favor on the venture, if you ask me."

"I still can't believe it at times," Phoebe told him. "I think I'm going to wake up and find myself in a dream, and I'll be my little old self again, hiding away from who knows what because I'm so scared."

"You were never hiding," *Daett* assured her. "The Lord was guiding you the whole time. That's what I'm thinking."

"Your blessing is so appreciated. That's all I can say." Phoebe took *Daett*'s hand and leaned against his shoulder. "Thank you."

"You are more than welcome." *Daett* glanced toward the barn. "And here comes David to enjoy this moment with us."

Phoebe stepped away from her father to greet David with a smile. "Isn't this sight just *wunderbah*?" She motioned toward the horizon.

He grinned. "*Yah*. I saw the sunset from the barn window and had to come out."

"I appreciate your help this week, David," *Daett* told him. "I'm comforted that I can leave my daughter in such *goot* hands."

"*Daett*," Phoebe scolded. "You make me sound downright helpless."

"Oh, you're quite capable, daughter. But David takes care of things you don't know much about."

"I'm sure that is true."

"I think Phoebe could handle everything if she set her mind to it," David said. "But I am honored to be included. I never thought I would have the chance to work on a project that will be so interesting and rewarding, to say the least."

"*Yah*, there's much potential for *goot* and for bad," *Daett* agreed. "That's why we will have to keep praying for the Lord's grace. With that granted, I'm sure things will be all right."

"I agree," David seconded. He leaned against the fence to gaze at the last of the lingering sunset.

Phoebe remained with him while *Daett*'s footsteps faded away into the distance.

"You're staying for supper?" Phoebe finally asked.

"I would love to. Thanks for being my friend, Phoebe."

"I...well, it's that..." She stopped. "I guess Grandma was right, but I honestly didn't have any grudge against you, David. I never thought less of you. It's just that with..." She paused again.

"Our family's history," he finished. "But you didn't let that stop you from befriending me."

Phoebe hung her head. "I guess I trusted Grandma, but now I see for myself. You know I couldn't have gotten to the place we are without your help."

"I suppose so. But I also couldn't have done this without you. In fact, the farm never would have happened without your input."

"Come on, David. You don't have to say all these nice things about me."

"Maybe I want to," he said with a grin. "But really, Phoebe, I do appreciate what your family has done for me and for Ruth. Your *daett*'s offer yesterday was most kind."

"Yesterday? Kind?" Phoebe glanced toward him. "Is Ruth helping on the farm too?"

"No, but the school board is offering Ruth the teaching job this fall. Your *daett* broke the news to her during the tour yesterday."

"Really? That is so *wunderbah*. I can't believe it. Then Ruth is staying in the community? Grandma's prayers have been answered again?"

"I don't know about that." He hung his head over the fence. "Ruth hasn't made her mind up yet, but I hope she accepts."

Phoebe hugged herself and laughed. "Oh, what more blessings could be thrown upon our heads? The Lord is making things right, isn't He?" Phoebe looked toward David and sobered. "I'm sorry about your *daett*. It must have been difficult growing up under him, and being associated with his surly behavior when you didn't deserve that at all."

"We made it," he said, attempting to smile.

"But barely. I can't imagine how that must have been for you.

He's so unreasonable, David. Throwing things together that don't belong, like presuming you and I would be..." Her arm fluttered in the air but stopped when she saw the look on his face. "Oh, David, I'm so sorry. I hope you know that I never thought poorly of you. The times I was around you while Grandma still lived, you were nothing but decent and kind to me. Your *daett* was so wrong to accuse you of—"

"It's okay, Phoebe," he interrupted, but his face was quite pained.

"I know that I am...I'm not much of a catch, David. I'm sorry your *daett* thought you'd settle for something so—"

"Phoebe, that's not—"

"You don't have to defend me. The facts are the facts. I am what I am, and I'm almost twenty-five and unmarried. I mean, I've been on a few dates, *yah*." Phoebe looked away at the now-darkened sky. "I'm not complaining. You are the one who has everything to complain about after what you suffered from the community."

"You undersell yourself, Phoebe, by an awful lot. You are—"

"Stop, David. You don't have to lift my spirits. I will think on this no more and be thankful for all the *goot* things I have. I want to enjoy this last evening before *Daett* and *Mamm* leave for home." Phoebe took a step toward the barn.

"Any man who could win your heart would have won a great treasure," David told her, his voice low.

Phoebe stopped and laughed. "With a tongue like that, you should be able to win the heart of any girl you choose to pursue."

"You don't see me with a girl, so that must not be true."

"And you don't see any man seeking to unlock my great treasure!" she retorted. "So we're even."

"I suppose so," he allowed, falling in behind her.

She turned to face him by the barn door. "Things have changed for you now. Have you got someone in mind? Maybe I can drop a bug in her ear that starts buzzing?"

He laughed. "I doubt that. I'm a hopeless case, Phoebe."

She pushed open the barn door. "You know that's not true. Look how efficient you've been these past weeks with the *Englisha* forms and with arranging that tour."

"That was Ruth's doing."

"But you get the point, David." She gave him a smile in the low light of the barn. "Let me help you. I can say what I have to say in the hearing of this charming woman, and the little fly will begin to buzz."

He laughed again and hurried past her. "I need to join your *daett* for some chores I have to finish before supper," he called over his shoulder.

Phoebe stilled the protest that rose to her lips. David needed time before he could fully come into his own. But his healing had begun, and had been ongoing since Grandma began to pray and plan. Phoebe took a quick look out of the barn window, but the sunset had faded from sight. She heard the snap of a lantern from behind her and turned her head.

Daett smiled in the flickering light. "Are you going to help *Mamm* with supper?"

"Yep," Phoebe chirped. "Sorry. I forgot about supper for a moment. I was watching the sunset and talking with you and David."

Daett stopped her as she hurried past. "I wasn't scolding, Phoebe. And I want to say this in case I don't catch you alone again."

"*Daett*." Phoebe made a face. "You make it sound so serious."

He chuckled. "It's not serious. I just want to make sure you understand that I would have no objections if you and David...well, you know."

"*Daett!*" Phoebe gasped. "Surely you're not also..."

"Also what?" He tilted his head sideways.

"Thinking that David—"

"I'm not thinking about David," he interrupted. "I'm telling you, Phoebe, in case your heart should be drawn to the man. I think he would make a decent husband for you."

"*Daett*, I can't believe this!"

"Hush. David will hear you."

"But *Daett*, why? You know David and I don't have anything going on. Leroy claimed David was...oh, this is awful. Please don't join the party, *Daett*. Not you."

"You make it sound like a horrible idea, Phoebe," *Daett* chided. "I think you and David would make a decent couple."

Phoebe tried to breathe. "You're just saying so to make me feel better about my lack of...well, you know what. You're pushing us together out of desperation. I appreciate that, but trust me. David has no interest in this plain girl, just as no one else does."

"Stop, Phoebe. I see this conversation isn't going well, and I'm sorry I brought it up. You will find someone as the Lord wills. I'm not trying to interfere. Come!" He held out his arms. "Give me a hug. You are a lovely woman, daughter. I don't care what the unmarried men have to say."

Phoebe laughed and wiped away her tears before giving *Daett* a hug. This evening had continued as it began, filled with both sorrow and joy. "I'll be missing you," she told him. She looked up into his bearded face. "Thank you for all that you have done for me this week, and the effort you put into raising all of us children."

"I wouldn't have it any other way," *Daett* told her, planting a kiss on top of her *kapp*.

"*Daett*," Phoebe protested. "I'm not a little girl anymore."

"You will always be my little girl. Don't forget that. Now run along and help *Mamm* with supper."

Phoebe ducked her head and hurried out of the barn to cross the lawn at a fast pace. Darkness had fallen, but the lantern in the living room window threw light along the walk. She went up the porch steps and into the house. Ruth was setting the table when Phoebe entered the kitchen. *Mamm* was bent over the stove.

"You're here too!" Phoebe exclaimed.

Ruth smiled. "*Yah*, your *mamm* was kind enough to invite me yesterday, but I didn't know until this afternoon whether I could make it."

"I'm glad you could join us," Phoebe told Ruth as she busied herself at the counter with slicing the bread. Apparently her parents had all sorts of secrets they kept from her, but that was okay.

"Did you enjoy the sunset?" *Mamm* asked as she pulled the chicken casserole from the stove.

"It was awesome! *Daett* and I watched from the pasture fence with the ponies around us. It couldn't have been a more perfect send-off for the two of you leaving tomorrow."

"*Yah*, that's what I was thinking," *Mamm* agreed. "Did anyone tell you that Ruth plans to teach school for the community this fall?"

"I haven't—" Ruth began.

"She's still thinking about it," *Mamm* amended. "But the Lord has His hand in all of this. That I can say. Your grandma was a praying woman."

Phoebe glanced at Ruth, who had her head down and her fingers busy with the last of the silverware. *Mamm* seemed to understand and said no more about the tender subject.

"I hope you take the job," Phoebe told Ruth when she looked up.

Ruth nodded but didn't say anything. Moments later, *Daett* and David came in from the barn and took their places at the table. Thanks were given, and the food was passed around. Light chatter filled the kitchen as *Daett* and *Mamm* made their plans for the trip home to Lancaster tomorrow.

"When will you be coming back for a visit?" David asked.

Daett smiled broadly. "The road goes both ways, you know."

David chuckled. "I'm thinking we'll be right busy here on the farm, but maybe there will be an opening over the holidays."

They all laughed. David knew there wasn't money for trips down to Lancaster, and *Daett* and *Mamm* would be back before long unless Phoebe missed her guess. Their happy smiles showed that plainly enough.

Daett pronounced his benediction. "May the Lord watch over you in the months ahead, as I'm sure He will."

"Thank you," David responded. "You have been a great help this week."

"That's what parents are for," *Daett* said as he dished out another helping of mashed potatoes and gravy. "And we wish you the best also," *Daett* told Ruth. "Even if we aren't your parents."

Ruth nodded and looked away. Phoebe was sure there were tears on Ruth's cheek, so she wasn't the only one who experienced both joy and sorrow tonight.

"This is awesome eating," *Daett* declared, and laughter rippled around the table.

FOURTEEN

On a Monday morning two weeks later, Phoebe stepped out on the porch and closed the front door gently behind her. The sun had burst over the horizon, and the rays streamed across the front lawn to splash against the side of Grandma's barn in a blaze of white.

The breakfast dishes were still on the kitchen table, but she needed a few moments of quiet reflection before the busyness of the day thundered down upon her head. The first two children from Child Protective Services were due to arrive at nine o'clock. They would stay for the entire week. Phoebe stilled the rapid intake of her breath and breathed a quick prayer toward the heavens. "Help us, Lord, as I know You will." That was more statement than request, but everything about this venture was strange and new. Why not say prayers of faith for the day? At least it calmed her nerves. David would be here before long, and she would lean on his strength. Not literally, of course, but his manliness and stability were great comforts.

Mamm's letter had arrived a week ago.

Greetings, dear daughter. The trip back to Lancaster has gone off without a hitch. We are back into the flow of the season, it seems.

Daett is ready to harvest the cornfield with the back forty going for silage. We need more cow feed this winter with the extra heifers we are keeping.

Phoebe's thoughts drifted from her mother's letter to the present. The arrival of the farm's first children took precedence over tales of Lancaster's midweek sewing circles and news of who might have their wedding plans in place for this fall.

A figure took shape in the distance, walking north on the main road, and Phoebe leaned over the porch railing for a better look. Had David set out this early? Phoebe smiled as she focused. No, this was Ruth, headed up the road to open the schoolhouse for the first day of the new term. Ruth had chosen to accept the position. Phoebe knew the decision couldn't have been easy for her friend. Ruth was committed to ending her *rumspringa* and settling down for the baptismal class this fall without any prospects of finding a husband in the community. She was more than two years younger than David, but twenty-four was still old in the Amish world. Phoebe could identify with that feeling. Thankfully, she had the farm to occupy her thoughts. Perhaps the schoolteaching job would do the same for Ruth.

She would have taken the schoolteaching job if Grandma hadn't made other plans. That would have left Ruth out in the cold, so things were better this way. Her situation hadn't changed, though, when it came to attracting the attention of the community's eligible bachelors. There weren't any men, but if there had been, her chances still remained around zero. Who wanted a *frau* who ran a farm for *Englisha* children? On that score, she had chosen the losing card, but feeling sorry for oneself was not wise.

Phoebe waved when Ruth came close enough. She called out, "*Goot* morning! You're on the road bright and early."

Ruth didn't answer until she had hurried in from the road. "It's *goot* to see you this morning, Phoebe. My nerves are all a-jitter. Even though it's out of the way, I just had to come up and speak with you.".

"Is it that bad? I thought I was the one on pins and needles this morning."

"You're getting your first children today, aren't you?" Ruth sounded sympathetic. "David's talking about little else. He's so excited. Thankfully, *Daett's* no longer complaining now that the community approves. In the meantime, I keep wondering if I'm doing the right thing."

"Oh, you are. Don't doubt now."

Ruth sighed. "I know I shouldn't. I should be thankful instead. Your family is doing so much for me, and I do appreciate that. In fact, that's the only reason I'm giving teaching a chance. It's my heart that won't agree."

"Ethan Thompson?" Phoebe guessed. "He is handsome. There is no question there, and he's quite charming, but..."

Ruth sighed again. "That's what your *daett* said. It makes so much sense, but still...oh, I wish letting go were easy."

"We'll pray for you. I'm sure Grandma did while she was here. In fact, her prayers may be the reason we all are where we are."

"Everyone's right about Ethan. I guess I was fooling myself. I haven't heard a peep from him in two weekends now."

"Oh, let me give you a hug." Phoebe came down the porch steps, and the two embraced. "You must feel awful."

"Have you ever walked away from love?" Ruth asked.

Phoebe made a face. "I had my dreamy sort of love interrupted quite rudely, if the truth be known."

Ruth appeared astonished. "Really?"

"It was a long time ago. I'm just trying to find my courage again."

"Running a farm takes courage. You underrate yourself, Phoebe."

"This was Grandma's idea, not mine. I'd be schoolteaching otherwise."

"I didn't mean to take that away from you. Please believe me."

"I know you didn't. And I'm not wishing I were teaching. I like this idea much better."

"I appreciate this job. I guess I've always liked such things but never thought them possible here in the community with our..." Ruth looked away. "Sorry, I don't want to bring that up all the time."

"I'm sorry too. And I think you'll be much better at teaching than I would have been. You're more studious and into books. Aren't you?"

"*Yah*, I guess," Ruth allowed. "Maybe things did work out for the best."

"You'll have some unmarried man giving you the look before long," Phoebe told her. They both laughed.

"Well, I have to get going," Ruth said moments later. She hurried across the lawn with a quick wave over her shoulder.

Phoebe watched until Ruth disappeared from sight. Then she returned to the kitchen and washed the dishes. David's heavy tread sounded on the porch before she finished, and Phoebe set down the dishcloth to rush into the living room. He had already let himself in and stood inside the front door with a grin on his face. "Ready for the day, are we?"

"Oh, David! It's so *goot* to see you. You don't know how your being here comforts my heart. So much lies ahead of us today."

"You'll be great," he promised. "Just relax and love them, and give the children time to adjust. That will be the biggest trick every time, I'm thinking. What, with the clash between our cultures." His grin grew again. "But that's also our strength. If we don't act strange or nervous, we'll just be part of the new experience and seem perfectly normal to them."

She could have hugged him, but that wasn't proper. So Phoebe bounced up and down a few times, which produced a laugh from David. "You are nervous this morning."

"I'm always scared around something new, David. You know that."

"Come." He took Phoebe's hand to lead her back into the kitchen. "Shall I help with the kitchen work, perhaps?"

"Now you're treating me like a *boppli*," Phoebe said, but she didn't pull back her hand. His attentions felt like those of a big brother, but that wasn't quite it. David was a huge help, and she wouldn't try to figure things out. She needed him, and that was *goot* enough.

"I see the dishes aren't done." He motioned toward the counter. "I will help."

She gave in. "Only because I want you around until the children arrive. Otherwise you're never doing my dishes. And there aren't but a few pieces anyway."

"We'll check on the ponies afterward. Not that they need checking on, but doing so might calm our nerves."

"Calm *my* nerves," she corrected him. She washed the dishes, giving them to him to dry.

He didn't speak again as they worked.

She broke the silence. "I want to show you something. Have you ever seen Grandma's prayer journal?"

He shook his head. "Ruth mentioned something about it, but..."

"Then that's what we must do first. I want to show you the prayer Grandma prayed over her dream of a pony farm."

David smiled. "Okay. I have great faith in Grandma Lapp's prayers."

"You are a jewel."

"For believing in Grandma's prayers? Come on, Phoebe! Who wouldn't?"

"Maybe," she allowed. "But you are still a special person to have known Grandma."

"That could be," he agreed. He looked away.

"Sorry. I didn't mean to embarrass you."

"It's okay. Shall we go see the prayer book?"

She hung the dishcloth over the center of the sink and led him back to the living room. He took a seat on the couch and waited while she retrieved the tablet from the bedroom. She handed him the open page, and he read without comment.

"Well?" she asked when he finished.

"That's so Grandma Lapp."

She was sure she saw tears in his eyes.

"Can I read another page?" he asked.

"Of course!" Phoebe seated herself beside him as he turned toward the back and read aloud. "'My precious granddaughter is coming soon to take care of me in these last years of my life. I pray, Lord, that Phoebe's journey up from Lancaster will be blessed, and that You would comfort her heart. I know she isn't used to changes, and doesn't take to them well. Something must have happened to her when she was young that injured her, but You are the unchanging One, and You are the Lord of her life. Give Phoebe peace and safety on the journey. I know she will be a great blessing once she arrives. I believe You have a special plan for her in the years ahead and will use her to bless many in this world with her love. She is a dear girl with a great heart, but not many know this. I pray worry will not grip her too much as she grows older. I ask that her heart become ever tenderer toward You. I believe that someday the love of a man will find her, and that You will bring her healing. I ask that You would guide Phoebe's—'"

"Stop, stop, stop!" Phoebe ordered. She leaped to her feet. "I had no idea there were things in there about me. I—oh, David, I'm so embarrassed. You probably think..." She paced the living room floor in front of him.

"I don't think anything," he assured her. "I didn't know what Grandma wrote." He closed the book. "But what happened to you, Phoebe?"

"That was in the past. I dealt with it and moved on."

"Okay." He stood as well. "Shall we go see the ponies?"

"But David, this is awful."

"It's not awful. It's true. You are what Grandma Lapp said you were, but I'm sorry I didn't stop reading. I shouldn't have embarrassed you like that."

She clung to his shirtsleeve. "What you must think of me!"

"I think you are a *wunderbah* friend," he said with a smile. "And nothing is going to change that. Someday you will find what Grandma Lapp said you would."

Phoebe let go of his sleeve. "I don't know about that, but if I'm red and blushing all day, you'll know why."

"You'll just be...ah, forget it," he said. He hurried out the door.

She caught up with him at the porch steps. "You will finish that sentence, David Fisher."

He only increased the speed of his steps.

She caught his shirtsleeve again, and he stopped.

"Tell me," she ordered.

He didn't meet her gaze. "Blushing makes you appear more beautiful, Phoebe."

She groaned. "Now I have stepped in it."

"Come. Just forget what I said. Let's go see the ponies."

"You'll have to let me collect myself. I..."

"I'll be out there then." He turned to leave. He was halfway to the barn door before she ran to catch up.

"David, wait!"

He paused a moment, and then they entered the barn together with careful efforts to avoid looking at each other. The ponies hung around the back barn door and whinnied when they walked up. David and Phoebe stroked the ponies' noses and pressed their faces into their manes. They were like two little children in so many ways. Both of them were near twenty-five years of age and burdened with the responsibility of this farm, yet in their hearts...

"Did you really mean what you just said?" Phoebe asked him. "About me? That I am..." She couldn't say the word.

"I think you are very beautiful, Phoebe, blushing or not."

"Do you think I am wild and wicked?"

A look of horror crossed his face. "Whatever put such a thought into your head?"

She bit her lower lip. "That doesn't matter."

He reached over to touch her hand. "You are the loveliest woman I have ever seen. Both inside and outside."

"Did you have to say that at a moment like this?" Phoebe wailed. "We have two children coming, and I have to be at my best and strongest instead of a weeping mess."

"You are at your best now," he assured her. "And I spoke only the truth."

"Your opinion, *yah*. But how are we supposed to work together now? I'll be so embarrassed I can't even look at you."

"Is it really that bad? My opinion of you?"

"No."

"It's okay," he comforted her. "We all have thoughts we shouldn't have, but never again think that you are wicked, Phoebe. You are like your grandma, and she was a woman of the Lord."

Tears came, and Phoebe wiped them away.

"I'm sorry. I didn't mean to disturb you."

"You're not the one who disturbed me." She forced a smile. "Just give me a moment to collect myself."

"Okay."

"Let's be adults about this," she finally said. "I greatly appreciate you, David. The truth is, I found myself looking forward to your arrival this morning. You will be a great help to me, and I will take comfort in your presence on the farm both now and in the future. So that's that."

"That's that," he agreed, his gaze fixed on her.

"What?" she demanded.

"I still think you're pretty."

"And I like to have you around, so we're even."

A smile spread over his face. "*Yah*, I suppose we are."

"Then let's forget this happened."

"I agree."

"There's the van coming in the driveway," she said, but he had already heard and turned toward it. She smiled and hurried after him.

FIFTEEN

Minutes later, Phoebe paused behind the half-open barn door, hidden by the wooden frame.

"You should go ahead of me," she whispered to David. Her courage had flown right up through the roof and vanished into the blue sky.

"You have it in you," he said, his voice low. "They need to see you first. You are in charge, you know. This is the Lapp Family Farm."

Phoebe pasted on a smile and stepped forward. David was right beside her as they crossed the barnyard together. She had not exaggerated the comfort of his presence. And he thought she was pretty... and a saint like Grandma! But she could not think on that right now or she would pass out.

The van had parked near the front walk. Phoebe waved, and Mrs. Broman's face appeared in the passenger's window. The door swung open, and Mrs. Broman stepped out, smiling and waving back. "Good morning, Phoebe. We thought for a moment you were still all sleeping."

"We were just taking a last-minute check of the barn—"

"Phoebe, dear," Mrs. Broman interrupted. "I'm teasing. How are you?" She gave Phoebe a hug and a quick peck on the cheek. "Are you okay?"

"Do I look that scared?" Phoebe managed.

"No, you look fine." Mrs. Broman patted Phoebe on the back.

"She's okay," David echoed as he squared his shoulders.

Mrs. Broman seemed pleased. Thank the Lord Grandma had somehow foreseen this moment and provided her with David, who was the exact person she needed by her side.

The driver's side door of the van slammed, and Ethan appeared. "Howdy," he said. Then he shook their hands.

"How's Ruth?" Ethan asked David. "I haven't seen her in town the last few weeks."

"She's..." David stopped. "Maybe I should leave the explaining to her," he finished.

Ethan didn't give up. "Something serious?"

Mrs. Broman cleared her throat. "Maybe we should focus on the task at hand, Ethan. We have two young boys to settle into an Amish farm. That's like settling aliens, I'm thinking."

"They'll take to it like ducks to water," Ethan assured her.

His bravado seemed forced, but Phoebe gave him a warm smile. "Thanks for the vote of confidence. That's kind of you to say."

"You are a gentle and decent people," Ethan told her. "George and Bill will pick that right up."

"That's certainly what they need," Mrs. Broman agreed. "So shall we begin?"

Ethan nodded and opened the van door. Two small boys of no more than ten or eleven years of age were seated on the front seat, staring back at them. "George and Bill," Ethan said, "this is Phoebe and David, your hosts at this lovely Amish farm. You will be spending a wonderful week riding horses and climbing mountains and enjoying yourselves immensely. Tell Phoebe and David hi."

Neither of the boys said anything.

"Come on," Ethan encouraged them.

"They're kind of shy," Mrs. Broman whispered in Phoebe's ear. "For good reasons. But you'll be perfect for them."

David nudged Phoebe's arm, and she forced herself to step forward. "Hi, George and Bill." Her smile felt crooked and tight on her face, but at least she could smile. Neither boy seemed to mind as they scooted closer to the open van door and peered out. Skeptical looks filled their faces.

"This is not Mars," Ethan said with a chuckle.

"Don't encourage them," Mrs. Broman chided.

"Come, boys." David stepped forward. "I'll take you to see the ponies."

"Ponies?" they said together. Interest sparked in their eyes.

"Yep." David grinned from ear to ear. "Real Assateague ponies from the salt flats of northern Virginia."

"Where is that?" George asked.

"Certainly not in *Dungeons and Dragons,*" Ethan quipped.

Mrs. Broman shushed him with a tap on his arm. The two boys hopped down from the van and followed David into the barn.

"I like him," Mrs. Broman said. "You two will make a great team."

Phoebe nodded but said nothing.

"Well, shall we be going?" Ethan asked. "I put the suitcases on the front porch, and everyone seems settled in at the moment."

Mrs. Broman turned to Phoebe. "You have my cell phone number. And also Ethan's. Call either of us at the slightest problem, day or night. I'll be checking in tomorrow for the first time, and we'll go from there. Do you think you can handle this, dear?"

"David and I can," Phoebe replied. Her courage seemed to have returned. "He seems to know exactly what needs doing."

"He has a down-to-earth quality," Ethan agreed. "They'll listen to him, and everything will be fine."

Mrs. Broman seemed to breathe deeper than usual. "And no

religious instruction, Phoebe. Remember that part of your training. I don't want them going back to their parents quoting Bible verses. That will be the end of your little venture right there."

"I wouldn't do that, and neither would David," Phoebe assured her.

"Just saying." Mrs. Broman's face softened. "I didn't think you would—"

"They are decent people," Ethan interrupted. "But tell me, Phoebe. What's up with Ruth and her disappearance?"

Phoebe studied the ground for a moment. "Ruth has ended her *rumspringa*. The school board offered her the teaching position for this term. Ruth accepted, and she won't be in town anymore."

"That must mean—"

Mrs. Broman interrupted him this time. "You know what ending *rumspringa* means. You should have seen this coming, Ethan. If you were thinking that…" She let the sentence hang.

Ethan's smile was bright. "Well…so. Shall we get going?"

"Remember, call if there are problems!" Mrs. Broman repeated the instructions as she hopped in the van. Ethan was inside moments later, and they both waved on the way out of the driveway. The van headed south toward Little Falls, and stillness settled over the farm again.

Ethan had inquired about Ruth. Was he serious? She had always been the one who had pursued the relationship, from what Phoebe could tell. Surely Ethan wouldn't interfere with Ruth's plans. And Ruth knew what the rules were. She had to cut off contact with Ethan—which was the right step. Grandma's plan had unfolded seamlessly right in front of their eyes…but now this? Surely Ruth would soon find an Amish man from somewhere who could capture her heart. Ruth wasn't unattractive, and now that she was the community's schoolteacher, there was no reason…

Phoebe pinched herself. She was not about to descend to

matchmaking. Enough duties stared her in the face already. David was a great help, but she was still in charge of the farm and had to act accordingly. Lunch was a few hours away, but her duties extended well beyond the house. Grandma had seen to that.

Phoebe turned to walk quickly toward the barn. She never would have dared to undertake this venture on her own. Not in a thousand years. And no one in her family would have dreamed her capable or supplied her with someone to walk with her. Only Grandma had seen the possibility in both David and her. Had Grandma seen more? Had Grandma seen...

"No! I will not go there," Phoebe told herself.

She entered the barn with a firm stride and hurried to the back barn door. She stopped short at the sight in front of her. David had all three ponies around him with their saddles on, and he stroked their necks as he spoke with George and Bill in a soft voice. Bill appeared ready to join David in touching the animals, but George still stood back a few feet. David knew what he was doing, though. She could tell at a glance from the intense looks on the boys' faces. Maybe she would hang back for a moment and not interfere.

Then David looked up and called out, "Come, Phoebe. Join us. The boys are just getting up the courage for their first ride."

Phoebe took a deep breath and walked toward them. The skeptical looks on the boys' faces had returned. She should have stayed out of sight.

"Jump on and show them," David encouraged her with a smile.

"How are you two doing?" Phoebe asked George and Bill before she returned David's smile with a nervous one of her own. "You were doing so great," she whispered to him. "You shouldn't have called me."

"I'm doing better with you here," he whispered back. Then he raised his voice. "Watch her, boys, as Phoebe hops on. There's nothing to it at all."

There seemed no option but to follow David's instructions. Hesitation would only sow doubt in the minds of George and Bill. Phoebe grabbed the saddle horn with one hand and Snow Cloud's mane with other, swinging herself into the saddle. She settled in with a smile and gripped the reins to steer Snow Cloud a short distance away from the other two ponies.

"See, there's nothing to it," David encouraged the boys. "I'll hold the reins, and I'll lead you after Phoebe. We won't go faster than a walk."

Bill was the first one up onto Lady's back, and David patted the pony's neck with one hand while he held the reins with the other. "How about you, George? Want to try?"

"I think I'll walk him," George said, reaching for the other pony's reins.

David shrugged. "As you wish. I'll lead Lady."

"What's this pony's name?" George asked. He held onto the leather reins with both hands.

"Aladdin," David told him, "after the tale—"

"I know," George interrupted. His eyes were fixed on the white-faced pony.

"There's no magic here, though," David said. "Just the farm and fun and..."

The look on George's face said he wasn't convinced that magic didn't exist in the horse. Phoebe watched him approach. Despite the troubled times this boy had seen, perhaps there was magic here on the farm...or rather, grace. That was more like it. This was another world for George and Bill. Maybe the peace and quiet could supply them with what they lacked. She couldn't begin to imagine what their lives were like in the world they came from. Maybe she would find out in the week ahead. Maybe healing could come for these torn children. There was an awful pain in their hearts. She could tell by the look on their faces.

Phoebe continued to watch as George approached her, leading Aladdin.

"How's it going?" she asked him with a warm smile.

"I'm doing it," he said.

Phoebe nudged Snow Cloud's ribs, and the pony moved slowly forward. She led the way out of the barnyard gate with George on foot behind her and David with Lady's reins right behind him. They must make a strange sight as they worked their way slowly across the pasture to the far side, but she didn't care.

Bill spoke up first. "That was fun. You should try getting on, George," he encouraged.

George skeptically eyed his pony.

"You can pretend you're Luke Skywalker," Bill suggested.

This brought a wry smile to George's face. "This is a long stretch from a Tauntaun, and there is no snow."

"You can pretend," Bill said. "And a pony is much easier to ride."

That seemed to clinch the matter for George, who swung himself up into the saddle in one easy move. David hurried forward to hold the reins, but George waved him away. "This is easier than a Tauntaun. Shall we go for a ride, Bill?"

"I'm game," Bill shot back. "But not faster than a walk. At least today. My Tauntaun isn't completely tamed yet."

George chuckled and turned Aladdin toward the barn with Bill on Lady right behind him. David had let go of the reins and stood transfixed as the boys moved away from him. "Should I have let them go?" he asked Phoebe.

"They'll be okay," Phoebe assured him. How did she know that? She wasn't sure, but this seemed right. And George did keep Aladdin to a steady walk. The ponies would not dash off on their own. They didn't like anything beyond a slow amble on their own initiative.

"What's a Tauntaun?" David asked, his gaze fixed on the departing two.

Phoebe grinned. "I have no idea, but it seemed to work."

"I'm going to ask them what a Tauntaun is," David declared.

"I don't think I would. I have a feeling it's something everyone out there knows about, and we would appear…"

"Out of touch," David finished for her. "Naive and weird."

"Something like that."

He regarded her for a moment. "But we're not."

"It depends on your perspective, I suppose."

"I can live without Tauntauns," he declared. "Whatever they are. I'll take this any day."

"*Yah*. I would too."

"My guess is Tauntauns aren't pretty like you are."

"David!" she scolded. "No more talking about that subject."

He grinned. "I do know what I'm talking about when it comes to you."

"I didn't hear that." She nudged Snow Cloud. "Are you coming?"

He laughed and followed her. She kept Snow Cloud to a walk so David could keep up. He appeared handsome striding beside her, but maybe her mind was colored by his charming remarks.

"This has been a *goot* start to the day," he remarked, sober faced now. "You are doing very well."

"And so are you."

He kept his gaze on the boys in front of them as they approached the barnyard again.

SIXTEEN

That evening, with dusk still a few hours away, Phoebe spread the kitchen table with tasty supper dishes. She had worked inside since two o'clock, while David entertained the boys in the barnyard with another long pony ride through the back pasture. They had begun the chores soon after four, and David had taken his time. She had seen the trio lingering whenever they stepped outside the barn, David waving his arms about and engaging the boys in long conversations. David must be giving George and Bill instructions or explaining things. There weren't that many duties on the small farm, not enough to last the three hours it had taken to complete the tasks. David knew what he was doing. How wise the man was to take the time to include George and David in his activities rather than simply doing the work himself.

Phoebe smiled as she sampled the pot of potatoes with a small spoon. "Perfect," she declared.

What a *wunderbah* day this had been so far. Things had been almost too easy, but she must not doubt. Grandma's blessing was on their venture, and she should not be surprised if things worked out so well.

Phoebe heard footsteps on the back porch. As she laid down the spoon, the mudroom door burst opened without a knock. Excited voices filled the room on the other side of the kitchen wall, David's deep voice mingling with the two younger ones. Phoebe quickly laid out the last of the supper plates and arranged the silverware before she cracked open the mudroom door to peer out. They were gathered around the washbasin, but none of the three noticed her.

"Watch me," David was saying. "It's as simple as it looks. You run a little water into the sink, and then you wash with soap. Take your time, hit the plunger when you're done, and wipe your hands over there on the towel."

George and Bill laughed together. "Now you're teasing us," George said. "We know how to wash our hands in a sink and wipe them on a towel."

David kept a straight face. "I'm just going over the main points so you know for sure."

"He's teasing us," Bill said.

David ran the water and chuckled. "*Yah*, I am. But you both have done very well this afternoon with the chores. I'll have you doing them alone by the week's end."

"I can see where this is headed," George said. "Free labor."

"Slave labor," Bill added. "What do we get out of this?"

David reached for the soap. "Now that lesson you haven't learned yet. Amish boys learn how to work for the pure joy of labor. The reward is the open skies, the accomplishment of a task well done, the pleasure of a body honed by hard labor, a soft bed to sleep in for the night, and slumber that leads to sweet dreams."

"He didn't say anything about being a con salesman," George told Bill.

"That's right." Bill grunted. "Now I know he's selling us a bill of goods."

"Just remember this afternoon," David said, his voice muffled as he splashed water over his face. "And when you're sleeping so well tonight, you'll know it was no con job."

"And supper," Phoebe added in her sweetest voice from the open door. "Food is what David missed."

Both boys turned about to face her.

"Where did she come from?" Bill demanded.

"This is the kitchen doorway," Phoebe told him. She opened the door wider. "Supper is on the table."

George and Bill both stared.

"*Yah*, that's the final reward," David said as he wiped his hands on the towel. "A man can eat a whole plate of food after a hard day of work and feel the full satisfaction of his labors."

Both George and Bill turned toward David.

"Next," David said with a smile. He motioned toward the sink. "You'll see that I'm right."

Phoebe left the mudroom door open while the boys washed. David fell silent as he waited for the two. Phoebe transferred the last dish to the table and took her place. David came in moments later, followed by George and Bill. The two boys took in the food-laden table with quick glances but made no comments.

"You can sit beside me," Phoebe told Bill. "And George can sit beside David over there." Phoebe pointed to the chair near the head of the table.

David didn't hesitate as he took his place. She had half expected him to object because this wasn't his home, but he appeared properly placed, sitting there with a big grin on his face. This was how they would venture into the unknown. David would always be there, and she would be the hostess. There was nothing wrong with that.

"What is all this food?" George asked with bated breath.

"That's best discovered by tasting and not by asking," David answered. "Some things in life can't be explained."

"But..." Bill fell silent.

He didn't appear displeased, though. Why should either of them be unhappy with *goot* food? Likely this was simply the latest novelty of their first day spent on an Amish farm. *How sad,* Phoebe thought, *that tasty meals were something one should find astonishing.* She felt they were indeed blessed beyond measure with the life they lived in the community.

"Shall we say the blessing?" David suggested.

He didn't wait for an answer but bowed his head. Phoebe followed. Neither George nor Bill knew what was expected of them. They simply stared, but Phoene would not say anything. Mrs. Broman could not accuse her of religious instruction at the end of the week, especially if neither of the boys bowed their heads through grace.

"Our Father which art in heaven," David prayed out loud, with Phoebe mouthing the familiar words along with him. George and Bill still hadn't closed their eyes when Phoebe looked up after David said "amen." The boys didn't have to join them, but their prayer time at the kitchen table was not negotiable.

"We say a prayer before we eat every meal," Phoebe explained. She had allowed the practice to slip at noontime when she had served the sandwiches and cold milk in the barn, but David hadn't objected. He simply had taken off his hat and briefly bowed his head. Neither George nor Bill had noticed the gesture.

"We have mashed potatoes and gravy, pot roast, and a tossed salad," Phoebe informed the boys with her best smile. "Have you ever had a meal like that? And pecan pie. That's cooling over there on the counter."

Both of their gazes went toward the plates, and their eyes grew round.

"Fall to it," David commanded, leading the way with a generous helping of mashed potatoes. The steam rose high from his plate as he poured on gravy. "Now for a thick slab of Phoebe's wheat bread to finish things off, slathered with fresh butter and strawberry jam." David prepared his piece with a big grin on his face.

Neither George nor Bill had moved yet.

"Shall I dish it out for you?" Phoebe offered. The two seemed frozen in place.

"What is this stuff?" Bill asked, his eyes fixed on the food dishes.

"You have to taste it to find out," David teased again.

"Actually, these were once potatoes," Phoebe explained. "Those are round things that grow in the ground." From the looks on their faces, neither of the boys understood. She continued undeterred. "I peeled them, boiled them, and then mashed them in a bowl. After that I added salt and a touch of butter and milk, and this is the result. The accompanying bowl holds gravy, made to add flavor and seasoning to the mashed potatoes. There is meat over here in this dish for protein, and a salad to balance things out. You really have to try this, boys." She wasn't getting through to Bill or George, who still hadn't moved. So she tried David's angle and dipped out generous portions for them. "You worked all afternoon. You must be hungry." Phoebe added the gravy, and the warm steam rose into their faces.

Apparently this did the persuading. George went first, and a smile crept across his face. "This is good, Bill."

Bill already had his mouth full and was nodding with delight. Mission accomplished. But who would have thought a battle would be fought on such strange ground?

"What do you boys usually eat?" Phoebe asked.

George swallowed before he answered. "Chips, pizza, or hamburgers if we can get them, and sodas sometimes. Breakfast cereal if nothing else."

"Moon pies." Bill's face lit up. "We had those all last week, and Twinkies the week before."

Phoebe hid her disapproval. "No one cooks for you?" From the looks on their faces she shouldn't have asked the question. "Sorry," she murmured.

George tried to smile. "It's okay. Mom works all the time, and when she doesn't there's always something to watch on TV. Which, by the way—what's on for tonight? Monday night football hasn't begun, but something good should be playing."

Phoebe glanced at David, who cleared his throat. "There is no TV."

"No TV?" George stopped chewing.

"No TV?" Bill repeated. He looked at his brother. "No one told us about that."

"As no one told you about mashed potatoes and gravy," Phoebe chirped. "Life is so much better without TV."

Neither of the two appeared convinced. They peered down at their plates as if the potatoes and gravy were the cause of this betrayal.

"So what do you do all evening?" George finally asked. He glanced up at the kitchen clock. "It's not even seven o'clock, and the sun's still up."

"It normally is at this time," David said, but no one laughed. Clearly this was a serious matter for the two boys.

"We'll think of something," Phoebe told them. "You can help me with the dishes, and then we can walk down to David's place and meet his parents."

David loudly cleared his throat.

"Oh, sorry about that. Change of plans," Phoebe rushed on. "Perhaps a buggy ride then?"

Mild interest flashed across their faces but soon vanished.

"You'll just have to get used to things," David said. "You are here for the week, and you'll see that life is more than video games and Monday night football and..." David stopped, apparently out of breath, or more likely overcome with his own boldness. She had never heard him lecture like this before, and with such authority in his voice.

"I agree," she joined in. "The first evening might be a little rough, but the Lord has filled the hours with beautiful things that live all around us. We miss them when we are off in a world of modern technology."

David stared at her. He appeared quite impressed with her little speech. Now to place the plan in action. Neither of the boys was convinced in the least. Their faces were quite fallen, with their appetites apparently gone.

"You should finish your plates," she told them. "Then there is pecan pie."

They hesitated for a moment, as if they would rebel, but George's fork moved first.

Bill followed his brother's example. "Is pecan pie like Twinkies?" he asked.

"Much better," she told him. "Much, much better. There is no plastic wrap and no preservatives added. Just freshness straight from my stove to your plate."

George's grin was crooked. "I thought you said there was no TV in the house."

"There isn't. Why do you say that?"

"You sounded like a commercial," Bill said. He snapped his fingers. "Which one was that? The—"

"Some pizza commercial," George finished. "That last part sounded just like it."

Phoebe could feel her face reddening as David grinned from ear to ear. "Well, then. Now let's talk about something else."

"She's very humble," David told them in a conspiratorial tone. "She's also bashful at times."

She wanted to bonk David on the head with her fork. He knew better than to tease about such things. TV! The very idea! Phoebe jumped up to grab the pecan pie and cut the pieces. Thankfully, the boys were busy with the last of their food. She slid clean plates toward them and waited while George took the first piece. David could wait as payment for his transgressions. He noticed and grinned even more. She couldn't help but make a face at him, and she felt her cheeks flush again. David almost laughed out loud. Fortunately, both of the boys were busy with dessert.

"How is it?" Phoebe asked them, more to distract herself from David's glances than anything. She liked the man, but he had to stop this teasing.

"It's good," said George.

"More like heavenly," Bill added. "I've never tasted anything like this."

Both boys looked at each other and nodded, clearly impressed.

"I'm glad you like the pie." She helped herself to a small piece. David had no such compunction. His piece was large, but he had worked outside all day, and men didn't have to worry about putting on the pounds the way women did. Phoebe made another face at him, but he was deep into his pie and didn't notice.

They all savored the delicious dessert in silence, and then Phoebe rose to run the hot water for the dishes. David glanced at her, but she shook her head. There would be no final customary prayer of thanks. Some concessions must be made for the greater good while they kept *Englisha* children in their home. She wouldn't be accused of forcing religion down anyone's throat.

The evening stretched out in front of them. "You will stay until dark?" she asked David, who had risen to his feet.

"Come, boys," David said. "I think I will take you down to our farm after all and show you the sheep. We should find something to keep you busy."

He had apparently forgotten that they could help with the dishes, but that hadn't been a *goot* idea anyway.

"Thanks," she mouthed to David as he led George and Bill out the mudroom door.

He nodded and smiled. She would tell the boys Grandma's story when they came back and David left again. Maybe this could become a tradition each new week. She couldn't sidestep all religion because Grandma's life was a testament of faith. Afterward, George and Bill would probably be tired and ready for bed. The boys could take showers and do their final unpacking, by which time they should fall asleep. Likely they weren't used to early bedtimes or rising with the sun, but that would change this week. David would be here right after breakfast to begin the day, and she would be ready.

Phoebe cleared the table and began to hum a tune. The blessings of the Lord were with them. How could things be otherwise when Grandma's prayers had been lifted well before her granddaughter had ever dreamed of a pony farm?

SEVENTEEN

The following morning David strode quickly up the slight incline of the road toward Grandma Lapp's farm. Toward the east, the first blush of dawn hung over the Adirondack Mountains. He had been up well before daylight, unable to sleep half the night. He had gulped down a bowl of oatmeal for breakfast and left right after the family's morning prayers. No one at the Fishers' house had seemed surprised by his rush to leave. Ruth was also wrapped up in her schoolteaching work. Everyone understood the urgency that came with a new job.

He had introduced George and Bill to the farm animals when they visited yesterday evening. *Daett* had been in bed when David returned from dropping off the boys and had remained silent on the subject this morning.

The heavy weight on David this morning was Phoebe. His steps quickened at the thought of her. What if George and Bill had proven troublesome or rowdy overnight? Though they were young, they were city boys who were probably used to being awake at all hours. In their world, television and video games were likely always at their disposal. The first night spent in the stillness of the old farmhouse could have caused all kinds of disturbances to their routine.

What if Phoebe hadn't slept a wink? She might have beaten a path up and down the stairs seeing to the young boys' insomnia. He should have been there to share the burden, but that wouldn't have been decent. He had to trust the Lord. Phoebe was able to cope. He should have remembered that last night. Perhaps then he could have slept a few more hours instead of tossing and turning in bed.

David slowed his walk as the glow of the gas lantern in the kitchen window came into focus and he turned into the driveway. Phoebe was up, but he had expected that. What were George and Bill up to? He couldn't stop the questions in his mind, and he hurried past the barn and up the front steps. With only a light knock he entered.

Phoebe's soft voice called from the kitchen. "Come on in."

He stopped and took off his boots before he continued. Tomorrow morning he would enter through the mudroom door, but he didn't want to send the wrong signal. Phoebe might withdraw if she thought he took privileges that didn't belong to him.

The dim light of the lantern cast a shadow out on the living room floor. Phoebe appeared in the kitchen doorway, a weary smile on her face and dark rings around her eyes.

He sprang forward. "Phoebe! Did you have a rough time last night with the boys?"

Her smile faded. "Nothing I couldn't handle, David, but I must say my nerves are pretty much shot."

He wanted to take her in his arms and hold her close, but that was way out of bounds. "I'm so sorry," he managed.

"Don't blame yourself, silly." She tried to laugh. "No one is to blame except me, perhaps. Thinking I could handle all this." Her hand motion took in the whole house in a quick swoop.

"Phoebe." He stepped closer. "Can you tell me what happened? And sit, please. You look as if—"

"Don't say it. I know. I look awful, and that only after *one* sleepless night. I'm sure everyone goes through this for whatever reason—family, sick children, concerns, wayward sons and daughters."

She was prettier in her disheveled state than he had ever seen her, but what an awful thing to think at this moment. "You...I..." He faltered again.

She sat on the kitchen chair with only a brief glance toward the food laid out on the table. "I've served eggs, bacon, sliced cheese, bread and jam, and oatmeal. I couldn't awaken them." She choked. "I tried ten minutes ago, but they were so fast asleep I didn't get further than the bedroom door. They only fell asleep an hour ago—something like that. What was I thinking?"

"You must tell me what happened," he said as he took the chair beside her. His hands rested lightly on the kitchen table.

"Nothing much. I way overreacted, I think, but after..." Phoebe gave a deep shudder and covered her face with her hands. "I can't speak of this, David. I can't."

He leaned closer. "You must, Phoebe. I must know. If it's serious..." He let the threat hang.

"Oh, it's not serious." Her hands fluttered about. "The boys didn't misbehave. They just...oh..." Phoebe groaned. "It was such an awful story they told me—about a worm." Phoebe froze, unable to finish.

"Tell me. What story?"

"Did they tell you stories yesterday afternoon?" She asked instead. "Those kind of stories?"

"I don't know. You haven't told me anything. I heard more about *Star Wars*, but that's all. About this character Luke Skywalker and the movie where the Tauntaun thing came from."

"But you haven't seen it?" Horror filled her face.

"Of course not."

"But you could talk to them about it?"

"Phoebe." He dared to touch her hand. "The movie was nothing. It's all make-believe."

"You could speak to them about the movie?" She drew back her hand.

"*Yah.*"

"Have you seen a movie called *Poltergeist?*" Her gaze was intense.

"No." He didn't hesitate. "I've never heard of it."

She studied his face for a long time.

"What? Tell me."

Slowly her face softened. "None of our people should hear of such a horror." She shuddered again and reached for his hand. "You are such a comfort, David. Such a sea of sanity after what I went through last night."

He didn't dare move with the softness of her hand in his.

"I was sharing Grandma Lapp's story with them," she continued. "We got to the part about Grandma's dream for this farm, and how her prayers no doubt were what made this possible. I said I was sure Grandma somehow knew how things were going..." Phoebe's voice died out for a moment. "Bill spoke up and said, 'That's just like *Poltergeist!*' I asked what that was, which was the wrong thing to say. Maybe I'll know better next time."

"I'm sure you will."

Phoebe continued. "'You don't know about *Poltergeist?*' George asked me. 'Why, that's like the best movie ever, about the dead coming back and haunting us.'" Phoebe clung to David's hand until his fingers throbbed. "They told me awful things, David. Words that should never be heard in this house, and yet they were. The worse tale was of an awful thing that came out of...and grew...and..." Phoebe's voice failed again, and tears streamed down her face. "I can't say it, David. I just can't even say the horrible words."

"It's okay," he comforted her.

She shook her head. "I'm so ashamed of myself. I lost all my courage and all my *wunderbah* plans for the evening. I couldn't finish the story or tell them to quit or bring out the Monopoly game after that. They tore about the upstairs until all kinds of hours this morning, and I still didn't dare say a word—as if they would have listened. I can usually sleep through anything. What is happening, David? Is this all some horrible mistake? How am I to deal with what these boys have seen?"

"The Lord will help us." He squeezed her limp hand.

She didn't even try to smile. "I can say that, too, but how is that possible? I feel so...oh, it's so awful." Her hand withdrew to her lap.

"The Lord takes care of such things, Phoebe," he assured her. "We must believe that, and we must pray."

"I guess so," she said, but she didn't appear convinced. She stood. "Will you help me eat this breakfast? The boys certainly aren't getting up, and I can keep warm what's left over."

"I already..." he began but stopped. "Of course I will. It looks delicious." He turned his chair to face the table.

"Will you pray, then?"

He nodded and bowed his head. This was more than a prayer. It was a test, perhaps, or a cry for help, and this was his chance to come to her aid. He sent a silent cry heavenward before he opened his mouth: *Help me, dear Lord.* Never before had he prayed out loud in his own words, let alone in front of Phoebe Lapp. If he passed out, he would blame himself for the rest of his life.

"Lord, come to our aid this morning," he began.

"Amen," Phoebe muttered from the chair beside him.

"Forgive us where we have sinned in thinking too high thoughts of ourselves," he continued. "In thinking we could do things which are too high and mighty for anyone but You, O Lord. Comfort our hearts this morning, especially Phoebe's, after all the things she heard last night that are not pleasing to You. Give us fresh grace today and mercies anew with the dawning of a new sun. Rest our weary bodies and minds, and restore what has been lost through a sleepless night. We will rest again today, confident that You will still be with us. And bless this food and all the many other blessings You are giving us with this day. Be with Phoebe, and give her great blessings for preparing this food after a weary night, and let her find favor in Your eyes and confidence that all will be well in the end. Amen."

"Amen," she whispered, raising her eyes to him. "Thank you, David. That was so kind of you." She passed him the plate of eggs. "This is small thanks. I just wish they were still warm from the frying pan."

"They are perfect," he said as he helped himself to three of them.

She passed him the bread plate and the butter.

"You should eat," he said. "Don't just serve me."

Her smile flickered, and she turned to her own plate. He watched while she took one egg and hesitated.

"*Yah*," he told her. "You need two at least."

Her laugh was soft. "Now you're spoiling me, but I do need nourishment after a night like..." Her voice faltered again, but she ate without comment in the stillness of the kitchen, the hiss of the gas lantern above them.

David kept his gaze away from her face. It was enough that he had been granted such access to her heart this morning. He'd sat at Phoebe Lapp's kitchen table and not only listened to her troubles, but also had been able to soothe her ruffled spirits. And where had the stumbling words of that prayer come from?

David lifted his head as he heard buggy wheels in the driveway. Phoebe leaped to her feet and raced to the kitchen window. "Uncle Homer!" she exclaimed. "He's come to check on things." She smoothed her apron twice and checked the kitchen window again.

"You'll be okay. Just tell him it was a rough first night. He'll understand."

"Certainly nothing about *Poltergeist*." Her laugh was nervous.

"Certainly not," he agreed as she hurried to the front door. He stayed at the table and continued to eat.

A moment later he heard Homer's booming voice from the kitchen doorway. "*Goot* morning, young man. I see you're on the job bright and early."

"Just trying to help out." David offered his best smile. "But I think Phoebe has things under control."

"Had a difficult night, though, I hear," Homer said. He pulled out a chair. "Care if I have some breakfast, Phoebe?"

"Help yourself," she told him. She passed the eggs. "I'm afraid they're a little cold."

"*Goot* enough for me." Uncle Homer chuckled as he piled several onto his plate.

Phoebe gave David a grateful smile as her uncle spread his bread with a thick slab of butter and topped it with a generous helping of jam.

"Do you have any suggestions for getting the boys to bed earlier?" Phoebe ventured.

"Hard work!" Uncle Homer proclaimed. "There's nothing like physical labor to get unruly boys to bed at night."

"That sounds simple enough." Phoebe turned toward David. "Do you think you can find chores for them?"

"I'll try."

Uncle Homer pounded him on the back several times. "You'll do just great. I know you will. If you run out of tasks, bring them over to my place, and we can find plenty that needs doing."

Phoebe beamed at him as David nodded in agreement.

Taking the boys to Uncle Homer's place for work wouldn't be approved of by Mrs. Broman, but he would consider it as a last resort. Anything to make the week more peaceful for Phoebe.

EIGHTEEN

On Friday afternoon Ruth paced the schoolhouse floor on Peckville Road. The children had left ten minutes ago, and a mound of ungraded papers lay on her desk. An experienced teacher would finish them in an hour, but she was new at the task. Dusk would fall by the time she completed her weekly duties. Last week she had trudged home, weary but satisfied with her accomplishments. Today was different.

The emotions of the past had returned. The memories of bygone rejections from the community had bubbled to the surface. All week they had percolated, stirred by the things David had told her about the happenings at Grandma Lapp's place.

"Phoebe's really holding up well," he had said, and his eyes shone with happiness. "But George and Bill sure are a handful."

Ruth knew her brother well enough to know he wasn't telling the whole story. David was in love with Phoebe. Where had he found the courage?

How both of their fortunes had turned! She was the community's schoolteacher, and he had designs on Grandma Lapp's granddaughter. David was happy. His dreams would be fulfilled if Phoebe returned his affections. But was Ruth happy? Was her heart truly in this change? She told herself she was. She could smile and cheerfully answer any questions about her schoolteaching job, but David's casual statement yesterday evening after supper had upset the applecart.

"Keep us in mind," he'd said. "Ethan's picking up George and Bill. He'll spend Friday afternoon at the farm to see how things have gone this week. We need a *goot* report to keep this going."

She and *Mamm* had been the only ones in the kitchen at the time. *Mamm* had smiled and nodded, and Ruth had studiously ignored the remark, though David must have noticed the sudden intake of her breath. Had he meant the words for her ears? Was there a subliminal message? Did David mean she should be there if she wanted to see Ethan? That's what her heart whispered. *Walk up and see him, Ruth. Show Ethan you still care.*

Only she didn't...but she did. What a mess this was! Which was exactly why she should stay here in the schoolhouse until her work was completed and Ethan had driven safely away from Grandma Lapp's farm.

Ruth paused her pacing in front of the schoolhouse window and gazed across the road to the Yoders' farm. She had to see Ethan. He was so close.

A team of horses stood in front of the barn door attached to a wagon, and Emil Yoder or one of his boys would be out any minute to drive them into the fields. With Emil out of the way, she could amble down the road and wave to women working in their kitchens. They would assume she had completed her work early and was walking down to see how things progressed with her brother's new undertaking. No one need know about conversations with Ethan.

Which was wrong and dishonest if she planned to end her *rumspringa*. Hadn't she broadcast those intentions with her acceptance of the schoolteaching job, not to mention her plans to join the baptismal class this fall? That was all true.

Ruth paced again. Ethan was still in her heart. He was an ache that wouldn't cease. How did one pull such affections out and cast them aside as if they had never been? She had consoled herself that Ethan had never returned her feelings with the intensity she had felt for him. Her efforts had not convinced him to show her more than a passing interest. Did she hope to change that? Why take this risk? Why continue to expose her heart to pain? Was she unable to accept the kindness or acceptance the community offered her?

Ruth sighed and stared across the road again. The wagon was still there. She was foolish to think that all would be well now that she was the community's schoolteacher. The community's approval was a balm for the soul, but she still loved Ethan. David might win Phoebe's love, but no Amish man would take Ruth as his bride. Not in a thousand years. She was a Fisher. She was *goot* only for the status of an old maid, not as someone's beloved *frau*. So what if she changed her mind or Ethan came to his senses? Shouldn't the bridge back to Ethan be maintained? At least she could see if the link was still there. Perhaps that would decide the matter. If Ethan was cold and distant, her heart would receive the message and act accordingly.

Ruth hurried back to her desk and straightened the stack of papers before laying a book on top of them. They would appear less formidable to anyone who should stop in while she was out. At the front door she paused. The wagon was gone. Was it a sign? With quick steps she made her way out to Peckville Road. Someone moved in the kitchen window of the Yoders' home, and Ruth waved with a cheerful smile. She was a bold one, but her heart pounded.

Ruth turned north at the intersection and approached the Lapps' farm at a slower pace. No sense in arriving all breathless even if Ethan welcomed her—which was uncertain. A van was parked in front of the barn, so he was here. She would see him again after weeks of silence. Ruth slowed her walk further. What if he ignored her? Or her appearance disturbed the activities of the afternoon?

The front lawn was empty, and so was the kitchen window. She would leave again if she wasn't welcome and lick her wounds at the schoolhouse.

Ruth approached the barn and pushed open the door. The dusty interior was lit by light from the barn windows, and the murmur of voices—laced with bursts of laughter—rose to the rafters. The past week must have been a success for the two boys and for Phoebe's venture with David by her side. Ruth crept past the unused cow stanchions and tiptoed up to the cluster of people gathered by the back barn door.

David noticed her first and turned with a smile. "You've come down for a visit."

"*Yah*. Is that okay?"

"Of course it is!" Phoebe exclaimed, giving Ruth a quick hug. "Welcome to the end of our happy week."

Ruth tried for a light tone. "So everything went well like David claimed?"

Phoebe laughed. "We followed Uncle Homer's *goot* advice and kept the boys busy with work around the place, and they didn't keep me up all night after that."

"Oh!" Ruth said. "So I guessed right. There were problems."

"Didn't David tell you?"

"You said you were handling things," David muttered.

"He undersells himself, I see." Phoebe gave his arm a playful slap. "You shouldn't, David."

Ruth stepped away from them to catch sight of Ethan out in the barnyard, where he and the two young *Englisha* boys stroked the necks of the ponies.

"Are you done early at school?" Phoebe asked from behind her.

Ruth jumped. "Not really. I just thought I'd slip down to see how things are going. I'm planning to run right back up again."

"That was so thoughtful of you. But like I said, David has been *wunderbah*, and I learned so much this week."

"I'm glad," Ruth responded. "So this is George and Bill? I haven't met them yet."

"Come, then." Phoebe motioned Ruth forward and hollered through the barn door, "George and Bill! Come meet Ruth. She's David's sister."

Ruth kept her gaze away from Ethan's smiling face as she shook hands with the boys. "Hi. Did you have a *goot* week?"

They both shrugged.

"It was different but okay," George finally managed. "I'm looking forward to a good horror movie this evening."

Phoebe made a choking sound, but George didn't seem to notice. "We've enjoyed the week," he admitted. "But don't get me wrong. Peace and quiet is...well, it's been different."

Bill nodded his agreement, and the two turned their attention back to the ponies.

"They've gotten more out of the week than they know," David whispered in Ruth's ear. "Don't let them fool you. Phoebe impressed them both deeply, and so did their stay on the farm."

"Shh," Phoebe whispered. Her face reddened as Ethan approached them.

"So who have we here?" Ethan proclaimed. "Ruth, the Amish schoolteacher, I hear."

Ruth's heart pounded. All of her boldness seemed to have flown far away.

"Cat got your tongue?" Ethan teased. When she didn't answer, he continued. "I'm quite impressed with the farm. This idea of yours, Ruth, was an excellent one. The boys say their week was very enjoyable, and I sense a peace about them. I think the stay was good for both of them."

What did you expect? The sharp retort died on Ruth's lips. Instead, she smiled sweetly. "That's kind of you to say. But I knew Phoebe was up to the task."

"Seems you were right," he agreed.

"And this wasn't all my idea," she corrected him.

"That's not the point. This is working, and I'm glad. We'll do a physiological analysis on the boys next week, but I suspect the findings will only confirm my instincts. Farm life and exposure to animals in a peaceful setting will improve a lot of things. All you need is a dog, and this place will be perfect." Ethan laughed.

"That's not impossible," David told him. He joined in the laughter.

"I'm thinking a dog and a couple of cats would be *goot* for girls when they come," Phoebe added. "There are some coming, aren't there?"

"Perhaps. Mrs. Broman makes those choices, and I don't interfere." They all chuckled.

"Can we take a ride on the ponies?" Bill called from the barnyard. "One more before we leave?"

"Help yourself," Ethan hollered back. "I'm here for another hour or so."

"They're becoming experts," Phoebe commented as the boys mounted and rode out of the barnyard. Everyone stepped outside to watch them leave.

"I think I have to agree," Ethan said. "Good job, Phoebe and David. I'm glad to see it."

As they watched the boys ride, Ethan eyed Ruth sideways. "How's schoolteaching going? Somehow I can't picture you—"

"Don't say it," Ruth snapped. "I know I don't have a degree, but Amish don't have things like you do. Be thankful we can read and write, unlike some of your students I've heard about."

"Careful there!" Ethan chuckled. "I wasn't trying to insult you. I'm impressed. Not everything in the world must be done according to formula. Abraham Lincoln split rails and learned to read by a stone hearth."

"There you go," Ruth said. "Don't forget that."

Ethan laughed. "You are touchy today...but you're here."

"What does that mean?"

Ethan motioned with his chin over his shoulder. "Can I have word with you? In private?"

Ruth nodded and avoided David's and Phoebe's glances. She shouldn't do this, but neither should she have come up here. It was too late to turn back.

"What?" she asked once they were out of hearing distance. She had no right to snap at Ethan, but she had to mask her feelings.

"Where have you really been? What's going on with us?"

She looked away. "I think you know. I've been—"

"What does this mean?" he interrupted. "Why haven't I seen you in town?"

"Did you want to?" She sneaked a glance at his face.

"Of course, Ruth. I miss you."

"Really?" Her cynicism was also unnecessary, but she couldn't help it.

"I thought our relationship was—" He stopped. "Well, never mind. I guess I was wrong."

"Ethan." She reached for his arm. "I...we..." How could she say this?

His gaze pierced her. "I thought we were going somewhere. That you were trying to..."

"Reach you?" she finished. "*Yah*, I was. But I never knew if I was getting through. I guess I gave up."

"So you're gone for good? After all that?"

Her fingers tightened on his arm. "Maybe not, Ethan. I don't know."

"What do you mean you don't know?"

"If I can change things now, or rather...maybe I should have changed them to begin with."

His smile was grim. "Typical female, I see."

"That wasn't nice. I tried. I did, and I was given a chance by the community, which—"

"Doesn't include me."

"I wouldn't say it quite like that, but—"

"But it's the truth?"

"*Yah*, if you insist."

"And do you want it like that?"

"Oh, Ethan, are you serious? About us? Would you?" she beseeched him.

His gaze shifted. "Maybe I'm in the same shoes."

"Then why—"

"We should try," he said. "I really think so. How else will we know for sure, whether, at least on your part, it was worth it? I'm not the one who would have to make the most changes from the appearance of things."

"So what are you saying?"

"Can I see you next week sometime? Pick you up for supper in town? We can talk and go from there."

"Oh, Ethan." She covered her face with both hands.

"Then it's a go." A smile flickered.

"Why not?" She tried to still the pound of her heart.

"Tuesday night," he whispered. "But where?"

"At the junction of 170 and Peckville Road. I'll be walking home from the schoolhouse at six."

He nodded, and she turned to rush out of the barn and down the road toward the schoolhouse. A song rose unbidden in her heart. How could something so wrong make her heart sing? But the music was simply there, and she allowed the joy to flood all the way through her.

NINETEEN

Aunt Millie's buggy pulled into Grandma Lapp's driveway early on Saturday morning. Phoebe jumped up from the breakfast table and hurried outside to help her aunt unhitch. Aunt Millie was already out of the buggy with the tie rope in her hand, and she greeted Phoebe with a cheerful, "*Goot* morning!" and a concerned, "How are you doing, dear?"

"You didn't have to come over and check on me," Phoebe protested.

"Now, you know that's not true," Aunt Millie chided. "I saw Homer in town yesterday, and he told me he had stopped by on Monday and that everything was under control. But I could tell from the tone of his voice that trouble lurked in the air. I had to come right over this morning to see whether you were still alive after the week was done."

Phoebe forced a laugh and reached for the tug on her side of the buggy. "It wasn't *that* bad."

Aunt Millie waved her away. "I'm only tying up. I can't stay long."

Phoebe stepped back and waited. Now that Aunt Millie was here, a flood of emotions threatened. To make matters worse, her aunt clucked her tongue and took Phoebe in her arms. "You poor dear. Just as I expected. A rough week."

"Not bad enough that I should be blubbering like a *boppli*."

"I'm thinking you held up quite well," Aunt Millie comforted her. "But I still had to come and visit. That's the least I can do. This will give you a chance to tell me all about it. Talking does much *goot* after rough days."

Phoebe tried to smile. "I already told David about the first night with the boys. That was the worst spell, what with the horrible stories they told me. David was such a comfort."

Aunt Millie's face was full of questions. "Horrible stories from the boys and telling everything to David? Come up to the swing where we can sit."

"I still have breakfast on the table. You could join me," Phoebe offered.

"That would be even better." Aunt Millie smiled and followed Phoebe into the kitchen, where she pulled out a chair.

"Help yourself." Phoebe swept her arm over the plate of eggs and toast. "Not much, but it's all I had the energy to make. I'll have oatmeal for lunch, I think."

Aunt Millie clucked her tongue again and studied Phoebe's face. "Now what was this about stories and David?"

"He comforted me," Phoebe began. "I couldn't have recovered as I did without...well, I guess Uncle Homer came later in the morning, but David was better."

"What were these stories?"

"Nothing you would want to know." Phoebe studied her plate. "Young people live in a world I know nothing about. It's not even decent to repeat the horror movies they watch."

"But you told David?"

"*Yah*, but that's different."

Aunt Millie didn't appear convinced.

"Of course, I would have told you that morning if you had been here, but it seems such things shouldn't be revisited after a week. I don't want to think about them again."

Aunt Millie gave in. "We must pray then. But I'm worried, to say the least. These things might be affecting you, and you don't even know it. Have you been sleeping okay?"

Phoebe nodded. "Since Monday night. Well, the boys didn't settle down until well after midnight on Tuesday evening, but I made them get up at six, and on Wednesday evening they were asleep by ten. So you see, I'm feeling my way along and getting up my courage. Now I'm ready for next week."

"So you're sticking with it?"

"*Yah*. I can't let Grandma down, to say nothing of myself."

Aunt Millie laid her hand on Phoebe's arm. "Dear heart, no one would blame you if you decided this was too much, or that the dangers were of the kind no one had anticipated. This farm can be sold in a jiffy, and you can go back to Lancaster next week—or you can stay on in the valley without the least disparagement cast on your character."

Phoebe sighed. "I know. That does comfort me, but really, I'm okay. David is just great. He couldn't—"

"David," Aunt Millie interrupted. "Has he been..."

Phoebe laughed. "He's been nothing but a big help. I've seen no signs of the reputation the Fisher family has in David. He is decent, hardworking, and dependable, and he's someone I can talk to with confidence." She finished with a smile.

Aunt Millie nodded. "That *goot* to hear, but if things get too rough, I hope you will let me know. I could come over for the night. I'd be more than glad to."

"*Yah*, I know. And thanks." Phoebe took another bite from her plate. "Aren't you eating?"

Aunt Millie smiled and seemed lost in her thoughts as she slid an egg onto her plate and buttered a piece of bread.

"Here's David now!" Phoebe exclaimed. She hopped to her feet to wave at the kitchen window. "He said he'd come up sometime this morning to get things ready for next week."

"Are you falling in love with the man?"

Phoebe gasped and pulled back. "Of course not!"

"Are you sure?" Aunt Millie persisted.

"I'm sure! He's...well, he's....." Phoebe sputtered. "I can't fall in love with him, and I don't want to."

Aunt Millie took a bite of bread. "You're protesting a lot, Phoebe."

"He's a nice man, like I said, and...but, no. I'm not going there, and neither is he. You're sounding like Leroy now, trying to imply wrong where there is none."

"Falling in love isn't wrong, Phoebe. It happens all the time to people like you and David who work together."

"It's not happening!" She sat down again and contemplated her empty plate. "And I'm *not* thinking about it. I need David to help me, and that's that. You would take that from me?"

Aunt Millie's smile was thin. "I'm not trying to take anything away from you, dear. It's just that...well, so much has changed suddenly. You have to admit you wouldn't have looked at him twice not so long ago, and now you're singing his praises. He's still Leroy Fisher's boy, and you would be a Fisher if you married him."

"Aunt Millie! Enough of this. So what if his name is Fisher? David is stepping up to the plate. Who would have thought I'd sit through a *Poltergeist* story not that long ago either?"

"So that's what the story was about," Aunt Millie muttered.

"You know this movie?" Phoebe stared.

Aunt Millie's face reddened. "I wasn't all I should have been in my *rumspringa*, Phoebe. And *yah*, we did see it, much to my regret. The others in my group and I vowed never to try out that kind of thing again. But that was a very long time ago. That movie's old by now. Those boys must have really dug to find it."

Phoebe bounced to her feet. "I'm not discussing the stories again."

"Sorry." Aunt Millie rose and followed Phoebe to the kitchen

window, where they watched David lead the ponies out of the back
barn door.

"He is handsome," Aunt Millie observed. "I have to admit that."

"Would you stop it? I have to work with him, and I can't..."

"I should be going, dear." Aunt Millie's hand was light on Phoebe's shoulder. "Shall we pray before I go?"

"*Yah*, of course." Phoebe didn't hesitate.

She bowed her head while Aunt Millie held her hand and led
out, "Dear Lord, thank You for protecting Phoebe this week from
the evils of the world, and for giving us all grace when we stray from
the narrow path. Be with Phoebe and David next week as they continue this journey of ministry to needy children. Help us stay alert
to danger and not be afraid to ask for help. Bless both of them, and
let Your will be done. Amen."

"Amen," Phoebe echoed. "That was just like the prayers Grandma
has written in her tablet."

Aunt Millie smiled. "Of course the Lord is the great teacher of
all, but I am her daughter, and she taught us well. And don't forget
that you are *Mamm*'s granddaughter."

Phoebe tried to laugh. "Now you scare me. Those are big shoes
to fill."

"You're doing quite fine." Aunt Millie reached up to tuck several
stray hairs back under Phoebe's *kapp*. "Not so long ago you were
a little bundle, and now look at you, all grown up and doing the
Lord's work."

"You'll have me crying soon," Phoebe whispered as the two
embraced.

Aunt Millie let go to lead the way toward the front door, where
they parted with another quick hug. Phoebe watched from the door
until Aunt Millie had untied her horse and hopped in her buggy to
drive out of the lane. David showed his face in the barn door but
stayed there. He must know that everything was under control. She

waved to him, and a big smile filled his face. Phoebe ducked back into the house as her face reddened.

Aunt Millie's words buzzed in her ears: *"Are you falling in love with the man?"*

There was no sense in being a blushing mess about things. David wouldn't use their work situation to his advantage. They were partners in this venture. She should go out and wish him *goot* morning and face important subjects, such as Ruth. There hadn't been time yesterday after Ethan left to discuss the matter, and she hadn't wanted to mention the point to Aunt Millie this morning. Her suspicions could be wrong, but what if they weren't?

Phoebe shuddered and closed the front door behind her to hurry across the lawn. David was gone from the doorway, and she paused just inside the entrance. He was silhouetted by the sun's rays against a stall door with his back turned. He was spreading straw with both hands. She drew in her breath and waited. David hadn't heard her enter. He was apparently caught up in his task. His arms were moving sculptures of strength—etched, hardened muscles under his long-sleeved shirt. His hair came to his shoulders and hung long over his ears. She knew how to give someone a trim.

She almost called out, *"Surprise! Time for a haircut."*

But was such a thing decent? Maybe Ruth always did the task, or more likely David's *mamm*, Priscilla. Phoebe had never thought to wonder. His thick locks would be a match for any scissors, but her fingers would make the cut evenly. She could feel them snap shut as she pressed down his hair with her free hand.

Phoebe gasped when David glanced over his shoulder. "Howdy there. I didn't hear you come in." A grin formed on his face.

"Hi. I...*yah*, *goot* morning," she stammered. "I just came out after Aunt Millie left. She...how is Ruth?" Her face flamed bright red. David had caught her staring at him. There was no hiding the fact. At least he didn't know what her thoughts had been.

"Ah, Ruth," he said, obviously puzzled.

"Don't you think she acted a little strange yesterday?" Phoebe rushed on. "She and Ethan had quite a long conversation together."

David shrugged. "They knew each other before Ruth's *rumspringa* ended. I figured it was old friends talking, that kind of thing. You don't think Ruth would..." David appeared concerned. "Phoebe, you're not accusing her of something, are you?"

"Of course not!"

David's smile was crooked. "Thanks. Ruth seemed perfectly normal when she got home last night from the schoolhouse. Did Ethan say anything unusual to you before he left with George and Bill?"

"No." Phoebe's mind raced. "Nothing like...Sorry, I'm just..." She tried to laugh, but the result was a wild cackle. "Aunt Millie was just here," she finished, which didn't make the least bit of sense.

"Did she say something?" He stepped closer, the straw in his hand dribbling to the floor. His muscles rippled under his sleeve, and Phoebe felt her face blaze again.

She jerked her eyes away. "No. Aunt Millie was very supportive. I told her about *Poltergeist*, and she said she had seen the movie when she was on her *rumspringa*. Of course she was also horrified and would never watch the thing again."

David studied her with concern. "Are you okay, Phoebe?"

Just blubbering, she almost said. She never blubbered. Never!

"Just the stress of the week working itself out," she said instead. "I came out to say *goot* morning, and to wish you well, and to thank you for all you did last week."

He nodded. "The first week is the rough one." He smiled. "At least we hope so, but you are the one who did well, Phoebe. A little meltdown is in order, I guess." He came closer and seemed ready to reach for her hand.

She pulled back. "I'd best be going. I have the house to clean and

sweep, and I need to get ready for whatever comes next week, and..."
There came the cackle again.

Thankfully, David seemed unconcerned when Phoebe turned
and fled. She almost ran across the lawn and back into the house.
Why did Aunt Millie have to say what she did about David, and love,
and falling...Phoebe was not in love, and David was not...

"Confound it all!" Phoebe exclaimed. "I *will* get over this, whatever it is. It shall pass. I will be my levelheaded, secure, normal self
come Monday morning. I will! I will!"

She plopped on the couch with a thud. This was a meltdown.
That's all it was. A little one, thankfully, and David was so understanding. She would never be able to repay him, but he didn't ask
her to. So there! Take that!

Phoebe took deep breaths and willed the pounding of her heart
to slow down. David didn't think she was wild and wicked. The look
in his eyes said that plainly enough.

TWENTY

On Monday morning, Phoebe waited on the front porch as the van pulled into Grandma Lapp's driveway with Mrs. Broman at the wheel. There was no sign of Ethan in the passenger's seat. Instead, Phoebe caught a glimpse of a young girl's face. There would not be a repeat this week of all boys. Even if three boys had climbed out of the van, Phoebe could have handled them and remained calm and collected. There would also be no repeat of her melt-down. Her composure was back after a long weekend of rest, and Bishop Rufus had preached a *wunderbah* sermon at the Sunday service about trusting the Lord in all situations. There was no way the bishop could have known of her personal needs, but the Lord had still provided.

Phoebe came to halt at the end of the walk and waved as Mrs. Broman climbed out of the van. David appeared in the barn door and approached cautiously on the other side.

"*Goot* morning," he called out.

Phoebe hurried to join him in greeting the new arrivals. The van door opened, and a young girl climbed to the ground, dressed in a pretty yellow dress with flowers.

"*Goot* morning, sweetheart!" After her words burst out, David looked strangely at Phoebe. The girl, though, said nothing.

Mrs. Broman appeared with two more girls in tow, both younger than the first.

"Thank You, dear Lord," Phoebe whispered. She had been prepared for the worst.

David reached over to squeeze her hand. "The Lord is at work indeed," he whispered.

She squeezed back but let go at once.

Mrs. Broman turned to face them and announced with a big smile, "Good morning, folks. Here we are again with Sadie, Eva, and Bella." Mrs. Broman patted each head in turn. "And girls, here are Phoebe and David, the people you will be staying with this week."

All three pairs of eyes studied them, while David smiled his brightest. Phoebe hurried forward to open her arms. None of the girls flinched as she gave them hugs, but they didn't respond either.

"Shall we show you around the place before I leave?" Mrs. Broman bubbled with forced joy.

None of the girls appeared impressed as they peered around.

"We can start with the ponies," Phoebe suggested.

There was no answer from the three.

"How about I take you inside?" Phoebe tried again. Mrs. Broman gave her a quick nod, so that must have been the correct answer.

David seemed to know that he should make himself scarce as Phoebe took the youngest girl's hand and led the way forward. "How old are you?" she asked Bella.

"Six. What is this place?"

At least someone was talking.

"A farm," Phoebe told her. "We have..." She stopped. The ponies were the staple of the place, but her instincts warned her to steer in another direction for the present.

Phoebe turned to give Sadie and Eva a warm smile. Mrs. Broman walked behind them with her arms outstretched as if afraid the two would bolt.

"Are they orphans?" Phoebe mouthed the question to Mrs. Broman over the tops of their heads.

"No," Mrs. Broman mouthed back.

Then why were the girls here? But now was not the time for such questions.

Phoebe paused near the front porch steps and motioned with her hand. "There's our swing, Bella. You can sit there on warm evenings and read a book or chat with your sisters. Would you like that? Maybe you'd like to try the swing out now?"

Sadie piped up. "Can I bring Forrest out to sit on the swing with me this week?"

"You will do no such thing," Mrs. Broman retorted. "This is a week to get away from your world and explore new horizons."

Sadie snorted. "New horizons! This looks like the fifth century to me."

"Hush!" Mrs. Broman ordered. "I don't want any of you making any trouble for Phoebe. She'll have enough on her hands with three children."

"I can leave," Sadie offered.

"You will not." Mrs. Broman pasted on her bright smile again. "You will be in love with this farm by the week's end. Last week George and Bill couldn't stop talking about their time here on the ride back into town. They wanted to stay an extra week. So be thankful you get to be here."

"Come." Phoebe took over. This lecture was obviously doing Sadie no *goot*. All three girls were beginning to grow long faces.

"Let's go inside," Phoebe suggested. "We'll sit on the swing later, maybe at lunchtime, and have a porch picnic."

None of the girls said anything as Phoebe led the way through the front door. The kitchen was the first stop, which didn't provoke any spark of interest. She should have prepared food, but the thought hadn't occurred to her. What better way to welcome her visitors to the farmhouse than with a warm breakfast of bacon, eggs, and oatmeal, even at midmorning?

"I should have made something to eat," she told them. "I'm sorry, but we'll have a big breakfast spread tomorrow morning. We can even prepare pancakes if you want, along with maple syrup."

Slight smiles appeared on the girls' faces.

"You're spoiling them already," Mrs. Broman chided, but she appeared pleased.

"So now the upstairs," Phoebe announced. They followed her through the kitchen doorway, their faces lifted toward hers.

She opened the stair door, and Sadie chirped, "What have we here, a secret stairwell to the witch's castle? Where are the cobwebs?"

"I swept them all up," Phoebe shot back. Sadie laughed, but the girl had been serious.

"Be nice," Mrs. Broman lectured them.

Phoebe forced herself to chuckle. "Up here is where the three of you will be sleeping," she told them.

The stair squeaked, which produced a squeal from Sadie. "I told you, the witch is above us."

"Hush it," Mrs. Broman lectured again.

Phoebe set her face and moved on. The *Poltergeist* tales had been bad enough, and now there would be witch talk all week. "Help me, dear Lord," she prayed quickly.

"How perfect!" Sadie exclaimed at the top of the stairs. "This is a haunt."

Phoebe bit back her protest. "This will be your room, Sadie." She held open the first bedroom door. "This was my room before Grandma Lapp passed."

"Where did she die?" Sadie asked.

Considering the circumstances, there was no safe answer.

Phoebe motioned for the girls to enter. "There's a dresser and a warm bed and a window over the barnyard. It's the nicest bedroom up here."

Sadie hadn't moved from the hallway. "Where did she die?"

"Ah…" Mrs. Broman began.

"Downstairs," Phoebe told her. The truth might as well be told. "As have many other people before my grandmother, I suspect. And just for your information, Grandma's in heaven with the Lord, and her life was a great blessing to all of us."

Sadie wrinkled up her face but remained quiet. This apparently had not been the expected answer.

"Do you want to see your room, Sadie?" Phoebe asked.

Sadie entered and looked around for a long time, as her sisters ran over to the bed and bounced on it.

"A real quilt!" Eva exclaimed. "I want this room."

"This bedroom goes to the oldest girl," Phoebe told her. "Unless Sadie doesn't want it?"

"I'll take it." Sadie didn't hesitate, and Eva's face fell. Sadie cautiously approached the bed to run her hand over the handcrafted quilt.

"It's a Texas Star pattern," Phoebe told her. "Grandma Lapp made it while she was still alive."

Sadie grunted but didn't respond.

"Now for Eva's room," Phoebe told them. "Follow me."

They crossed the hallway without Sadie, who stayed behind on the bed.

"It's okay," Mrs. Broman whispered to Phoebe. "She likes the room."

Phoebe was sure there were tears in Mrs. Broman's eyes. That seemed strange, but nothing should be surprising after the last week she had spent with George and Bill. She should have learned that lesson well.

Phoebe held open the bedroom door, and Eva cautiously entered. Her gaze stopped on the doll seated on the dresser, its face blank. Phoebe froze by the door. Would there be a negative reaction again? Perhaps a ghost story this time? Instead, Eva moved forward and reached with both hands to grasp the doll to her chest.

"That went over well," Mrs. Broman whispered in Phoebe's ear.

"*Yah*," Phoebe agreed. But why? *Englisha* girls weren't accustomed to faceless dolls.

"She looks at me so kind." Eva held the doll at arm's length. "And she is so real."

"Do you like the bedroom then?" Phoebe exhaled slowly.

Eva's face glowed. "It's even better than Sadie's bedroom, but don't tell her that."

"I'm staying too," Bella piped up.

Phoebe shrugged and glanced at Mrs. Broman. "Why not? There are no hard and fast rules."

Mrs. Broman wiped her eyes. "That's what this is all about. Getting away from hard and fast rules. That works for me."

"We're off to a *goot* start, then!" Phoebe exclaimed. "And I haven't said this yet, but I am glad I have three little girls with me this week. Last week George and Bill were here, but now I have you."

Bella ignored the little speech to reach for the doll in her sister's arms. Eva complied with regret written on her face. "I want my turn again soon."

"We have a boy doll in the other room," Phoebe suggested, but her words fell on deaf ears. Both Eva and Bella were wrapped up in their own world as they took turns cradling the doll.

"I really should go," Mrs. Broman whispered again. "I see that you will be getting along great with them."

"Thanks," Phoebe whispered. She followed Mrs. Broman out into the hallway. "What about their mother?"

"She abandoned them a month ago, poor things," Mrs. Broman

told her. "Ran off with a new boyfriend, we think. She'll be back eventually. All such things have their end. In the meantime…" Mrs. Broman sighed. "You don't know how much good this will do the girls. I wish I could leave them with you full-time, but things are what they are. We might have a nice foster home on the horizon. Hopefully, we can take them straight there next week. We're trying to keep them together. That's all they've ever known or trusted, really—one another. It's hard, I know, but that's the world out there." Mrs. Broman gave a little laugh. "A thousand miles from here, that's for sure."

"That's very kind of you to say. Will you check on us later in the week?"

"We'll see. Maybe Wednesday, but I really think you'll be fine without me. If not, you can call. I'll be back Friday afternoon." Mrs. Broman squeezed Phoebe's arm. "Make it good, dear heart. You're the best."

Phoebe held back her tears as Mrs. Broman disappeared down the stairs. She wiped them away and returned to the front bedroom. Sadie was still seated on the bed, apparently lost in deep thought.

"You okay?" Phoebe asked with a smile.

"Yep," Sadie replied. "Can you sit with me?"

"Certainly." Phoebe lowered herself onto the quilt, sitting beside the young girl's thin frame.

"Tell me about your grandmother," Sadie said, peering up into Phoebe's face.

Phoebe took a deep breath. "I would be glad to," she began. "See Grandma Lapp's the reason…" The story flowed easily, and Eva and Bella soon joined them with the doll to curl up on the quilt. Neither of the three said a word until Phoebe finished.

"That's no witch's story," Sadie observed.

"No, it isn't," Phoebe agreed as she slipped her arm around Sadie's shoulders to pull her close.

TWENTY-ONE

The following morning, the dawn sky over the Adirondacks glowed red through a blanket of clouds on the horizon. Phoebe dressed and held the kerosene lamp in one hand while she pushed back the drapes of her bedroom window to peer out over the valley. There would be rain today—perhaps a thunderstorm, considering how the sky was painted. The attempt at horseback riding with the girls would be postponed, but things were going well otherwise. The three had slept through their first night in the old farmhouse without awakening with nightmares or worse. That was much better than last week's frightening stories from George and Bill.

Phoebe trembled at the memory. Thankfully David had comforted her the next morning, but there would be no repeat of anything like that this week. The girls had listened respectfully to the story of Grandma Lapp's dream yesterday. They seemed uplifted afterward, even hopeful about life. What must the poor creatures have endured with a mother who abandoned them?

Phoebe jumped at the soft knock on the front door. She allowed the window drape to flutter back into place. She held the lamp up to the bedroom mirror and peered at her image. Everything was in place to greet whoever was at the front door.

The knock came again, and Phoebe hurried out of the bedroom. Who could be here this early? Aunt Millie wouldn't call at this hour, but David might. After last week, he would likely be concerned with how the first night with the girls had gone, but she was okay.

Phoebe cracked open the front door, and David's face danced in the shadows outside.

"*Goot* morning," he whispered. "Are you okay?"

"*Yah*. I just got up, but you shouldn't have worried."

"Did they behave themselves last night?"

"You mean, did they try to burn down the house?" she teased.

Concern still rippled on his features. "Did Sadie attempt such a thing?"

Phoebe suppressed a nervous giggle. "I half suspected her, but no. They slept the night through in silence. I haven't been upstairs since I put them down for the night."

"Then they are still here?" David stepped back to peer at the upstairs windows.

Phoebe laughed this time. "They aren't Amish girls who sneak out of windows in the dead of night on their *rumspringa*—and they're not old enough to do that anyway."

David managed a grin. "Girls are girls."

"David," she chided. "I never snuck out of windows. That's a joke."

"I know," he said, but he didn't believe her from the look on his face. She could easily imagine Ruth sneaking out of bedroom windows for secret meetings in the night.

"Are you sure everything is okay?" He stepped closer to study her face.

"*Yah*, David. But now that you're here, why don't you come in for breakfast?"

"Really?" He seemed pleased. "I still have time to run home for *Mamm*'s breakfast."

"Don't you like mine?"

"I haven't eaten too many of them," he shot back.

"Well, we'll have to take care of that problem." She smiled at him. "Come in, and I'll start the preparations."

He followed her inside. "Shouldn't you check on the girls?" He glanced at the stair door.

"I'm not going to awaken them that way." She grinned. "Let the smell of a *goot* breakfast cooking be what brings them out of their sleep on their first morning in Amish country."

"You are a romantic," he said. He seated himself at the kitchen table. "Can I help with something?"

"Now *that's* romantic," she told him with a smile.

He chuckled. "Until I spill bacon grease all over the kitchen floor."

"I'll watch you." She motioned toward the stove. "Start the fire, and I'll get the pan and the bacon."

He shrugged and got to his feet. His movements were slow and careful, and he did everything right.

"You've done this before!"

He made a face. "I started the fire a few times for *Mamm*, and I've made a few pieces of bacon on the sly when the family was gone for the day. Breakfast at lunchtime isn't something I brag about. But I can make popcorn now."

"I'm sure you did a great job with lunch," she encouraged him. "My brothers would have made *Mamm* leave them something for lunch."

"It was edible. At least I didn't die."

They laughed together as the bacon began to simmer. He watched over it while Phoebe busied herself with eggs and toast. She couldn't help but take frequent glances toward him. She wasn't used to a man working in the kitchen with her, especially one who was frying bacon. Popcorn-making with the family present was one thing. This turn of events must be kept from Aunt Millie's ears. Who knew what her reaction would be? Probably a knowing smile and a wise comment about Phoebe falling in love.

Phoebe's face flamed, and she stepped closer to the oven. If David noticed her blush, she needed a convenient excuse. He would never think such thoughts about their relationship, and she wouldn't either if Aunt Millie hadn't planted them.

"Am I doing okay?" he asked, glancing quickly in her direction.

Had David seen her face?

"We won't die," she quipped, and thankfully he laughed.

The hinges of the stair door creaked, and they both turned to see Sadie's sleepy face in the kitchen doorway.

"*Goot* morning," Phoebe sang out. "Did you sleep well?"

"I guess so." Sadie appeared befuddled. "Where am I? And you're..."

"*Yah*, I'm cooking breakfast with David." Phoebe smiled her warmest. Maybe that would cover the continued heat that rushed up her neck in long flames. "He's being very nice to us this morning. He came up early from his parents' place to help out."

"Is he your boyfriend?" Sadie asked.

Phoebe laughed. "No. He helps out with the farm. David is part of Grandma Lapp's dream. Remember the story I told you last night?"

Sadie nodded but said nothing. Phoebe dared give David a quick look. He appeared pensive and seemed absorbed in frying his bacon, but the pan didn't need that much attention at the moment. Did he think she might be his girlfriend someday? Was this why he fried bacon in her kitchen? Was he in love with her? But how could that be possible? She was the one who had invited him in. Still...Phoebe pushed the thought away. She must focus on the task at hand.

"Do you want to wake your sisters?" Phoebe gave Sadie a bright smile. "And help them get dressed?"

"They usually dress themselves."

"How about we change the routine this week?" Phoebe suggested. "Helping one another is something we do on the farm. Can you, dear? That would be very sweet of you."

Sadie appeared to waver for a moment, but then she turned to leave and climb back up the wooden stair steps.

"You are a *goot* teacher," David said. He lifted the first of the golden bacon slabs out of the pan. "Are these okay?"

"*Yah*," she told him. "And thanks for the praise. I'm—"

"I mean it, Phoebe. Don't run yourself down."

Phoebe glanced away as her heart pounded. A man's words didn't usually affect her like this, not after…but David spoke the truth. She did have too low of an opinion of what she could handle. Grandma Lapp had thought her capable of more, and so did David. She was the one who always objected.

"Maybe I should go help Sadie." Phoebe still didn't look at him. "Isn't that what a *goot* teacher would do?"

David smiled and continued flipping his bacon slabs. She left him to hurry up the stairs. Sadie was seated on the bed beside her sisters, with tears running down her face.

"What is wrong?" Phoebe exclaimed. She joined Sadie on the bed to wrap her arms around the thin shoulders.

"They won't listen and get up," Sadie told her.

Phoebe glanced at the sleeping children. "That's okay," she said, wanting to comfort the little girl. "Aren't they sweet? Maybe we should let them rest. I can warm the breakfast things for them later."

Sadie nestled against Phoebe. "Are you always this nice to people?"

Phoebe looked away. "I have many faults, just like everyone else."

Sadie appeared skeptical, and Phoebe laughed. "It's true."

"Well, I like you. I hope we can stay here always."

Phoebe pulled back from the embrace. "Dear, you know that's not possible. You're here for—"

"I know. But don't tell me right now. If only Mom would..." Silence fell, and fresh tears came.

"You poor thing." Phoebe pulled her tight again. "Shall we go down and eat breakfast with David? Maybe that will help."

Sadie shrugged, but she stood and followed Phoebe down the stairs. Her tears were dry by the time they arrived in the kitchen, but David must have noticed her tearstained cheeks.

He sent Phoebe a sympathetic look and pulled out the chair for Sadie to seat herself.

"The best seat in the house for you!" he proclaimed. "This is where the man will sit once Phoebe marries and settles in with him—" He seemed to catch himself midsentence.

Phoebe looked away. Obviously he imagined someone else here besides himself as her husband. She hurried over to the stove to hide the heat that rose up her neck again. She seemed to be blushing continuously this morning, especially at the thought of David as her husband and head of the house.

Phoebe grabbed the plate of eggs from the corner of the stove. David must have fried them while she was upstairs. They looked well done, with perfect yolks in the centers. The man had extensive experience in the kitchen despite his denials. She had never thought of a man as capable of cooking, but the idea was intriguing, to say the least. When Phoebe turned around, the plate of eggs nearly flew out of her hand.

"Careful there," David warned from his place at the table.

He had taken the chair beside hers. Did he mean anything special by the gesture? She should take the one on the other side of the table, but she wanted to sit beside him. The heat flamed once more into her face, and there was no stove close enough to blame. Thankfully, David didn't notice, but Sadie clearly did. The girl wore a slight smile. At least she approved of Phoebe's heart's capers when it had a mind all of its own.

"These are perfect eggs," Phoebe said, her voice squeaking.

David nodded, but all he said was, "Shall we pray?"

"Certainly!" Phoebe closed her eyes. Finally they were back on familiar territory.

Phoebe's eyes flew open when David began to pray. "Our most gracious heavenly Father..." She hadn't expected David to pray out loud again.

"We give You thanks this morning for Your gracious hand toward us," David continued, his voice steady. "Thank You for Phoebe's hospitality this morning, and for her willing and open heart to help people, and for her kindness to us all. Thank You for this food we have before us. Bless it, and bless us as we go through this day. Let no evil come our way that You are not with us. Keep our hearts..."

Phoebe tried to breathe quietly. She wanted to cry—but why? David did nothing that unusual, and yet he did. She knew it deep down inside. He was a very special person, and she had never noticed. Grandma Lapp had, but she...

"Amen," David said. He lifted his head with a smile.

"Thank you," Phoebe managed, but she avoided his eyes. "That was nice."

"Do you always pray like that?" Sadie asked.

"We always pray for our meals," Phoebe told her as she passed the plate of eggs.

A crunch of tires was heard on the driveway, and David paused with an egg halfway onto his plate. "Who would be coming here this time of morning?"

Phoebe shot up and rushed to the kitchen window. "It's a strange car."

When Phoebe turned around, Sadie had disappeared.

David shrugged. "She went shooting into the living room."

As if in answer, Sadie reappeared in the kitchen doorway. "It's Mom!" she exclaimed, her face white. "She must have come to get us."

"Your mother." Phoebe sat down to steady herself. What other shocks were in store for this morning? Was the week with the three girls to end before it began?

"I'm not leaving," Sadie said. "I don't care what she says. She'll just leave us again next week."

"I...we..." Phoebe gave up. What was there to say?

"You must talk their mother into staying," David told her. "Begin by inviting her to breakfast."

Phoebe tried to breathe. Did she dare? Could she? But here she went again, doubting herself. This was a brilliant idea.

"What's your mother's name, Sadie?" Phoebe asked.

"Melissa," Sadie spat.

Phoebe stood and steadied herself. She could do this. Somehow she could. Phoebe walked out of the kitchen and opened the front door moments before the woman came up the porch steps.

Her face was angry. "Is this where my children are?"

"*Yah*." Phoebe breathed deeply. "Eva and Bella are upstairs asleep, and Sadie was getting ready to eat breakfast with us."

The woman's face seemed to soften.

"Would you like to join us, Melissa?" Phoebe put on her best smile.

"I suppose I could. I am hungry, and the Amish do cook well, I'm told."

"We try," Phoebe replied as she held the door open.

Melissa walked inside and headed toward the kitchen. *So far so goot*, Phoebe told herself. Maybe with David's prayers and his *wunderbah* ideas, they would make it through this week.

"Help us, dear Lord." Phoebe sent a prayer heavenward before she closed the door behind them.

TWENTY-TWO

Minutes later, Phoebe still lingered by the closed front door. All of her courage seemed to have fled. Her feet wouldn't move to follow the girl's mother into the kitchen. She could hear the murmur of voices clearly, but she couldn't understand the words. At least they didn't sound angry. Perhaps if she waited a few more minutes David would solve this problem with another splendid idea. Or he might have convinced Melissa to stay for the week. Melissa would want to take her children home with her, and Mrs. Broman wouldn't allow that. Reconciliation took a long time in the *Englisha* world. The least they could do is give this family some immediate time together.

Phoebe breathed another quick prayer heavenward. "Give David the wisdom to say what needs saying, Lord."

Phoebe forced her feet to move. When she walked in, Melissa was seated at the table with her plate filled.

"There you are!" Melissa exclaimed. "I thought you had left me with your husband."

"Ah..." Phoebe began, but the words stuck in her throat.

David smiled kindly. "I'm just the hired hand on the farm. I walked up this morning from—"

"He's the boyfriend," Sadie added.

"That's not—" Phoebe stopped again. "David's a dear friend," she finished.

Melissa had a sly smile. "I see. Well, he's been regaling me with tales of the farm's beginning. Seems like quite the fairy tale you people are living here."

Phoebe seated herself and kept silent. Grandma's dream wasn't a fairy tale, but a denial seemed inappropriate at the moment.

"Excellent cooking, though," Melissa told her. "On that the reports were accurate."

"I'm going now." Sadie jumped to her feet.

"You're going nowhere, young lady." Melissa's command stopped her. "You're staying right here until I finish eating, and then we're leaving."

Sadie's face grew stony. "I'm not going. You left us, and now we're here for the week."

"Watch your mouth! I am your mother."

"Then why don't you *act* like our mother?"

Phoebe jumped into the conversation. "Sadie, why don't you get your sisters up for breakfast?"

"I already tried that, remember?"

Apparently all *goot* will had been cast out with Melissa's arrival.

"I'm sorry. What was your name?" Melissa peered at her.

"Phoebe," she managed, "but that's okay. Sadie's—"

"She's a spoiled brat. Don't pay her any mind. I'll get the girls up in a minute. They don't eat until noon anyway."

David cleared his throat, and Phoebe forced the words out. "Sadie has been a jewel since she arrived yesterday. I have no complaints. She's..."

Melissa frowned. "Of course you would think so. She knows how to put up a front for strangers."

"Like my mother does," Sadie snapped.

Melissa's face turned thunderous. "Sadie! That will be enough out of you!" she yelled.

Phoebe stared at the kitchen wall and breathed deeply. Outside the rain had begun to fall. Silence filled the room while the tears rolled down Sadie's face. Melissa ignored the girl to take another egg and butter a piece of toast. How could a mother be so unfeeling? Phoebe had to do something. But what?

David spoke up. "I really think you should stay here for the week and see what life on an Amish farm is like. Phoebe has plenty of room upstairs, and you could—"

Melissa glared at him, but David smiled and continued. "I think the Lord wants to touch all of your hearts with a special time here on Grandma Lapp's farm. Not that we are special people, but the Lord can minister here where Grandma's tender heart used to live. I know I can bear record to how she touched my life. She gave me a chance to work on the farm and help Phoebe. I will always be grateful."

Melissa stared at him. "You have your nerve, meddling in my business."

"It seems as if you could use some help," David said, nonplussed. "Your girls are in the care of Child Protective Services, and I'm thinking I should give them a call." He let the threat hang for a moment. "I don't know how you found out where they were, but I don't want to make that call. We do things differently here. Perhaps..."

"Perhaps what?" Melissa demanded. "And for your information, I have friends who keep track of my kids."

Phoebe clung to the edge of the tabletop with both hands. She wanted to slip down through the kitchen floor, right into the darkness of the basement. How could David be so brave?

Yet he continued without missing a beat. "Your life is not what it should be." David gave Melissa a kind smile. "Spend some time here with your girls." He waved his hand outward toward where the rain drummed against the side of the house. "Who knows? Perhaps the Lord will minister a special healing to your family this week. I know Grandma Lapp's prayers were offered up in this house, and surely they still rise before the throne of the Lord."

Phoebe tried to breathe. Never had she heard David speak like this. What would Melissa's reaction be? The woman's face displayed flashes of anger and shame, but she hadn't replied yet.

"Yes, Mom. Let's!" The words burst out of Sadie's mouth.

"I'll have to think about this," Melissa finally allowed. "In the meantime, my breakfast is getting cold."

Phoebe dared to breathe again. "Thank you," she mouthed to David, who smiled in return.

Sadie's face glowed through her tears. She raced around the corner and disappeared up the stairs.

"Where's she going?" Melissa demanded.

Phoebe stated the obvious. "Upstairs." Thankfully, Melissa didn't pursue the girl.

"We should pray again and give thanks for the food," David said. "I need to tend the animals in the barn."

"Pray!" Melissa exclaimed, but David had already bowed his head.

He spoke in a firm voice. "Our gracious heavenly Father, thank You for the food we have eaten and for Melissa's arrival. Thank You for the pleasant week she and the girls will spend at Grandma Lapp's farm and for the great mercies You will show them through this time. Thank You for all the kindness You have shown to us and will show in the future. Amen."

Phoebe never closed her eyes. The astonished look didn't leave Melissa's face. The woman still had not spoken when David stood and left the kitchen. Phoebe pushed her chair back and hurried after him.

He paused at the front door. "*Yah*?" he asked when he heard her behind him.

"Oh, David." Phoebe came to a stop in front of him. "That was so brave of you, and so right."

"I'm glad to hear you say so," he said. His smile flickered.

"That prayer was *so* perfect," she assured him. "And your words? I just know it."

"Even if Melissa up and leaves?"

"If she does, we have to call Mrs. Broman. They won't let Melissa keep the children for a while yet. That's how they do things." Phoebe reached out to touch his arm. "Thank you so much for everything. And for this morning, for coming up early, for breakfast, and now that *wunderbah*...This was much better than making popcorn together." She paused to gaze into his face. He was so manly and so handsome.

"I'm happy you think so."

Phoebe touched his arm again. "Grandma was right, David. About so many things. About—" She couldn't get the word *you* out. *Grandma Lapp was right about you.* What would he think? That she had been unable to form her own opinion? Or see what was right in front of her eyes?

"Phoebe."

"*Yah?*" She looked up at him.

"You know that Grandma Lapp was also right about you?"

She dropped her gaze. "Well, I don't know about that."

"Don't say so," he said. His fingers caught her chin gently.

She gave in and gazed up at him. His face was a conflict of emotions.

"David," she said as she reached for him. This was Grandma Lapp's living room, but what better place to show the man what a jewel he was, how much she admired him this morning. How deeply he had moved her heart with his brave words, while his spirit had trembled just like hers. She, too, had to move past the horror of those words and the sting of that pain.

"David," she repeated as she pulled him closer. "Can I tell you something?"

He nodded and waited.

"Outside on the porch," she whispered.

He opened the door, and she followed.

"I..."

"Phoebe." His fingers touched hers. "Please."

"I have to tell you. I have to. I want to." Tears stung.

He held her hand as she collected herself. "In the schoolyard, after classes one day...you know how it was back then in our schooldays. They were the same in Lancaster as they were here in the valley. That day I stayed behind, and so did he. Paul Mast. We were in the same grade. I liked him, and I thought he liked me. Out of sight around the corner, I kissed him on the cheek. Twice, David. His older brother Willie caught us, and he slapped me on the face. Hard! He said I was a wicked and wild woman, and that I would never find a husband in the community. That Amish men only wanted submissive women."

"Phoebe, stop. None of that is true. You are—"

"I have to say it, David. I have to." Phoebe looked up at him. "Paul smirked afterward, and he slapped me too. They both ran off, and Paul never talked to me again."

"Phoebe." He reached for her.

She clung to him. "Can I, David? Will you let me?"

He resisted for a moment as she touched the bristles on his chin with both hands. He must have rushed over this morning without his usual shave, concerned about her first night with the girls. His face was inches from hers. She had dared once to imagine this moment, this preciousness, this nearness, this overwhelming sense of a man's presence.

He came closer, and she lifted her face to his. His lips were gentle,

and he wrapped his arms tightly around her shoulders. She didn't
let go for a long time.

He pulled slightly away and stared down at her, wide eyed.

"Oh, David," she whispered.

He came close again, and the kiss was longer this time. Soon she
wouldn't be able to breathe. He let go, and Phoebe gasped.

She turned toward the kitchen doorway.

"They didn't see us," he said.

"I don't care. I don't care if the whole world saw us."

"I love you, Phoebe." His voice was tender, and she melted into
his arms again.

"Oh, David," she mumbled into his chest.

After a moment, he held her at arm's length to gaze into her face.
"What does this mean, Phoebe? I just..."

"It's okay. We'll figure it out. In the meantime, I'd best get back
to the kitchen."

"Of course." He reached for the front door.

"David." She stopped him. "I love you too. Don't forget that, and
don't be sorry for what happened. You have...oh, David, you don't
know what you have done for me this morning."

"I have...you have..."

"The Lord will help us. Hasn't He so far?"

"He has," David agreed, rushing off the porch into the rain.
There was a raincoat in the mudroom, but he was already out of
sight in the mist that hung heavy between the barn and the house.

Phoebe gathered her wits about her. She smoothed her dress
and straightened her *kapp* the best she could. She had kissed David
Fisher—a man, a strong man, a man who loved her. The weight of
the years seemed gone. They had disappeared into the mist beyond
the front porch railing. She was not a wicked and wild woman. She
was just a woman. They were two sane young people who followed
the Lord's will. Phoebe entered the house and crept toward the

kitchen doorway, but Sadie's face appeared before she arrived. She grinned and vanished.

"So he is the boyfriend!" Melissa declared when Phoebe walked in.

Sadie nodded knowingly. At long last, mother and daughter were unified.

"He's...ah..." Phoebe gave up. Appearances would negate any denial she made. They would have to straighten things out later. How that would be done was beyond her. David hadn't even taken her home from the Sunday evening hymn singing, and here she had kissed him.

"I've decided to stay the week," Melissa announced, all smiles. "I think I like this place."

"I'm glad to hear that. David said many wise things this morning."

"Is he a preacher or something?" Melissa asked.

Phoebe laughed. "No, he's just a neighbor..." She stopped to think about Melissa's words. David had acted like a preacher this morning. Maybe he would become one someday, if the Lord willed it so. But she must not think about such things right now. "Let me go wake the girls."

"How about if I do it?" Melissa stood. "Just show me the way."

"Up there." Phoebe told her. "The bedroom door that's closed on the left."

Melissa nodded, and the stairs squeaked as she climbed the steps.

"I can't believe Mom is staying with us this week," Sadie gushed when silence had settled in the kitchen.

"Neither can I," Phoebe agreed. "But in the meantime, are you helping me with the dishes? I'd appreciate it."

Sadie hesitated only a moment. "Okay, but you have to show me how. You don't have a dishwasher."

Phoebe managed a smile. "Nope. *We* are the dishwashers around here."

Sadie giggled. "Human dishwashers and an Amish couple kissing outside the front door. I agree with Mom. I like this place."

Phoebe hid her bright red face with a quick rush to the kitchen sink and a long stare out of the window into the falling rain.

TWENTY-THREE

David rose early on Wednesday morning at the Fishers' homestead, but he lingered in the barn after breakfast. How was he to proceed with life from here? He had kissed a Lapp girl. Maybe the whole problem would be solved by a rebuff from Phoebe this morning. Things would be easier on that familiar road. Even a little hesitancy on her part would help, but she wouldn't go back on what they had shared. When he left last evening, she had come out on the front porch to holler, "*Goot* night!" as he ran through the rain.

Phoebe would have stayed inside if she had regretted the precious moment they had shared that morning. His face burned with the sweet memory of her in his arms. Somehow he had managed to appear normal last evening around his family. He had retired early, exhausted from the day's efforts, and had slept uneasily all night. And not only because of the decisions that lay ahead of him, but also because Ruth hadn't come home from her schoolteaching job until well after the big clock in the downstairs living room struck twelve. Apparently he was the only one in the family who had noticed.

David pushed open the barn door and glanced out. Ruth had appeared at the front door with a bundle of books clutched in her arms, headed out for her day's work at the schoolhouse. He caught up with her at the end of the driveway.

"Why are you still here?" She turned to look accusingly at him.

"What's wrong with walking my sister part of the way to her schoolhouse?" He forced a grin.

Ruth looked away and held the bundle of books tighter to her chest. "You've always gone early up to Phoebe's these past days. Have you two fallen out?"

. "No." David laughed. "She has things well under control this week. She doesn't need me at the moment. The woman's a marvel."

"You don't have to tell me that," Ruth retorted. "She's a Lapp, and we're Fishers. Remember that, my darling brother."

"Why the bitterness this morning?" David kicked a loose stone deeper into the ditch. "And why have you been coming home so late in the evenings?"

"I had a lot of papers to check the other night. Isn't that what *goot* schoolteachers do?"

"And last night?"

"Maybe I had a load of work all week."

"You went out with Ethan, didn't you?"

"And you're getting sweet on Phoebe," she shot back. "Or rather, is Phoebe getting sweet on you? That's what we're waiting for, isn't it?"

David kept his gaze on the road. "So what if she is? Does that mean you have a right to bend the rules to suit your own purposes? The community is giving you a fair chance, Ruth. Why are you tempting fate? If someone—"

"If someone finds out? I know. Always it's *if someone finds out*. What if I want both worlds, David? What if Ethan finally has come around right when I've been given this...whatever you want to call it...this glorious chance? What if love is the other glorious chance I've been waiting for? The man loves me, David. Finally!"

"And how do you know that? Because he took you out for a

night on the town until after twelve o'clock? What's wrong with you, Ruth? If *Mamm* and *Daett* weren't so wrapped up in their own worlds, they would have noticed when you came in."

She gave him an accusing look. "The stairs didn't squeak once. Don't tell me you hear that well."

"I was up…"

She searched his face. "I know you, David. What's wrong?"

"Nothing. Everything's right, in fact. It's just that…"

"David, tell me!" Her voice was sharp.

"I'm not begging, Ruth. You have to live your own life. I've always let you do that."

She whistled in the still morning air. "So you think you have a chance at Phoebe Lapp? Is that it? And you don't want me messing things up?"

"It's more than a chance, Ruth." He lowered his voice. "And I didn't try. I just followed…whatever. I don't need to explain things to you, but *yah*, you could make plenty of trouble for me if it's found out that you're seeing Ethan on the sly. Especially since you are the community's schoolteacher and plan to join the baptismal class in a few weeks."

"So we have a few weeks," she chirped. "Don't get all huffy, David. I'm very careful."

"That's what they all say. And they all are found out."

She sighed. "The Fishers always get caught. That's for sure."

"You don't have to let this bitterness rule your life. There is another way. Grandma Lapp is giving us this chance. *Daett's* way isn't the right way."

"And you think there's love for me in the community? I don't see a handsome young man knocking at my door."

"Is that why you're flirting with Ethan?"

"No! It's because I love him, and I've worked long and hard to get this attention. Now I have it."

"By slipping away with him while taking on the teaching job and planning to join the community?"

She laughed. "You are perceptive, dearest brother. Nothing else worked."

"You shouldn't do this, Ruth. Nothing *goot* will come out of it."

"Says the man who's making a play for the Lapps' daughter."

"It's not what you think, but you and I are not going there today."

"Do you really think she's going to stick with you?" Her gaze was piercing. "Everything is going well at the moment. The sun's shining and all that. You must have really impressed her, but then the rain clouds will gather and the sun will go behind the clouds. Then Miss Lapp will be gone. Don't you think that's what will happen once her family catches on? Can you really imagine Phoebe Lapp standing in front of Bishop Rufus and saying the wedding vows with you? Come on. You know better."

He shuffled along. Ruth's words stung. He had thought them himself only weeks ago, before Phoebe had been in his arms and the glow on her face had drawn so close to his.

"Maybe things will be different."

Her laugh was bitter. "We will always be Leroy Fisher's children, David. Let's get that straight."

The road forked ahead, and he didn't speak until they reached the point of parting. "I think Phoebe has a true heart."

Ruth shrugged. "And so does Ethan. So we're even on that point. And thanks for not spilling my secret. You always were a dear brother." She gave him a quick peck on the cheek before she whirled about and hurried off with her books in both arms.

He waited until she vanished around the bend. *We will always be Leroy Fisher's children.* Ruth's words were a flame that consumed beautiful things, and it burned brightly right now. But could the bitterness she carried erase what Phoebe had given him? The love, the admiration in her eyes, the nearness of their hearts at Phoebe's kitchen table. Never had a woman given him anything like that. Could he help it that Phoebe was a Lapp? She drew deep things from his heart. Things he hadn't known were there.

David quickened his steps. He must trust in the Lord, who had led him this far, and in Grandma Lapp's dream. Hadn't that been where all this started—Grandma Lapp's faith in him, which had born fruit in her granddaughter's heart?

David straightened his shoulders. Ruth might say harsh words, but he knew her heart was tender. He would pray for her to see the light of day before she did irreparable damage to herself and the rest of the family. Jumping the fence into Ethan's arms would benefit no one—Ruth, the least of all.

David whispered a quick prayer as he turned his feet into Grandma Lapp's driveway. "Lord, help us."

A hand waved at the kitchen window before he was halfway to the barn, and he caught a glimpse of Phoebe's smiling face. Moments later the front door burst open, and she ran across the yard toward him to pause breathless a few feet from him.

"David! You're late. I was expecting you for breakfast."

"I...we..." he sputtered. "I didn't think." He gave up amid the light of her sweet smile.

She took his hand. "But you did have breakfast. Surely."

He managed a laugh. "*Mamm* fed us as usual. I—"

She tugged on his hand. "We haven't had devotions yet. I know we can't preach to people, but having devotions is a normal Amish activity, and Melissa needs all the godly input she can get. She'll only be here until Friday, when she will be separated from her family again. You'll read a chapter and pray with us, won't you?"

He gave in. What else could he do? The admiration and happiness in her face filled him with the greatest joy. Their kiss had opened doors behind which lay things he hadn't even imagined.

He attempted a protest once they reached the front porch. "You can lead out in devotions when there are only women present. I can wait in the barn."

"I know you can." She smiled and squeezed his hand. "I'll do that for the rest of the week if you don't show up early enough. But this morning you'll be with us, won't you?"

He continued on as an answer and entered the living room right behind her. Melissa was already seated on the couch with all three girls around her. The youngest, Bella, had her head in Melissa's lap. They had waited for him. A lump formed in his throat. He swallowed, but it wouldn't leave.

"Good morning, David," Melissa greeted him. "Phoebe said you would be up before long. I'm looking forward to this Amish tradition of devotions after breakfast."

David forced a smile and seated himself. No words would come out at present, but they would have to soon. Phoebe handed him the Bible and sat beside him on a chair.

"You can read whatever you wish," Phoebe told him after a few moments of silence.

He nodded and turned the pages. The rustle of the paper calmed him, but it was the quick touch of her hand on his arm that loosened his throat. He scanned the words in front of him for a passage that would do—something safe, something familiar to all of them, but especially to Melissa. Surely she had heard the familiar passage somewhere in her life.

David began to read, "'The Lord is my shepherd; I shall not want. He maketh me to lie down in green pastures...'" When he finished, Melissa had a smile on her face.

"That was sweet," she said. "My grandmother used to take us children to church years ago." Her face became dreamy. "We were just little girls then, my cousins and I." Slowly sorrow formed on

Melissa's face as she stroked her daughter's head. "But that was a long time ago, and now is now."

Phoebe's hand found his, and a lump formed in David's throat. He forced the words out. "We should pray."

Phoebe smiled and nodded. David prepared to kneel, but the sound of buggy wheels in the driveway stopped him.

Phoebe bounced up to look out of the living room window. "It's Aunt Millie come for a visit!"

David's legs propelled him out of his chair. "I should get to the chores in the barn."

There was no way Phoebe's aunt would catch him leading morning devotions. The action had seemed right when there was only Phoebe and him present, but Aunt Millie would see things differently. And if she found out he had kissed her niece yesterday...

David fled the house and ran past the surprised aunt, who had tied her horse to the hitching post.

She stopped him short. "What are you doing in the house at this time of the morning?"

"Can I unhitch your horse?" He lunged at the tugs.

"Thank you for the offer, but I'm not staying that long." Aunt Millie glanced meaningfully toward the front door.

Explanations were useless, and she would find out soon enough that Melissa and her daughters were inside.

"I'll be going then," he said. "There are the chores to do."

Let her think him a bumbling fool. Wasn't that how a Fisher was supposed to act? David's face burned as he turned and hurried on toward the barn. He heard Aunt Millie's exasperated snort behind him, but he didn't look back.

David rushed about with the chores, heedless of the flying straw or the heaviness of the manure he forked into the wheelbarrow from the horse stalls. Time passed in a blur until Aunt Millie's buggy went down the driveway again. He kept on working, his arms aching from the strain as the fork rose and fell.

The barn door opened behind him on a creaky hinge, and a shaft of light filled the dusty interior.

"David?" Phoebe called.

He didn't answer but continued to work.

"David?" she repeated. She came closer until she stood in front of him. "You shouldn't have run. There was nothing to be ashamed of. Aunt Millie would have joined in with the prayer."

He hung his head and didn't protest.

"David." Her fingers touched his arm. "Please don't act like this. You don't have to."

He lifted his gaze and met hers. The truth was written there. He had to believe Phoebe was right.

She spoke as if she had read his thoughts. "I know you can do this."

"I'm sorry. I shouldn't have left."

"Promise me you'll come earlier tomorrow morning and lead out again—even if Aunt Millie or Uncle Homer visits?" She searched his face.

The lump was back, but he swallowed hard and let the words out. "I will if you want me to."

"David, you know I do."

"Then I will." He took both of her hands in his. "Thank you."

She smiled, her fingers tight in his. "I should be going. We have a full day ahead of us with Melissa in the house. Aunt Millie is coming back later to help bake pies and to make sure we are behaving ourselves, I think." Phoebe giggled. "What did you say to her that got her all in a tizzy?"

He hung his head. "I'm sorry. I'll try to do better next time."

"Hush." She touched his lips with a finger. "It's not all your fault. I know that."

"I wasn't going to say that," he protested.

"I'll see you later when we come out to ride the horses for the first time. I'll need your help."

He nodded, but she had already turned and hurried off. He watched her leave until she passed the barn door and stepped out into the full blaze of the morning sunlight.

TWENTY-FOUR

Ruth paused in her brisk walk home from the schoolhouse on Friday evening. The sun hung low in the sky, and darkness was only an hour away. A buggy appeared, its horse stepping high as the rig trotted toward her. Ruth waited and waved as Emil Yoder passed. His beard was parted by the late evening breeze. Emil smiled and nodded, and his hands clutched the reins of his frisky horse.

The Yoder family had yet to notice her capers with Ethan, but David's words lingered in her ears. *That's what they all say. And they all are found out.* David wouldn't spill her secrets, but neither did he approve. She had been foolish to think he would. No one approved of how she was sneaking about—not even Ethan. He had frowned on Tuesday evening when she instructed him to pick her up on the road home from the schoolhouse for their next date.

Yet he had agreed. He wanted to meet her. She finally had his attention, though she couldn't help but wonder if the secrecy routine was part of her allure even though Ethan denied it. Men were like that. They didn't always know why they did things. If she broke faith with the community and jumped the fence, would Ethan return to his blasé disinterest in her? The question was a valid one.

Why couldn't he have given her the attention she wanted when she had been available to him?

Ruth sighed and resumed her walk. There was no use wrestling with the matter. She wanted to see him, and he would pick her up in a few minutes. She might as well enjoy the evening and see where things went from there. If she backed away from the relationship, she would always regret the missed opportunity to know for sure.

In the meantime, she thought about her bitter words to David. They were true, even if he didn't think so. Or perhaps he thought things could change for them in the community. David was optimistic—but of course he was. He had Phoebe's friendship to help him along, and his shyness stood him in *goot* stead in the community...the same community who saw her display of strength as rebellion.

Knowing this, she had accepted the schoolteaching job with humility and grace, but maybe that was what rankled. She didn't want such obvious charity. She wanted acceptance on her own terms, which included Ethan, and he could never be a part of the community. What a mess she had gotten herself into. But what was new about that? Life had always been a mess at the Fisher household. She had yet to succeed at anything.

Ruth jerked her head up as a pickup came over the horizon from Little Falls. She stepped off the road a few feet and waited. With her luck, Emil would choose to drive past again and catch her red-handed as she hopped into Ethan's pickup. Thankfully, there was no sound of horse's hooves on the pavement behind her as Ethan slowed and she climbed inside.

"Hi." She fastened her seat belt as he took off.

"Sorry I'm late. I had to pick up the children from the Lapp farm at the last moment. Mrs. Broman had a medical emergency."

"Anything serious?"

Ethan shook his head. "Her youngest boy had a toothache, but they made it to the dentist's office before the weekend." He chuckled. "I can't imagine living with Kaleen while he's suffering an abscessed tooth—even with an ice pack and Tylenol."

"Don't you like children?"

Before he answered, another buggy appeared in the distance, and Ruth ducked her head until it had passed.

"Still hiding?" he asked. He didn't sound pleased.

"Isn't that part of the mystery?" she shot back.

"Feisty tonight, are we?"

Ruth forced a smile. "Sorry. I'm touchy right now, that's all."

"We can do this some other time, if you wish," he offered. "I'm available most nights next week."

"Tonight's fine." Her answer was terse.

"You sure?"

"*Yah*, I want to be with you, Ethan. This evening!" She paused. "Well, I just like being with you."

His smile seemed genuine. "That's a compliment. Thanks. So... shall we try for the steakhouse in Utica? We haven't been there in a while, and I could use a hearty meal."

"Okay," she agreed at once. "Did you have a difficult week?"

"Not really. Stressful today, that's all. Just that everything landed on my lap this afternoon with the family at your brother's farm."

"You mean Phoebe Lapp's farm."

He shrugged. "Correct."

"What happened?" She sat forward on her seat as they drove through Little Falls.

"Looks like things could get a little interesting," he said. "Much more than we expected. I haven't told Mrs. Broman yet, but the mother showed up and stayed there for most of the week. No one reported in to us—which will *not* happen again. I told your brother and Phoebe so in no uncertain terms. We have to know those details.

The strange thing is that everything went well. The mother—Melissa is her name—seemed to enjoy her time at the farm. In fact, she enjoyed it immensely, and she wants to take full custody of the three girls again, which is against policy. When I told her it would take some time, she eventually accepted after a fit of temper. Such people don't take well to instructions or restraints, to say the least."

"Maybe my brother and Phoebe did her some *goot*," Ruth suggested. She settled back into her seat. What did she expect? David was moving up in the world, but she was tempting fate.

"The therapy farm seems to be a success," Ethan agreed. "Thanks for your part in smoothing the way."

"Do you want to start one?" Ruth asked.

Ethan laughed. "Now you're being funny."

"I wish we could do something like that together, and I'm not trying to be funny."

"Ruth, come on. Isn't that rushing things a little?" Ethan gave her a quick sideways glance as they drove out of Little Falls and north toward Utica on Interstate 90. "Me, working on a farm?"

Why should Ethan wish to work with her—on a farm, no less? She was dreaming. Ruth stared out of the windshield in silence.

"You okay?" He sounded concerned.

She nodded. "Just thinking, that's all. And looking forward to the steak. Thanks for taking me."

He smiled, obviously confused by the random track of their conversation. "I guess we should wait until we get to the restaurant, but now that you've brought up the point, I'd like to at least mention it."

Ruth waited. "Mention what?" she finally asked when he didn't continue.

"This thing about us. I received a fresh insight this afternoon into your way of life when I picked up the three girls. You are a very religious people. Not only through your words, or your intentions, but it's in you, like..." For once he seemed at a loss for what to say.

"It's our life. It's who we are," she offered.

"That's it! Exactly!" He nodded. "So I'm thinking you are that way too, even if you don't act like it sometimes."

"But I do act like it—"

He continued undeterred. "You seem a little different from them, but yet you are not."

"What's that supposed to mean?"

"Exactly what I said." He waved his hand about.

"I seem conflicted. Is that it?"

"Yes! Thank you." He seemed pleased. "So what are you going to do about that?"

"I wasn't conflicted before this," she objected. "I was...I would have...never mind. I'm not going to say it."

He grinned. "I think you've always been conflicted, ever since I've known you. Only lately you weren't, and now you are again."

She stared out of the pickup window as he slowed for the Utica exit. "So that's it? That's the reason you were suddenly interested in me, but now you aren't as much?"

"Are you talking to yourself?"

She ignored him. "So if I settle in as an Amish schoolteacher, you find me fascinating, but when I don't, you find me..."

"Maybe that's it!" He laughed. "I'm not that analytical, but you pretend well, which—"

"Which you don't like," she finished. "What a mess."

"You're as pretty as ever," he teased at a red light. "You'd be even prettier without that thing on your head, and with a decent dress on and your hair done up. You came close to all that not that long ago. Why don't you come all the way, Ruth?"

She regarded him with a serious face. "Will there be a marriage proposal?"

He laughed. "You mean an engagement ring?"

"I suppose so. But...sorry. I shouldn't have said that."

"Always the two worlds," he mused. "Somehow we have to bring them together."

"Can it be done?"

"You could join me in my world," he responded.

"And would there be a ring?"

He laughed heartily.

"That's a real endorsement."

Ethan said nothing as he pulled into the restaurant lot and parked. "We have tonight and good food ahead of us. Shall we go in?" He motioned toward the building.

Ruth hopped out and waited. Tentatively she took his hand, and he didn't object. They entered the restaurant and were ushered to their seats. The waitress appeared with menus and took their orders for drinks.

"I have a little surprise for you," Ethan teased after the waitress left.

Ruth ignored him to scan the pages of the menu.

He held up two thin pieces of paper. "Tickets to Chicago."

"Chicago? You want to go there?"

He laughed. "No, silly. The band! Chicago! They are playing in Syracuse at nine. I want you to go with me."

Ruth dropped the menu to the table. "I..." She looked down at her dress and pointed to her head. "In this!"

He shrugged. "You always got rid of those before."

"But those *Englisha* clothes are at home, and we'd be gone most of the night. I mean, Syracuse? Driving there and back, and the concert..."

"I'll get you back in one piece." He grinned. "And this might help you decide about..." His rapped his knuckles on the table. "About what we discussed earlier."

"You want me to cut off my limb at the trunk."

His grin spread all over his face. "In a manner of speaking."

"And is there a ring in your pocket?"

He stifled his laughter as the waitress returned and took their orders.

"I take it there is not," she told him once the waitress had left.

"There is not. You have to walk out on your own two feet, Ruth—without promises. I'm not going to carry you over the threshold only to have doubts linger in your mind the rest of your life. I can never be a part of your world—not even a little bit. There will be no wading in both waters, so to speak."

"Not even for love's sake?"

"Especially not for love's sake."

"That makes no sense."

"Neither does double-dipping. Now, will you go with me tonight or not? It's not as if I could find anyone else on short notice."

"Which means you were certain I would go?"

"Exactly, my dear. I know you well."

"Then divine who I am instead of placing this ultimatum in front of me."

"That, sweetheart, is not possible. Some things even I do not know. They become clear only when choices are made."

"Then to Syracuse," she said, "and to burning the bridges."

"Keep your voice down. The waitress is coming back. And you're not burning bridges. That I do know about you."

"I'm coming exactly like this."

"See? What did I say?"

She didn't respond as the waitress set their dishes in front of them. The steaming goodness filled Ruth's nostrils. She was hungry—starving, in fact. Mental wrestling with Ethan was a brutal task, but she had made it this far and would spend the evening with him at a wild concert. She had been to enough of them to know what to expect. Paper napkins would serve as earplugs if worse came to worst, and she could lose her *kapp* easily enough.

"I'm glad you're coming," he said, cutting into his steak. He lathered the piece with a generous helping of steak sauce.

There had been no prayer of thanks, but she was far from home and would travel even further by the time the evening was through. Maybe Ethan was correct. Maybe she would finally make up her mind and land solidly on one side of the fence or the other.

TWENTY-FIVE

On Monday morning Phoebe peered out of the kitchen window toward the south. There was no sign of David, and there would be no children arriving this week. David was late, but she was sure he would arrive soon. There were chores in the barn she needed help with.

Phoebe plunged the last of the breakfast dishes into the soapy dishwater. She might as well be honest: She wanted David's presence near her, even if he stayed in the barn all day. But there was nothing wrong with her feelings for the man. David's family was complicated, *yah*, but Grandma Lapp had approved of him. What the rest of the family said at this moment was beside the point.

Phoebe set a wet plate on the drainer and reached for a dish towel. After a long lecture on Saturday, Mrs. Broman had decided against bringing more children this week. There had been nothing in her classes about allowing a child's *mamm* to stay for the week, even if she had guessed that the relationship would not be allowed to continue.

She hadn't told Mrs. Broman this but simply apologized and promised to call at once if anything like that came up again. Likely what saved David and her from worse recriminations was that Mrs.

Broman also needed time to gather her wits after the *wunderbah* healed relationship last week between Melissa and her daughters. Mrs. Broman could not have expected such a result from the three girls' stay on an Amish farm.

Phoebe drew a long breath. She had her own astonishment to deal with. She cared about David. She had feelings in her heart for him—and they must have been there all this time. She obviously had buried them under those hurtful words from the past. Not in her wildest imagination had she thought that David could heal her heart.

Phoebe fanned herself with her towel. The wedding vows were where these things led. She knew that, and so did he, and he would be here again this morning.

"Oh!" she exclaimed. "How can this be?" But it simply was. The feelings were there, all of their own accord.

She trembled around David. He was unsure of himself and a little afraid of her, but he had a *goot* heart underneath all that. How blind she had been. Thank the Lord Grandma had seen through all of his insecurities to the gold that lay beneath the surface. The same went for Ruth. Look at how both Fisher children had blossomed in the last months. Ruth was the community's schoolteacher—a high honor only a few attained. Grandma had not been wrong.

Phoebe jumped when a sharp knock came on the front door. Could that be David? He wouldn't knock with such insistence. Phoebe draped the towel over the drainer and tiptoed out of the kitchen. Ruth was framed in the living room window with her hand raised to knock again. Phoebe hurried forward to open the door.

"Hi, Ruth! What—"

"I'm on my way to school," Ruth muttered. "I guess I am." She looked as if she hadn't slept all night.

"What is wrong?" Phoebe held the door wide open. "Do come in."

Ruth hesitated. "I should be at school."

Phoebe turned to check the time on the living room wall. "It's only seven thirty. Sit down."

Ruth seated herself on the couch. "I'm really sorry about this," she began. "I know you will be shocked beyond belief by what I'm about to tell you, but..." Ruth's hand went to her heart. "I'm so torn up, and...I guess I don't trust anyone else."

Phoebe took one of Ruth's hands in both of hers. "Has something happened at school?"

Ruth gave a strangled laugh. "I only wish things were that simple. See..." She seemed to falter. "Oh, how can I say it, Phoebe, after everyone has been so nice?" The words stopped again, and Ruth's gaze moved to the far living room wall, as if answers could be found there.

"Ruth, whatever this is, we can get through it," Phoebe encouraged her.

The strangled laugh came again. "I...if only that were true."

Phoebe tried another angle. "Did you speak with someone at church yesterday about this issue? People can be a little—"

"I wasn't at church." Ruth turned to Phoebe. "You didn't even notice."

"I'm so sorry, Ruth. I..."

"That's okay. I wasn't—" Ruth stopped with a frown. "Why can't I behave myself or fall in love with the right man?" Her fingers dug into Phoebe's hand.

"What did you do?" Phoebe demanded.

"I went out with Ethan on Friday evening."

Silence filled the living room.

"*Yah*, see? This is what I expected." Ruth tried to stand. "All is lost now. My schoolteaching job, the respect the community has for me, and their trust. It's gone because I can't..."

"Ruth." Phoebe pulled her back. "We have to talk about this."

"What is there to talk about or do? Should I make a confession at church, perhaps? That's what lies ahead of me. That and failure, and expulsion from the school. How will I live down that shame? *Daett* is enough of an embarrassment."

Phoebe tried to breathe evenly. "Perhaps there's something that can be done. I don't know what, but don't go telling anyone yet. Not if this was the last time you'll do something like this."

"*Yah*. See, that's the problem." Ruth leaped to her feet. "Ethan and I have a date set up for later this week. I love the man, Phoebe."

"But that's another world, Ruth. It's time to come back and let go. That's what you promised to do when you took the job."

"I know, but my heart is in his hands." Ruth's face was desperate. "I've worked so hard to win his love, and on Friday night I think I finally convinced him..."

"What?"

"That he and I could make a go of it if I—"

"Stop talking like that. It's not going to help. That's not what you really want. If you did, why would you be here this morning?"

Ruth sat back down on the couch. "Do you think so? I mean, I'm so confused. I think one thing and then another. On Friday night I had such feelings for the man, and then..."

"See?"

"He held me tight, Phoebe," Ruth wailed. "All the way home in the pickup truck. He loves me. I know he does. Why else would Ethan have asked me out again this week? He's never done that before. Oh!" Ruth threw her hands in the air. "I'm going mad. There can be no other explanation."

Phoebe patted Ruth's arm. What was she to say? Her heart pounded at the thought of what Uncle Homer would say when he found out what Ruth had done. "You must call off this date and tell no one," Phoebe finally said. "One slipup isn't so bad if you choose the right path again."

Ruth gave her a serious look. "Do you really mean that?"

"*Yah*, of course I do. We can keep this our secret, and you can talk with me anytime you wish. Such as when Ethan becomes too big a—" Phoebe stopped. Referring to Ethan as a temptation might provoke Ruth unnecessarily.

Ruth clasped and unclasped her hands. "And I'm just supposed to walk away from what I've worked so long to obtain, from what my heart wants—Ethan's love?"

"I..." Phoebe paused again. "I don't know the answers. Maybe we can just walk through this together, but don't do anything rash. Think long and hard before you see him again."

Ruth stood. "I have thought about it plenty, Phoebe, and thinking doesn't help. But I had best be going before David comes and catches me here."

"So he doesn't know?"

"He suspects, I'm sure. As does the rest of my family. It's not the first time I've done this, and I was out until three o'clock on Friday night. But we're Fishers. We don't tattle on each other." Ruth's face hardened. "I hope you don't tattle either."

Phoebe held onto Ruth's hand. "I told you I'm not going to tell, Ruth."

A tear rolled down Ruth's face. She pulled away and rushed out of the front door. Phoebe followed her but stopped on the porch steps. Ruth was running down the lane and across the fields, taking a shortcut to the schoolhouse road.

Phoebe's gaze lingered until Ruth disappeared from sight behind a row of trees. What a mess. But she could understand Ruth in a way—if Ruth was in love with Ethan. How could anyone expect her to cut off the relationship at the drop of a hat? Yet Uncle Homer wouldn't feel the same way. He would throw Ruth out of her school-teaching job the moment he learned of her indiscretion. Difficult decisions lay ahead. How could Ruth join the baptismal class next month while feeling the way she did? Unless the situation was resolved, something would slip out—and the community would learn that their schoolteacher hadn't forsaken her *rumspringa* after all.

Phoebe drew in a sharp breath. That would mean the end of so much—Ruth's future in the community and further deterioration of the Fisher family name—all right on the brink of a great victory. She should have chewed Ruth out royally this morning, but she didn't. Grandma had loved the girl, and Grandma would have been most understanding. She was that way, and Phoebe was Grandma's grandchild. Hadn't she offered all kinds of understanding and compassion to Melissa last week? The girls' mother had done worse things than Ruth ever would.

She would keep her mouth shut. Let someone else spill the beans on Ruth's shortcomings. In the meantime, maybe this explained why David had not appeared on the road from the south. The poor man must be totally heartbroken over his sister's actions. David would be racked with feelings of guilt on his sister's behalf. That's how he would see things, and with *goot* reason. David was accustomed to his family's faults being made known to everyone.

Phoebe breathed a quick prayer heavenward before she returned to the kitchen. "Please help us, dear Lord." She still needed David's help with the chores. Should she walk down to the Fishers' place and clear the air with David? Her appearance would be suspicious, and if Leroy learned that she had kissed his son last week...Phoebe's face flamed at the thought. Leroy would have much to say on the subject. She didn't want to hear the man's criticism or his gloating.

Was she ashamed of her kiss? Didn't she want anyone to know about her feelings for David, especially now that Ruth had a secret to keep? Was she like everyone else who spread stories and rumors about the whole family?

"I will not." Phoebe set her chin. "Grandma left me in charge of this farm, and she must have known I would fall in love with David."

A man cleared his throat behind her, and she spun around to see David's red face in the kitchen doorway. "I'm so sorry. You didn't answer the door, and I—"

"Did you..." The answer was obvious, and Phoebe's hands flew to her face.

"I really am sorry," he repeated. "I didn't mean to hear you talking to yourself."

Phoebe lowered her hands and peeked at him. Only pain was written on his face. "You know about Ruth," she whispered.

He didn't answer, but he lowered himself onto a kitchen chair with a groan. "If you know, does everyone know?"

"I don't think so. Ruth stopped by on the way to school this morning and told me."

"Ruth..." His mouth moved almost soundlessly.

She pulled out a chair to sit beside him. "*Yah*. She told me everything, and I feel quite bad about the struggle she's going through."

"She was out till three the other morning with Ethan," he said in horror. "Do you know what that means?"

"Of course, but no one else needs to know."

"You would cover this up? Phoebe, you know what happens when people do such things."

"Not like that!" She shook her head. "I want to help Ruth through this. Putting pressure on her isn't going to help."

"But you can't keep things like that secret for long."

Phoebe shrugged. "Then we'll deal with it when the news breaks. In the meantime, I'll be praying that Ruth makes the right choices."

"Do you know what her future plans are?" His gaze was desperate.

"David." She laid her hand on his. "Let's be strong. Let's believe that Grandma knew what she was doing. Ruth jumping the fence is not what the Lord wants, but she must come to that conclusion on her own."

"You expect her to give up Ethan?"

"I don't know. I hope so. Maybe the Lord will send a handsome young man from the community to charm her heart now that she is the community's schoolteacher."

Skepticism played on David's face. "People are not chomping at the bit to marry into our family, Phoebe. You seem to forget that."

Kiss me, she wanted to tell him. "We have chores to do," she said instead. "Can you help me today?"

He nodded. Chores, David could do.

TWENTY-SIX

The sun had risen high in the sky when Phoebe slipped out of the house and crossed the lawn. David was in the barn, where he had gone after their conversation in the house earlier that morning. Other than brief glimpses of him while he tended the ponies in the barnyard, she had not seen him. The Lord must have known this problem would arise with Ruth. Here was the real reason they needed the quiet week to sort through things. How much worse would Ruth's problem seem if Mrs. Broman had arrived an hour ago with another van-load of children to stay the week? David and Phoebe could not have hidden their troubled faces.

"Thank You, Lord, for helping us this far." Phoebe sent the prayer heavenward as she entered the barn. "And thank You for helping us through this week." She was sure the road wouldn't be easy, but the Lord would be with them.

"David!" she called out. She heard a muffled grunt. "I've come out to help you," she told him, moving farther into the barn.

He appeared, his hat coated with straw particles. He brushed them off and grinned. "The grain bin needed cleaning."

"Are you finished?"

"No, but—"

"Then I'm helping you," she said firmly.

He relented at once and led the way back.

She grabbed a broom hung on the wall. "Where shall I begin?"

"I have most of last year's chaff loose. Maybe you can reach up the wall as high as you can, and I'll get the rest."

She wielded her broom, and the dust stirred.

"A handkerchief?" He offered his.

She gave him a smile through the dust-filled air and produced a square of white linen from her pocket. "I have my own."

"Let me," he said. He stepped closer to take the handkerchief from her hand. Gently he slung the cloth around her face and tied a knot in the back. "Better," he said, peering around at her.

She nodded, and he tied on his own. They worked—a broom in her hand and a shovel in his—until the cobwebs were gone. The floor was dusty with bits of chaff, and they stepped outside to catch their breath. David went to empty the wheelbarrow while Phoebe untied her handkerchief.

"What next?" she asked when he returned.

"It has to be close to lunchtime," he suggested.

She glanced around. "There is no clock out here."

"Either way, I'm hungry. How about I walk home and grab some lunch?"

"You will not. Come in the house, and I'll fix sandwiches."

Doubt flickered on his face.

"Please, David," she begged. "Don't let this trouble with Ruth come between us. What happened last week…" She paused.

"I shouldn't have, Phoebe." His gazed dropped to the floor. "It was my fault."

"There is no blame." She reached for his hand. "Listen to me. I wanted to…" Her words stalled again.

"I am unworthy of you. You know I was out of my place."

The protest died on her lips as she heard buggy wheels in the lane.

A sharp whinny from a horse called out and was answered by the ponies' cries from the back pasture.

"That's Uncle Homer! I'd know his horse anywhere."

"Do you think he knows about Ruth?" Fear filled his eyes.

Phoebe forced the words out. "That has nothing to do with us, regardless." She took his hand. "Come with me, David. Don't feel this way."

He hesitated, but then he followed her.

Uncle Homer was out of his buggy when they stepped through the barn door. "There you are," he called out. "Can you come with me, Phoebe?"

"What's wrong?" she asked. She rushed forward with David by her side.

Uncle Homer looked worried. "There has been an accident at the schoolhouse. Deacon Matthew's daughter, Mary, was hit on the head with a bat at the first recess. The Yoders—"

"How badly was Mary hurt?" Phoebe interrupted.

"Badly enough. I didn't see the girl, but the Yoders drove her to the hospital in Little Falls. There was blood from a cut, I was told." Uncle Homer winced. "The Yoders thought of calling an ambulance once Ruth sent for help, but they figured they'd be in town by the time the ambulance arrived. Emil has a fast horse."

"Has there been an update on Mary's condition?" Phoebe inquired. David still hadn't said a word.

Uncle Homer shook his head. "They may have taken her on to Utica. You never know. The concussion was severe, we suspect."

"What happened?" David finally said. "Was Ruth to blame?"

"I don't think so," Uncle Homer told him. He sounded none too certain, though. "Ruth wasn't out on the playground when the accident happened."

"I'm sorry," David replied. "Is there anything we can do?"

"*Yah*, I think." Uncle Homer gave David a quick glance. "Could you come along with me and stay with your sister for the rest of the day? She doesn't appear disturbed, but this must have been a shock. It would be best if someone stayed with her."

David didn't hesitate. "Certainly."

"Can Phoebe spare you with the children?" Uncle Homer's glance took in the house and barn.

"We don't have any this week," Phoebe told him. "David can go, and I'll make some sandwiches and bring them up to him. We haven't had lunch yet."

"You are here by yourselves this week?" Uncle Homer's eyes made the rounds again.

"*Yah*, we were cleaning out the grain bin," Phoebe told him. "It's sort of an off week. Although it looks as if we won't get much time off with the amount of excitement we've had already."

"What else has happened this morning?" Uncle Homer's gaze fixed on Phoebe.

"I...we...." Phoebe stalled. "Never mind. I'll make sandwiches and walk up to the schoolhouse. You can drop off David on your way."

Uncle Homer watched her walk into the house. That had been mighty stupid of her to cut him off like that. She couldn't run away, and Uncle Homer wouldn't rest until she gave him a full explanation. He felt responsible for her.

Phoebe peeked out of the kitchen window as the buggy went out the driveway. David was perched inside as if he would fall out the door. Then it occurred to her: Uncle Homer didn't have to wait until he saw her again to dig deeper into the morning's happenings. She had left David with him. Uncle Homer would assume correctly that David knew what she had not been able to say. Phoebe's mouth dropped open.

"Oh, no!" she groaned. David was no match for Uncle Homer. All of Ruth's secrets would be spilled before the buggy arrived at the schoolhouse. Uncle Homer would know that she had tried to protect Ruth. This only grew worse and worse.

She should run after the buggy, but how dumb would that be? She could never catch Uncle Homer before he disappeared from sight. Already his buggy was a dot in the distance as the two turned left onto Peckville Road.

"Dear Lord, give David courage," Phoebe prayed. But courage for what? Telling the truth? For once she wanted to hide the truth. Maybe the Fishers were having a bigger influence on her than she had imagined. Uncle Homer would likely have that figured out too.

Phoebe rushed about fixing the sandwiches. Duty always came first—even when one was being shady. But she hadn't lied, and she wouldn't lie. This was for a *goot* cause. Ruth must be given the chance to make up her own mind. Force would only send her over the fence. If only Phoebe could persuade Uncle Homer of that truth, but her uncle would be as receptive as a cow having her tail twisted sideways.

She would have to think of something.

Phoebe slapped pieces of bread on the table and lathered on butter. Meat and cheese came next. There was no time to waste. Uncle Homer might have the schoolhouse emptied out of students before she arrived. That would be his natural instinct if David told him of Ruth's escapades on Friday evening.

Phoebe shoved the sandwiches into a paper bag and nearly ran out of the lane. She kept up her pace until she reached Peckville Road, where she slowed to a walk, panting fiercely. My, she felt out of shape. As a young girl she could run on the school playground for twenty minutes with barely a catch of her breath.

Phoebe still breathed heavily when a buggy appeared in front of her. She stepped off the road, prepared to wave, and pasted a smile firmly in place.

Phoebe gasped when she recognized the horse. Uncle Homer

was on his way back. Had disaster struck already? She trembled and the smile fled.

Uncle Homer came to a stop in front of her. "Get up in the buggy, Phoebe."

A protest died on her lips. Doomsday had arrived. She pulled herself up onto the seat and avoided his gaze.

"David told me what happened."

No words would come, but Uncle Homer didn't appear to mind.

"I don't know what to think," he said. "I guess it was bound to happen, but still. I don't know what is right."

She stared at him. "You approve?"

A hint of a smile played on his face. "I didn't say that."

"But Ruth—" Phoebe stopped. Something wasn't right. "What exactly did David tell you?"

Hope ran across Uncle Homer's face. "So the boy exaggerated."

"You're making no sense. What did David exaggerate?"

He was puzzled now. "His interest in you. Don't you share it?"

She felt blood rush to her face. "Oh! That..." She stopped. Relief flooded her, and she blubbered the words. "I did kiss him last week, and—"

"Wait. He didn't tell me that. So it is serious?"

Phoebe clutched the side of the buggy seat. "Are you going to tell me I shouldn't like the man?"

Uncle Homer jiggled the reins, and his horse headed back to the schoolhouse. There was only the beat of hooves on the pavement for a long moment. "I don't know what to say, Phoebe," he finally ventured. "A kiss? This all seems a little fast moving to me. David made it sound as if he had an interest in you and you shared his feelings. I might have accepted that—after a warning to you, of course, about praying and making sure the Lord's will is being sought. But David didn't say anything about a kiss." Uncle Homer grunted. "Just like a Fisher. Taking advantage of the situation."

Phoebe kept her gaze on the road. "He didn't take advantage of me, Uncle Homer. I was quite willing." What else was there to say? Blaming David would doom them.

"You are a Lapp, and he is a Fisher. Maybe things can change, but that takes time, Phoebe. If you're already kissing the man, that's—"

"You gave Ruth the schoolteaching job!" The words slipped out.

"I know," he allowed, "but that's different. Schoolteaching is serious enough, but marriage is for life. You can fire a schoolteacher, but our people do not believe in divorce. You know that."

"David wouldn't divorce me."

"You don't have to be so touchy. That is a bad sign, Phoebe. Maybe you should slow down, and perhaps David shouldn't be there every day working on the farm."

She bit her lip. A hasty response would not help.

"Think about it, Phoebe," he continued as he brought his horse to a stop near the schoolyard lane.

"Thanks for the ride," she muttered. She hopped off.

Uncle Homer was off with spinning buggy wheels. Students filled the playground, busy with another ball game. When David met her halfway to the schoolhouse door, his face was wrinkled with concern. "I am so sorry, Phoebe," he whispered. "But I had to say something."

"The other would have been worse," she agreed. Should she tell him everything? How else was their relationship to survive? They couldn't begin to hide secrets from each other. "I told him about our kiss. And that I was most willing."

Horror filled his face. "How could you?"

"It slipped out when—oh, David. I said the right thing."

"It's okay," he told her, but he didn't sound convinced.

"Uncle Homer wants you to stop working on the farm until things can slow a bit."

"And you agreed?" His face went pale.

"It doesn't matter what I agree with. He won't listen to me."

"But I want to hear it from you."

She glanced around the playground. No one was paying them any attention. "I want you to stay, David. I don't regret our kiss one bit, and I never will."

Relief flickered on his face. "In that case—"

"We'll weather the storm." She reached for his hand. "They always blow over."

"This is a big one, Phoebe," he said, his hand over hers. "But I would do a lot to earn your affections. I hope you know that. If it comes out about what Ruth is doing..." The threat hung in the air. "We may not survive that."

"Come." She pulled on his hand. "I have the sandwiches ready. You must eat."

He didn't resist but followed her.

"How's Ruth?" she inquired.

"A mess. But it's all on the inside."

She looked and saw Ruth in the schoolhouse doorway. Phoebe hurried up to her and opened her arms. Ruth flew into them, and they embraced. "Have you heard news about Mary?" Phoebe asked.

Ruth shook her head. "It was awful. Blood was everywhere, and that horrible cut lay open on her forehead. The accident was all my fault. If I had been on the playground—"

"You must not blame yourself," Phoebe interrupted. "I'll stay with you for the rest of the day, and we'll get through this."

David stood beside them with his hands clasped, and Phoebe handed him the bag of sandwiches. "Eat," she ordered. "I'll be with you in a moment."

He nodded and hungrily eyed the bag. Life would go on. It must, and the Lord would not leave them.

"Come and sit with us while we eat," she told Ruth.

"I had better go out on the playground," Ruth demurred. "But I am so grateful you came, Phoebe. I can't thank you enough."

"You're welcome." Phoebe forced a smile.

Ruth turned and dashed outside, and David waited until Phoebe sat on the long bench beside him. He handed her a sandwich before he took a bite of his. They ate in silence to the sound of the children playing in the schoolyard outside the long glass windows.

TWENTY-SEVEN

Two days later, Phoebe stepped out of the house into the brisk morning air. David had entered the barn with only a brief glance toward where she waved from the kitchen window. Now, she approached the barn with quick steps, and the hinges on the door squeaked as she pushed it open. The familiar, dusty interior greeted her along with the whinnying of the ponies. David had the back barn door open, ready to release them into the pasture for the day. The man was efficient, even if his courage failed him.

"Why didn't you come up yesterday?" she called to him.

He turned to face her. "I figured you had things under control, and *Daett* needed my help on the farm."

She didn't argue with him. He had his reasons. "I'm glad you're here now," she told him instead. "Even if there isn't much to do."

"I had to make sure everything was okay."

"Have you had breakfast?"

"The rest of the family did."

"David," she chided. "There is nothing to worry about. I'm okay, and the rest of my relatives will eventually approve of us."

He hung his head. "I wish I had your confidence."

She stepped closer. "Come to the house. I'll fry eggs and bacon, and maybe make toast and oatmeal."

A hint of a grin played on his face. "That would be nice."

"And we can talk while you eat."

"There's not much to say," he objected.

"Then we can chat, or…" She let the sentence hang. *We can simply enjoy each other's company* didn't sound right. She tried again. "We'd better catch some downtime this week, don't you think? Next week could be quite hectic again."

"I know. I'll be right in after I've let the ponies out."

Phoebe retreated and closed the barn door behind her. She hurried across the lawn and had bacon sputtering in a pan by the time David arrived.

He seated himself at the kitchen table with a nervous smile. "Have you heard that Mary's home from the hospital?"

She shook her head. "I was wondering about her."

"Ruth said the concussion only needed observation for one night. The cut took nine stitches, though. That must have been some blow from the bat."

Phoebe made a face. "You know eighth-grade boys. They don't always know how to manage their newfound strength."

He grinned. "That was a long time ago, but *yah*, you are right. Charles is so sorry for what happened. I guess he'll be more careful from now on about who stands behind him when he's batting at home plate."

"How's Ruth doing?" She turned back to the frying bacon.

"Okay, I guess."

Should she ask if the Friday night date was still on?

"Ruth is still going out with Ethan," he said, as if reading her mind.

"We must pray," Phoebe told him. What else was there to say? A discussion about something they couldn't control would only sink

their spirits. She gave him a warm smile. "Do you have any suggestions as to what we should do today?"

"Not really," he said. He studied the tabletop. "The horse stalls
could be mucked out..."

"We should go help someone," she suggested. "That would get
our minds off our troubles."

"I suppose so. But who?"

"I could visit Mary and help Fannie around the house for the rest
of the day. There should be plenty of work with a sick child on her
hands. And you..." She stopped when his eyes grew round. "David,
you can ride with me in the buggy. Deacon Matthew is sure to have
work that needs doing. All his boys are young yet."

"You want to spend the day at Deacon Matthew's with me?"

"What? Am I such a bore?"

He grinned in spite of himself. "You know what I mean."

"This would be *goot* for both of us, and Deacon Matthew could
see us together. He knows you work on the farm."

"You're trying to get him used to the idea of us," he said. "A Fisher
and a Lapp?"

"I don't mean it like that," she protested. She cracked open the
first egg. "How many?"

"Two, please." He looked thoughtful. "I don't think this is a wise
idea. Suppose your uncle spoke with the deacon about his disapproval. You'll be seen as manipulating church opinion."

Phoebe laughed. "Me? Come on."

David joined in. "I guess that is a stretch."

"It'll be okay," she encouraged him. "Let's go. We should get
away from the farm while we have the chance. Remember? Next
week!"

"Do you think things will get worse? Are you prophesying?"

Phoebe laughed. "Let's think positively." She turned the eggs
over. "The Lord will be with us."

The struggle was evident on his face, but he finally smiled. "*Yah*, let's go. I would enjoy that—mostly spending the day with you."

"Come now," she teased. "I'll be in the house, and you'll be in the fields with Deacon Matthew."

His smile didn't fade. "Are you eating with me?"

She set the plate in front of him. "I'll have a little oatmeal." She brought the pot over from the stove, and the steam drifted across the table. "I ate earlier."

They bowed their heads and finished their food in silence. There was much she wanted to ask, to talk about. What would happen if Ruth continued to pursue Ethan? Would Uncle Homer's fear about Phoebe's interest in David subside or grow worse? Would next week's children bring fresh worries or further joy? But these were questions for which there were no answers.

David's smile was weak when she caught his gaze. "What's Deacon Matthew going to say when we drive in together?"

She shrugged. "We'll explain that we're having an off week. He'll be glad for the help after Mary's injury."

From the look on his face, David wasn't convinced—but he didn't object. "That was a *goot* breakfast," he finally said.

Phoebe pushed aside her bowl. "I'll take care of the dishes if you'll hitch Misty to the buggy."

He nodded, and they bowed their heads for a brief prayer of thanks. She reached over to touch his hand. "It'll be a *goot* day, David. Thanks for coming with me."

He stood. "I'll have Misty ready in a few minutes."

She gave him another smile when he glanced over his shoulder from the mudroom door. A look of joy filled his face for a moment before the shadows drove the light away again. "I'll be right out," she called after him.

The back door slammed, and Phoebe cleared the table. As she

washed the last dish, she caught a glimpse of David at the barn door with his hand on Misty's bridle. With the towel draped over the drying rack, Phoebe left the kitchen and hurried across the front lawn. David was ready, the reins clutched in his hands. She hopped up, and they pulled out of the driveway.

"Old Misty's perky this morning," Phoebe commented.

David grinned and didn't answer.

"She likes you," Phoebe added.

"She's become used to me," he allowed. "I've been around for a while now."

"Were you working for Grandma before I arrived from Lancaster? I can't remember."

His smile was gentle. "I've always worked for her, even during my school years. She had a kind heart."

"That she did," Phoebe agreed as the buggy climbed higher up the grade on Highway 170. At the junction of 29, they turned left and pulled into Deacon Matthew's driveway moments later. The beauty of the countryside from the high plateau still took her breath away. She was enraptured with the sight when David pulled up to the barn.

"It's so beautiful up here," she whispered.

"*Yah*, it is—oh, and here's Deacon Matthew."

Phoebe pulled her attention away from the mountains to call out, "*Goot* morning, Deacon." She climbed down from the buggy.

His smile was broad. "To what do we owe this visit on such a fine morning?"

Phoebe returned his smile. "How is Mary?"

"We're keeping her in bed, but that's becoming harder each passing moment." He grinned. "The girl was determined to go to school this morning."

"That's *goot* news," David said.

"How is your sister doing at school?"

"She enjoys the job," David managed. He dropped his gaze to the ground.

"I'm glad to hear that," Deacon Matthew replied. "Did Ruth take the shock of the accident well?"

"She keeps most of her feelings inside, but she's coping."

"Some people are that way," Deacon Matthew said, nodding. "I hope she talks with someone. Bottling things up isn't *goot*."

Phoebe tried to keep her smile firm. If Deacon Matthew really knew what his schoolteacher was up to…She pushed the thought out of her mind. The Lord would provide somehow, and Ruth would make the proper choice.

"Well." Phoebe forced cheerfulness into her voice. "We've come to help for the day. This week is our downtime on the farm because no children came to visit. Next week will be hectic again, I'm sure, but we are yours for the time being."

"This is *wunderbah*." Deacon Matthew clasped his hands. "I see the Lord does provide."

"He always does," Phoebe agreed. "I learned that lesson from Grandma."

"A godly woman indeed," Deacon Matthew responded. "So let's get this horse unharnessed and begin our day."

"I'm sure you two can handle that," Phoebe told them over her shoulder. She was already on her way up the walk when horse's hooves beat in the distance, and a buggy appeared to turn in the driveway. Aunt Millie's face was clearly visible through the windshield, and she appeared quite troubled.

Phoebe turned back and was standing by the buggy's wheel when Aunt Millie pulled to a stop. "Is something wrong?"

Aunt Millie's lips were pressed tightly together as she took in David and Deacon Matthew. "Why are you here, Phoebe? And with him?"

"Aunt Millie, I..." But what was the use? Her aunt's attention was clearly elsewhere. "What is wrong?" Phoebe repeated.

"Homer's Eugene was gone this morning when the family awoke," Aunt Millie said through clenched teeth. "But I'm still asking, Phoebe. Why is David here? I don't..."

Aunt Millie stopped speaking when she saw David and Deacon Matthew hurrying over, the deacon's brow wrinkled in concern. "Is there a problem, Millie? You drove in the lane quite fast. Or am I to get more help for the day?" He attempted a laugh.

"We think Homer's Eugene ran away last night, and Homer's out looking for him with the sheriff." Aunt Millie divulged the information with a shiver through her whole body.

"But the boy's only sixteen!" Deacon Matthew exclaimed. "He's barely begun his *rumspringa*. And what did you say? The—"

"*Yah*, the sheriff," Aunt Millie repeated. "Their neighbor's truck was s-s-stolen." Her voice gave out, and tears trickled down her cheeks.

"Lord, help us," Deacon Matthew prayed out loud. "I can't believe this. Homer Lapp's child?"

Aunt Millie found her voice again. "I know. This shames us all, and to have the sheriff involved!" Aunt Millie's voice rose to a wail. "One of the men would have come over to tell you, but they are all busy with the search, and we felt you should know."

"Of course," Deacon Matthew agreed. "Has Bishop Rufus been told?"

Aunt Millie shook her head. "You were the closest, but I must go there next, although my heart nearly fails me with the task."

"I'll go with you," Phoebe decided on the spot. "I'll come back later to visit with Mary, and David can stay here for the day as we planned." David cleared his throat but didn't say anything. "Is that okay with you?" she asked him.

"I would be glad to," he said, and she gave him a grateful smile before hopping up into the buggy. Aunt Millie shook the reins, and they hurtled out the driveway.

"My thoughts and prayers are with you and the rest of the family!" Deacon Matthew called after them.

Phoebe hung on to the buggy seat. "Why are you driving so fast?"

"I don't know." Holding the reins with one hand, Aunt Millie wiped away her tears. "This is such an awful tragedy. I guess I've lost my senses. Who would have thought that Homer's oldest would so quickly jump the fence into that awful world?"

"I know," Phoebe comforted her. "But perhaps Eugene will see his mistake and something can still be done."

"But stealing a truck!" Aunt Millie's voice was a wail again. "How will our family live down such a wicked act by one of our young people? We'll—" Aunt Millie gave up and clutched the reins as they raced through a stop sign. Thankfully, there was no cross traffic.

"Aunt Millie, you had better slow down," Phoebe warned.

Her aunt nodded and pulled back on the reins. The bishop's driveway appeared in front of them, and Aunt Millie whimpered, "How am I going to find the strength for this? Why didn't Homer come himself to confess the family's sins?"

"We'll do it together," Phoebe told her. "I'm with you."

TWENTY-EIGHT

The following morning, Phoebe responded to a knock on the front door and found David on the porch.

"Are you okay?" he asked. There had been little time for conversation since their abrupt separation the day before.

She attempted a smile. "It's been a rough week to say the least, and this was supposed to be our time to rest up."

David joined in with a halfhearted chuckle. "When did you get back yesterday? I had to leave Deacon Matthew's place at chore time, and then I puttered around here until almost dark."

"Aunt Millie dropped me off after a late supper. Sorry I missed you."

"It's okay," he assured her. "It was nice of you to stay with your aunt during this time. How's the family taking it?"

"It's rough, as can be expected. Eugene is sitting in the jail in Little Falls." Phoebe shuddered at the thought. "Who would have expected things would come to this?"

"How long will he be there?"

"Uncle Homer's paying the bail today. That was one reason for the lateness last night. The whole family was at Uncle Homer's talking about the situation. After Deacon Matthew and Bishop Rufus were consulted, they decided it might be best if Eugene wasn't left in prison." Phoebe shuddered again. "Can you imagine what that must be like, even if the boy stole a truck? Too much of a bad thing can't be *goot*."

"I'm sure he learned his lesson. Paying the bail is the right decision."

"Homer's a strict parent. He wants to make the right choice." Phoebe held onto the front door. "Have you had breakfast?"

He nodded.

"Would you hitch Misty to the buggy for me, please? Now that you're here." She reached out to touch his arm. "I need to finish my visit from yesterday."

"You know I will," he said. He turned to leave.

"Thanks!" she called after him.

He gave a little wave over his shoulder before disappearing through the barn door. She rushed about the house and put away the last of the breakfast dishes. David had Misty ready when she came down the porch steps. She hurried up to the buggy and climbed in, and he handed her the reins.

"Thanks again for hitching Misty to the buggy for me," she told him. "I'll be back this afternoon sometime."

"I'll be here," he called after her as she trotted the horse out of the lane and up the incline toward Highway 29 and Deacon Matthew's farm. Mary would be recovered by this time, but Phoebe should still visit. Fannie had understood the interruption yesterday and would express nothing but encouragement for the beleaguered Lapp family.

Phoebe turned left at the stop sign, and Misty settled into a steady trot. She took a moment to observe the *wunderbah* view again. Cousin Eugene might make dumb life choices, but the Lord's handiwork still stirred joy inside of her.

"Whoa, there," Phoebe called out to Misty as she turned in the driveway. When they pulled up to the barn, the door swung open at once.

Deacon Matthew hurried out. "*Goot* morning, Phoebe. You're back."

"*Yah*," she responded. She hopped down from the buggy. "My visit yesterday was interrupted so abruptly. I wanted to come back today for a little bit at least."

"That's very thoughtful of you. How's the family and Eugene?"

"Taking it hard, as you can guess. They're embarrassed." Phoebe made a face. "Thanks for the advice yesterday. I think leaving the boy in jail until his trial would only have made things worse."

Deacon Matthew bowed his head. "Those are difficult decisions for parents to make, but kindness goes a long way sometimes after a tragedy."

"Thanks again." Phoebe started to unfasten the tug on her side.

Deacon Matthew waved her away. "I'll take care of your horse. Go on in for a chat with Fannie. She'll be glad you came."

"How is Mary?"

Deacon Matthew laughed. "I should have let her go to school this morning. The poor girl is beside herself, but I'm a little on the cautious side."

"Then I'll get to see her." Phoebe turned to head up the walk.

Fannie met her at the front door with a big smile. "You're back. So *goot* to see you, Phoebe."

The two embraced, and Phoebe was ushered inside.

Mary was lying on the living room couch with a pout on her face. "I'm all better, and I want to go to school."

"You can go on Monday," Fannie told her. "Another day of rest won't hurt you in the least."

Phoebe sat on the couch beside the pouting girl. "So what happened when that big bat hit you on the head?"

"I don't know." Mary wrinkled up her face. "One moment I was watching the ball game, and the next it was all dark."

"Oh, you poor thing." Phoebe gently ran her hand over Mary's forehead. The bandage was on the left side above the hairline. "At least no one will see your scar unless they are looking for it."

"I guess so," Mary said, without much enthusiasm.

Phoebe couldn't hold back a smile. "Those things don't mean much to you yet, but they will."

"With or without scars, Mary's going to marry whom the Lord has planned as her husband!" Fannie declared from the kitchen opening.

"I won't argue with that," Phoebe responded. She gave Mary a quick kiss just below the bandage. The girl grimaced, and Phoebe left her to enter the kitchen.

"So how are the Lapps doing? I didn't want to say anything with Mary in earshot."

"Troubled and disturbed and trying to make the right choices. Uncle Homer is paying the bail today, so Eugene should be home by this evening."

Fannie clucked her tongue. "Parenting is a hard road. Like keeping Mary home from school today. The poor thing. She's suffering."

"Parents do what they think is best," Phoebe replied. "I'm not a parent, but next week we get several more children. I pray I can be a blessing to them and make the best choices during the short time they are at the farm."

"How are things going at the farm?" Fannie poured two cups of hot water and set one of them in front of Phoebe. "Sit. We can chat for a little bit at least."

Phoebe added cocoa and stirred slowly as Fannie did likewise. "Adventurous, I guess. The children pull at my heartstrings."

Fannie nodded. "A sure sign the Lord is with you. We can't change what we don't love."

"That sounds like something Grandma would have said."

Fannie smiled. "Then I am honored. Grandma Lapp was a godly woman."

"That she was."

"So what about you and David?" Fannie probed. "Matthew had nothing but *goot* things to say yesterday after David helped him all day. They even finished harvesting the sweet corn field."

"He didn't tell me that." Phoebe smiled. "David's a *goot* man. We haven't spoken much since yesterday morning. Aunt Millie didn't drop me off at the house until after supper last night when David was gone."

Fannie tried to smile. "*Yah*, it's a tough time for everyone, but I think the Lapp family is handling things well."

"They're following your husband's advice, and Bishop Rufus's too, of course."

"Who can go wrong with the deacon's advice?" Fannie quipped, and they laughed together.

"In all seriousness, though, how are you and David getting along?"

"I can't complain. He helps with the farm, and he's been there through every crisis we've had so far."

"I mean, how are *you* and *he* doing?" Fannie leaned closer and gave Phoebe a meaningful look.

Phoebe's face flamed. Confessing things to family was one thing, but this was the deacon's *frau*.

"Serious, then," Fannie guessed. "I'm not surprised."

"Do you have objections?" Phoebe managed.

Fannie shrugged. "It's a little early to tell, don't you think? Are you officially dating?"

Phoebe shook her head. Kissing wasn't dating, which usually happened before the kissing. She guessed her face was turning the color of red beets.

Fannie fixed her gaze again. "I see. You've grown quite fond of the man. Does he share your feelings?"

"I think so," Phoebe whispered. The memory of David's lips on hers left her weak.

"You haven't forgotten about his family's problems, of course."

"Can't people change?" The words came out much too loudly. "Grandma seemed to think so," she said much more softly.

Fannie took a long sip of her hot chocolate before she responded. "Far be it for me to argue with Grandma Lapp. And Ruth seems to have settled into her schoolteaching job, so maybe..." The sentence hung in the air, full of peril and promise all at the same time.

Phoebe looked away. Her red face would give her away soon, if that hadn't happened already.

"You like the man," Fannie continued. "He is a member of the church, as you are, and you are both in *goot* standing. Who could object?"

"My family." The words slipped out.

Fannie shrugged. "You can't blame them, can you?"

"Sorry. I shouldn't have responded like that."

"Neither should you keep such things to yourself, Phoebe. I take it you don't know about your family's history with Leroy Fisher."

"What history?"

"I should not be the one telling you, but perhaps it's time. You seem sweet on his son."

"I have no idea what you are talking about," Phoebe said.

"Leroy Fisher was at fault in your grandfather Tobias's death, Phoebe. He carelessly drove a wagon to a community threshing day with a cracked single tree, thinking things would be okay. Your grandfather ended up paired with Leroy on his wagon and was driving when the single tree broke. Their wagon was empty, and Leroy's wild horses, which were never properly cared for, bolted over the creek bank. Leroy was able to leap off, but your grandfather stayed with the wagon. There was a terrible tangle at the bottom, and the rest you know."

Phoebe stood halfway to her feet and sat down again.

"Perhaps you understand better now why Leroy has the reputation that he does." Fannie came closer to give Phoebe a quick hug. "I'm sorry that I'm the one to tell you."

"This changes nothing between David and me," Phoebe said through clenched teeth. "I'm sure Grandma forgave Leroy a long time ago."

"I'm sure she did," Fannie agreed.

"Maybe I should help you with the housework." Phoebe stood quickly. Her hot chocolate splashed across the tablecloth.

A concerned look crossed Fannie's face. "Perhaps I should not have told you."

Phoebe reached for a washcloth that was hung on the sink, and she wiped up the mess before answering. "You did the right thing. I thought I was the one who couldn't deal with the past, but I see other people have the same problem."

"We have to be honest," Fannie told her. "That's very hard sometimes."

"I don't think Uncle Homer should object to my liking David, even considering this news. Look what wrong Uncle Homer's own child has committed. Isn't that a whole lot worse than anything David has ever done? He is not to blame for his *daett*'s careless ways."

Fannie tried to smile. "That's a natural reaction to have, Phoebe, but you shouldn't blame your uncle for his concern."

"That is true. Thanks for telling me, because it explains a lot. I wonder if David knows."

Fannie shrugged. "I doubt if he does. Few people talk about what happened on the day of your grandfather's death. Accidents like that occur. In the meantime, I am glad Leroy's children are growing out of his shadow. Ruth, I think, is also turning out well."

"She struggles," Phoebe said. She had to say something.

"I expect she does." Fannie's concern sounded genuine. "The road back from where Ruth has been will not be easy."

"Then you understand why one should have patience—" Phoebe bit off the words. She had already said too much.

"As long as Ruth isn't going back to what she used to do," Fannie agreed.

"I don't think she will." Phoebe's heart pounded. That was the truth, even if Ruth gave in to temptation and went out with Ethan tonight. She had to believe this, but if Fannie knew...

Fannie was looking at her strangely.

"We'll have to pray for Ruth," Phoebe finished. She rose to her feet. "I really have to either get back or help you so I don't feel useless."

"Talking about these things is not time wasted," Fannie assured her. "The heart needs tending from time to time."

"I'm sure it does." Phoebe gulped down the last of her hot chocolate. "Thank you so much for your council and your listening ear, Fannie. Also for what you told me."

"Anytime." Fannie followed her into the living room. "I'll be praying for your family's healing and restoration."

"We sure need it," Phoebe agreed. She stopped to give Mary a quick hug. "You get better, now."

"I *am* better," Mary declared, sitting up on the couch.

Phoebe left her and whispered to Fannie at the front door. "You are the perfect deacon's *frau*."

"I don't know about that," Fannie demurred. She waved from the front porch as Phoebe made her way down the walk.

The barn was empty when Phoebe stepped inside, but Misty whinnied from the closest stall. Phoebe led her out and hitched the horse to the buggy, and then they left the lane and turned east.

David came to the barn door when she arrived back in Grandma's driveway. He took Misty's bridle as she climbed down.

"Did you have a nice vis—"

"David, you have to speak with Ruth this afternoon!" The words burst out. "She can't go out with Ethan tonight."

"I agree, but I can't stop her, Phoebe. Do Fannie and Deacon Matthew know?"

"No, but I came close to both spilling the beans and lying." Phoebe rubbed her forehead. "I'm dizzy from lack of sleep, and heart-to-heart conversations don't help."

"You need to talk to someone," he said. "About us."

"David!" She came closer. "I know how I feel about you."

He tilted his head sideways. "We've been dodging bullets all week, Phoebe. You know the questions are there." He paused to sweep his gaze over the place. "Grandma Lapp only asked me to help you, not to—"

She laid her hand on his arm. "David, what can I say? Not much, but we..." The words fizzled out under his intense gaze.

"Do you know how much I love you, Phoebe?"

"*Yah*," she whispered. "And there's nothing wrong with that."

He didn't answer but came closer to touch her face. She lifted her head until her lips touched his, and he let go of Misty's bridle to pull Phoebe close. His strength filled her whole body, and they clung to each other.

"David!" She tried to breathe. "See! There is nothing wrong with your love for me, or with my love for you."

His fingers traced her cheek. "I will speak with Ruth after she gets home from school. You are right. She can't go out with Ethan. That would—"

"It would," she agreed. "And this has been a *goot* week, even with all the trouble. The Lord is with us."

"To many more then." He grasped Misty's bridle again. "I'll be leaving in an hour. I have to help *Daett* on the farm, and there isn't much that needs doing around here."

She nodded but stopped him with a touch on the arm. "I have to tell you something else, David."

"*Yah?*" Concern rippled across his face.

"Fannie just told me that your *daett*'s carelessness was at fault in my Grandfather Tobias's death." From there, the story spilled out quickly.

"So that is what's been going on," David muttered when she finished. "Now I am doomed."

She reached for him with both hands. "Don't say that. This changes nothing between us."

He was clearly unconvinced.

"Remember a moment ago, what we shared? I'm telling you about Grandfather Tobias only because we must have no secrets between us. Our love will survive everything but lies."

Hope filled his face. "You are like your grandma."

"I am Phoebe, and I love you."

His hand trembled in hers.

"I'll see you on Monday when the van comes." She gave him a warm smile and raced back to the house.

Once she was inside, Phoebe found the prayer journal and paged through it until she found the correct date. The words were there written plainly.

O God of heaven, the agony of my soul tears me apart. The death of my Tobias, the ripping of our love to pieces while it lay young in our hearts through the foolishness of an exceedingly foolish and careless man. How can I forgive the reckless squandering of such glory? How can I look the man in his face and tell him that I have let go and require no vengeance? How can I go on with empty arms while his are full?

How can I, oh God? How can I, and yet I must.

TWENTY-NINE

The late evening dusk hung on the horizon as David made his way north on foot. At the junction he turned right onto Peckville Road. Ruth must still be at the schoolhouse. His sister would likely remain there until dark on the pretense of some schoolwork. After that, she would have Ethan pick her up on the walk home for a few hours spent in town—unless David could persuade her otherwise. He had promised Phoebe he would try, and even after the shocking news of *Daett*'s past mistakes, he must make it work with her. *Daett*'s failures must not be his. If Ruth jumped the fence from her exalted position as the community's schoolteacher, it could jeopardize his relationship with Phoebe. The memory of Phoebe's sweet face so close to his only moments ago quickened his steps.

David paused to look back at Grandma Lapp's farm. Many were the happy hours he had spent there in his childhood. What sacrifices the woman had made, while her own heart was bruised and broken. Ruth had been with him for most of those times, but the effect had been different on his sister. Grandma Lapp's kindness had healed the deep hurt in his heart, but Ruth had seemed to react in the opposite way. Perhaps the contrast between the community's rejection and Grandma Lapp's acceptance had only made things worse.

Ruth had always wanted to leave. When the school board had offered her the teaching position, she had changed her mind for a moment. But her heart had already left. He knew this, and therein lay the problem. Did he dare ask his sister to forsake her love so he could find the same? Was that not too much of a sacrifice to ask of any human being?

David sighed and turned his footsteps toward the schoolhouse again. Never had he dreamed that a woman like Phoebe would give him a second glance. Not even Grandma Lapp's kindness had persuaded him. But maybe her confidence in him had given him the courage to believe Phoebe when she opened her heart to him. He had held her in his arms now, and kissed her. This was much more than he deserved—a thousand times more. David took another look over his shoulder at Grandma Lapp's farm. The Lord had truly made a *wunderbah* thing when He created a woman's love.

He wished to wed Phoebe, and she seemed to have no objections. She knew where their feelings would lead. An Amish woman didn't play with a man's heart only to withdraw her hand at the last moment. But he and Phoebe needed the approval of her family. They couldn't elope. He didn't wish to. He wanted the simple life of the community. He wanted to fall into routines along with others of like faith, to grow old in the traditions that had served so many generations before them.

David glanced toward the darkened sky in the west. Could he ask Ruth the question that must be asked? Did she really love Ethan the way he loved Phoebe? Somehow he would have to find the courage to say the words, and if the answer went against him, he would have to live with the consequences.

A light was on at the Yoders' house, but David didn't pause. If they noticed him visiting his sister at the schoolhouse this late, they would likely think it was a perfectly normal thing to do. He turned in the lane and crossed the playground. So much had happened here this week—the drama with little Mary's injury and Phoebe's deep concern for Ruth. The woman had her grandma's tender heart. He had known that for a long time, almost since the day Phoebe arrived from Lancaster. She hadn't noticed him back then, but he didn't blame her. Phoebe had unfolded like the petals of a rose blossom since she had taken on the responsibilities of the farm. Grandma Lapp must have known she would. Thankfully, he had waited with patience in his heart for the beauty that he now could hold in his arms.

David entered the schoolhouse with only a brief knock. Ruth must have seen him approach because there was no surprised look on her face.

"Hi," he greeted her. "How are you doing?"

"You might as well come right out and say it," she retorted. "Don't go out with Ethan tonight!"

He attempted a smile and slid onto the seat of a student's desk. "Actually, I have a question. Do you love him the way I love Phoebe?"

She looked surprised. "Now, that I didn't expect."

"That is the question."

She studied her papers and didn't respond.

"Perhaps you love this job, then?" His hand covered the schoolhouse in a quick sweep. "That would be a *goot* thing."

"Or out there," she added. "Why does it always come down to us and them, David?"

"Don't count me in, Ruth. I'm on their side for this round."

"So you've forsaken me?"

"This is what I want. This world..." He raised his hand again. "And Phoebe, of course."

"Have you kissed her yet?" she teased.

His red face was enough of an answer.

"Just think," she mused. "A Fisher boy kissing a Lapp girl. My, my, how things have changed."

"And you are teaching school," he added.

"We can't forget that!" Her voice was bitter.

He sighed. "Can't you let them go, Ruth—all those years of our youth? You know things have changed, and other people also have their problems. Look at Homer Lapp's boy this week. I don't think a sibling of ours has spent time in jail in recent memory. *Daett* has his own problems, and we should leave those to him."

"That's just it," she spat. "That's been true for years. Back when we did nothing worse than being born to Leroy Fisher. Yet they made us..." She sputtered to a halt.

"It wasn't that bad," he objected. "And *Daett* did something pretty awful."

"Says you, who suffered the worst." Her glare could have melted the vinyl floor were it not directed out of the window.

"Is that why you can't let go, Ruth? Because of me? Because you saw me suffer?"

A tear trickled down her cheek. "Maybe. You were the oldest, and it wasn't fair, David. You were as handsome and charming and dashing as the rest..."

"But we were Leroy Fisher's children," he finished. "That's behind us, Ruth. Grandma Lapp has seen to that. Why throw it away?"

Her gaze pierced him. "You have a Lapp girl to console you. Do you see anyone taking a chance on me?"

"You are beautiful. You always have been."

"Says my brother. You didn't see Albert Mast saying so when he got ready to settle down."

David searched his memory. He hadn't been paying attention to Ruth's affections when it came to men. "You cared about Albert?"

"He's a married man now. But *yah*, I would have considered him..." Her voice trailed off, and her gaze scorched the window glass again.

"I'm sorry, Ruth. I really am."

She tried to smile. "It's not your fault. The Lord knows you deserve everything that's fallen your way. Is she sweet to you?"

David looked away as his face flamed.

Ruth's smile was tender. "I wish you nothing but the best. You'll survive even if I don't."

"But I won't," he insisted.

"So you want me to let go of what I have so you can have what you have?"

"It does sound awful," he agreed. "But no. If you love Ethan like I love Phoebe, I wouldn't want you to walk away from that."

"I think that's a high standard to meet." She gave him another smile. "We'll have to see, I guess."

"So you don't know?"

She sobered. "I think you'll make it with or without me, David. Your heart is in the community, unlike mine. It's always been so, and you are being rewarded with the woman of your dreams."

He swallowed, unable to speak.

"Phoebe is like her grandma—if you haven't figured that out yet. That's why I had the courage to speak with her the other morning. I struggle, even if it looks as if I don't. I wonder what is right. I really do. I toss and turn in my bed at night thinking about what I will lose." She nodded her head to indicate the interior of the schoolhouse. "This is what I never dreamed I would have: honor, respect, and trust. It has been handed to me because of you."

"I—" he began, but she stopped him.

"Let's not pretend that's not true. I would not have this if it were not for you and Phoebe. Does that rankle me? I'll be honest. *Yah*. Do I owe you a debt? *Yah*, again. But do you want me to make my decision based on my obligation to you?"

"I want you to let go of your bitterness. That's all I ask. And whatever happens, happens."

She came close to kiss him on the cheek. He saw tears glistening in her eyes. "You are the best, big brother. The Lord won't take Phoebe from you. The Lord couldn't."

He stood. "I'd best be going, then. I've said what I wanted to say."

"Did you promise Phoebe you would come up?" she guessed.

"*Yah.* But I would have come anyway."

"I know." She stroked his arm. "You'll be okay. They believe in you, but they don't really believe in me."

"I wish you wouldn't say that."

"It's only the truth. I have to face it, David."

He dropped his gaze. "I don't know what to say to that."

"You don't have to say anything. Are you stopping in at Phoebe's place on the way back?"

He hesitated. "I hadn't thought of that."

"You should let her know tonight that you spoke with me. Tell her what I told you."

"That we'll make it?"

She laughed. "I guess that is a little forward."

"I wish you would treasure the lives we have, Ruth. What has been given to us doesn't compare to what is out there."

Her tears came again. "Your faith is a beautiful thing, David. I just don't know if I share it."

"But you can."

"I am not you, David. Nor am I Phoebe."

"You are you, Ruth. You don't belong with Ethan."

Her face hardened. "I have to decide that. Not you, or Phoebe, or anyone else."

"I agree," he said, stepping back. "I should be going. I'll keep the back door unlocked."

"Thank you." She tried to smile. "And thanks to both you and Phoebe for giving me the room to decide. You should stop and tell her that."

"Good night." He placed his hand on the doorknob, turned it, and went out into the darkness. The dim light from the gas lantern inside cast his shadow until he reached the playground. He paused to allow his eyes to adjust and continued cautiously. A few moments later his shoe dinged on home plate. With his hands outstretched he avoided the swing set and found his way back to Peckville Road.

The starlight helped as he headed westward. Should he follow Ruth's suggestion and stop in to see Phoebe? The hour wasn't that late, but still. What would he tell her? Much of the conversation couldn't be repeated, especially Ruth's assurances that his and Phoebe's relationship would survive if Ruth jumped the fence. They loved each other, but such words should not be spoken at this junction of the road. If Phoebe were his promised one, then maybe.

He must pray in this hour of need. Grandma Lapp had been a praying woman. Maybe that was why Phoebe had opened her heart to him, and where he found the courage to believe. Phoebe would wish to pray with him tonight.

David turned north, and a few minutes later his feet crunched on the gravel of Grandma Lapp's driveway. Phoebe cracked the front door open to his tentative knock. "Who is it?"

"David," he whispered. "I'm on my way home from seeing Ruth."

The door opened all the way. "You will come in then."

He stepped inside. "Just for a minute. We must pray."

She met his anxious gaze and took his hand. "Is Ruth struggling with her decision?"

He nodded.

"Do you want to sit on the couch?"

"I shouldn't stay," he objected. "I just wanted to let you know."

"We can pray now," she said, still holding his hand.

He hesitated before he bowed his head. Her tenderness overwhelmed him, and the words wouldn't come.

"Dear Lord," she whispered. "You know Ruth's heart better than we do. Bring hope and healing whatever she decides tonight. Let her not regret the decision she has to make, and take away all the bitterness. Forgive us our sins, Lord, as we forgive those who have wronged us, and we thank You for what You have done in the past, and for what You will do in the future. Thank You for being with us this week in our troubles—and whatever comes, give David and me the courage to face those challenges. Amen."

"Amen," he echoed.

She still held his hand with her eyes closed.

"Send Your angels to minister to Ruth tonight," he began. "Let her see clearly what lies ahead, and help her make the right choice, whatever that is. And help me go on." His voice broke, and her hand tightened in his. "And thank You, Lord," he continued. "I know You will help me."

She was smiling up at him when he opened his eyes. "We'll make it, David."

He nodded and stepped back out into the darkness again as the door closed softly behind him.

THIRTY

An hour later Ruth found her way out of the schoolhouse lane and slipped down Peckville Road. The lanterns were still lit in the Yoders' house, but that was no surprise. They were known for their industriousness and late work hours. At home *Daett* would have retired by now. To his credit, *Daett* rose before dawn, but that didn't necessarily ensure success. He should have plied some trade other than farming, maybe a harness shop or a bulk food store. *Daett* would have been *goot* with numbers and people, but he was who he was. The lessons of farming had never taken.

The opinion of the community was correct. *Daett* did mow his hay the day before the rains arrived. Sometimes he missed the dreaded occurrence, but usually not. Others could call the weather to the hour and have their hay mower in the field while the last drops of the spring showers cleared the sky. *Daett* waited, cautious as ever, wanting to see the sun well up, and the fields dried out before he ventured forth. By the time his hay was on the ground, the others were ready to bale, and storm clouds gathered on the horizon again. *Daett* would stand in stunned disbelief as the others threw the last of their hay bales into the barn loft, while he watched his almost dried hay swell with the soaking rain.

Surely he must have tried to change his ways, but he couldn't. His instincts of caution drove all else from his mind. Was this why she was so reckless, wanting to walk anywhere but in her father's footsteps, wanting to escape the shame of the years?

"She's Leroy Fisher's daughter." How often the words had been whispered within her hearing. She first heard them being spoken by children on the school playground, advising their visiting cousins or some new family who had moved into the valley, of who was whom.

"He cuts his hay in the rain," had been a child's interpretation of her father's doings.

Which was close enough. The pain was what mattered, the deep cutting sensation of knowing that the man who had given you life didn't know what he was doing. What hope was there after that? She was a mistake at best. Ruth pressed back tears and left the Yoders' lantern light behind to hurry down Peckville Road. Ethan was to meet her at the junction below the schoolhouse in ten minutes. She would be there ahead of time. Perhaps as she waited she would shed these bitter memories. Her brother didn't seem to suffer from them, which was *goot*. She wanted happiness and joy for David and Phoebe. He wouldn't be like *Daett*. Already he knew farming. Didn't Grandma Lapp's acres prosper under David's care, and now the venture with the *Englisha* children? David was a success, and Phoebe had noticed before anyone else did. This was to her credit, but no one had noticed Ruth until David's shadow reached her. She would not hold this against him but against the community. The pain had always come from home.

Ruth stopped short at the sound of a horse's hooves beating from the north. Buggy lights turned down Peckville road moments later. Who would be out this late? She pulled her head up high. She was the community's schoolteacher, on her way home from work. She would not be ashamed of herself. No one need know about her evening plans.

Ruth stepped to the side of the road as the buggy came closer and slowed. The horse stopped across from her, the reins taut. "*Goot* evening, Ruth," Deacon Matthew called out cheerfully. "Heading home from a hard day's work?"

"*Yah.*" She managed to smile as she turned her face toward the buggy lights. She had not lied.

Deacon Matthew chuckled. "I'm out a little late myself. Going up to the Yoders' place, but they should still be up." The chuckle deepened.

"They had lights on moments ago," Ruth replied. "How's Mary?"

"Getting along. How are you doing after the accident this week?" The deacon's voice was concerned.

"Okay, I guess. I spend more time on the playground."

"That's *goot*, but you must not blame yourself. The injury could have happened no matter what."

"I suppose so. But I still should have been out with the students. I'm sorry about that."

"I'm glad to see your *goot* heart demonstrated." Deacon Matthew clucked to his horse. "I should be going. It's late, you know."

She attempted another smile, but he had already let out the reins. Ruth watched the lights retreat and grow dim in the distance. She was the community's schoolteacher. There was no other reason for Deacon Matthew's friendliness. Months ago he wouldn't have pulled to stop for conversation if he had passed her on the road. Couldn't people see her behind the family's reputation? Apparently not. Nor could any men of marriageable age. There were too many other options available to take a chance on one whose *daett* was such a disgrace.

Ruth forced her steps forward. She would go out with Ethan tonight and forget all of this—at least for a few hours. He might have another concert they could attend until the early morning. David might suffer from her choice, but he would survive. Phoebe would see to that, while she...

Ruth paused as headlights appeared from the south, but they didn't slow when they drew closer. The car roared past, and darkness settled again. Ethan would arrive any moment. The intersection ahead was visible in the starlight, and he wouldn't be scared away by Deacon Matthew's passing. Ethan would laugh at such fears, but he hadn't grown up under the community's watchful eye or tender loving care.

Ruth laughed bitterly. She needed a distraction. Badly! So where was Ethan? He should have been here by now. He wasn't known for his tardiness. She paced across the intersection to peer into the darkness in either direction. There were no headlights anywhere. Should she return to the schoolhouse? But she would miss him if he was in one of the passing vehicles.

Ruth thought of the phone shack near the schoolhouse. She could call his cell phone from there and keep a watchful eye on the road at the same time. Ruth turned her steps backward when buggy lights came out of the Yoders' driveway ahead of her. This would not work. With a wild look around her, she fled into the ditch and hid behind a growth of bushes. What a fix she'd be in if Ethan chose this moment to make his entrance. She could imagine him stopping and asking Deacon Matthew if he had seen her on the road. That's how little Ethan understood or was willing to learn about her people.

Deacon Matthew's horse passed with a steady clip of hooves on the pavement. Ruth didn't move until the buggy lights were out of sight. There was still no sign of Ethan. Ruth moved forward again but stopped a few feet away from the shadowy phone booth. A record would be kept of the call, but she would take the chance.

Ruth opened the door and punched the numbers in by starlight. The phone rang in her ear, once, twice...nothing. Finally, Ethan's voice mail greeting: "You have reached Ethan. Please leave a message."

Was the man on call? Had an emergency come up? There would

have been no way to notify her. Or had he forgotten about their date? Ruth grimaced. That was not like the man she knew, and Ethan wasn't unkind. Not like the community.

He was an oasis, a calm in the storm, a hope where she had never had one before. Ethan gave her new life, the promise of a fresh start, a way out where only pain and suffering existed.

Ruth paced and waited. She walked down to the junction and back again. She dialed once more with the same result. How could he know she called from the phone shack? He wouldn't know the number, so he would pick up. Unless...Ruth took a breath. The pain was too much. There must be some explanation. Ethan had never done this to her. His word was his word. They trusted each other. They were friends. They would work through this. Yet he wasn't here. She must give him the benefit of the doubt. The dawn would arrive, and he would have an excuse that made sense.

The barn door across from the road burst open, and the lantern light spilled across the yard. Ruth gasped and threw herself behind the phone shack. Thankfully, the thin plywood sides kept out the light and could hide her securely. Unless she already had been seen? In which case, there was no ready explanation for why the community's schoolteacher would hide behind the phone shack at ten thirty on a Friday evening. The Yoders would have a field of gossip about that, and Deacon Matthew would become involved.

There was no way she could talk herself out of this situation. Especially since Deacon Matthew had seen her earlier heading harmlessly toward home. Perhaps the hour for the truth had arrived. The moment would be a relief in a way. No more sneaking around. She would be out of a schoolteaching job on Monday morning, but she could join Ethan in his world without a backward glance.

Ruth held her breath as footsteps approached and entered the phone shack. Numbers were punched, and the faint ring of a phone reached her ears.

"Hi, sweetheart," the youngest of the Yoder boys, John, said plainly enough.

Ruth stilled a gasp. Now she was listening to a private conversation. Could things get worse?

"*Yah*, I'm missing you too," John cooed, "but I can't get away tonight. Tomorrow night maybe."

John wasn't of *rumspringa* age yet. The boy couldn't be more than fifteen. Maybe fourteen. Hadn't he been in school last year in the eighth grade?

"What are you doing tonight?" John continued sweetly. "Thinking about me?"

There was soft laughter. Apparently John was having endearments whispered into his ear.

Did Emil Yoder approve of his youngest son's early foray into *rumspringa*? Did Emil even know? Ruth's mind swirled, and her anger stirred.

"You'll be picking me up down at the junction then," John was saying. "The usual time, *yah*? Dim your lights. Don't forget." There was silence for a few moments, then, "You're sweet, dearest. The sweetest and the best."

Young John had a sugar tongue for sure. He'd be able to talk milk out of a bull cow.

Ruth dug her fingers into the ground. She had to keep her anger in check. Nothing would be gained by an explosion, and no explanation would save her reputation—unjust though this all was.

John was wrapping up his conversation. "You sleep tight now, dear heart. Love you. Remember that. Always and forever."

Ruth heard deep chuckles and a kissing sound coming through the receiver. She stilled a bitter protest as the phone clicked and young John laughed. "Isn't she the sweetest? They don't make Amish girls like that."

Ruth's fingers twitched. She wasn't going to move. She couldn't.

His footsteps faded away along with the glare of the lantern he'd brought with him. Ruth peeked around the edge of the phone shack, and when the light went behind a clump of trees, she fled down the road. Here she was, running away when John was at fault. But if he ever learned that she had listened in to his conversation, her reputation wouldn't survive even though she was the community's schoolteacher.

Ruth paused to catch her breath at the junction. There was still no sign of Ethan. He wasn't coming. She might as well face the facts. She knew he answered his phone even when he was on emergency calls. He didn't want to speak with her tonight. She might as well bear the pain. Right now there was only numbness from this rejection, this dashing of high hopes and dreams. Not once in her life had she known a man who truly loved her. Tears stung again as Ruth pushed her feet southward toward home. Only, Leroy Fisher's place wasn't home to her. Nowhere was home. Not really. The north, the south, the east, the west—what difference did it make?

THIRTY-ONE

Phoebe stood on the front porch on Monday morning and waved as Ethan drove the van into the driveway. David stood silently beside her.

"Good morning, folks." Ethan hopped out. "I have Wesley with me this morning." He helped the boy down and patted him on the head.

The new arrival, a young boy of ten, seemed frozen to the ground where Ethan left him. David approached their latest charge while Ethan lowered Wesley's suitcase to the ground and motioned for Phoebe to follow him behind the van.

"I think you can handle Wesley, but I have to mention this. The boy has a speech impediment. He stutters. We think that a week on the farm may do him more good than the psychological counseling and speech therapy we've been giving him."

Phoebe shrugged. "A lot of young boys stutter."

"There you go. You are just the right people for him." Ethan gave her a bright smile and hopped back in the van to drive out of the lane. Phoebe followed Ethan's progress as he disappeared from sight. Wesley seemed like a small problem compared to the weight that had been on her shoulders all weekend. What had Ruth's decision been last Friday? There hadn't been time to ask David before Ethan arrived. Surely Ruth had made the correct choice and cut off her relationship with Ethan. This would explain why David had been late this morning. He must have been encouraging his sister's broken heart. Ethan's abrupt departure pointed toward this conclusion.

Phoebe stepped closer to David and ruffled Wesley's hair. "Shall I fix you some breakfast?"

Wesley didn't move. He appeared to be in shock after being left alone with two strange Amish people. She would be petrified herself in such a situation. But they had all week to get to know Wesley better. Who knew what great things the Lord had in mind for all of them? Hadn't *goot* things come about before? She was confident they would arrive again this week, even with only one child in their care.

"Are you sure you're not hungry?" she tried again. "And we have ponies in the barn."

Wesley didn't look up. "Your Aunt Millie's coming," David muttered, and Phoebe glanced toward the north. Sure enough, a buggy had appeared and turned into the driveway.

Aunt Millie had said nothing at the Sunday services about a morning visit. What could her aunt want? David didn't say anything, but he hurried down the walk as Aunt Millie came to a stop.

"Are you okay?" Phoebe inquired of Wesley. "This is my aunt visiting, and we all drive a horse and buggy."

Wesley still didn't respond. Phoebe reached for his hand. "Do you want to come with me? We have to say hi to my Aunt Millie."

Wesley's hand moved and slipped into Phoebe's. Finally there was a response. She slowly moved down the walk with Wesley by her side. Aunt Millie waited for them in the buggy while David held her horse's bridle.

"*Goot* morning," Phoebe greeted her.

"*Goot* morning," Aunt Millie responded as she hopped out of the buggy. "Who have we here?" She gave Wesley a bright smile.

Wesley stared but said nothing.

Phoebe mouthed, "I think he's scared. He stutters."

"Oh," Aunt Millie responded. "Did I come at a bad time?"

"I don't think so." Phoebe brightened. "I believe Wesley might be hungry. Maybe you can help with breakfast?"

Aunt Millie mouthed the words this time. "And draw him out of his shell?"

Phoebe nodded. "Do you have the time? I don't know why you came over, but—"

"I'll make the time," Aunt Millie assured Phoebe. "Come," she addressed Wesley. "Surely all little boys like to eat hot breakfasts right off the stove?"

The first smile flickered on Wesley's face.

"See, you are good for him," Phoebe said in Pennsylvania Dutch. Wesley gave her a strange look.

"Sorry," she told him. "I didn't say anything bad about you."

Aunt Millie smiled at him. "We speak another language, but don't worry. This is a safe place, and Phoebe takes *goot* care of little children."

"Shall we go then?" Phoebe led the way toward the house in answer to her own question. "So why did you stop by this morning?"

"I just had to check on you." Aunt Millie made a face. "Nothing in particular, but with Eugene's arraignment in court this morning, it seemed like the right idea. Trouble always comes in bunches, it seems."

"You don't think so," Phoebe responded with a quick glance toward Wesley. Aunt Millie was overreacting. "He's harmless enough," she said in Pennsylvania Dutch.

Aunt Millie whispered in the same language. "*Englisha* children have been known to burn down houses before. I've heard the stories."

Phoebe forced a laugh. "You came over because of that?"

"I know I'm silly." Aunt Millie sighed. "My nerves are raw with Eugene's problem, and now you have a child in your care who stutters. Maybe I do have some reasons for concern."

"Lots of Amish boys stutter," Phoebe told her. "But we need to stop talking about him in a language he doesn't understand."

"Don't worry about us," Aunt Millie said in Wesley's direction. "We are just chattering away."

Wesley's face didn't register any emotion.

"Let me get David," Phoebe suggested. "We can eat together and figure this out before you leave. That way, you don't have to worry."

"That's a great plan." Aunt Millie appeared relieved.

"I'll be right back," Phoebe told them before she hurried toward the barn.

She left Aunt Millie bending down in front of Wesley, speaking gently. "In just a moment Phoebe will be back, and we'll have breakfast cooking on the wood stove with smoke curling..."

Phoebe moved out of earshot and pushed open the barn door. "David!" she called.

"What is it?" he asked, appearing suddenly in front of her.

"Breakfast," she told him. "Why don't you come in, and we can eat together. Aunt Millie is worried about Eugene's court date this morning, and we have a scared child on our hands who has a stuttering problem. You would be *goot* for him."

"I think your aunt has charmed him." David grinned, having stepped to the barn door to peer out.

Phoebe joined him and agreed. "I think she has. So are you coming?"

He shook his head. "I've had breakfast."

"David."

"I can't this morning, Phoebe. Please?" he begged. "Wesley will be okay. Millie will figure out something."

She changed the subject. "I'm assuming Ruth ended her relationship with Ethan."

"I don't know," he replied. "She wouldn't talk all weekend, but she came in early on Friday night. Well, before midnight."

"Thank You, dear Lord," Phoebe whispered toward the heavens.

"She's hurting, though," David added. "We should pray for Ruth. I don't think her battles are over."

"I know." Phoebe sobered and gave his hand a quick squeeze. "But that was a brave choice she made."

"If she did," David cautioned.

"We should still pray," Phoebe told him. "And I should go help with breakfast. Looks like we have a long week ahead of us, but the Lord will help us."

"You should go." David motioned toward the house, where Aunt Millie stood on the front porch with Wesley's hand in hers.

Phoebe gave him a gentle smile. "So maybe a pony ride is what he needs after breakfast."

"Go," he said. "I'll have them ready."

"I love you," she whispered, and he smiled.

Phoebe made her way back up the walkway with a brief glance over her shoulder. David was troubled because of his sister, as he should be. She would walk up to the schoolhouse this afternoon and speak with Ruth. That was the least she could do. Too much sorrow was not *goot* for anyone. Sharing would lighten Ruth's load, even if she wasn't willing to open fully to anyone about her troubles.

Phoebe entered the house to find Wesley ensconced at the kitchen table with a hint of a smile on his face. Aunt Millie had kept up a constant chatter from the sound of things. "These are eggs." She pulled one out of the carton. "And this is bacon." Aunt Millie displayed a sliced piece.

Wesley had to have seen these items before. This was her aunt's way of keeping the tension out of the air.

"How are you doing?" Phoebe asked Wesley.

The hint of a smile faded.

Phoebe pulled out a chair to sit beside him. "Did you know the man who dropped you off, Wesley? His name is Ethan Thompson."

There was a slight shake of the head.

"Do you know Mrs. Broman? Have you met her?"

Again the shake.

Phoebe reached over to lay her hand on his. "I want you to know that you are very welcome in our house for the week. This is my Aunt Millie, and I live here alone. She came over to check on us, and she is staying to help with breakfast. The man outside is David. He comes up each day to help out. He's a very nice person."

Aunt Millie made a face at her as the bacon splattered in the pan.

"Well, he is." Phoebe tried for a lighthearted tone. "And your breakfast is the exact thing we need to begin a *wunderbah* week."

Wesley didn't show any emotion, but Aunt Millie smiled. "Thanks. That's kind of you to say."

Phoebe gave her aunt a quick glance. Last week had taken a bigger toll on her family than she had suspected. Aunt Millie was usually a bundle of confidence. Praise was the last thing her aunt usually needed.

Phoebe stood to slip her arm around Aunt Millie's shoulders. "I'm so sorry for what happened last week. Should we pray for a *goot* outcome from the court date this morning?"

Aunt Millie glanced at the clock on the kitchen wall. "It's at ten." She gave a little gasp and buried her face in Phoebe's shoulder for a moment. "Sorry to be so overcome, but if there is a jail sentence by the time this is all over...we've never had a Lapp child in jail before." Aunt Millie ended in a whimper.

"Dear Lord, help us," Phoebe prayed quietly.

"Amen," Aunt Millie echoed. "I feel better already being in *Mamm*'s house. She was such a praying woman, and you've so taken after her. The courage you have, Phoebe." Aunt Millie glanced at Wesley and then quickly looked away to crack open an egg. "Thanks for reminding me about prayer. One can so easily forget when real trouble strikes."

"Wh-wh-what? Who is in jail?" The stammering voice came from the kitchen table.

Both Phoebe and Aunt Millie turned to give him kind smiles.

"You poor child," Aunt Millie cooed. "It's okay." She lifted his chin to look at him. "My nephew is the one who will be in court today. He did a very wicked deed last week and stole someone's car. He—" Aunt Millie's voice broke, and she sat down beside Wesley. "It's hard on all of us, thinking about Eugene going to jail."

"So-so-so, he got ca-ca-caught?" Wesley asked.

Aunt Millie stroked his face and drew him close. "It doesn't matter if Eugene got caught or not, dear. It's the stealing that was very bad. That's wrong whether anyone finds out or not."

Wesley didn't appear convinced, but he remained silent.

"Breakfast is almost ready," Aunt Millie told him. "Phoebe already ate, but I can always use some more. Shall I eat with you?"

Wesley nodded, his smile broader this time.

"How about pancakes?" Aunt Millie asked him. "Shall I make you some?"

"Th-this is g-good enough," Wesley said.

Aunt Millie gave him another hug. Phoebe turned to leave the kitchen, but she paused when Aunt Millie's footsteps followed her.

"I just had the perfect idea," Aunt Millie whispered in Phoebe's ear. "Come over for supper at our place tonight, and bring Wesley with you. We all need comforting after this horrible court date, so I'll invite Homer and Noah and their families. We'll find peace in one another's company and encourage our hearts together. That would also do Wesley wonders, I'm thinking."

Phoebe gave Aunt Millie a hug. "I knew there was a reason you came over this morning. The Lord had His hand guiding us all the time."

"*Yah*, He did," Aunt Millie agreed. "And now I'd best get back to Wesley."

"I'll be in the barn when you're done," Phoebe told her. "Wesley might be ready for a pony ride after your *wunderbah* mothering this morning."

Aunt Millie was already halfway to the kitchen, so she didn't respond to the praise even if she heard it. Phoebe slipped out of the house to find David busy in the barn running a brush over the ponies.

"Wesley stutters badly," she told him.

He winced. "The poor boy."

"Maybe we can help him this week," she suggested. "Although I don't know where to begin."

"We can pray," David replied, smiling.

Phoebe nodded. "Aunt Millie has invited us to supper tonight at her place. I think you should come."

"I will."

"I'm glad you're with me this week, David, walking through these problems."

"It is an honor, Phoebe," he said, smiling again.

THIRTY-TWO

Phoebe paused to squint into the late afternoon sun. She waved toward the pasture, where David had his hand on Wesley's back. The boy appeared expertly balanced on the pony, and David grinned and waved back. This was not Wesley's first ride of the day. David had worked for hours to reach this point. Wesley had bonded so well with Aunt Millie this morning and with David once Aunt Millie had left that Phoebe had kept her distance. Too much pressure wasn't *goot*, and a relationship with David seemed the proper next step. She would have plenty of time as the week progressed to nurture her friendship with Wesley.

Phoebe waved one last time before she headed south and turned left at the junction. She stopped in at the phone shack and called the number Mrs. Broman had left her to report on the evening outing with Wesley.

"*Yah*," she told the secretary who answered. "I am taking Wesley to my aunt's place for supper. Not for overnight, just an evening visit." She paused, listening to the woman on the other end of the call. "So no problem then? Thank you."

Phoebe stepped out of the shack. Schoolchildren filled Peckville

Road ahead of her, so she had timed the visit perfectly. Ruth could probably use a short break to catch her breath after a long day of classes.

Phoebe smiled and nodded to the schoolchildren as they passed her. Most of them were on foot, but an occasional buggy trotted by filled with youngsters. Young John was outside the Yoders' barn when he hollered out, "How's it going there, Phoebe?"

"*Goot!*" she answered. John was a friendly fellow, due to begin his *rumspringa* soon.

Phoebe's face clouded as she headed up the schoolhouse lane. Would John end up like Eugene—in trouble with the law? The boys were close to the same age. Surely some new trend had not been established by Eugene's transgressions. So far, there had been no word yet on the morning's court proceedings.

Phoebe pasted on a smile to knock on the schoolhouse door.

"Come in," Ruth called out.

Phoebe entered. She closed the door gently behind her. "How are you doing?"

Ruth leaned back in her teacher's chair. "I'm just a little tired." She had dark rings under her eyes, so she was obviously understating things.

"I thought I'd run up and say hi. We have a new boy this week. His name is Wesley. David is giving him a pony ride right now."

"That's *goot*." Ruth attempted a smile, but the effort failed.

Phoebe paused a moment before saying, "Ethan dropped him off this morning."

Ruth's face darkened, and she focused on the papers in front of her.

"How are things between you?" Phoebe ventured. "I'm assuming..."

"We'd best not discuss that," Ruth snapped. "The less said the better."

"It can be hard, doing the right thing." Phoebe stepped closer. "I'm sorry for how this must be hurting you."

Ruth raised her head. "I appreciate your concern, Phoebe, but we shouldn't talk about this. I've already said too much."

"I know you must feel awful, Ruth, so don't take this the wrong way, but with the choice you made last week, the worst should be over."

"How do you know what my choice was?" Ruth's words were clipped.

"David said you came in early that night. I'm sorry if that's interfering, but I was concerned, as was he."

"Considering that your lives were on the line, I can understand that." Sarcasm dripped from her words.

"The Lord would have taken care of us," Phoebe assured her. "That's what I told David."

"You did?" Ruth's face softened. "It seems as though you and I were on the same page. I told him much the same thing. There's nothing a Lapp can't weather, or a Yoder." Ruth's gaze moved across the road, toward young John as he drove his team of horses into the back field.

"Eugene had his court date this morning, Ruth. No one is above failing. You should know that."

"Knowing it and having the community believe it are two different things. Maybe I can snag me a Yoder for a boyfriend." Ruth's laugh was bitter. "As if that is going to happen."

"I am really sorry about all this," Phoebe tried again. "I know it's not right the way things have been, but..." She stopped. There was no reason to belabor the point.

Ruth took a deep breath. "*Yah*, I know. I am the community's schoolteacher. Be thankful."

"I didn't mean to chide you."

Ruth was silent for a moment. "I didn't go out with Ethan on

Friday night because he didn't come by to pick me up, Phoebe. That's not very virtuous the last time I checked."

"Oh!" Phoebe rushed forward to stand by Ruth's chair. "He jilted you?"

Ruth gave a muffled choke. "Something like that. But you should be happy."

"Not over an awful thing like that. Let me give you a hug." Phoebe leaned over to pull Ruth into her arms.

"I don't need that," Ruth objected.

"It's all I have to give."

"I'm not making any promises about the future," Ruth mumbled. "I tried calling him twice from the phone booth, and he wouldn't answer."

"The Lord will bless you someday with a real love, Ruth. I just know it."

"That's easy for you to say."

"Not really. The road hasn't been easy with either the farm or with following Grandma's dream. And poor Wesley this morning. You should hear him try to talk."

Ruth wiped her eyes. "I know. I shouldn't pity myself."

"I'm not trying to make you feel bad. Why don't you come with us to Aunt Millie's tonight? She's having family over to comfort one another after all our troubles. I'm sure the community's schoolteacher would be welcome."

"And if I wasn't the teacher?"

"I would have you come along even if you weren't a schoolteacher, Ruth. Didn't Grandma feel that way about you?"

Ruth blew her nose before she answered. "Okay. That is true, and you are so much like her. Why not? I'll come."

Phoebe gave Ruth another hug. "Thank you. And now, can I help you with something? I've taken up some of your time, and I don't need to be back just yet. David has things under control."

"I'm fine," Ruth assured her.

"Then I'll be going."

Ruth stopped her. "My brother loves you, Phoebe. You know that, don't you? For that reason alone, I'm glad Ethan didn't show on Friday."

"Don't say that," Phoebe chided. "I wish you no pain."

"You are a kind soul."

"You'll have me crying soon," Phoebe warned.

A hint of a smile played on Ruth's face. "I've changed my mind. Maybe you can help me with some of the schoolwork." Ruth pointed to a stack of papers and a teacher's manual. "Can you check the third-grade spelling papers? That would help a lot, and I wouldn't have an excuse to show up late at your Aunt Millie's."

"I'll do that gladly," Phoebe assured her. She grabbed a red pen before seating herself in one of the smaller chairs.

Silence settled in, broken only by the scrape of chair legs on the hardwood floor and the faint rustle of pen on paper.

"How are they doing?" Ruth finally asked.

"Mostly 80s and a few 90s," Phoebe replied.

"Anything worse?"

Phoebe made a face. "Just one. A 60. The last of the Yoder girls, Darlene."

Ruth's face flared. "I've told that girl *many* times that she has to study, but what does she do? Stares out the window and throws winks at the boys."

"I suppose some children have that attitude," Phoebe allowed.

"The Yoders!" Ruth fumed. "I wasn't going to say this, but I had to hide behind the phone booth on Friday night after I tried to call Ethan, and young John surprised me. You should have heard him carrying on with some *Englisha* girl on the phone. The boy's not even on his *rumspringa* yet."

Phoebe's face paled. "I had feared some such thing after Eugene's capers. They are close, those two. What is going to happen to our young people, Ruth?"

Ruth glared, but she appeared to stifle her bitter words. "I guess I shouldn't be angry. I should be as concerned as you are, Phoebe. You shame me."

Phoebe winced. "I am concerned, but you have suffered more from the community's hands than I have."

"You need to stop saying kind things to me." Ruth lowered her head over her papers and fell silent.

Phoebe waited a few moments before she continued her work. There were no more grades lower than an 85, and she finished the stack and carried it to Ruth's desk. "Anything else?"

Ruth forced a smile and shook her head. "You have done enough. Thank you."

"Shall we pick you up tonight?" Phoebe offered.

Ruth chuckled. "With what? The surrey? Your single buggy will be full with David, Wesley, and yourself."

"That is true, but there's always room for one more." Phoebe attempted a laugh. "Or David can pick you up, and I'll drive myself."

"You'll do no such thing," Ruth retorted. "David would never let me hear the end of it if I deprived him of a buggy ride with you. Has he asked for a formal date yet?"

Phoebe reddened. "No, but we see each other almost every day of the week."

Ruth reached up to squeeze Phoebe's arm. "I know I'm short tempered and bitter about things, but I want to say that I fully approve. David deserves a *wunderbah* woman like you to return his love. The man has a heart the size of an ocean. You'll never regret opening your life to him, Phoebe."

"Now you do have me crying." Phoebe leaned over to give Ruth a kiss on the cheek. "Thank you," she said. She hurried out of the schoolhouse before more tears appeared. That she had not expected from Ruth.

"See you!" Ruth's parting words lingered in the air.

Phoebe waved through the large window and continued across the schoolyard. Young John had his team working busily in the back field, and he gestured heartily as she passed.

A chill crept over her. Why would John already be calling an *Englisha* girl and likely meeting with her in secret? Wasn't a proper *rumspringa* observed among the young people anymore? But on the other hand, she had covered up Ruth's transgressions, and Ruth still wasn't in the clear from the sound of things. What if Ethan changed his mind and made contact with her? Even so, Phoebe shouldn't feel above anyone else. Eugene, Ruth, and John needed her prayers, not her condemnation.

Phoebe breathed a quick prayer and turned north again at the junction. "Help us all, dear Lord." David was still in the field with Wesley when she arrived back at the farm. He had seen her approach and waved a greeting. Phoebe crossed the barnyard instead of heading to the house and leaned against the wooden fence to watch Wesley ride Snow Cloud. The all-white pony's mane streamed out behind them as the two trotted across the field.

"He's doing quite well," David said, walking up to her.

"You are a *goot* teacher." She gave him a warm smile.

He sobered. "If only I could do something about his speech. Isn't there something that can be done? The poor boy tries, but nothing comes out at times."

"There has to be something," Phoebe mused. "Our people usually let such things work themselves out, but I don't think this one will."

David nodded. "How was your talk with Ruth?"

"She wasn't telling you everything," Phoebe told him. She ran over the basics of her conversation with his sister.

"So the storm clouds still hang on the horizon."

"That was my feeling."

"I don't want to lose you, Phoebe." His voice broke.

"You won't, David," she assured him. She reached for his hand. "Things will look better after tonight. Ruth is also coming. I invited her."

"You did?" David appeared pleased. "That was thoughtful of you."

"That's what I am—thoughtful," Phoebe laughed.

He grinned. "That you are, and that's why I love you." He sobered, watching the pony trot by. "That, and a thousand other reasons."

"It looks as if I'd best get myself in the house," Phoebe warned. "You're saying too much, and it's time to get ready to leave for Aunt Millie's. I called and let Mrs. Broman's office know."

"You just want to get away from me," he teased.

"I do not, but..."

"See?"

She raced for the house before his hand could catch hers. They behaved worse than teenagers in love. She was sure he would have kissed her right there in the open if she hadn't fled. She would have allowed the endearment if she had waited a moment longer. But she did love the man, and his care of Wesley warmed her heart. David would be *wunderbah* with *kinner* of his own—with their *kinner*. Her face flamed at the thought. They were nowhere near thinking about marriage yet. The Lord would lead in His time. Their love was young and should not be rushed. With the Lord's blessing, they would have years ahead of them in which to live and grow old together.

Phoebe entered the house and slipped into her room to change into a clean dress. With her hair freshly combed, she refastened her *kapp* and tucked loose strands of hair underneath. David was in front of the barn with Misty in the shafts of the buggy when she came back outside. Phoebe hurried up and fastened the last tug on her side.

"Did you like the pony ride?" She smiled up at Wesley, who had perched himself on the buggy seat.

"It-it was lots and lots and lots of-f-fun." His face glowed.

"I'm glad to hear that," Phoebe told him. "Has David told you where we are going?"

He nodded but fell silent. Still, this was progress from the silent boy of this morning.

"Ready to go?" David chirped in her ear.

She kissed him on the cheek before she hopped into the buggy, and Wesley's grin nearly split his face.

"I like him," she whispered, and Wesley laughed. "See, he approves," Phoebe told David when he climbed in.

David's smile was the only answer she needed. Together, they trotted out the driveway with Wesley between them on the buggy seat.

THIRTY-THREE

The supper table was spread from one end of Aunt Millie's dining room to the other. Only a small space remained behind the chairs on either side so the women could serve the food. Phoebe held a large bowl of steaming mashed potatoes aloft as she maneuvered in from the kitchen.

"Over here!" Uncle Noah hollered out. "We're empty."

Phoebe turned in his direction and deposited the bowl in front of him. "Don't eat it all yourself," she teased.

He chuckled and slapped his stomach. "Do I look like I'd do such a thing?"

"You are quite handsome even with a rolling middle," his *frau* Hettie spoke up from beside him.

Phoebe joined in their laughter. Uncle Noah had no rolling middle. He kept himself in shape from his hours of hard work on the farm. That's why teasing was such fun, especially tonight, when there was such a sense of relief in the air. She hadn't heard the details, but Eugene had been given a suspended sentence this morning, along with a stiff warning from the judge. Much worse could have happened. Their neighbor must have put in a *goot* word after Uncle Homer had paid for the damages to the stolen pickup. No doubt, all those things had been taken into consideration by the judge, coupled with Eugene's sincere apology. The lad was seated across the table at the moment. His head was bowed, and Eugene showed no inclination to join in the merriment—which was how things should be. A proper display of repentance for such a public embarrassment of his family was in order. They would all love and forgive him, and life would go on with its lessons learned.

Ruth deserved the same treatment, which was why she was here at Phoebe's invitation. Ruth was a little nervous being seated beside Uncle Homer's *frau*, Mary, but Ruth would relax as the evening progressed. This had been the right decision, as was Aunt Millie's surprise supper.

"Woo-hoo!" Aunt Millie waved her hand in Phoebe's face. "The next bowl of gravy's ready. Wake up!"

Phoebe pretended to jerk her eyes open.

"So what were you dreaming about?" Aunt Millie asked. "Is Cousin Herman making eyes at you?"

Phoebe awoke for real. "Is he here?"

"Then you didn't notice." Aunt Millie's face fell. "He's sitting right across from you when you walk up to the table."

"I thought he was leaving Sunday for the trip back to Lancaster."

"He stayed over, so I invited him for supper." Aunt Millie batted her eyes. "That must mean he has an interest somewhere..." Aunt Millie let the sentence hang, full of implications. "He's only your cousin by marriage, remember."

"My heart is set on David," Phoebe whispered back. "You'll have to accept that. So no matchmaking."

"I was just hoping..." Aunt Millie made a face. She handed Phoebe the gravy pot. "But David's a decent man too."

"*Yah*, he is," Phoebe retorted. "Thank you for saying so."

Aunt Millie sighed. "Go now. I give up. They're waiting for you, and don't drop off into your dream world."

Phoebe took a firm grip on the gravy pot but didn't move. "Thanks also for letting me invite Ruth tonight. Things are going on in her life that most people don't know about, but it's *goot* that we are kind to her."

"I suppose so," Aunt Millie allowed. "Kindness and understanding are always *goot*."

"Eugene is getting plenty of our forgiveness," Phoebe told her. "We should extend that to Ruth too."

Aunt Millie tilted her head. "What is she doing?"

"She's troubled with her schoolteaching job and its newness," Phoebe managed. "There are lots of adjustments." She knew this was half of the truth.

Aunt Millie's face softened. "We should be praying for her, *yah*. But you know a schoolteacher is always welcome at my table."

Phoebe bit off a retort and made her way back to the table. She had said enough for the moment. Ruth was being accepted for now, and that was all she could ask. Not everyone had Grandma's ability to see the hearts of people.

Phoebe entered the dining room with the bowl of gravy held firmly in her hands, the steam rising halfway to the ceiling.

"There she is!" Uncle Noah hollered. "Over here again!"

She headed that way and set the bowl with its heating pad on the wooden tabletop. Uncle Noah bent low to take a long breath. "*Wunderbah*. It's like I'm at home."

Laughter rippled, and Uncle Noah dipped out a large spoonful of gravy. Phoebe slipped halfway around the table to where Wesley was seated beside David. "How are you doing?" she whispered in his ear.

He gave her a smile but didn't say anything.

"Is the food *goot*?"

He nodded.

"You can go out to play with the other children after supper," she informed him. "The games will probably be strange to you, but they'll explain if you ask."

Wesley's face was troubled.

"I'll ask one of them to tell you the rules," she told him, and he brightened considerably. She patted him on the back, and with a smile for David, she moved on.

Cousin Herman stopped her. "Hi, Phoebe. Are you ignoring me?"

"No." She turned toward him. "Just busy."

"I see. Aren't you going to eat?"

"Pretty soon. We're swapping off with two of the other aunts for dessert."

"I have an empty chair beside me," he said with a grin. "You're welcome."

"I might just take it," she replied. She hurried on.

In the kitchen, Aunt Millie's eyes had grown big. "What did I just see? And at my dining room table?"

"You didn't see anything," Phoebe assured her. "He wouldn't court me in public."

Aunt Millie's face fell. "I suppose not. Herman flirts with everyone."

Phoebe paused, searching her memory.

"What is it?" Aunt Millie asked.

Phoebe shook her head and grabbed the pan of fried green beans. She was not about to say what she was sure she had seen. Ruth's face had been tinged with a blush of red, and Ruth sat one chair down from Cousin Herman. Had the two been talking? Cousin Herman would chat with any woman within earshot, which was why he had invited Phoebe to sit beside him. But did Ruth know this? Would Ruth's wounded heart misinterpret the attention Cousin Herman had doubtlessly shown her? Cousin Herman was a single man who had never found quite what he searched for in a *frau*. Did

Ruth interest him? Or did he simply know Ruth as the community's schoolteacher? All they needed to completely alienate Ruth's heart from the community was for Cousin Herman to reject her once he discovered the whole truth. Phoebe hoped Ruth was simply flustered with the newness of being a welcome guest at Aunt Millie's dining room table.

Help us, dear Lord, Phoebe silently prayed.

She delivered the fried green beans and stepped back to sneak a glance at Ruth. She had her head down, but her face flamed. Cousin Herman was laughing and was turned in her direction. Clearly something was going on, but no one else seemed to notice. But why would they? Cousin Herman chatting with women was not an unusual occurrence. The man was well traveled and well versed in the ways of the *Englisha* world.

Aunt Millie tapped Phoebe on the shoulder. "Time to sit down and eat. Hettie and Mary will take care of the desserts in a moment."

"Glasses are empty," Uncle Noah hollered.

Aunt Millie smiled at him and whispered to Phoebe. "I'll get that. Start eating."

She did, taking the seat beside Cousin Herman.

"Here we are, with the local beauty at my right hand." Cousin Herman grinned. "I was beginning to think I was being jilted."

"You'll be gone tomorrow, and my heart will be broken and shattered," Phoebe quipped.

He threw his head back and roared with laughter. "This supper is doing my heart a lot of *goot*. I'm thankful I stayed another day or two, and that Millie asked me over."

"It was sort of a cobbled-together affair," Phoebe assured him.

Cousin Herman passed her the bowl of mashed potatoes. "I hope they're not cold."

Phoebe dipped out a spoonful. "I'm sure they'll be okay."

"And the gravy."

"Are you always this solicitous?" she teased.

"You don't know what you've been missing."

Thankfully, Ruth joined in the laughter. Perhaps Ruth would gain the full measure of the man by their light banter and know that Cousin Herman meant nothing by his attentions.

"So I hear you have quite the decent venture at Grandma Lapp's farm—after my ample part in it, of course." He gave himself a quick pat on the back.

"Cousin Herman," Phoebe chided. "One must always be humble."

He grinned and then tilted his head toward Wesley. "He's a nice-looking young man. A little shy, though. I couldn't get a word out of him so far."

Phoebe lowered her voice. "He stutters. Badly."

"Oh, my." Cousin Herman wrinkled his face in concern.

"Do you know of any solutions other than hoping he grows out of it?"

He shrugged. "Not really. Children normally do grow out of such things, but some of them don't. Come to think of it, there's a new program in Lancaster." Cousin Herman gestured in a southerly direction. "Sort of under the radar among our people. They help the children to talk real slow, drawing out the words until they can get through the sounds. The logic is that stuttering people never have trouble singing, so it's a copy on that. Not that you can speak that way—real slow, but the method builds confidence and allows the child to know that there is a way around the block they feel in their mouths."

"That's interesting." Phoebe took a piece of bread and spread on the butter. "I only have a week, but anything would help. Maybe I'll try that."

"You're *goot* with him," Cousin Herman observed. "Wesley likes you and that young man beside him." His head tilted again.

"David Fisher," Phoebe informed him. Cousin Herman didn't

react negatively, so she added, "And this is David's sister, Ruth, our schoolteacher you've been talking to."

Cousin Herman nodded and sent Ruth a warm smile. "I know. She's been regaling me with school stories. All I can say is, I admire schoolteachers for their grit and stamina. Not to mention their smarts." He sent another smile in Ruth's direction.

Her face flamed bright red. What had Phoebe gotten Ruth into? Cousin Herman must know about the Fishers' reputation, and Ruth was taking his banter seriously.

Phoebe looked away. Thankfully, Hettie appeared with the pecan and lemon cream pies, and Cousin Herman was soon occupied with his dessert. Phoebe stole a glance toward Ruth, who had her head down.

"Excellent, excellent, eating!" Cousin Herman declared. "I am glad I stayed for Millie's supper invitation."

"I thought it was my excellent company," Phoebe shot back.

Cousin Herman roared with laughter again. "I am blessed, to say the least. I've known you for a long time, Phoebe, but not Ruth." He gave her a meaningful glance. "Where has this woman been?"

Phoebe bit back a retort. Ruth kept her head turned, but a flush of red went all the way up her neck into her white *kapp*.

"Excellent, excellent," Cousin Herman repeated, and he dipped back into his two pieces of pie, oblivious to the reaction he had created in Ruth. But how could he not see?

The chatter continued around the table as Cousin Herman concentrated on his plate and Ruth studiously ignored both of them. Phoebe was ready for a piece of pie when the others finished, and then the last prayer of thanksgiving was offered. She motioned with her finger for Millie's oldest daughter to come over. When Beth approached, Phoebe whispered in her ear, "The *Englisha* boy, Wesley, can't talk very well. He stutters. See that the games are explained to him without his having to ask."

"We'll do that," Beth assured her, and she walked over to offer Wesley a smile and her hand.

"We're ready to go out and play," she told him. "Do you want to come with me? I'll explain things."

He nodded and followed Beth out the front door.

"That was sweet of you," Cousin Herman commented. "You are a lot like Grandma Lapp. Did anyone ever tell you that?"

"I am not," Phoebe protested. But the praise still warmed her. "But thank you," she told him a moment later. "Maybe I did need to hear that."

He nodded wisely and smiled. "We all do from time to time."

Ruth leaped up and scurried into the kitchen while Phoebe finished her pie. Cousin Herman turned his attention to the men's conversation. Then Phoebe gathered up a stack of empty plates and maneuvered her way back through the dining room. She would have to speak to Ruth about Cousin Herman before the evening ended and explain his tendencies—unless she should let things run their course. But Ruth as Cousin Herman's *frau*? Now wouldn't that be the Lord's way of bringing about *goot* from a bad situation.

She must keep her finger out of this pie and simply trust in Him.

THIRTY-FOUR

Darkness had fallen outside Aunt Millie's kitchen window as the women worked to clear the dining room table and wash the dishes. Phoebe stood at the sink with soapsuds up to her elbows and Ruth at the drying strainer beside her. Questions niggled at Phoebe, but she suppressed them. She must not inquire about Ruth's feelings for Cousin Herman.

Phoebe gave Ruth a gentle smile. "The children are sure having a great time tonight."

Ruth nodded. "Seems like I hear children's voices in my dreams of late. I wasn't used to having them around me all day."

"*Kinner* are a blessing of the Lord," Phoebe mused.

"Especially one's own," Ruth whispered, and her face flamed again.

Cousin Herman must have gotten to her for Ruth to express such pensive thoughts. "Has Ethan contacted you?" Phoebe asked out of the corner of her mouth.

A pained look crossed Ruth's face.

"I'm sorry, I shouldn't have asked," Phoebe hastened to say.

"He didn't, and it's okay," Ruth told her. "I'd be surprised if he ever does, but maybe..."

Phoebe plunged her hands into the soapy water. She scrubbed the stubborn stains on the mashed potato bowl until the suds rose even higher.

Thankfully, Ruth changed the subject. "How are things going with Wesley?"

"He's out there playing. I'm happy about that, and Beth is looking out for him..."

She paused as Ruth stared out the window. "That looks like fire."

"Fire!" Phoebe jerked her head up. "Where!"

The answer was obvious, and Ruth had already turned to press through the crowd of women. "The barn is on fire!" Ruth shouted into the living room.

Loud thumps and crashes and thudding of feet were heard as the men hurriedly exited the house. Phoebe tried to move away from the sink, but her path was blocked by the women who rushed toward the mudroom door en masse. She pressed forward but was still the last one outside. Ruth was nowhere in sight, and children stood transfixed everywhere, with the women gathering them into their arms. Several single girls raced back and forth on the lawn, apparently trying to account for everyone. They appeared satisfied.

"Where's Wesley?" Phoebe called out.

"Over here!" Aunt Millie called.

Phoebe ran toward the sound to find Aunt Millie holding Wesley's hand. The boy trembled from head to foot as he stared at the flames that shot out of the open barn door. The men ran around in front of them, organizing a bucket brigade from the water trough in the barnyard, while several of the older boys wrestled with hoses they had dragged out of Aunt Millie's garden shed.

Uncle Noah's clear voice rose above the racket. "Has anyone called the fire department?"

There was a muffled reply, apparently in the affirmative. Phoebe took over Aunt Millie's post by Wesley's side while her aunt hurried back into the house. The flames were growing quickly, seemingly unfazed by the buckets of water hurtled through the barn door. One of the boys came racing up with the end of the water hose, the coils finally untangled enough to work the water through. A thin stream rose skyward, and the fire hissed in response.

Would the whole barn go? Someone had opened the doors into the barnyard, and the wild whinnies of the horses filled the air.

Wesley gulped. "I-I-I-I...th-th-this, th-this is m-my f-f-fault."

"Your fault?" Phoebe peered down at him for a moment. The boy seemed serious. She knelt in front of him. "How could this be your fault?"

"I-I-I tr-tripped over..." He gave up and stared at the flames.

How could Wesley have caused the fire?

"What happened?" Phoebe called to Aunt Hettie, who was the closest woman to her.

"I don't know." Aunt Hettie had two of her children wrapped in her apron.

The oldest pointed toward Wesley. "He did it."

"Wilma!" Aunt Hettie gasped. "How could he do such a thing?"

"He fell over the gas lantern!" Wilma declared. "It went to the ground with a crash."

Aunt Hettie appeared dumbfounded, joining in her daughter's frequent glances toward Wesley. Thankfully, they were soon distracted by the flames that continued to dance out of the barn door and had reached the windows on both sides. In the distance, the wail of sirens rose and fell. Phoebe clutched Wesley to her side as they waited.

"Move back! Make way!" Uncle Noah was walking about the yard and waving his arms. "Don't get in the path of the fire trucks! Give them room!"

Everyone obeyed, pushing backward into Aunt Millie's garden, the vegetables still in the ground forgotten for the moment.

"I-I-I wa-wasn't, wasn't wa-wa-wa-watching where I was going," Wesley stammered. "I-I-I'm sorry."

"It's okay," Phoebe told him. "Accidents happen."

"Th-th-they were chasing me."

"You were supposed to join in the games," she assured him. "You were not a bad boy."

He still trembled. Maybe she should call David to comfort the lad. She hadn't been around him too much today. What a shock this fire must be. Here he was, dropped off on a strange farm and among strange people, and then taken to a strange place for supper to play games he didn't know. And now he had caused a fire.

"None of this is your fault," Phoebe tried again. She hugged him, but he still shook.

Aunt Millie reappeared with a blanket as the first of the fire trucks blasted into the driveway. With a tight pull she secured the quilt around Wesley's shoulders.

"For shock," she hollered to Phoebe over the racket. "We have to keep him warm and talk to him."

How thoughtful of Aunt Millie. Her aunt must know that Wesley had caused the accident by now. Phoebe kept the blanket wrapped around Wesley's shoulders and a running account of the firefighters' activity.

"There's the first truck set up."

"Looks like they will have no problem keeping enough water in the water trough. The windmill will keep that full."

"There goes the first blast of water right through the barn door."

"Looks like it made a dent."

"And now another one through the window."

"All they need is a third hose and the barn might be saved. Don't you think so?" Phoebe peered down at Wesley. His shaking had stopped, but he didn't answer.

"There's another fire truck coming," Phoebe said as a distant siren wail rose from Little Falls. "Thank the Lord the station is so close and we aren't way out in the country somewhere."

With Wesley calm, Phoebe ceased her chatter, but she stayed with the boy. Aunt Millie set up a small table near the mudroom door, and the women began setting out the remainder of the pies from the kitchen along with tall pitchers of water. Aunt Millie planned to feed the firefighters once they were finished. Phoebe wanted to help, but her first responsibility was to Wesley. There would be plenty of questions to answer when Ethan or Mrs. Broman picked up the lad on Friday evening. Questions she didn't want to contemplate.

She must pray. That was about all she seemed to accomplish of late.

"Shall we go inside?" Phoebe asked Wesley.

He shook his head. "I-I-I wa-want to watch."

"Okay." She led him over to the porch, and they sat down. Others were doing the same thing with their children. Was she right in thinking the flames had gone down? How could they be otherwise with the amount of water being pumped into the barn? Firefighters were now inside. The barn door was open, and their hoses flopped against the door frame. The barn would be saved, and the damage would be manageable. The Lord was extending His mercy again.

"Thank You, dear Lord, for Your mercy," Phoebe whispered toward the heavens.

Aunt Millie reappeared to tousle Wesley's hair. "How's he doing?"

"He's not shaking anymore," Phoebe answered. "Did they save the barn?"

"It appears so," Aunt Millie confirmed. "Praise the Lord."

"*Yah*, I know, but I'm still sorry it happened."

"But no one was hurt," Aunt Millie said. "We have much to be thankful for."

She bustled off as the first of the firemen reappeared in the barn door. Smoke continued to bellow out of the windows, but the worst must be over. Aunt Millie served her pies to any fireman she could wave over. A few came while the rest kept a watch on the smoking barn. They soon swapped places, and the vigil continued. This would not be over for a while yet, and Phoebe knew she and Wesley should get on home.

"Can you stay here while I find David?" she asked Wesley.

He nodded, and Phoebe slipped off the porch to search the crowd. She found David gathering up a garden hose. "Is there any way we could leave?" she asked. "I want to get Wesley back."

Soot lined David's face, but he nodded. "I don't see why not. I'll find Misty in the barnyard once I finish here."

"Do you know who started the fire?" she asked him.

His face grew grim. "I heard."

"Are they blaming Wesley?"

"Not really. Children are children. It could have happened to anyone."

"I know," Phoebe agreed. "The Lord continues to be with us. The barn could have burned down."

He didn't answer, his hands busy with the garden hose. She took the other end and straightened the tangled knots for him. "We unfolded them in an awful rush." He grinned.

"But you got the fire out."

"The firemen did," he corrected.

"But you helped contain the flames until they arrived. I know. I was watching."

His smile was still there as he disappeared into Aunt Millie's garden shed.

Phoebe left to find Aunt Millie beside her small table, serving pieces of pie and large glasses of water. "We're leaving," she whispered in her aunt's ear.

"It was still a *goot* evening, even with our loss," Aunt Millie assured her.

Phoebe forced a smile and went to search for Ruth. She hadn't seen a buggy leave, but Ruth was nowhere around.

"She left," one of the younger girls finally told Phoebe after her second trip through the house. "She tied her horse down by the ditch."

Her departure could mean anything, but Phoebe hoped Ruth would also see the Lord's hand of protection on the evening and would bear no ill will against anyone.

Phoebe tapped Wesley on the shoulder and led the boy out to where David had hitched Misty to the buggy. She paused to stroke Misty's neck and coo, "Were you frightened, you poor thing?"

The answer was a wild whinny and a shake of Misty's head. Clearly horses didn't like unmanaged fires, but neither did anyone else.

Phoebe helped Wesley up the steps of the buggy then hopped in herself. David clucked to Misty, and they were off down the lane. She turned around for one last look at the flashing lights and the flood of people spilling over Aunt Millie's lawn. "What an evening."

"You can say that again."

Misty's hooves beat a steady drum on the road as silence settled on the buggy.

"Did I see something tonight?" David finally asked.

She presumed he was talking about his sister Ruth. "*Yah*, I think you did," Phoebe told him. "Do you think it was what I thought?"

"I don't know," he mused. "Ruth still has her heart set on Ethan. Those things don't go away easily, but Herman Yoder did get her attention."

"That's what I thought." Phoebe fixed her gaze on the darkened countryside as they drove past. "We have to pray. That's all I can say. Cousin Herman is not always that serious about such things."

"D-d-do you always p-pray?" Wesley asked from the seat between them.

"You poor dear." Phoebe gave him a quick hug. "Are you over your shock?"

"I-I-I..." He gave up and nestled against her.

Phoebe glanced over at David. "How must he feel?"

"I hope the rest of the week calms down." David exaggerated a groan, and they laughed together.

"At least there is a bright side to everything," Phoebe told him, as Misty's hooves continued to beat on the pavement.

"I know," he said, and his hand found hers in the darkness.

THIRTY-FIVE

The following morning, David strode north from the Fisher homestead while the dew was still heavy on the roadside grass. He stooped to moisten his fingers and held them aloft. As he felt his hand cooling on its southern side, the smile grew on his face. With the breeze from the valley floor moving toward the Adirondacks, the weather would be warm and clear. He would be able to keep Wesley outside in the fields all day. The boy needed to spend some time with nature after the traumatic events of last night. Thankfully, Rueben Yoder's barn hadn't burned to the ground. After a few days of repairs, it should be restored. David ought to offer his time later in the week if Phoebe could spare him on the farm. Not that Wesley was to blame for the accident, but the community pitched in to help each other when calamities occurred—even small ones.

David slowed his pace as he approached Grandma Lapp's driveway. A light was on in the kitchen window, and he headed toward the front door of the house instead of the barn. How things had changed since Grandma's passing. Phoebe now welcomed him into the house without any hesitation. She returned his feelings, and a light glowed in her eyes. He couldn't believe a woman like her would really love him. He was afraid that one morning he would awaken to find this a dream. He'd be simply David Fisher again, with a family mark on his forehead that nothing could remove.

But for now...David drew a deep breath as he climbed the front porch steps. Would Phoebe stand with him in front of Bishop Rufus someday and say the sacred marriage vows? Would he dare ask her if she would be his promised one? That came first, but fear held him back. He didn't want to rush things, even if Phoebe wouldn't say no. That would be his excuse. The summer spent helping Phoebe run Grandma Lapp's farm was a joy in its own right. He didn't want the days to end, certainly not by an ill-timed question that would damage their budding relationship. A kiss wasn't a promise of marriage—it was only the hope of a future together. Whether Phoebe had ever been held in another man's arms he hadn't dared ask and didn't want to know. Certainly no girl besides Phoebe had been in his.

He knocked on the door and heard Phoebe's cheerful voice call out, "Come on in."

"*Goot* morning." He stepped inside. "Am I too early?"

"Depends on if you've had breakfast," she teased.

He glanced at the floor. The truth was, he had forgotten about breakfast.

"Worried about Wesley?" Her eyes twinkled. "You didn't have to be. He slept real well last night."

"Well, last night was quite a dramatic time," he ventured. "Not something the boy's used to seeing."

"Sit down," she ordered. "I'll have breakfast ready in a moment, and then I'll call Wesley."

He complied and watched her as she worked. "Let me help you," he finally offered.

"Can you fry the bacon?" she teased.

"I sure can," he replied. She handed him a fork.

He stepped in front of the stove, and she lingered near him.

"I'm going to mess everything up if you watch," he warned.

She squeezed his arm gently. "I'm glad you're here this morning, David. Your presence is a comfort."

"My presence..." He turned to face her. "I'm frying bacon."

"That you came early means a lot." Her voice was a whisper. "And I'm sure Wesley will feel the same way. He needs a father figure in his life. I spoke with him for a long time after you left last night, and I prayed with him—but he needs more. Will you take him riding on the ponies again today, and maybe keep him with you for the fieldwork?"

"Of course," he promised. He tried to breathe normally. Her nearness overwhelmed him. Thankfully, she moved away to stir the pot of oatmeal.

"I read Wesley some of Grandma's prayers last night." She glanced at him. "Will you read the Scriptures with us this morning?"

"*Yah*," he said. He flipped the pieces of bacon in the pan.

She came close again to peer over his shoulder. "You are an expert, I'm thinking. A real natural with the bacon."

He concentrated on the pan as she left the kitchen and went up the stairs. He had the bacon on the plate when she returned with Wesley in tow.

"*Goot* morning," he greeted the boy. "Did you sleep well?"

"Di-did I-I almost b-burn d-down a barn last night?" Wesley stammered. "Or...or..."

"It wasn't a dream," Phoebe assured him. "But it also wasn't your fault."

David stepped closer to wrap his arms around Wesley's thin shoulders. "Accidents happen," he told him.

Reassurance seemed to flicker on the boy's face, and he nodded.

"Sit," Phoebe ordered both of them as she transferred the food to the table.

Once she had joined them, David bowed his head for the prayer of thanks. Phoebe had already closed her eyes, and Wesley didn't hesitate to close his also. The boy must be accustomed to their ways already. Maybe this week could be a time for the Lord to minister to all of them despite the rough start yesterday.

"Amen," David declared, and Phoebe's smile greeted him when he looked up.

"Fall in," she ordered. "I'm sure we have a big day in front of us."

"Wi-wi-will we r-ride the ponies?" Wesley stammered.

Phoebe passed the plate of eggs and gave Wesley a big smile. "I'm sure David will give you all the rides you want. The weather should be great, and you can work outside with him all day."

A pleased look crossed Wesley's face.

Phoebe appeared ready to say more when a knock came at the front door. David glanced at her. "Are you expecting anyone?"

Phoebe shook her head before she dashed out of the kitchen.

"Is...is...?" Wesley's voice trailed off, his face filled with concern.

David guessed at the question. "Nobody is coming to blame you for last night." He reached over to squeeze the boy's shoulder, and Wesley relaxed. He had said the right words.

Murmurs came from the front door, and David strained to listen. Who would arrive this early at Phoebe's doorstep? Now he was concerned. He still couldn't make out the voices, so he stood and stepped closer to the kitchen doorway.

"Are you sure he's okay?" he heard his sister's voice ask. So Ruth had stopped in to show her concern for the accident last night. That was a *goot* sign.

"Everyone will be just fine, I'm sure," Phoebe was saying when David stuck his head into the living room.

"Hi," he called to Ruth. "Thanks for stopping by."

"I was concerned when you weren't home for breakfast," she told him. "Now I see where you've been keeping yourself."

"I had the same concerns you did," he told her with a smile. "But Wesley's okay."

"I have a few moments. Can I speak with him?" Ruth stepped closer.

David shrugged. "You'll have to ask Phoebe. That's her call."

Phoebe didn't hesitate. "Of course. You are always welcome to stop in and speak with the children. Grandma would have loved to see you involved, even if she didn't..."

Ruth had already hurried past them, and Phoebe gave David a confused look.

"I don't know what this is about," he told her. "But I'm glad she's showing an interest."

"Do you think this means Ruth has forgotten about Ethan?"

David reached for Phoebe's hand. "I hope so, but with Ruth you never know."

She smiled up at him. "We will take this as a sign of the Lord that Ruth's heart is turning. Shall we leave them alone for a moment?"

"I think we should go in," he said. He led the way back to the kitchen, where Ruth knelt in front of Wesley.

"Do you want to come up and visit my school today?" she was asking him. "It's not a big school like the one you're used to attending, and we do things differently."

Wesley hesitated. "W-we p-p-planned to r-ride the p-ponies today."

Ruth glanced up at David. "There's time for both, isn't there? I would love to have Wesley visit."

"Then I'll bring him up," David assured her. "And there is plenty of time for both."

"I'll see you later then." Ruth hopped to her feet and tousled Wesley's hair before she hurried out of the kitchen.

The front door slammed as Phoebe stared after her. "What was that about?"

"She's finding her way. That's all I know. Let's be thankful for whatever progress Ruth makes."

"Do you think..." Phoebe paused. "Forget it."

David took the Bible she handed to him, and motioned for Wesley to sit. He found the book of Psalms and sat down beside the boy to read. "'I will extol thee, my God, O king; and I will bless thy name for ever and ever. Every day will I bless thee; and I will praise thy name...'" His voice rose in confidence as he read.

Not many men were allowed the joy of courting the woman they loved in this way. Did Phoebe know what he felt in his heart? Did she know what they were doing? She had to realize that this meant so much more to him than the help he gave her on the farm.

David closed the Bible and they knelt. "Thank You, Lord, for the protection You gave all of us last night," he prayed. "The accident could have been so much worse than it was. Your grace must have kept the fire from burning down Rueben's barn and..." He couldn't say the words—*and making so much trouble for Phoebe and myself.* "Just thank You, Lord," he finished.

Phoebe's smile greeted him when he rose to his feet, and her hand reached over to hold his for a moment. "Thank you for that, David. It was exactly what I needed."

Seated on the couch, Wesley hid his grin.

It wasn't anything, he almost said, but he bit off the protest. "Can you ride the ponies with us?" he asked instead. "That would mean a lot to me and to Wesley."

"But what about the kitchen?"

"We will help you first," he declared.

A smile filled Phoebe's face. "Okay. Shall we begin?"

He followed her back into the kitchen.

"Wh-wh-what...wh-what can I do?" Wesley asked.

Phoebe pulled out a chair in answer and perched him near the drainer. Then she placed a towel in his hand. "David will wash the dishes, and you can dry them. I'll clear the table and sweep the floor. This shouldn't take long."

David waited while she ran the hot water for him and added a dash of soap. He stepped as close as he dared. That he was here this morning, had again read the Scriptures, and had stumbled through a few words of prayer were wonders beyond words. But he must be thankful and accept what came from the Lord's hand, both the *goot* and the bad. That was the way of the community.

Phoebe gave him a warm smile and transferred the first of the dishes to the counter. He washed and rinsed while Wesley wiped them dry.

"Have you ever done this before?" he teased the boy.

Wesley shook his head, but joy filled his face.

They finished, and Phoebe put the dishes away before leading the way outside to the barn. David saddled the white pony and helped Wesley to mount. Then the adults stood by the fence and watched the boy trot back and forth in the barnyard before David opened the gate to the pasture. A look of rapture filled Wesley's face as he guided Snow Cloud outside.

Phoebe whispered at his elbow: "Do you think he can stay on?"

"He'll be fine. Wesley has a level head like you do. He won't go too fast."

Phoebe pinched him on the arm. "You're just trying to flatter me."

"I speak nothing but the truth. You were great with him last night in that hubbub. Look how well he's recovered this morning."

"That's because of *your* influence."

He laughed. "Are we going around this all day?"

"Only half the day," she shot back as she chuckled.

Now was the moment. He should ask her if this could be forever. Would she join her hand in his for their walk through life? But he hesitated. Could he mar Phoebe's life with his family name after what his *daett* had done? The words got stuck in his mouth.

"I should be getting back to the house," she finally said. "Can I go up to the schoolhouse with you and Wesley when you're ready?"

"Of course. I wouldn't want to go by myself."

"Then after lunch perhaps?" Her sweet smile melted him, and he couldn't move. She seemed to understand. "I'll have lunch ready at twelve, then." She turned to hurry across the barnyard. He didn't dare watch her leave but fixed his gaze on Snow Cloud, who was trotting across the field with Wesley on her back.

THIRTY-SIX

Ruth walked to the window of the schoolhouse. The clock on the wall read minutes from two thirty. Phoebe should have brought Wesley to visit by now, along with David. Her brother was sure to come along. He was so moonstruck over Phoebe that he used every excuse he could to spend time in her presence. But Ruth must not be bitter about her brother's happiness. Phoebe had gone to extremes so Ruth could have a fair chance. Any other woman in the community would have spilled the beans about her shenanigans with Ethan a long time ago. How foolish she had been to believe that she could ever capture his heart. Ethan hadn't bothered to return any of her phone calls from the phone shack. At least he could have stopped by the schoolhouse and explained himself.

"We can't go on with our relationship," would have been painful to hear, but they would've been healing words at the same time. She would have known the situation was truly hopeless. But there had been no word from Ethan. Didn't he care even a little about her feelings? He knew how hard she had worked to reach him and how much she had risked.

Ruth pressed back her tears and turned away from the schoolhouse window. "Time for recess!" she called out.

Thankfully, none of the students seemed to notice her distress as they filed out in orderly fashion. Once the last child was through the door, Ruth scurried over to her desk and pulled out her handkerchief to dry her eyes. She could wipe away her few tears and be out on the playground for every minute of the recess. The horror of another injury haunted her. Strange how she risked her job with reckless behavior during off hours but hung on with both hands when school was in session. What a bundle of contradictions she had become.

Ruth pulled open the schoolhouse door and slammed into its edge. The pain shot all the way through her. She gasped, unable to breathe for a moment. David and Phoebe were standing in the playground with their backs turned to her, observing the children at play. She hadn't seen them walking up the road moments ago. Worse, Herman Yoder was with them and had noticed her performance at the schoolhouse door. A big grin filled his face as he craned his neck for a better look. What was the man doing here? He should have been gone from the community a long time ago. She had already wiped clean the memory of his friendliness from the other evening. She was not about to allow her heart to break again, or entertain thoughts that a man like Herman would have an interest in her. She didn't want his attentions. She wanted Ethan's love.

Ruth steeled herself and pushed the pain from running into the door out of her mind. She was not about to display more weakness than necessary around Herman. Instead, Ruth closed the schoolhouse door behind her and marched forward. David and Phoebe still hadn't seen her, but Herman's gaze was fixed—along with his big grin. He certainly seemed to be enjoying her discomfort.

"Do you always walk into doors at recess time?" he teased.

Ruth ignored him.

"Oh, Ruth!" Phoebe exclaimed and turned to face her. "Sorry.

I didn't see you come up. We were watching Wesley play. He just joined right in as if he has always been here."

"They are a nice group of schoolchildren," Ruth mumbled. She tried to ignore Herman's grin, which was still fixed on her. She was not about to grace his teasing with an acknowledgment.

"Cousin Herman came back at lunchtime to check on us," Phoebe continued. "That's why we are a little late. He couldn't stop talking, as usual." Phoebe gave her cousin a warm smile.

"Now, don't be running down my reputation," Herman retorted. "Some people are just *goot* with words, and they are needed in the world."

Ruth ignored the comment, and thankfully Phoebe did likewise. "Cousin Herman wanted to spend a few moments with Wesley because he is leaving tomorrow for Lancaster. Sometime during his travels, Cousin Herman came across some ideas our people learned of what can be done for stuttering children. He wanted to try them on Wesley."

"These are surefire methods," Herman declared. "They are things my nephews in Lancaster have tried on their own, and they work especially well on younger children. You simply use *goot* common sense and slow down the children's speech until they regain their confidence. What's simpler than that?"

Phoebe shrugged. "Wesley seemed to respond well to the few sentences Cousin Herman had him say after lunch. I'll try them willingly if they could help. The boy needs something."

"I don't know anything about speech therapy," Ruth demurred.

Herman's grin grew again. "I thought schoolteachers knew everything."

She gave in and glared at him, which only made things worse.

"You two stop fighting," Phoebe warned. "Or I'll leave you at home next time, Cousin Herman."

"That's right!" Ruth declared. She lifted her nose and walked away, but Herman didn't appear concerned as she left them to join the children's game. Soon David came over too and took his turn at batting. Ruth watched as David hit the ball clear over the back fence and trotted easily around the bases for a home run.

"Not fair, not fair," several of the children from the opposing side chanted. "We don't have a big person on our team."

Ruth answered at once. "That's right. The score doesn't count."

The children smiled at the ruling, and Wesley came up to bat next.

"Can I ring the bell?" one of the first graders interrupted to ask.

Ruth nodded, and the child dashed toward the schoolhouse. Wesley struck the ball on the second try and made the run to first base, his face aglow with happiness. Wesley was still there when the bell at the schoolhouse jangled. Ruth hung back to give him a pat on the back and wave the rest of the students back to the classroom. She entered the schoolhouse last along with Phoebe and David.

Herman had gone ahead and was sitting at the back of the schoolhouse. He surveyed the room as if he were king of his domain. Ruth almost glared at him again, but that was exactly what he wanted. Why did he keep pestering her? Herman was leaving tomorrow, and fortunately she need not see him again for a very long time.

The minutes ticked past as Ruth called the last classes and lectured in front of the schoolhouse. Herman's eyes seemed to follow her everywhere, while David and Phoebe were absorbed with each other. Wesley also tracked her moves, but Ruth didn't mind him. The boy would make a *goot* Amish schoolchild if the way he played at recess was any indication of his behavior. But Wesley wouldn't have the chance to live in the Amish world.

How different her life was from Wesley's. She had the opportunity of living in the community, yet so many times she had risked throwing away that chance for what lay outside the fence. Ruth bit her lip until she tasted blood. Was Herman trying to provoke her for some reason? But why? He couldn't care about her one way or the other. That simply wasn't possible.

Maybe he had learned of her indiscretions with Ethan. If so, that would explain the sudden interest disguised as affection. And if he knew, then Homer Lapp knew as well. Homer wasn't beyond using subterfuge to ferret out her wrongdoing. Ruth finished with the last class and then glanced at the clock. Thank the Lord this tortured afternoon was at a close.

"Time to dismiss!" she called out. A flurry of books closing and desktops slamming shut followed. "Not so loud," she admonished the room. "Now, everyone, please stand and wave goodbye to our visitors."

The students all did as instructed, and many were still waving on their way out the door.

Phoebe praised her friend once the schoolhouse was empty. "You have a very well-behaved classroom."

Unlike their schoolteacher, Ruth thought to herself. But no such words should be uttered in front of Herman. "Thank you," she managed.

"We really ought to be going," Phoebe said. "Thanks so much for your time, Ruth, and for giving David a chance at hitting a home run."

David chuckled. "That was fun. And worth the walk up here to relive my school days."

"You did great, David," Phoebe cooed.

"Thank you all for visiting," Ruth told them. As they turned to leave, she followed the group to the door. But Herman hung back and didn't go out with the others.

"Can I stay a few minutes?" he whispered.

What was she to say? Ruth waved from the schoolhouse door as David and Phoebe crossed the yard with Wesley in tow. After they had disappeared down Peckville Road, she turned to face Herman. "Okay, what do you want?"

"My, my. Aren't we snappy," he said, but his grin had faded.

"Just answer the question. If I've done something wrong, let's hear it."

He raised his eyebrows. "You run a very tight ship here, Ruth. And that decision on the playground when your brother hit the home run was right on target. Not every schoolteacher calls things to that precision. I'd say you've landed in your home court."

Sudden tears sprung to her eyes. The praise touched her, and she had to glance away. But maybe she shouldn't take the man's words too personally. "Thank you," she muttered anyway. Why be bitter about Herman's words? They were kind enough.

"I wanted to come up today to see how you were running things, and lo and behold I arrived at Phoebe's place to find they were already planning a walk up with young Wesley. What a coincidence, don't you think? But I would have come myself if I had to."

He settled onto a seat, as if he planned to stay. He vaguely glanced around. "What are your plans for the future after this year of schoolteaching?"

She drew in a long breath. "I haven't thought that far ahead. I mean, it's not as though I even planned to teach school in the first place."

"Your family's reputation complicates matters."

Ruth's eyes blazed, but she bit back a defensive retort. Where was Herman going?

"But your father's reputation clearly didn't predict your fate," he said with a smile. "Everyone should have known that, but apparently they didn't. Not until Grandma Lapp made her move."

Ruth looked away and remained silent. Grandma Lapp was a tender subject.

Herman forced a laugh. "I've traveled a lot. Maybe that's why I'm more open-minded."

What is he talking about? Ruth wondered. *Open-minded about my teaching school? Or open-minded about...*

He peered at her. "Have you traveled much, Ruth? And please— why don't you sit down? You look uncomfortable."

"You're grilling me. Why shouldn't I be uncomfortable?"

His grin returned. "I guess I am. Sorry. I didn't mean my questions to come across that way. I am genuinely interested."

She didn't meet his gaze. She'd cry soon—and she couldn't let that happen. Herman's "interest" was in her schoolteaching job— not in her as a woman. But oh, how she wished his words meant something else, something more. Maybe soon she'd get over the wound Ethan had given her.

"I think you're doing a great job," he told her.

She set her chin. "I'm glad you do."

She could make it through the next few moments until his interest faded and he left her alone. She would settle down for a *goot* cry before he was halfway across the yard, but he didn't have to know that.

He studied her again. "I like what I see, Ruth. You've turned the opportunity the community has given you into an accomplishment, as has your brother David." He gave a little laugh. "I think he has Phoebe's affections pretty much wrapped up."

"Not bad for a Fisher," she said, the words sounding bitter to her own ears.

"Now, there you go. You are sore, and yet you've done this." His hand took in the whole schoolhouse.

"I guess I manage. And I do like schoolteaching. I hadn't..." She stopped short. Why was she spilling her heart to him?

He wore a pleased look. "You have done well, and that's all I can say. I like your adventurous spirit. Are you sure you haven't traveled a lot? There's something different about you."

"You don't like me." The words came out unbidden, and Ruth's face flamed.

He tilted his head. "*Yah*, I do like you, Ruth."

She kept her breath even. She was not going to take this conversation further. Not in a thousand years. Herman Yoder was not interested in her in that way, and she did not care for the man.

He stood up and extended his hand. "Well, it's been nice chatting with you. Maybe we can do this again sometime."

"Maybe," she allowed. But what in the world did he mean?

Herman didn't elaborate on his words. He gave her a wave and left through the schoolhouse door. She sat unmoving for a long time before she peeked out the window. He was nowhere in sight, and Peckville Road was empty.

THIRTY-SEVEN

On Friday afternoon, Phoebe waited on Grandma's front porch swing with Wesley seated beside her. The boy had a peaceful look on his face. Any minute now Mrs. Broman was due to arrive with her van, and Phoebe's time with Wesley would be over.

"Did you enjoy your week with us?" Phoebe asked him. She knew the answer, but if she said anything else she might cry. Wesley didn't need to leave the farm with a teary-eyed host as his last memory. She had grown close to the child in the few days they had been together.

"I liked being here," Wesley said, taking his words slowly. "Y-you taught me so much."

"You're a wonderful young man," she whispered. "Don't let anyone tell you otherwise." She wrapped him in her arms and let her tears run into his hair.

He looked up at her. "C-can I c-come back sometime?"

"You are always welcome," she managed.

But that wouldn't happen. The program didn't work that way. Time moved on, and the next week would bring new challenges for both her and Wesley.

Concern filled Wesley's face. "Sh-should I-I-I tell Mrs. Broman about the accident?"

"You don't have to," she told him. "It was not your fault, but it's up to you."

"I-I m-might not," he said. "Sh-sh-she...she might not let me c-come back."

Phoebe hugged him again. "You may not be coming back soon, Wesley—no matter what you tell Mrs. Broman. There are many children and only one little Amish farm. Mrs. Broman wants the other children to have their turn here."

He seemed to ponder the point and finally nodded. "I s-suppose that's t-true. B-b-but I still won't s-say anything."

Phoebe thought about her own half-truths of late. She hadn't told Uncle Homer about Ruth, and things still hadn't blown to pieces as they would have if Uncle Homer knew of Ruth's struggles. These were the choices that came with adulthood and running a farm. She would have to bear them on her shoulders and follow her own conscience.

"It was a *goot* week, Wesley." She smiled down at him. "Let's not let a little bit of trouble cloud the whole sky."

His smile widened, and he nestled against her. "I will always remember you, Phoebe," he said. "And your s-stories about Grandma Lapp. I'm glad she dreamed about me."

"There's the van," Phoebe said. She stood and took Wesley's hand. He carried his small suitcase as together they walked down the steps and out to the lane where Mrs. Broman parked her vehicle. The woman bustled out and waved to them. "Good afternoon, everyone. How are things going?"

"Just fine," Phoebe called back. "Wesley wants to stay another week, I think."

"Well, that's good news!" Mrs. Broman exclaimed. "It means he must have enjoyed his time here on the farm. Did you?" Mrs. Broman knelt down to peer into his face.

"I-I had a great time. Can I live here with Phoebe and David?"

"Oh, that's sweet," Mrs. Broman cooed. "You are doing an excellent job, Phoebe. I must say, my confidence grows each week I bring children here. Your grandmother had a great vision, and I am glad it's working out so well."

"I took Wesley to visit relatives with me on Monday night," Phoebe offered. "We never spoke about taking the children off the premises, but it hope it was okay."

Mrs. Broman didn't hesitate. "I'm sure it was all part of the experience. Wesley seems no worse for the wear, and you did let us know." Mrs. Broman ruffled his hair. "Are we ready to go?"

Wesley nodded. He threw his suitcase on the seat and then hopped in the van.

Phoebe kept her voice low. "My cousin gave me some advice about his speech problem. We tried to get him to relax and slow down his words. I hope that was okay."

Mrs. Broman raised her eyebrows. "We have the boy in a speech class. I didn't know the Amish did such things."

Phoebe wrinkled her forehead. "We're not trained, but I hope we helped."

"I'm sure it's perfectly okay," Mrs. Broman assured her. "I have to go, but we'll see you next week. Ethan will drop off the children on Monday morning."

"Okay!" Phoebe called, but Mrs. Broman had already shut the van door.

What would the new week hold? Had they finally ironed all the wrinkles out of the system? Phoebe waved as the van pulled out of the driveway. Wesley's face was pressed against the glass, and Phoebe's tears stung again.

After the van disappeared from view, Phoebe turned and saw David framed by the barn door. "You should have come out to say goodbye."

"I thought about it, but one goodbye this morning was enough for me."

She stepped closer to reach for his hand. "He grew on us, didn't he?"

"*Yah.*" David hung his head. "And I'm not *goot* at goodbyes."

"You did so much for Wesley this week. He'll never be the same."

"You had more to offer than I did." He met her gaze. "You are *wunderbah*, Phoebe, in so many ways."

Warmth tingled on her neck, and she looked away. "What are you going to do for the rest of the evening?"

His hand slid out of hers. "The ponies are taken care of, and the rest of the chores are done. Maybe I'll go home and see if *Daett* needs anything."

"Will you be coming over to Uncle Reuben's tomorrow?"

He didn't hesitate. "Certainly. It shouldn't take but a few hours for the men to clean up and repair the damage from the fire."

"I'm going up tonight to help prepare food for the work party." She reached for his hand again. "Do you think next week will be as rough as this week was?"

He laughed. "The fire at your uncle's place was unfortunate, Phoebe. But I know what you mean. The protection of the Lord was very real during that fire."

"Grandma's dream is reaching so many hearts and blessing them. I just want it to continue."

"I'll be here. I know that's a small comfort, but—"

"Don't say that, David," she protested. "How would I run this farm without you?"

He looked away. "You'd make it. There is always someone to help in the community."

"But not like you," she insisted. "You have…I don't know…you've become very necessary to everything around here. I think Grandma always knew you would." She gazed into his face. "David, you are the one I depend on and go to for answers. Grandma knew I would discover who you are, and she planned for us to work together. You are not your *daett*."

"I hope not," he muttered. "Thanks for seeing that."

"But I should have seen it sooner."

He took her hand this time. "Let's just take what the Lord is giving and be thankful."

She beamed. "Then…to being thankful!" Joy bubbled up from her heart, and David was the cause. What wonders Grandma had envisioned.

"Can we sit on the porch swing for a few moments and enjoy the victories this week?" she asked. "Just for a little while."

He looked uncertain.

"Please," she begged. "Your *daett*'s work can wait."

"Okay." He gave in and followed her to the porch.

She made room for him on the swing, and the chains squeaked in the still afternoon air. She looked at him and asked, "Do you think we will love them all as much as we did Wesley?"

"Maybe," he allowed. "The emotions might not be the same, but our hearts can give as much."

She nestled against him, with the strength of his arm on her cheek. "You say such *wunderbah* things," she whispered.

He was silent as the chains continued to squeak.

She sat up straight again. "Have you heard anything from Ruth? Did she say what Cousin Herman discussed with her?"

He shook his head. "I haven't dared to ask."

She chuckled. "Do you think it might actually happen? That Cousin Herman has an interest in your sister?"

His face clouded for a moment, and Phoebe clutched his arm. "I didn't mean it like that, David. I really didn't. I was overcome with joy at the thought of Ruth finding the right home for her heart."

"I know. I have to stop being so sensitive about my family. But we'd best not ask too many questions of Ruth. She could easily go off in the wrong direction."

"I think happiness is possible for her!" she proclaimed. She leaned against him again. "Ruth and Cousin Herman would be perfect for each other."

"When are you leaving for your aunt's place?" he asked, ignoring that point.

"Anytime now," she mumbled into his arm.

"I'll get Misty harnessed," he said.

"Not yet," she begged.

He grinned and walked off the porch. "I'll have her out in a moment," he called over his shoulder.

She watched him walk toward the barn and vanish inside. She was not normally a dreamer—but if she were, she never would have imagined her love for David. Grandma was the dreamer, and Phoebe the recipient of Grandma's gift. David had so many things she needed, and he had been there for her the whole time.

"Thank You, dear Lord," she whispered to God. "Thank You for seeing what I didn't."

She stood up from the swing and entered the house. It only took her a few minutes to pack a small bag, and then she exited the house. David was in the lane and had hitched Misty to the buggy.

"Sorry I didn't get out in time to help," she told him.

He smiled and patted Misty on the neck. "No problem. I'll see you tomorrow." He tossed Phoebe the reins once she had climbed inside. "Have a *goot* evening at your aunt's place. I'll close the barn doors and shut things down tight."

"Thank you!" she called to him as he let go of the bridle.

Misty lunged forward, but Phoebe still managed to wave as they swung past. David appeared so happy, so contented, and so joyful. He must be in love with her—but more than that, he had shared with her the joys and trials of this last week. Together they were more than either of them would have been apart. Wesley could have made his way into her heart, but David made the moments come alive. The Lord came first, and He made all things *goot*, but had the Lord not also made a man and a woman to live and work together?

As she jiggled the reins, Phoebe felt warmth gathering at the base of her neck. She shouldn't arrive at Aunt Millie's red in the face like a love-struck teenager—even if she was in love. That must be what all the feelings that bubbled inside of her were about. Phoebe jiggled the reins again. Would David ask her to marry him someday? Could David be her husband? What did she expect in a husband? She had many questions but no answers. She hadn't spent time dwelling on matters of the heart the way other girls apparently did. Maybe that's why the wonder of David was so much greater. He was everything she desired, as if he had been there all the time.

"Whoa there," Phoebe called to Misty as they approached Aunt Millie's driveway. She pulled in and stopped by the barn. The charred door burst open, and Uncle Rueben hurried out.

"Howdy there! Who have we here?"

"Your niece! I hope you have a place for me to stay tonight," she told him with a grin. "I've decided to come over."

"You know you're always welcome," he assured her as he took Misty by the bridle. "Go on up to the house. I'll take care of your horse."

"Thanks, Uncle Rueben," she told him. "Is everything going okay with the plans for tomorrow?"

"There's just some smoke and soot and a few burnt boards. I could have taken care of it myself, but you know how people are. They want to help."

"That is as it should be. I should get on my knees and apologize for not keeping better tabs on my charge."

"Now, don't go there, Phoebe. It was an accident, and Wesley endeared himself to us."

"That he did," she agreed. "But thanks again for being so understanding about it."

Uncle Rueben smiled as Aunt Millie shouted from the front door. "Are you coming up to the house, Phoebe? Or are you sleeping in the barn?"

Phoebe grabbed her satchel and ran up the walk. Aunt Millie came down the steps to embrace her in both arms. They clung to each other for a long time.

"Is everything okay?" Aunt Millie inquired, holding Phoebe at arm's length. "Your eyes are red."

"I'm just happy," Phoebe whispered. "So very happy."

"Oh, dear!" Aunt Millie proclaimed. She wrapped Phoebe in her arms again. "I guess I was wrong about David."

THIRTY-EIGHT

On Saturday morning, Phoebe stood inside Uncle Rueben's barn. She held a garbage bag with both hands while Aunt Millie and Ruth shoveled soot and debris in with shovels. Several other women attacked the barn ceiling with brooms, leaving only the blackened undercoating from the fire. One of the men came in with a garden hose, and everyone moved back as he sprayed the water.

Aunt Millie giggled. "You look worse than I do, Phoebe. We'll have to wash up twice before we're fit to serve lunch."

"You'd better!" one of the men hollered above the noise of the water. "I don't want my food filled with soot."

"You should be glad we feed you at all after that insult," Aunt Millie shot back, and everyone laughed.

Phoebe stepped back with her garbage bag and waited until the water stopped dripping from the ceiling. Then she grabbed a broom to join the other women. In no time, they had the barn's beams almost back to their original color.

"Okay, everybody out," Uncle Rueben ordered. "Things are clean enough, and the men need to work. They've loitered around all morning already."

"Speak for yourself," someone hollered, and laughter rippled again.

Phoebe retreated with the women to the water trough, where they removed most of the soot from their arms and faces. Aunt Millie appeared with washcloths and soap, which took off the rest.

Phoebe dried her arms on a towel and caught sight of David near the barn door. He was busy sawing pieces of lumber while someone shouted measurements to him from inside the barn. She hadn't seen him earlier in the crowd, but that wasn't surprising. David wouldn't go out of his way to attract attention. Eventually, though, he would become the confident man in public he was around the farm. Phoebe followed the motions of his arm as he cut another piece of wood.

"You really are taken with him." Ruth's voice at her elbow made Phoebe jump.

"*Yah*, I like your brother."

A slight smile played on Ruth's face. "I'm glad. He deserves your love."

Phoebe hid her blush behind the towel. Ruth giggled at Phoebe's embarrassment.

"Has he gotten up the nerve to ask you?" Ruth asked in a sly whisper.

"Ruth," Phoebe scolded.

Ruth's smile only grew.

Phoebe gathered up her own courage. "How did you make out with Cousin Herman?"

Ruth sobered at once. "Maybe I shouldn't be asking questions."

"I'm glad if he has kind feelings for you," Phoebe assured her. "But I'm sorry about Ethan. I know his rejection must hurt."

Ruth nodded and looked away. Phoebe handed the towel to one of the other women, and the push of the crowd separated her from Ruth. She hoped she and Ruth could talk more later.

David, bent over his saw, held Phoebe's attention until she slipped into the house. Aunt Millie stood near the front door, giving instructions to the women as they came in.

"The pudding," she told Phoebe. "You would be the perfect person to make the pudding."

"Can Ruth help me?" Phoebe asked.

"Of course!"

Phoebe waited until Ruth entered the house. Then she grabbed her by the elbow and pulled her toward the kitchen. "You are to help me with the pudding."

"How's school going, Ruth?" one of the women near the counter asked.

"Just fine," Ruth chirped.

Phoebe found the ingredients and the bowls in Aunt Millie's pantry. She and Ruth set things up at a corner of the kitchen table. They read the recipe together and bent over their work, but their heads jerked up when they heard a commotion at the front door.

One of the children hollered, "Someone's been hurt!"

"Oh, no!" Ruth groaned. "Now what?"

The sentiment swept through the kitchen, and the women dropped their tasks to rush outside.

"Who is it?" everyone asked one another.

Phoebe kept close to Ruth as they made their way to the outskirts of the crowd. "You're not thinking what I'm thinking?" Phoebe asked.

"I'm afraid I am," Ruth whispered back.

Phoebe held onto Ruth's arm as they pushed closer to the small of group of men gathered in front of the barn. A few of them kept the children from coming too close. The spot where everyone focused was exactly where David had been working only a short time before.

Ruth clung to Phoebe, and somehow they managed to move forward. Phoebe choked back the sob that caught in her throat.

Surely not...David was here to help, not to suffer. And what if... She stopped the dreadful thought. She would not let her mind go there.

"It's David Fisher," one of the men said. "Come." He took Ruth's arm, and Phoebe stayed close on her other side. Her legs would barely hold her, but she must be with David—whatever had happened.

The sight made the earth move all around her. She only stayed upright because of Ruth's supporting hand. David was covered in blood and lay against the sawhorses, his head listing to one side. A scream threatened to come out of her mouth, a horrible shriek no Amish woman should ever utter, but she stifled the urge and struggled to gather her emotions. She must be strong, and David was not dead.

Silently, she forced her feet to move forward and then rushed to his side, nearly falling into his lap. Strong arms held her, and she didn't bother to look up to see whose they were. Slowly she was lowered to the ground beside David. She cradled his head and whispered his name. "David. David, can you hear me?"

She was not his promised one, and they weren't even dating officially, but this was not a moment to stand on technicalities. The men around her would have to think what they would. David worked on her farm. That would suffice as an explanation for the present.

His sister's concerned face came into focus, bent low over her brother. "He's cut his arm badly," Ruth told her.

Phoebe hadn't seen the tourniquet tied to David's arm. All she had noticed was his crumpled form. The horror of what might be had gripped her.

"I'm okay," David whispered. "I was just careless—rushing too much, I guess. The wood slipped, and the saw..." His words faded.

"Hush. Don't speak," Phoebe said softly. His head seemed heavy against her shoulder, his strength gone. But this was still David. Laid low, *yah*, but the man she loved. He would live. That was enough for now. "I'm so sorry," she sobbed. She pulled him closer. She didn't care who saw.

"You have to let him breathe," Ruth warned, and Phoebe released her tight hold on him a little.

No one took him away from her. There was a faint wail of sirens in the distance, followed by louder ones.

Phoebe asked the men standing around, "Why is an ambulance coming?"

"He'll need stitches, and maybe even surgery," one of the men answered. "An artery was cut, I think. That needs a doctor."

True, but she didn't want to let go of him, and she couldn't go along with him to the hospital.

"Will you go with him?" Phoebe asked Ruth. "And stay with him until he's safe?"

"*Yah*, of course," Ruth assured her.

"I'll be okay," David protested with some of his usual vigor.

His face was white, though, and his pulse weak. Phoebe realized she held his uninjured wrist and had been counting his heartbeats unconsciously.

The wail of the ambulance pierced Phoebe's ears as the vehicle bounced into Aunt Millie's driveway and pulled past the long line of buggies.

"I love you so much, David," she whispered in his ear. She kissed his cheek.

A faint smile played on his face. "I should have injured myself sooner."

"David Fisher!"

Ruth pulled on Phoebe's arm. "Time to let go, Phoebe. The EMTs are here."

The ambulance attendants examined David while they listened to the men's explanations.

"Nice tourniquet," one of the EMTs said.

Several of the Amish men chuckled. "That's my blue bandana tied to my brother's," Uncle Rueben told them. "Worked, I guess."

David was lifted onto a gurney and wheeled toward the ambulance. True to her word, Ruth stayed by her brother's side and hopped into the vehicle with him. Someone would see that things were taken care of from here. As usual, Leroy was nowhere in sight, having found more urgent duties on his own farm for the day.

But the family's reputation would change soon for David. Grandma had seen to that, and Phoebe had kissed David on the cheek in front of everyone. Heat rushed into her face as the ambulance backed out of Uncle Rueben's driveway. What thoughts to think at a moment like this. But she would kiss David a hundred times more in front of the whole congregation if doing so would bring him back to full health. Phoebe tried to slow her rapid breathing. The doctors would take care of David, and time would heal the cut. Nothing had happened which couldn't be made right again. She had to believe that.

Uncle Rueben echoed her thoughts from a few feet away. "He'll be okay."

Soon Aunt Millie appeared out of the crowd and slipped her arm around Phoebe's shoulders. Together they watched the ambulance leave.

"I'm so sorry that all these bad things happen to you on our place," Aunt Millie muttered. "Soon you won't come over anymore."

Phoebe managed to chuckle. "You know that's not true."

"At least David didn't burn down my barn," Uncle Rueben joked.

"Rueben!" Aunt Millie scolded. "How dare you."

"Sorry," Uncle Rueben said. "I was the one who got the tourniquet on the man so quickly, so don't be too hard on me."

"Oh dear me." Aunt Millie let go of Phoebe to scurry to her husband's side. "I didn't mean any harshness. All of our nerves are on edge. First the fire and now the accident."

"We should pray," Uncle Rueben said, and numerous voices echoed the sentiment. Men took off their hats and everyone bowed their heads in prayer.

"Our dear Father in heaven," Uncle Rueben prayed, "we thank You that protection has been given again as another accident has occurred. We do not question Your hand, but give You praise and glory instead. You know what is best, and do all things after the council of Your own will. Be with us now for the rest of the day, and shed Your grace and mercy upon Your weak and unworthy creatures. Amen."

The amen was repeated several times as the men turned back to their work. Aunt Millie appeared at Phoebe's side again. They made their way to the house, where Phoebe paused on the front porch to listen for the sound of the siren in the distance.

"The Lord will be with him," Aunt Millie assured her. "Come in and sit down on the couch."

"I will not. I will finish the pudding I was working on."

"No use for theatrics, dear," Aunt Millie chided. "There are plenty of people here to finish the lunch preparations."

Phoebe tried to protest, but her legs wouldn't hold her. Where had her resolutions flown off to? She should be strong in the face of adversity, but the memory of David's slumped form seemed to drain her blood. What if Uncle Rueben hadn't been so quick with the tourniquet? What if David had been working alone on his *daett's* farm when the wood slipped? David should never have been working with a saw today. He wasn't a carpenter, but a farmer. Her thoughts raced, and Phoebe stilled them. After settling herself on the couch, she smiled weakly at Aunt Millie. "I think you are right. I had best rest."

"That a *goot* girl." Aunt Millie patted her shoulder. "You stay right there until lunch is ready."

The bustle of the food preparations continued in the kitchen, and the occasional woman walked past her and offered her muttered sympathies.

"At least it wasn't a broken leg. Those can take eight weeks to heal," someone said.

"He'll be better quickly with a few stitches in his arm."

"You'll have forgotten this happened in a few weeks," another added.

Phoebe nodded her thanks each time but didn't offer a reply. She couldn't find the words. A great weakness gripped her that wouldn't leave. She had never loved a man as she loved David, and to see him... A shudder ran all the way through her. She must not entertain these dark memories. She would love David even more ferociously after this. She would trust the Lord and His almighty hand. How else would one dare love when the pain of loss could sting so deeply? She still had David, and he would be there once he had healed.

David loved her, and she loved him. He would not forget that. Phoebe hid her tears and tried to smile as the women bustled around the kitchen.

THIRTY-NINE

Sunday afternoon after the church service, Phoebe unhitched Misty and left her in Grandma's barn before walking south on Burrell Road. A warm breeze pushed stray strands of hair across her cheeks. She tucked them back under her *kapp* and bowed her head. How many times had David made this walk north, even though she hadn't been down to see his family since the children began arriving at the farm? Maybe the accident was the Lord's way of reminding her that the road ran both ways. David had never complained, but the truth was a visit to the Fisher family was long overdue. She had practically claimed David as her promised one, and now that she knew of Leroy's role in Grandfather Tobias's death, the tension between their families must be addressed beyond the conversation she had with David.

Phoebe quickened her step. "David's home from the hospital and in *goot* spirits," his *mamm* had told her this morning at the service.

She could barely wait to ask, "Can I visit?"

Priscilla's smile had come just as quickly. "Of course, dear. You are always welcome at our house." Clearly, Priscilla carried none of her husband's hostility toward the world or the Lapp family in particular.

Phoebe glanced around as she approached the Fishers' driveway. Their buggy sat by the barn with the shafts turned sideways. Leroy could not do anything right, even parking a buggy in its proper place—but David was not like his *daett*. Phoebe took a deep breath and knocked on the front door.

Priscilla's voice called at once, "Come in, Phoebe."

She opened the door and saw David propped up on the couch with pillows on each side of him. "David!" Her hands flew to her face. He appeared pale and weak, so unlike his usual healthy self.

"It's better than it looks. I'm fine. Do you want to sit?"

Priscilla produced a chair because David occupied the whole couch. Phoebe sat down before her legs gave way. "What did they *do* to you?" she asked. She stared at his bandage. "I knew it was bad, but—"

"A few stitches, that's all." He tried to grin. "Really. I'll be *goot* as new by Monday morning."

"You're *not* coming up to the farm," she ordered. "Not until you've regained your strength. I can manage for a week on my own."

"A week, Phoebe?" He appeared horror-struck. "I'm coming up the minute I can stand up."

Priscilla cleared her throat beside them. "Maybe I'll leave you two alone so you can talk this out. But let me assure you, Phoebe, that he's not leaving the house a minute before he should."

Phoebe let out a long breath. "I'm glad to hear that. Of course you wouldn't allow him to be foolish, Priscilla."

"I'm still his mother," Priscilla said. She smiled at her son before heading toward the kitchen.

David made a face. "I hate this mothering and smothering. I was ready to get back on my feet today. I could easily have gone to morning services."

Phoebe gave him a glare. "Thank the Lord *someone* has some sense." He chuckled, and she continued. "What happened yesterday? Can you give me more details?"

"I can't remember everything the doctor told me, but a large vein was severed. Thankfully, no tendon was snipped. The saw went lengthwise and not across."

"Oh, David!" She reached over to hold the hand of his undamaged arm.

"I remember our parting," he said with a grin.

"Stop it."

"The cut was almost worth the kiss," he teased.

Phoebe covered her face with both hands. "I'm so embarrassed, and to think that... Well, I was caught up in the moment."

"You have nothing to be embarrassed about. I love you."

Phoebe peeked out from between her fingers to see his big grin. "You are a very naughty boy," she told him.

"I don't take back one word," he said, his grin still in place. "I still have the kiss right here." He tapped his cheek with his finger.

Phoebe's hands covered her face again. "I'm leaving if you don't quit this," she warned.

David chuckled and reached over with his free hand. "I'm sorry. I'm just so glad to see you."

"Okay, that's better." Phoebe breathed a sigh of relief. "But I still want to know how the cut happened. You are not a careless man. Did someone trip over the sawhorse or walk into your board?"

His face darkened for a moment.

"I want to know, David." She held his arm again.

"It's not what you think," he finally said. "This was my fault. I was trying to..." He looked away. "I don't know. I don't want to say it, Phoebe. I'm still new at this. You and me..." He had tears in his eyes. "I was trying to impress your uncle by working fast. That's the truth, if you must know."

"Oh, David, you should stop that. No one needs to be impressed. The community accepts you and would accept the rest of your family if your *daett* would simply accept forgiveness. Grandma forgave him. I know she did because I read the words she wrote in her prayer journal after the accident."

"You are right," he agreed. "I shouldn't have been trying to impress anyone."

"Not if you injure yourself." Her own tears welled. "Look what could have happened. Those saws can cut off an arm. What would I do then?"

He attempted a tease. "Would you have fired me from the farm?"

"David!" She clutched his uninjured arm with both hands. "I would never have done that!"

"I know. I'll do better—or try. This is a hard lesson, you know."

"I'm with you, and I'm sorry for what happened. I'm partially to blame, you know."

He shook his head. "You are not to blame for anything. You couldn't be more blameless."

She forced a laugh. "Be careful what you say. I do have my faults."

He appeared totally unconvinced as Priscilla appeared in the kitchen doorway. She asked, "Are you staying for supper, Phoebe?"

She didn't hesitate. "Of course! And thanks for the invitation."

"Who's staying for supper?" At the sound of Leroy's voice, Phoebe jerked her head around. The man rubbed his eyes near the bedroom door, clearly having just awoken from his Sunday afternoon nap.

"Me, I guess." Phoebe managed a smile. "Is that okay?"

"I wish you wouldn't," he said. "Are you to blame for David's accident?"

"*Daett!*" David turned around on the couch. "Please stop this."

"Someone is to blame," Leroy muttered. "And it sure wasn't me."

Phoebe decided to speak up. "We should talk about Grandfather

Tobias's accident, Leroy. There is no need for the past to come between our families. Grandma—"

His face turned into thunderclouds. "How dare you come into my house and lecture me, Phoebe? Do not speak to me of your grandma and her spiritual ways. Haven't I put up with her meddling with my children? Now you intend to steal my son from me."

David tried again. "*Daett*! Please!"

Priscilla reappeared in the kitchen doorway. "The time has come to let go, Leroy. Phoebe speaks the truth."

"Are you turning on me too, Priscilla?" His look blazed into her.

His wife wilted, and tears streamed down her face.

"*Mamm* is right!" David declared. "This must end. You must forgive yourself and ask for the Lord's grace, which we all need."

"Now my son has turned on me as well," Leroy muttered.

"Phoebe is welcome in our home," David continued. "If you can't say the words, I will. Phoebe has done no wrong, and Grandma Lapp was nothing but *goot* to you after the accident."

"What do you know about accidents?" Leroy snorted. "If Tobias had driven carefully, the single tree would not have broken."

David appeared stunned. "I am not fighting the past, *Daett*. I wasn't there, and what happened, happened. I only know that I love Phoebe and that she is welcome to stay for supper. Will you at least allow that?"

Leroy said nothing but bolted out the front door.

"Grandma forgave you," Phoebe wanted to holler after him, but the words came out barely above a whisper.

David's face was grief-stricken. Priscilla rushed over to wrap her arms around Phoebe.

"I am sorry about that," David said. "I should have approached *Daett* about the matter before now."

"You did nothing wrong," Phoebe told him.

"Will you still stay for supper?" Priscilla begged. "Please? This would mean so much to us, and the Lord knows our hearts need healing."

Phoebe gathered herself together. "Of course I will. And I'm sorry Leroy feels the way he does about me."

"Leroy will see the error of his ways!" Priscilla declared. "I will speak with him after I have supper ready."

"Let me help in the kitchen, then. I might as well make myself useful."

"You don't have to help," Priscilla protested. "David likes your company in here."

Phoebe gave David a sweet smile. "I'll see plenty of him once he's well, but I'm not down here every day."

"Okay." Priscilla gave in and led the way. "How are things going up at the farm?" She turned to ask. "David doesn't say too much."

Phoebe took a deep breath. "I don't know where to begin. Your son has been such a blessing through everything. He pitches right in and helps with even the most difficult situations. Last week we had a young boy with a stammering problem, and David helped make Wesley feel right at home."

"He would do that." Priscilla's smile appeared again. "My boy has a tender heart. Thanks for letting him work with you, Phoebe. That has meant the world to him, and for your..." Priscilla paused. "I don't want to assume, but I guess you are..." She paused again. "We are so thrilled."

Phoebe ducked her head bashfully. "I know. We have a strange relationship, but it's going well."

She didn't know how much David had told his mother, but Priscilla must assume they were close after seeing Phoebe's open expression of affection at Uncle Reuben's place yesterday. Mothers usually knew what their children were up to.

"How many people know about Ruth's struggles at the schoolhouse?" Priscilla asked, her smile gone. "I'm assuming you know."

"*Yah*, I do," Phoebe admitted. "But I've not talked about them with anyone."

Priscilla sighed. "I don't know what will happen if Ruth is disciplined."

"We can pray." Phoebe laid her hand on Priscilla's arm. "And we can pray for Leroy. Maybe the worst is over with your family's trials. I keep hoping it is. Uncle Homer must know Ruth was tempted, yet he has given her the time to make her own choice. Isn't that a *goot* sign?"

"That would be the Lord's blessing indeed, and Leroy must change his attitude." Priscilla turned away and began to work, but not before Phoebe caught a glimmer of tears in her eyes.

"Grandma's dream has changed so many of us," Phoebe told her. "We must not lose faith."

"You are right," Priscilla agreed. "I wish Ruth were here this afternoon, but she went home with Lily Yoder. They seem to have a budding friendship of sorts."

"Look how the Lord is working already!" Phoebe exclaimed. "We must believe for the best."

Priscilla nodded and wiped her eyes. "You are such a blessing, Phoebe. I can't say how much."

"I would feel like more of a blessing if I made myself useful. How can I help with supper?"

Priscilla caught her breath. "Sorry about that. I am forgetting my manners. Here, slice the celery, and I'll get the lettuce from the basement. I'm serving sandwiches tonight with a tossed salad for a light meal." Priscilla paused to think. "While I'm out, I might as well speak with Leroy. Pray for me, Phoebe."

"I will," Phoebe assured her. "And take your time. I'll have things ready when you get back."

Phoebe busied herself after Priscilla disappeared down the basement stairs. The outside door soon slammed, and Phoebe took a peek through the kitchen window to catch a glimpse of Priscilla hurrying toward the barn door with her head bent low.

"Please help her, Lord," Phoebe whispered, returning to the food preparations.

Phoebe had finished her tasks when the basement door slammed again. Priscilla appeared with the lettuce, smiling but tearful. "You must have gotten to him because he didn't argue with me. He is coming in to eat supper with us."

"Thank You, dear Lord," Phoebe softly prayed.

"Amen," Priscilla echoed.

The lettuce was sliced and the sandwiches were completed when Leroy appeared stone faced, helping David hobble in from the living room. Leroy took his place at the table, and the smaller children came in from the outside as if they already knew when supper would be ready.

"Hi, children." Phoebe greeted them with a smile.

They grinned back but didn't offer any comments. Apparently everyone was used to tension in the family.

Leroy grunted when Priscilla placed the last dish on the table. He bowed his head and led out in a short prayer of thanks. After the amen, they passed around the sandwiches.

David caught Phoebe's eye. "These are *goot* sandwiches."

"Your *mamm* made them," she said, and everyone except Leroy chuckled.

"David thinks everything is made better by the touch of your hands," Priscilla added. "We are all glad to see that he has made such a *goot* choice in a girlfriend."

Phoebe kept her head down as even the smaller children grinned from ear to ear. Leroy grunted again but made no comment.

"I hope our teasing isn't too much for you," Priscilla ventured.

"It's okay," Phoebe assured her. "I guess I should come down more often."

"*Yah*, do," said a chorus of small voices.

"In the future, then," Phoebe replied with a smile, and the conversation moved to other subjects. Even Leroy joined in with a few short sentences.

After they finished, Leroy offered another short prayer of thanks. The smaller children dashed outside to play, while Priscilla waved Phoebe out of the kitchen. "Don't even think about helping with the dishes. Go into the living room with David. Leroy's going out to finish the evening chores, and I have plenty of time."

Phoebe agreed as Leroy helped his son back to the couch. She seated herself on the chair, but David moved his pillows after everyone had left.

"Sit here," he ordered. "I want you near me."

"What is this? An official date?" she teased.

He laughed. "Would you have agreed?"

"You know I would have."

"Thanks for speaking to *Daett*," he whispered. "That means the world to all of us."

They locked eyes as his fingers tightened on hers.

FORTY

Phoebe was waiting beside the barn door on Monday morning when Ethan pulled up with the van. He was grinning, but she didn't feel like responding in kind. She had been brave since she left the Fishers' home last evening, after that horrible explosion with Leroy. Now the new week had arrived, and David's absence hung like a weight over the whole farm.

Phoebe forced herself to paste on a smile. There was no reason the week should go badly, and she could manage. David would be back eventually, perhaps by Friday, and Leroy would find his own way toward healing somehow.

Ethan scrambled out of the van and approached her. "Where's David?"

"He's not here. He has an injury to his arm that required stitches."

"Do you know any Spanish?"

"No." She gave him a strange look.

"Well, we have two sisters from Guatemala. They'll be staying with you until we can find them permanent homes." Ethan shrugged. "Not the usual one week, but orders are orders. Political situation."

Phoebe froze in place. "Until..."

"Don't look so panic-stricken. If that's a problem, we can take them back for the weekend, but it would give them a more stable life if they could stay here. Two weeks, we hope—but with the bureaucracy, you never know."

"Why...I guess...okay."

Ethan opened the van door, and two bewildered-looking young girls stared back at her. They slowly climbed out of the van. Phoebe took small steps toward them before she hurried forward. So what if she couldn't speak their language? A hug was understood by everyone. Their smiles were tentative as she took the oldest in her arms. "*Goot* morning. How are you?"

"*Buenos días,*" Ethan muttered behind her. "I know that much." He shoved a dictionary in her hand. "That's the best I can do."

Phoebe hugged the second girl before opening the pages. There were English words on one side, with meaningless letters on the other. Did anyone in the community know Spanish? Considering all his travels, Cousin Herman might know a little—but he wasn't here.

"Time for Spanish lessons," Ethan said. He transferred the suitcases to the ground. "Sorry. At least you have my number. Call me if you need to."

She turned to face him, and the words tumbled out. "I don't approve of your relationship with Ruth Fisher, but it still wasn't decent of you to drop her without at least an explanation. You should talk with her and end things on a decent note."

"Whoa," he said. "What have we here?"

"Just human decency, Ethan. And for the record, I don't think you should date her."

"Ruth told you about us?" He scratched his head.

"Not everything," she told him. "But enough that I know. Ruth should be at the schoolhouse by now. I'll ride up with you and the girls, and you can speak with her."

He raised his eyebrows. "First it's secrecy, and now it's a chaperoned parting."

"I won't go inside, but if you're alone you'll only make things worse, so..."

"You Amish are strange creatures."

"And this from a man who doesn't keep his dates."

"Your tongue is sharp this morning," he muttered. "But your logic compels me, Phoebe. Maybe I will take you up on the offer."

Phoebe glanced at the suitcases by the sidewalk. "I guess these won't run off anywhere."

"Come on. We can go and then bring the girls back. Oh, and meet Maria and Juanita."

They both smiled at the mention of their names. Phoebe pointed at herself and said, "Phoebe" before motioning them back into the van. Then she slid onto the seat beside them. Ethan started the van and pulled out of the driveway, turning east on Peckville Road to slow for the schoolhouse moments later. John was standing outside the Yoders' barn with a bucket in his hand, and when Phoebe hopped out of the van, she waved at him. His curiosity satisfied, John vanished inside.

Ethan headed toward the schoolhouse without a backward glance. Phoebe stood by the van door to wait. Ethan's and Ruth's silhouettes were framed inside the front window. Arms flew around, and the sound of voices rose in the background. If Phoebe had to guess, she'd say the conversation was not going well.

Phoebe sighed. She had still spoken the right words, even if Ethan was getting his ears chewed off. Ruth was understandably upset, but closure would come quicker for her this way. She didn't want Ruth to be haunted for the rest of her life by an unresolved past. Leroy kept enough of those ghosts in his closet.

Moments later, Ethan appeared in the schoolhouse doorway still waving his arm about. Then the door was shut behind him with a slam.

"Just a minute," Phoebe told the two girls, who looked more confused than ever. "I'm going in to talk..." she tried again. Giving up, she crossed the schoolyard at a run to meet Ethan at the bottom of the steps.

"Where are you going?" he asked.

She rushed past him. "I'll be out in a minute."

Ruth was crying when she entered, and Phoebe hurried to her side. "I'm so sorry," she whispered, embracing Ruth. "Did he apologize?"

"You put him up to this?" Ruth asked, wiping her eyes on her handkerchief.

"*Yah*," Phoebe admitted. "Kind of a spur-of-the-moment idea."

"Perhaps it was for the best. I was going to bury him in a deep, dark corner of my life and never think of him again."

"Oh, you poor thing." Phoebe reached out, and Ruth buried her head in Phoebe's shoulder, sobbing. But after a few moments she managed to pull herself together.

"I should be going," Phoebe said. "Do you want to stop by and speak with me on the way home from school today? That might help, and I have two cute little Guatemalan girls who can't speak English." She made a face, and Ruth managed to smile.

"I'll be okay." Ruth wiped her eyes. "I needed a good cry, and to hear that it really was over between Ethan and me." Ruth glanced toward the ceiling as her tears welled up again. "I thought I knew, but deep down..."

Phoebe held Ruth until the wails subsided.

"You have to go," Ruth said this time. "I'll wash my face and be brand new by the time the schoolchildren arrive."

"Remember, you can stop by anytime."

Ruth followed Phoebe to the door, and they parted with another hug.

"What did you tell her?" Phoebe demanded of Ethan when she climbed back in the van.

He shrugged. "I apologized. You were right. I shouldn't have stood her up that evening, and I could have answered the phone when she called and explained that I didn't think we should see each other anymore. It was wrong to just dodge her. Are you satisfied?"

"Thank you, Ethan," Phoebe told him. "I appreciate it. Ruth is in a fragile phase of her life, and she needed a proper conclusion to the matter."

"Fragile phase!" He snorted. "The woman is a blazing firebrand."

"Not everything is as it seems on the surface," Phoebe chided. "But thanks again."

He pulled back into Grandma Lapp's driveway. "Are you sure you'll be okay with these girls? It's not as though we have much choice, but the tender side of my heart has been stirred."

"Just go!" She smiled at him before climbing out and then helping the two girls down.

Maria and Juanita grabbed their suitcases and headed toward the house before Ethan had the van turned around. With the dictionary tucked under her arm, Phoebe gave him a quick goodbye wave and followed the girls up the walkway.

This was a new situation indeed, and one she had not expected. She needed David now more than ever. He might know what could be done. Should she make a trip over to Aunt Millie's to search for Cousin Herman? That could turn into a wild goose chase. One never knew where the man would show up, and she had never heard Cousin Herman speak in a foreign tongue other than German anyway.

What would Grandma do? Phoebe asked herself. That was a better question—but Grandma had never spoken Spanish.

Phoebe approached the two girls, who were huddled by the front door. She gave them both hugs and smiles, which seemed to help. She flipped through the dictionary to the word *welcome*. "*Bien-a-ven...ben, ven...*" Phoebe tried to sound out the unfamiliar word.

Both girls giggled—which was an improvement—but they hadn't communicated yet beyond hugs.

She found the word *hunger* next. "*Hambre, ham...*" That must have been closer. They smiled and nodded this time.

"Then we'll make breakfast!" Phoebe proclaimed. "That is another form of language."

Their happy smiles seemed to say they understood, and maybe they did. The smells of bacon and toasted bread soon filled the kitchen. The girls watched her with wide eyes while she worked. Where had these two come from? Ethan hadn't given any details, other than their home country, but maybe he didn't even know.

They must have parents. Perhaps still in Guatemala? But what were two little girls doing here all by themselves? Maybe they had brothers who had been situated somewhere else. Phoebe left the bacon pan for a moment to flip through the dictionary. She stopped at the word *brother*. "*Hermano?*" She pointed at them. They nodded vigorously. Phoebe pointed around her. "*Hermano* here? Or *hermano* in Guatemala?"

"Here," they said together. The word was said clearly.

"So you can speak some English?" Phoebe asked. "That's a start, at least."

She dashed back to the bacon pan, where smoke had begun to rise toward the ceiling. When Phoebe transferred the bacon to a plate a moment later, she cracked in the eggs. Once they were cooked, she set them on the table. She heard a knock at the front door. Both girls jumped, and worried looks crossed their faces.

"It's okay," she told them. Her tone must have communicated assurance because they relaxed. Phoebe still tiptoed to the door and cracked it open. "David!" she exclaimed. "How dare you walk up here?"

"I didn't. *Mamm* dropped me off." He grinned. "She had to run a quick errand, and she'll pick me up afterward. You must be really into something not to have heard the buggy."

She let out her breath and almost gathered him into her arms. It was so *goot* to see him. "Two girls from Guatemala are here," she said instead. "I was told they don't speak a word of English."

"Oh!" He appeared amused. "Can I see them?"

Phoebe nodded, and they approached the kitchen together. Other than his bandaged arm, he showed little sign of his injury.

"Hi," he greeted the girls.

They smiled back.

"Would you like to eat with us?" Phoebe asked him.

Delight flooded his face. "Why not? I've had breakfast, but how can I pass up your cooking?"

"Sit yourself down."

He complied, and they bowed their heads for the prayer of thanks.

"So no English?" David asked the girls once the amen was said.

"Try the dictionary." Phoebe handed the book to David. "That's what I've been using."

David chuckled but made no move to open the pages. She passed the food around, and David waited until the girls had filled their plates. The man was as kind and gentle and *wunderbah* as always. For a while they all simply ate in silence.

"What's the word for *cute*?" David asked.

"You're not telling them that word in Spanish. I'm sure the girls have been told that often enough."

"I meant you."

Her eyes must have flashed because he laughed. "I mean it."

"I will ignore that comment. How is your *daett*?"

David's grin didn't go away. "*Daett* will find his way back eventually." He was obviously unrepentant to the core.

She changed the subject. "You really shouldn't have come up here. You might pull a stitch in your arm."

His grin turned into a sweet smile. "I couldn't stay away from you."

Her face filled with warmth, and she kept her gaze away from him.

"I guess I shouldn't tease you so much," he allowed. "I'm sorry, but I meant what I said, and I needed to get out of the house. I guess *Daett*'s attitude gets to me after a while, and I'm sorry I can't be of help with your farm today."

"It's okay," she assured him. "I'll manage. You can stay in the house and learn Spanish."

He made a face. "I'm not good at languages, but that will give me something to do."

"There you go." She got up to clear the table, and his gaze followed her. She ignored him and asked the girls, "Do you want to go out and play?"

They smiled but obviously didn't understand. "Find the word for *play*," she ordered David.

He did, mouthing the strange sound. "*Jugar. Ju, ju...*"

Phoebe giggled. "You sound worse than I do."

The girls seemed to understand, though, and they cautiously left the table and went outside.

David closed the dictionary. "This will be an interesting week, I'm thinking."

"Try a few weeks. Ethan said they are staying until other quarters can be found, and it may be a while."

"Then I'll have plenty of time to learn Spanish." He grinned.

She gave him a quick smile as she heard the sound of buggy wheels outside. "Your *mamm*?" Phoebe glanced toward the kitchen window.

"I suppose so." He got to his feet and came closer.

"You should be going, David. She will wonder why two little Spanish girls are in the yard."

He studied her face for a long time before he turned to go. She followed him to the door but stayed there until he had climbed in the buggy and was driving away with a wave of his hand.

FORTY-ONE

David strode north toward Grandma Lapp's farm. The road had become intimately familiar to him after many years of traveling the short distance. The stitches in his arm would come out next week, but it was time he spent a full day on the farm with Phoebe. She had plenty on her hands with the two little Guatemalan girls. Not that he could do much with one arm, but he could try. Phoebe would protest, but she would also be pleased.

His gaze swept over the surrounding countryside. Summer would soon be past, and another fall would arrive in all its brief glory of gold and yellow trees before the land settled in for its long winter sleep. His own life stood on the brink of spring, or so it seemed. Grandma Lapp had done so much for him and opened so many doors. Phoebe's heart had been the most precious gift of them all. Her love was a jewel of value incomparable to anything else in his life. If Grandma Lapp were still here, he would visit her this morning and express his heartfelt and perhaps tearful thanks.

In the meantime, *Daett* was still *Daett*. Family was still family, and he was still David Fisher. Perhaps his courage had grown, though, and the community was kinder and more understanding. They had been that way for some time, ever since the Lapp family had allowed Grandma Lapp's dream to unfold. Likely many of them had always hoped that the Fisher children would turn out okay, but it had taken Grandma Lapp to nudge everyone in the right direction.

So much could have gone wrong in the journey. Ruth could have jumped the fence. David paused and waited as her buggy pulled out of the driveway behind him. He stepped off the road, his injured arm wrapped to his side, and waved a greeting as Ruth approached in the buggy.

She pulled up and stopped. "Are you *sure* you don't want a ride?"

"I want to walk." He smiled up at her. "I wish to arrive on my own two feet."

She laughed. "Males are so stubborn."

"Speak for yourself."

"Okay." She chuckled. "Shall I pick you up after school?"

He nodded. "That I can handle."

She jiggled the reins and took off. Ruth was much happier of late. Perhaps she had made peace with her loss of Ethan. Ruth had never planned to settle down as an old maid teaching other people's children, but she seemed to be making the best of it.

David grimaced. That was better than jumping the fence and being married to an *Englisha* man. Much had hung on Ruth's decision. If Ruth had turned her back on what had been offered to her, the community might have reconsidered their opinion of Grandma Lapp's outreach to the Fisher children.

But Ruth hadn't, and he was thankful. He wanted Ruth to be happy. Maybe marriage was still on the horizon for her. He couldn't imagine with whom, but perhaps down the road some widower would present Ruth with a marriage offer. Whether his sister would accept was another matter. Ruth could laugh at him for his stubborn ways, but she was the most stubborn one of the family.

David continued north and hastened his footsteps the closer he came to Grandma Lapp's lane. The two girls were out on the front porch when he arrived, and they waved and giggled. He should go straight to the barn, but he wanted to see Phoebe before he made an attempt at the chores. She would come out otherwise, fussing over him like a mother hen. Phoebe cared for him from the bottom of her heart as no other woman had ever cared for him. When was he going to make the final leap and ask her if she would be his *frau*? The moment never seemed right, or his nerve was never high enough. Then *Daett* had created that awful scene the other evening when Phoebe had visited. David had wanted to hide his face in shame, but Phoebe's love kept him out of the despair that called from the distance.

He waved when she appeared in the front doorway and hollered, "*Goot* morning!"

The girls said something in Spanish he couldn't understand. "*Buenos días*," he sent their way, and they giggled again.

His accent was way off. He had tried to listen to their pronunciation on Monday, but it was difficult. The tongue needed to perform maneuvers for which neither the English nor the German language had given him preparations. Phoebe fared little better, but her voice was sweet by itself, so that helped.

He approached the house and smiled up at Phoebe from the bottom of the porch steps. "How are you doing?"

"You didn't walk up, did you?" she demanded.

"Ruth offered me a ride, but I need to be on my feet. I'm not an invalid."

"You still have stitches in your arm! You are *not* doing chores this morning. I'll do them myself later."

"I can do some of them. Please don't make a fuss, Phoebe."

She glared at him, but she also gave in at the same time. "Men! Well, don't hurt your arm."

"I won't," he assured her, seating himself on the porch edge.

"See, you're tired already." The front door slammed as she sat down beside him.

The girls raced around in front of them, jabbering away in Spanish, playing some game they must have learned in their childhood.

"Have you had breakfast?" Phoebe gently laid her hand on his uninjured arm.

"Yep."

Her gaze lingered on the playing girls. "I don't think Ethan is coming to pick them up today. If he is, he hasn't told me."

"Ruth should come up and stay with you for the weekend."

A pleased look filled her face. "Would she? That would be great!"

"She's picking me up tonight so I don't have to walk home. See? I have some sense. I can ask her then. You'll need help getting the girls ready for the Sunday services and other things."

"You always have such *wunderbah* ideas, David. And lots of sense." She laughed as her hand moved on his arm.

"I haven't learned Spanish yet."

"You've only had one week."

He laughed. "I know, but I doubt if I'll make much progress. How long do you think they will leave the girls?"

Phoebe shrugged. "I don't know, but they grow closer to my heart every day. I don't mind. I imagine someone will give them a home before too long."

David took a deep breath and reached for her hand. "I'm sorry about last Saturday, about my trying to impress people. It was all so unnecessary, but we learn bad habits, I guess. Now I have this." He motioned toward the bandage. "I'm so glad it will come off next week."

Her hand tightened in his. "You don't have to apologize to me, David. You have done well so far with what you've had to work with, and no one blames you. I am very grateful for all the help you give me on the farm. Grandma was right, you know." She leaned against him and sighed contently. "Do you think we are out of all the rough spots with our new venture and your *daett*?"

"There will always be rough spots, but the Lord will be with us."

"As He has been," she agreed. Silence fell between them, broken only by the rustle of the wind in the trees and the chatter of the girls as they played.

"We have not officially dated, Phoebe," he began. "But—"

"It's okay. Not everyone has to do things the same way."

He hung his head for a moment. "I know we haven't, but I like what has happened."

"*Yah*, I agree. The farm has been all that Grandma could wish for."

He cleared his throat. "What I'm trying to say is that I have grown very fond of you, Phoebe. In fact, I've been..."

She smiled and squeezed his uninjured arm. "You are very dear to me, David."

He rallied. "I'm still a Fisher, yet I want to marry you. I don't have a farm or a place to move to, but will you?"

Her face glowed. "You know I will. I would have agreed a long time ago." She gave his arm a pat. "You didn't have to go proving yourself."

He tried to breathe. "You will be my *frau* then?"

"*Yah*," she said, her eyes fixed on his.

He trembled but pulled her close. She didn't protest as he kissed her. He caught the movement of the girls out of the corner of his eye, but they didn't slow their play. To them it seemed that a couple kissing on the front porch was a common enough sight.

"I love you, Phoebe," he whispered after he let her go.

She nestled against him, and they watched the girls playing in silence.

Phoebe finally spoke. "I want to say something, David. Some people must step down, and others must step up. Yours is a step up in the eyes of the community, but you've always been upstanding.

That's what Grandma saw, and I have always been the woman who could love you with my whole heart."

"I don't know what to say," he murmured. "You are the one who speaks *wunderbah* things."

She smiled up at him. "You know we couldn't have gone on much longer like this. We have to wed this fall, and you have to move up to the farm. You're here every day—well, almost, and the community…" She raised her eyebrows. "They already know we are sweet on each other."

"You have such a way with words."

"I just speak my heart. Would you have it otherwise?"

"No. So when is this to happen?"

"We can plan the wedding. Pick out a date, and Aunt Millie will help me until *Mamm* can come up to the valley. I can't leave the farm, so the wedding can't be in Lancaster. Don't you like that better anyway?"

He paused for a moment. "We haven't done anything by the book so far."

"Should we have?"

"No. This works for me."

"Then it's settled!"

He couldn't take his gaze off her face. This had been too easy, too sudden, and yet it was as if it had always been. She and he, meant to be by some divine decree. They had been brought together by a dream, and yet Grandma Lapp had only seen what already was when others were blind. Phoebe had been reserved for him, to walk by his side, to be his *frau*.

"David, what are you thinking?"

Heat rose rapidly into his face.

She laughed and reached for him. "Just one more, okay? That's all. I know we've already—"

He silenced her with his kiss and then held her for a long moment before he let her go.

"You are so handsome, David. You're what I've always wanted even when I didn't know it."

He moved close again, and she stopped him with a touch of her finger on his cheek. "I have lots of work to do in the house, but don't do too many chores in the barn."

"I'm an invalid."

Her laughter rippled. "I'll see you at lunchtime, then." She stood to slip away.

"I'll talk with Ruth tonight!" he hollered after her, but she was already inside.

He turned to watch the girls playing as the sun rose higher in the sky. He and Phoebe had been on the porch for a long time, and miles had been traveled in those short moments. He was a man with a promised *frau*. In a few short months he would have Phoebe by his side for the rest of his life on this earth—if the Lord so allowed things to happen. There would never be another woman he would love as much, nor could he. Phoebe had known him when he was merely David Fisher. He still was David Fisher, but he wasn't. The impossibility of it all couldn't be explained, and neither could the love Phoebe offered him. He would believe that Phoebe Lapp loved him, unworthy though he was.

David stood up, and the girls stopped their play to look at him. "I'm going to the barn," he told them. "You want to come along and see the ponies?"

They couldn't have understood him, but they raced toward him anyway. Together, they walked toward the barn. David glanced over his shoulder. The kitchen window drapes fluttered as if they had been released rapidly by an unseen hand. David grinned. The woman loved him, and somehow it was as if she should.

FORTY-TWO

After Ruth finished grading her school papers on Saturday morning, she drove her buggy down Peckville Road and turned north at the intersection. The bright sunlight made the shadows dance along the roadway, moved by each burst of breeze blowing up from the valley floor. Her horse whinnied as they pulled away from the junction, and Ruth took a quick backward glance through the open buggy door. She had planned to meet Ethan here that long ago evening. His rejection had stricken her deeply. His apology, elicited at Phoebe's insistence, had helped, but things would never be the same. Ruth pulled back on the reins to turn into Grandma Lapp's driveway. She had promised to spend the weekend with Phoebe and her two young Guatemalan girls. David had asked last night with stars in his eyes, so she couldn't say no. And neither did she want to. Phoebe was a kind person, just like her grandma had been, and Ruth was caught up with her schoolwork.

Ruth pulled to a stop by Grandma Lapp's barn as another buggy appeared from the north. Was Phoebe's Aunt Millie visiting this morning? Perhaps Millie Yoder had come to check on her niece, not knowing Ruth was scheduled to help Phoebe for the weekend.

Ruth swung out of the buggy door and had started unhitching her horse when she glanced over her shoulder at the sound of footsteps behind her. "Herman Yoder! What are you doing here?"

"I could ask you the same, but I already know. You've come to help Phoebe for the weekend."

"That I have." Ruth shoved her nose in the air. "We'll take care of things. You can go now."

Herman chuckled. "I was greatly relieved when Phoebe told me you would be coming."

"You're welcome," Ruth snapped. "Now I have to get my horse in the barn and help Phoebe."

"I can do that." He reached for the tugs.

She hesitated. "It's not necessary. I've got it, and I know where the stalls are."

"Prickly, prickly. Are you always this way?"

"Only when I'm around you."

He laughed. "That's not very encouraging."

"I wasn't trying to encourage you."

"How do you manage to teach school without snapping off the children's heads?"

Ruth couldn't resist a smile. "They are sweet children, you know."

"Did I walk into a rattlesnake's nest, perhaps?" He tilted his head toward her.

The smile came again. "I might fit that description."

"I know about Ethan stopping by the schoolhouse the other morning, and I can imagine the rest."

She stared at him, her face paling.

"*Yah!*" He nodded for emphasis. "Did you really think you could keep Ethan and your troubles with him secret from me?"

"So you are the one they've chosen to throw me out of the schoolhouse?" she said bitterly.

"Ruth, no! I'm just saying this so we can understand each other and move forward on solid ground. We don't want this subject to come up later."

"You're not making a bit of sense. There is no later between you and me."

He studied her for a moment.

She quickly turned back to unharnessing her horse. He put out a hand to stop her.

"Ruth, please. It's not what you think."

"Then what is it?"

"You want me to speak when you have that kind of an attitude?"

"I am a Fisher. What else do you expect?"

"Maybe this very behavior," he allowed. "And I understand."

She sighed. "Can I go now? Nothing you are saying makes any sense."

"I want to…I wish…I…how many ways can I say it, Ruth? I want to become better acquainted with you. Like maybe on a Sunday evening. I would take you home from the hymn singing if you could calm yourself enough to give me a chance." Herman's hand twirled in circles. "I like your fire. I like a lot about you, and believe me—I've been around. You are the first woman to interest me in this way—romantically. Maybe that doesn't mean much to you, but I'm a determined man. I won't give up easily. I'm here this weekend, so why don't I take you home after the hymn singing? We can chat, and you might even bake me a few brownies." Herman laughed. "The way to a man's heart, and all that."

"You're not serious."

"What do you mean? The brownies or the date?"

"Both."

He shrugged. "The brownies are negotiable, but the date is not. Please?"

"You are asking me?"

"*Yah.* You are a woman. I do not command you, but I am interested in you."

Ruth clutched the bridle until her fingers hurt.

"So what will it be, Miss Fisher?"

She jumped. "Don't say Fisher."

"That's what you are."

She glared at him. "And that's not a problem?"

"No one's perfect. So, no. It's not a problem."

"You would come to my house?"

He took a deep breath. "I'm trying to be patient, Ruth, but you are trying me. *Yah,* I would come to your house. Now do you want me down on my knees or what? Usually that's the marriage proposal, not the first date."

"So what if—"

"There are no what-ifs with me. I hope you can learn to like me, and maybe..." His hand was in the air again. "Learn to like me enough that you would...well, that comes later, of course. We still need to leap over this first date hurdle."

"Okay! I'll do it, and if you decide you don't like my company after a few moments, you can leave. No hard feelings."

He clucked his tongue. "Thank you. That wasn't too difficult with a nice fellow like me, now, was it?"

She managed to smile.

"Can I take care of the horse now?"

She released the bridle and fled toward the house.

Phoebe met her at the door with a startled look on her face. "Is something wrong?"

"Herman Yoder asked me for a date!" she gasped.

"Cousin Herman? That's *wunderbah!*"

"Oh, it isn't," Ruth wailed. "What am I to do? Young John must have told him about Ethan stopping by the other morning, and he can imagine the rest, Herman said, and...and...and...oh, it's horrible. He'll hate me when this is all over, and I'll be in worse shape than I am." Ruth cut off the flow of words as the two Guatemalan girls peered at her with puzzled looks. "I'm sorry." She choked back her sobs. "I'm making a terrible fuss."

"Come." Phoebe helped her to the couch. "I'm sure the girls have seen tears before."

"But I'm supposed to help today, not—"

Phoebe shook her head. "First things first."

"But that's just the problem. I've agreed to a date with Herman Yoder." Ruth's voice rose to a shriek. "Your Cousin Herman!"

Phoebe hid her smile. "I'd say most girls would jump at the chance."

"But I'm not most girls. I'm Ruth Fisher, who was planning to jump the fence not a few months ago."

"Things change." Phoebe walked over to the living room window to glance out. "Cousin Herman's leaving now, so I don't think he regrets his decision in the least."

"The man's crazy!" Ruth proclaimed. "What other explanation can there be?"

Phoebe laughed. "You do care for Cousin Herman, don't you? Or you could learn to?"

"I don't know. I'm just confused right now. I'm having a breakdown, I think. A shock, and to think I said, *yah*."

"Do you want me to flag him down so you can change your mind?"

"No!"

"See there?" Phoebe smiled and seated herself beside Ruth. "You do like him. I do, and I don't see why anyone else wouldn't. Cousin Herman's adventurous and well traveled. You'd never have a boring life with him."

"It's his life with me that I'm thinking about." Ruth wrung her hands. "Oh, I can't bear it."

"I hadn't expected you to react this way to such *goot* news."

"I know, I know." Ruth tried to calm herself. "It's not like me at all. Nothing like this has ever happened to me. A man like Herman Yoder asking to see me home on a Sunday evening date?" She managed to end in a whimper instead of a wail.

"That's better," Phoebe said, obviously trying to hide her amusement. "I think you care a lot more for Cousin Herman than even you imagined you would."

"I didn't imagine anything," Ruth protested. "I didn't think about it, or dream, or plan anything with the man. I prepared myself to walk alone through life"

Phoebe raised her eyebrows. "All in defense against something. Would that something have been Cousin Herman?"

"Oh, I don't want to think about it. I just want my heart to stop pounding and my hands to stop shaking, and this horrible fear that I'm going to mess everything up to go away. What if I kill the man on Sunday night? He wants brownies."

"Cousin Herman told you what to bake for the date?"

"Something like that. He hinted."

"You couldn't kill a man with brownies even if you tried, Ruth."

"I know, I know." Ruth fanned herself with one hand. "It's all irrational, and I'm hyperventilating."

"Shall I give you a hug?" Phoebe offered. "Sometimes those help."

"I'm desperate enough to try anything," Ruth replied. She opened her arms. She shook while they embraced.

Phoebe's face was concerned when she let go. "Let me get something to read," she told her. "Grandma left me something that has helped a lot through this whole journey. Remember, how you told me about the mysterious prayer journal?"

Ruth stilled her breathing while Phoebe was gone. A few moments later she returned with the tablet in her hand. "This is Grandma's prayer journal, but I think you already know that. I read portions at times to the children. Maybe she said something that will speak to you, because you know that all of this wouldn't have happened without Grandma's vision."

Ruth's hand trembled as she transferred the tablet to her lap and opened the pages. Phoebe hurried into the kitchen with the girls in tow to give Ruth a moment alone. Ruth's eyes scanned the pages of words and settled on a paragraph.

Dear Lord in heaven, You know how blind we are sometimes, and how little we can see of what lies closest to us. I pray You would strengthen my heart to see better the needs of those around me. We say we love, but do we see clearly enough to love as You love? Open my heart to the possibilities of life as You see them. Let me feel as You must feel. Let me walk where You would walk. Let me not decline because I am too small, or reject what my heart would accept because of the pain I imagine might come. Let me not see the road that lies ahead, but the day given in which I am to walk onward. Let me take the step and leave the mile to You. Let me awaken tomorrow and leave yesterday behind. Let me always believe in what is good, even when I have done what I shouldn't have. Let me make the right choice when the wrong one is still fresh in my memory. Let me hope that tomorrow will be better when I know so well what the storm has done. Let me be what You see, and not what I do, and let me always dare to love again.

Ruth laid the journal down. She couldn't see at the moment, but that didn't matter.

"You were the one who gave Grandma the idea for this farm," Phoebe said from the kitchen opening.

Ruth nodded. The words simply wouldn't come even if she tried. She stood and flew toward Phoebe with open arms. They embraced, with her sobs buried in Phoebe's shoulder.

"You already like him, don't you?" Phoebe said.

Ruth's voice caught. "A little perhaps."

Phoebe smiled. "Everything is going to work out beautifully. Shall we pray and give thanks for what has been given us already?"

Ruth bowed her head and waited.

"Thank You, dear Lord, for precious Grandma," Phoebe prayed. "Thank You for her love, for her kindness, for the grace which has been brought to our hearts. What a gift she was to us. Amen."

"Amen," Ruth echoed.

When she opened her eyes, the two Guatemalan girls stood at their feet, smiling up at her.

QUESTIONS

1. What was your impression of Phoebe Lapp and David Fisher when they were introduced? What future did you see for their relationship?

2. Describe your thoughts when the extended Lapp family meets to discuss the proposed pony farm. What would your contributions have been?

3. If you had been able to meet Grandma Lapp, what questions would you have asked her?

4. How much sympathy did you have for David's quest to win Phoebe's heart? What advice would you have given him?

5. Would you have liked to read more of Grandma Lapp's prayer book? Do you have a family member who has left a similar spiritual legacy?

6. In what ways could the community have dealt differently with Leroy Fisher and his surly attitude? Do you think there are limits to community life and their control of unacceptable behavior?

7. Was Phoebe wise to cover for her friend as Ruth Fisher struggled to find her way?

8. As you watched Phoebe work with the different sets of children, was there any advice or encouragement you would have given her?

9. What caused Phoebe's heart to turn toward David? What struggles did David have accepting Phoebe's love?

10. Do you think Ruth will find the love she is looking for in Herman Yoder? Will she eventually make peace with the community?

A Beautiful Rose, Like True Love, Never Fades

Esther Stoltzfus considers herself to be down-to-earth, the way most Amish women do. Her marriage to her deceased husband was one borne out of practicality, and Esther sees no reason why God won't replace what He was taken away.

When Esther moves to a new community with her daughter, Diana, she meets the handsome minister Isaiah Mast, who has experienced his own loss and appears to be a logical fit to complete their family. But everything changes when Esther is introduced to Joseph Zook, her widowed neighbor down the road.

While tending to his treasured roses, Joseph tells stories of his passionate love for his late wife, Silvia—stories that stir a place in Esther's heart she never knew existed. What if she and Isaiah could have the kind of love Joseph and Silvia shared?

In the meantime, Joseph gets his own second chance at love with the eccentric Arlene King, even as he knows he will never find another *frau* like his beloved Silvia.

Silvia's Rose is a beautiful story filled with redemption, romance, and risking it all for the reward of true love.

How to Heal a Broken Heart

Mary Yoder's life couldn't get much better. Engaged to be married, spring is in the air and love is in her heart as she looks forward to the fall wedding she's always dreamed of.

Six months later on a crisp November morning, Mary awakens in a lovely little valley near the Adirondack Mountains on what was to be her wedding day, heartbroken and alone.

Her sister, Betsy, tries to protect Mary from the romantic overtures of Stephen Overholt, a longtime Amish bachelor. Betsy is considering jumping the fence for the *Englisha* world and encourages Mary to follow.

Meanwhile, Mrs. Gabert, an elderly *Englisha* grandmother, launches her own matchmaking effort on behalf of her grandson Willard, who is a missionary to Kenya and nursing his own broken heart. She hopes that Willard and Mary can find comfort in one another despite the fact they come from two different worlds.

As Mary struggles to accept the Lord's will, she must determine whether or not one of her potential suitors can give her the future that was denied her.

To learn more about Harvest House books and
to read sample chapters, visit our website:

www.harvesthousepublishers.com

HARVEST HOUSE PUBLISHERS
EUGENE, OREGON